Dear #47, You're the Worst

Seattle Havoc Hockey Romance

Vivian Wood

Chapter 1

Juliet

My feet are screaming in these five-inch heels and I've got about thirty minutes left on my shift at Foxies. Thirty more minutes of smiling at drunk assholes who think my uniform is an invitation to grab whatever they want. The white crop top barely qualifies as fabric, the purple shorts are more like a suggestion, and the push-up bra underneath makes me feel like a caricature of myself.

I hate this outfit. It fits my five-foot frame like someone who thinks women exist purely for decoration designed it. Customers look at my chest and assume I'm too dumb to be anywhere else. I know it, and it fills me with incandescent rage.

They don't see me. They see a sexy body with a name tag.

If I could make this kind of money anywhere else, I'd already be gone.

The table in section three has been nursing the same pitcher of beer for two hours, getting progressively louder and grabbier. The guy in the backwards baseball cap just tried to pull me onto his lap when I dropped off their wings. I laughed it off like I'm supposed to, like their disgusting comments are the highlight of my evening, because tips pay my rent and my student loans.

Two ass grabs tonight. Three lap-pulling attempts. One guy literally offered to take me home for two hundred bucks. Like I'm some kind of bargain-bin escort? I don't even have words for that one. All of that harassment and I only made three hundred and fifty dollars. Not even enough to cover my credit card payment.

I head for the back of the house, rolling silverware in Foxies-branded napkins and trying not to check my email every thirty seconds. Our manager Derek is a five-foot-nothing Napoleon with a clipboard fetish and a serious power complex. He's been hovering around the kitchen all night, making notes about our *customer engagement* and *brand representation* like we're high-level executives instead of servers in glorified lingerie.

I know all about customer engagement and brand repre-sentation. They are my bread and butter for Monroe Strate-gies, the boutique PR firm I run out of my tiny apartment here in Seattle. By boutique, I mean just me. A company of one.

Hopefully, I can get out of here someday and make ends meet by pulling in some bigger clients. Clients who hire me for my strategy deck, not my bra size. Until then, I'm still here. Rolling silverware. Pretending this is temporary.

My phone buzzes on the stainless steel counter. Another voicemail from Mom, probably reminding me that my LSAT scores are still valid and I should reevaluate my life choices. I delete it without listening. The only thing worse than corpo-rate law would be corporate law with a side of body glitter.

This job is temporary. That's what I tell myself every single shift. The tips are decent, I'm saving money, and it's just until I land a real PR client who isn't a toddler pageant mom or a used car dealership that wants influencer synergy with a ton of cleavage. But if I'm being honest, I feel like I'm treading water, and the shore keeps getting farther away.

My phone lights up with a text from Jessa.

Jessa: Got tix to the Havoc box for tonight. You in?

I stare at the message. Hockey. Of course it's hockey. I swore off hockey players, hockey games, hockey anything after the disaster that was my relationship with Patrick. He liked his women pretty, agreeable, and quiet. I could never manage all three. Five years of my life wasted on a man-child who thought advanced stats were more important than basic human decency.

She's my roommate. And one of the few people who doesn't treat me like a punchline. Plus, she works part time for the team, which means these are fantastic seats, not nose-bleeds behind a pillar.

Me: Can I dress up? I need to feel pretty after being here all day. BTW when I quit, I'm burning these shorts.

Jessa: Yes! I'll dress up too. Meet you at the arena.

I finish my closing duties, change out of the uniform from hell, and drive home to our tiny apartment. Jessa's already gone, probably setting up whatever promotional nonsense the team has her doing tonight. I stand in front of my closet like I'm preparing for battle.

Which, honestly, I am.

I pull out my emotional armor. Slinky black cocktail dress, perfectly tailored. Black heels, sky-fucking-high. They're not comfortable, but damn if they don't make my ass look amazing. I twist my wavy black hair into an updo and secure it with a billion bobby pins. Bright red lipstick that's as sharp as my wit. When I look in the mirror, I see someone who belongs in a corporate stadium box. I can't be dismissed or categorized so easily.

If I look like I belong, they won't touch me. If I'm composed, I'm safe.

They are men, mostly. There are a few exceptions; some are ladies, too. People look for flaws in everything and everyone they see.

I'm *flawless*.

The arena is buzzing when I arrive. I hate how easily I still know my way around this place. Patrick dragged me to enough games here before he went pro that I know this place as well as I do my college campus. We came to almost every game before he was drafted to play in Texas; it's no great secret that Patrick wanted to play here with the Havoc. But they never put in a bid on him, so when Houston offered him a stellar signing bonus, he didn't hesitate.

The ushers at the corporate level eye me like they're trying to figure out what I'm doing here. I get that look a lot. My chest enters every room a beat before the rest of me, and no matter what I wear, some people only see cleavage and assume I'm dumb.

Smart women with curves make people uncomfortable. I learned that early.

As Dolly Parton once said, "There's a heart under all this hair and a brain beneath these boobs." Dolly is an icon, especially for a petite woman built like me. Her being hysterically funny is just icing on the cake.

"Juliet!" My roommate Jessa waves me over to our suite. We've only been roommates for a few months now, but I absolutely love living with Jessa. It's really freeing, especially after I moved back home, fleeing living with my ex.

The rink is nicer than I remember. Having grown up in Seattle, I used to come to games and concerts here at the

Havoc Dome. The Seattle Havoc hockey team has been in this city forever; the players themselves have insanely devoted fans that border on psychotic.

The view from the box is incredible, right at center ice, with actual comfortable seating and a server who brings us overpriced wine without making it feel like a transaction.

I settle in and try to look like I belong here. Watching the team as they skate around the ice, it's impossible to keep my thoughts to myself.

"If their point man can't keep the puck in the zone, that power play's just cardio."

"You didn't tell me you were a hockey nerd," Jessa says, watching me track a power play setup.

I shrug and take a sip of wine. "My ex was a pro. You pick things up when you spend five years pretending to care about advanced stats and penalty kills."

"Five years. Damn."

"Five years wasted," I mutter, mostly to myself.

The words taste bitter, but they're true. Patrick taught me to love hockey, then used it as another way to make me feel small. Every game was a test I didn't know I was taking. Every new rule just proved I didn't belong.

I force my mind away from him. He's not allowed to take up any more of my brainpower.

On the ice, something violent is happening near the boards. A massive player in a Havoc jersey just laid out someone from the visiting team, and now he's dropping his gloves. Even from up here, I can see the rage radiating off him as he starts throwing punches.

Hunter Huxley. *The Chainsaw*.

I swallow.

Jessa points to the crowd erupting around us. Half the arena is on their feet, waving foam chainsaws and screaming for blood. "His fans are insane. Look at them. They cheer every time he punches someone. Bloodthirsty little freaks."

I don't answer. But I know all about Hunter. We both went to the University of Washington at the same time. He was on the hockey team. And me? I was the girlfriend of his rival.

Once, I thought we would be more than just acquaintances. But Hunter let me know just how wrong I was.

I know Hunter. He's not misunderstood by his fans. He's just an asshole. If I had to write a letter to him about my feelings, it would start with:

Dear #47,

You're the worst.

And it would only get darker from there.

Hunter is enormous. 6"6'. His height is always mentioned in his stats. He's just a big guy. His wingspan is huge, his hands are giant, and his build resembles Frankenstein's monster. Except his movements aren't jerky and spastic. No, they're graceful.

Damn him.

He moves across the ice like a shark cuts through deep water. Focused, intent, his mere presence threatening. A player on the other team seems to take issue with Hunter and drops his gloves.

I watch Hunter shed his gloves faster than it seems like someone that big ought to move. Then he skates right up to the guy, landing a right hook that sends the other player sprawling. A jet of blood sprays across the ice. Hunter has a smug look on his face that makes me want to scream.

Asshole.

The guy that he's fighting with comes back with a weak blow to Hunter's nose. Hunter straight up uppercuts the guy and the other player collapses like a puppet with its strings cut. Hunter pulls at his helmet, pulling it off. He has dirty blond hair with a messy cut and gray-blue eyes absolutely furious as the refs herd him backward from the other player. He skates toward the penalty box, jaw clenched, blood on his knuckles and his face. When he passes the rinkside camera, something low in my stomach tightens.

I hate how hot he looks when he's pissed off. Ugh, I hate that I notice.

My dress smoothed, I straighten, remembering why I avoid this. Men like Hunter are exactly the problem. All heat and impulse, all rage and recklessness. He reminds me of everything I swore off after Patrick. I'm not the girl who falls for chaos anymore. I crave control, safety, and a future I build myself.

Because I've always liked hotheads, I can't trust my opinion. But Hunter isn't just hot-tempered. He's actually violent, throws punches for a living. That's a hard no from me. Besides, I will never, ever date another hockey player. That's a promise I made to myself, and I'm keeping it.

Not that he'd ever ask me out. I'm pretty sure he hates me as much as I loathe him.

After some breathtaking action, the game goes to overtime. The Havoc lose in a shootout and I watch the players skate off the ice looking defeated and pissed off. Patrons in the corporate box clear out, but Jessa grabs my arm.

"Come on, let's go watch the interviews. It'll be fun to see them up close."

I follow her down toward the media tunnel, even though *fun* isn't the word I'd use. This is actually where I want to be, but not as a fan.

As a *professional*. I've dreamed about working for a team like this, crafting their image, managing their brand. But I didn't even bother applying after my last PR interview, where the hiring manager looked me up and down like I'd shown up in lingerie instead of the modest blouse and slacks I'd carefully chosen.

It didn't matter what I wore. People had already sorted me into a category. One glance at my curves and managers wouldn't even bother giving me a chance. *Figures*.

The media tunnel is cramped and loud, full of reporters and cameras. Jessa knows her way around, flashing her team ID to get us through security. I'm trying to look professional and invisible when I nearly walk directly into a wall of muscle and rage.

Hunter Huxley, still in his gear, still radiating fury from the loss.

I freeze, not sure if he'll recognize me. We weren't exactly friends in college. Barely acquaintances, really, just two people who occasionally ended up at the same parties. But he looks right at me with those storm-gray eyes and his jaw tightens.

"What are you doing here?" His voice is a growl, rough and irritated. "Aren't you supposed to have followed your loser ex to Texas?"

The question hits me like a slap. I did not know he even knew about Patrick, let alone that he'd been paying attention to my life. We may have spoken ten words to each other in four years of college.

"Huxley." I force a smile, the same one I use with difficult customers at Foxies. "Good news. I'm back! I finally dumped Patrick, so now I'm staying here in the city again."

Hunter's glare could melt steel. "Not sure why you're in my arena."

My arena. Like he owns the place. I introduce Jessa, mentioning that she works for the team and is my roommate, hoping that might make him back off. Instead, he just keeps staring at me like I'm something unpleasant he stepped in. Being under his gaze is acutely uncomfortable.

"That's great for you," he says flatly. "Now move."

The dismissal is so sharp and unexpected that I actually jump backward. Jessa's eyes go wide as Hunter pushes past us toward the interview area.

"Yikes," Jessa whispers.

"It isn't us." I glare at his retreating form. "I've known him for years. Hunter's always been a flying bag of dicks."

Jessa laughs, but I'm completely serious. He's a rude, growling grump with no redeeming qualities except he is good at hitting a puck with a stick. He's just lucky that people in this city are hockey-crazy enough to worship him for it.

Well, he's hot too. But I would never, ever admit that out loud.

We find spots near the back of the media scrum as Hunter steps up to the microphone. He looks like he'd rather be literally anywhere else, answering questions with grunts and one-word replies, refusing to make eye contact with anyone. His post-game interview technique is basically a masterclass in how to make reporters hate you.

Then some idiot in the third row asks, "Hunter, have you heard from your mom lately?"

I inhale sharply. The question hangs in the air like a live grenade. Every reporter in the room knows that's off-limits territory, but this guy either doesn't care or doesn't know better.

"What's the story there?" Jessa whispers.

Unfortunately, I know the story. Hunter, Patrick, and I went to college at the same time. I met Patrick exactly one day before I met Hunter and was as bowled over by Patrick's charm offensive as I was Hunter's growly presence. They were on the same team, so when I started dating Patrick, I was around Hunter a lot.

Unfortunately.

When Patrick and I were living in Houston, with Patrick playing for the Houston Stars, the news broke about Hunter and his mom having a major falling out. I remember, because Patrick made a massive deal out of Hunter's very public scandal.

Looking at Jessa, I keep my voice low. "His mom Darla used to be his agent. She stole a ton of money from him, tanked some of his deals, talked crazy shit about him to the papers, and then just disappeared. It was a whole *thing*."

"Oh, shit!" Jessa hisses. "I didn't know that."

Hunter doesn't handle the question well. His glare could cut glass as he leans into the microphone and growls, "Suck my dick," before stalking away from the podium.

The room falls into mortified silence. Camera flashes pop like fireworks as the reporters realize they just got the quote of the night. A young guy in a team polo shirt races up to the microphone, sweating bullets and stumbling over an apology.

"That's Julien," Jessa tells me. "He's the new PR guy. He's temporary. At least, I hope he is. He sucks."

I watch him fumble through damage control, practically begging the media to go easy on the team. He's a mess. Apologetic, nervous, completely out of his depth. I frown.

"He's not doing his job," I mutter.

"Who?" Jessa blinks. "The reporter?"

"No. Julien, the PR rep. If they respected him, they wouldn't have dared ask about Hunter's mom. Someone should have stopped them from asking that question."

Jessa studies my face. "You get kinda intense when you talk about PR stuff."

I don't answer. I'm too busy watching the chaos unfold,

seeing all the ways this could have been prevented. A good PR person builds relationships with reporters, establishes boundaries, controls the narrative before it controls you. Julien is just reacting, which means he's already lost.

This is why I love PR. I love finding the angle, controlling the story, building order out of chaos. I know I could do this better than anyone else in that room. And after Patrick, proving myself matters more than anything.

As we walk toward the parking garage, I can't stop thinking about what I just witnessed.

"The team managers have got to do something about Huxley," I say, almost talking to myself. "Have him adopt a kid. Rescue puppies. Get him a fake fiancée. Anything to change the narrative."

Jessa raises an eyebrow. "Fake fiancée? That's dramatic."

"Not if you sell it right. A few photos, sappy social media captions, gala appearances. Let the press eat it up and forget about tonight's disaster. I could build the entire campaign in my sleep."

"Does he even have a girlfriend?"

I snort. "Doubt it. He's too much. Too gruff, too pissed off at the world. And he never liked puck bunnies, not even in college. He'd need someone who can play the part but won't fall for the act."

Jessa side-eyes me as we reach my car. "So… you looking for a good side gig?"

I stop walking. "What? No. God, no. We can't stand each other. He once ruined my entire internship track with one stupid quote to a reporter about how female sports journalists were just quote *looking for attention*. I didn't even get to interview for the position after that."

She screws up her mouth. "But you already know him. And you're clearly the one with the plan."

I wave a hand dismissively. "Take the idea. I'll have a hundred more by tomorrow."

But as I drive home, I can't stop thinking about Hunter's interview disaster, about Julien's incompetence, about the way the whole situation should have been handled differently. I tell myself this is just a coincidence. One night, one sighting, one awkward run-in with someone from my past.

There's no way this horrible man will ever factor into my life again. I have better things to focus on. Better plans to make. But as I drive home, I can't stop thinking about Hunter's interview disaster, Julien's incompetence, and how someone could have handled the whole situation differently.

I intend to forget about him completely.

Chapter 2

Hunter

Another day, another fight waiting to happen.

It's game night and I'm sitting in Coach Cross's office with my arms folded and my jaw locked, already knowing what's coming. Cross is behind his desk looking like he'd rather be anywhere else, and Ryan Haart is standing nearby trying to look supportive. They're about to give me the talk. Again.

Cross doesn't bother pretending this is a check-in. It's a warning. One I've heard too many times before.

"Hunter," he says, drumming his fingers on the desk, "we love the Chainsaw act. The fans eat it up. But sponsors?"

I wait.

"Not so much."

There it is. The line. The threat wrapped in a compliment.

"You've had three suspensions this season. Two fines. The Department of Player Safety has your name pinned on a dartboard."

I clench my jaw so tight it clicks. The numbers don't lie. I know what nobody says out loud: how many people flinch when I walk into a room. How many wait for me to blow.

The numbers don't matter. Not to me. What matters is that many of the names on this roster play like cowards and expect me to save their asses. No wonder I can't stand being around them.

If it weren't for my brothers and a few players who have forced me into a friendship-slash-headlock, I wouldn't like anyone.

I already know this. Lost another family-friendly brand last week. Some breakfast cereal companies decided I wasn't the right role model for their target demographic. Kids aren't buying cereal based on which hockey player endorses it.

Moms will buy my face on cereal boxes because a 6"6' monster with tattoos who demolishes his enemies makes their fantasy lives much hotter. I get the fan mail they send me. Reading enough of their confessions tells me what women see when they look at me.

I'm not exactly in the position to contradict them, either. What you see is very much what you get.

Cross leans forward. "I fought to keep you here last year when upper management wanted the entire team gone. When we cleaned house, I could only keep you and a handful of other players. Jim Greene demanded fresh blood, new sponsorships, and a team that would win. I know you. I know that you're one of the most passionate players out there."

If he had just stopped there, I would've been happy as a clam. Coach Cross doesn't exactly hand out praise like candy. But he just sucks in a deep breath before continuing. "I think that passion has crossed over into something dark. The fans love you, cheer on your every move. But the sponsors don't want their brands to be associated with violence. If you don't shape up, we'll have to ship you out. I don't want to do that, but I have no choice."

I drop my gaze to the floor. Seattle is my hometown. It's

the only place I've ever lived. Not only that, but my brothers Jett and Silas are on this team. Leaving the team would mean leaving them. I wouldn't willingly do that.

"I can't get traded," I mutter. "Staying in Seattle is non-negotiable."

Not because I give a shit about this team. When it comes down to it, I don't. I'd torch the entire locker room tomorrow and not lose sleep. Leaving my brothers behind, though... that can't happen.

"You're going to have to do something radical to prove to the few companies that still sponsor you that you're a changed man." Cross throws his hands up. "You got ideas? I'm willing to listen."

I glance up at him, shaking my head slowly. "No. Let me think about it."

"Yeah, you do that, Huxley." Cross looks over to his assistant coach, who's a recently retired hockey player from Atlanta. "Ryan? You got anything you want to add?"

Ryan tries the softer approach, clapping me on the shoulder like we're buddies. "Just block out the noise and focus on the puck, man. You're one of the best players I've ever seen when you're locked in."

I shrug him off. "I don't need buddies. Half the guys in that locker room are knuckle-draggers. I'm not here to make friends with them. Winning is everything."

I learned not to let people get close anymore, not since the person I trusted most used my career to destroy me. My mother sold me out for attention and a quick payday.

The coaches are still talking, but I've stopped listening. I know what they want. They want me to be the Chainsaw when it sells tickets and jerseys, but dial it back when it hurts their profits. They want me to be exactly violent enough to be marketable but not so violent that I scare away the corporate sponsors.

I can do that. …can't I?

I walk the tunnel toward the ice, and the crowd is already a wall of noise. Chainsaw signs everywhere, foam props, drunk fans chanting my name like they actually know me. I used to think it was fun, all that energy directed at me. Now it makes my skin crawl. I'm not their mascot. I was never supposed to be anyone's entertainment.

The announcer drags it out, one name after another.

"Number four, Alexander Thorne!"

Thorne goes first, because of course he does. The captain skates out smooth as glass, every inch the sponsor's dream. He gives a clean little wave, just enough to get the crowd frothing. He's polished and unshakable. That's his whole brand.

"Number seventy-seven, Beckham Tate!"

Tate pushes out next, the Beast on the blue line. Co-captain. He doesn't acknowledge the roar, doesn't crack a smile. He just sets his shoulders and skates steady as a stone. The kids in the lower bowl chant Wolfie and he gives them the smallest nod. That's all they'll get from him.

"Number thirty-three, Silas Huxley!"

Silas doesn't look at anyone. He slides onto the ice and posts up near the crease like a statue. Tall, calm, coin in his hand between shifts, statistics running through his head. He won't say a word unless something's wrong. I trust him more than anyone else .

Silas has always been the steady one, the brother who never flinched no matter how loud the world got. When we were kids, it was his voice that cut through Mom's screaming, his calm hand on my shoulder that kept me from swinging first. Trusting him isn't a choice. It's muscle memory.

He doesn't need to be the loudest guy in the room, never has. He'll sit back and let everyone else blow smoke. When he finally speaks, it's the only opinion that matters. I've learned the hard way that ignoring my younger brother's advice never ends well.

The thing is, he doesn't demand attention. He earns it by always showing up, even if it's in that quiet, brooding way that makes people underestimate him. Not me. I know better.

When the world tilted after Dad died, it was Silas who steadied me. I didn't see it then, but I see it now. He's the anchor we never deserved but always had.

"Number nineteen, Grayson Reed!"

Grayson cuts a line across the ice, scowling already. Doesn't wave, doesn't smile, doesn't bother. He mutters at a rookie who's too slow to move out of his way. The cameras catch it, and the fans laugh, chanting Oscar. He hates it.

"Number seventy-nine, Jett Huxley!"

My oldest brother makes a show of it, because that's what he does. The Wildcard grins, tosses a wink at a group of women pressed against the glass, skates a half circle like he's headlining a concert. Brilliant one second, chaos the next.

Then it's me.

"Number forty-seven, Hunter Huxley!" A pause for dramatic effect. "The Chainsaw!"

The nickname used to feel like armor. Now it feels like a muzzle. Like the only version of me they'll ever want is the one who makes them scream. I step out anyway. In my first shift, I throw a hit, squaring up with their enforcer before the puck even drops. I'm following the script because it's the only role I've been allowed to play.

Decker and Moose get called after, the vets still hanging around. Moose yells about food or fantasy football every damn day. The rookies bring up the rear, Connor bouncing like he owns the place, Shane looking like he wants to disappear. Golden retrievers, both of them.

The game hasn't even started, but the roles are carved in stone.

First period, some asshole on the other team takes a cheap shot at Thorne behind the play. I react before I think. Drop the gloves, land my hits, set the tone. The crowd loses its mind.

All that noise used to hype me up. Now it just sounds like applause for a crash I can't stop.

The coaches grimace because they know what comes next. By the time I hit the penalty box, I'm already thinking about the next fight.

Through the glass, I see rookies staring at me like they expect blood. Like that's what I'm here for. Maybe it is. With so many fresh faces and the team still figuring out who the hell we are, nobody else seems ready to do the dirty work yet.

I look up into the stands, scanning the crowd out of habit, and that's when I spot them. Jessa Laramie, who works for the team part-time, looking sweet and harmless. And right next to her, Juliet fucking Monroe.

She's maybe five foot four in those heels she always wears. Always in those goddamn heels like she's trying to prove something. She's wearing a short sapphire blue dress, looking as impossibly expensive and out of reach as ever. Her red lipstick catches the arena lights, too red and too precise, like she wants people to look at her mouth. It's always perfect, never smudged, never faded. In college, it left marks on everything she touched. Napkins, pens, coffee cups.

Even her lipstick was trying so hard. With one look, you knew that she'd be impossible to please.

Two drunk fans with foam chainsaws wedged her and

another girl between them, and they are getting rowdy. One of them jostles her hard enough to spill beer on her knee. The other leans in close, saying something in her ear that makes her jaw tighten. She pushes him away, but the guy barely budges. He's twice her size and drunk enough to think he's being charming.

Something red-hot flashes behind my eyes. Like hell one of my fans is going to hurt a woman, especially not right in front of me.

I slam my gloved hand against the penalty box glass. The impact makes the plexiglass shudder and both guys jump. Catching their eyes, I make a slow, deliberate motion across my throat with one finger.

Letting them know that I'll kill them. Take their bodies out into the Sound on my boat and weigh them down, sinking them as deep as the fucking ocean.

The men laugh, thinking it's part of the show. But Juliet rips her arm free from the grabby one while they look at me. Juliet and her friend get up, fleeing their seats for somewhere safer. I turn around and cross my arms.

What I won't do is look for pretty little Juliet again after that. I don't need that kind of hassle in my life.

Third period, I get into another fight. This one isn't even about a hit or a dirty play. I just don't like the look of #32. He plays to the cameras, a smile on his face. And me? I just need a release, need to hit something before I explode. I check him into the boards and the guy goes down easy. The crowd erupts as if I just won the Stanley Cup.

I grunt and skate off. It means nothing to me. I used to feed off that roar. Now, it just sounds like permission to lose control.

The game ends with our losing in overtime. Not surprising by any means. I'm skating toward the tunnel when some jackass fan leans over the railing and shouts something that stops me cold.

"Hey Huxley! Darla was right! She dumped your ass just in time!"

I freeze with one foot still on the ice and the other on the rubber matting. My mother's name coming out of some stranger's mouth like he has any right to say it. Like he knows anything about what she did to me.

Silas skates up beside me smoothly. "Leave it."

I don't.

I spin around and punch the guy square in the mouth. Hard. He drops like a sack of cement. Suddenly, security is swarming and phones are coming up to record the whole thing.

And somehow, through all the chaos, Juliet fucking Monroe is there. She worms her way between bodies and presses her small hand against my chest, right over my heart. Her dark brown eyes flash.

"Hunter. Stop."

I jerk back automatically. Her hand drops as though I burned her. She takes a half-step back, eyes wide.

Not scared of the crowd.

Scared of me.

It's the worst expression I've ever seen. People have looked at like a lot of things, but damn. She saw the mask slip. I saw the thing my mother warned the world about.

It guts me. Makes me feel worth less than gutter trash. She doesn't know I'd rather throw myself through the glass than ever hurt her.

But how the hell could she know that, when half the world thinks the same thing? When my mother sold that exact story to the press?

And still… Juliet stepped between me and the ledge and pulled me back.

I stare wide-eyed at Juliet. Did she see it? My mother described me the same way in every interview. A monster in skates. Just a heavy breather who can't tell the difference between the ice and real life.

From the side, the fan's arm swings at my face, yet I don't flinch. Don't react. Don't move at all. I'm too busy watching Juliet watch me. He crushes his plastic beer cup into my neck, thankfully missing my face. The guy doesn't know how to punch for shit, but there is wet foam and bits of a plastic cup on my neck, my shoulder, my chest. Hell, there's even a drop or two on Juliet.

She flicks the drops away with a disgusted look, then grabs my wrist and yanks me backward into the tunnel with surprising strength for someone so small. I let her. Not because I'm done. Because she's the first person all night aside from my teammates who doesn't give me that look.

The one that says that I'm an out-of-control maniac. Juliet knew me before I was the Chainsaw. Before the money, the fame, the fans screaming for me to wreck other players and pound them into the ice.

I stare at that red lipstick of hers and watch as her lips twitch.

"You get in fights like it's your job," she says, still holding my wrist. "But being good at hockey doesn't excuse being a dick."

I grunt something noncommittal and dismiss it. She doesn't know what she's talking about. Hockey excuses everything.

Coach Cross is waiting for us in the tunnel. I cringe. He doesn't even look at Juliet, who finally lets go of my wrist and backs toward where Jessa is standing. Cross is bright red, his expression absolutely ballistic.

Well, shit. I probably earned that look.

The guys hate it when I lose it. Good. It's not as if I like them either. I'm not here to be anyone's favorite teammate. What I am here to do is scare the shit out of the opposition and maybe my locker room while I'm at it.

"You just gave the league a fucking field day," Cross says through gritted teeth. "We're going to have to do something drastic. Really drastic, Huxley."

Fuck me. I don't even know what he means, but I already hate it.

I don't speak as I trudge down the hall toward the locker room. Juliet's vanished by the time I turn around. Good riddance.

But later, sitting in front of my locker and slowly untying my skates, I can't stop replaying it. The way she looked at me. Not just with fear, but with something else. Recognition, maybe. Like she saw exactly what I was but stepped in anyway.

Is that really how she sees me? Just a blunt instrument with decent footwork and anger management issues? I know it's all that most people see.

That's how the rest of the team sees me too. They don't talk to me unless they have to. I prefer it that way. If I had my choice, I wouldn't talk to most of them either.

I'm the Chainsaw. The enforcer. Forever the guy who solves problems with his fists because I learned no other way. Or maybe I did learn. Maybe I just forgot how. Or maybe it's easier to be the monster they already see than the man I'm scared I'll never become.

Thanks to my mom's big mouth, most hockey fans also know that I'm the son who couldn't see his own mother's betrayal coming because he was too busy trying to make her proud.

I listen to the rookies joke around as they change out of their gear. Usually their noise grates on me, but tonight I don't join in and I don't glare either. I just sit there, quiet. Neutral. It's the closest thing I have to trying anymore.

Despite myself, I can't stop thinking about how small her hand felt against my chest. Or the way she grabbed my wrist like she actually gave a damn what happened to me. She could have just walked away. Should have walked away. Any smart person would have.

But she didn't.

She saw what I saw at that moment. The violence that lives just under my skin, ready to surface at the wrong word or the wrong look. The part of me that my mother turned into a commodity and the media turned into a brand.

And she still grabbed my arm and pulled me back from doing something even stupider.

My phone buzzes with a text from my agent. Probably damage control for tonight's incident. I don't check it. I don't want to know how much this latest outburst is going to cost me.

Instead, I think about red lipstick and small hands and the way Juliet Monroe looked at me like she could see straight through all my bullshit.

Chapter 3

Juliet

Six Years Ago

The Delta Tau Delta house is alive tonight. Music blasts from the open windows, Cardi B rattling the glass, the bass thumping so hard I feel it in my chest before I even step through the door. The lawn is a mess of students and lights strung across the trees. Someone has set up a shot luge on the cracked flagstones. Vodka and Jager stream down the slick ice chute into open mouths. Everyone's screaming, already drunk, already reckless.

Patrick told me to meet him here for our fifth date. He's a brother here, preferring to live in the house as opposed to living with a bunch of hockey players. I've been to the hockey house and found it so gross that I'm actually glad Patrick lives here, in this haven for douchebags.

I tug my cardigan tighter and make my way up the steps, trying to look like I belong, like I've done this a thousand times before. My dress feels too short under the floodlights, my heels wobble on the stone, and my heart is already racing.

Inside, it's suffocating. The air is scorching, heavy with

sweat, beer, and perfume. People crammed the hallway wall to wall, pressing together and shouting over the music. Someone shoves a red cup at me, beer sloshing onto my hand. I smile politely and keep moving, scanning the crowd for Patrick.

Bodies jam into the kitchen, making me work to get past them. Bottles line the counter, cups pile in the sink, and a girl in glitter kisses a guy right in front of me. I duck out quickly, cheeks burning, pretending I wasn't watching.

The living room is worse. A beer pong game has the packed room screaming. A couch sags under six bodies, everyone halfway in someone else's lap. I stand on my toes, looking for Patrick, but he isn't here.

I push through the crush of people to the back door. The music dulls a little when I step outside. Cool night air washes over me, smoke from the fire pit stinging my nose. I suck in a breath and shiver. Maybe I shouldn't be here.

I'm turning away to head back the way I came, to leave this stupid college party, when I see him.

Hunter Huxley.

He's impossible to miss. He stands near the fence, a red cup dangling from his hand, broad shoulders blocking the light behind him. Even when he's doing nothing, he takes up all the space. He has a sharp, dangerous energy that makes people turn to look at him without knowing why.

My pulse stutters. He's too much. Too tall, too intense, too sharp. A walking red flag. Everyone knows it. He sneers at professors, fights on the ice, and makes every girl with sense steer clear. But my eyes still find him. They always do.

He isn't alone. Jared Garrison, the overeager reporter from the school paper, is beside him. Jared doesn't belong here, not really. He clings to athletes like his life depends on it, begging for quotes, desperate to be seen.

I smooth my hair. Maybe I'll say hi. Maybe tonight I'll finally act normal instead of turning red whenever Hunter looks at me.

Then Jared laughs. Hunter's voice carries through the yard.

"Juliet Monroe? She's not all that great. She's not even hot. Just a control freak with no sex appeal. She probably has a spreadsheet to track her own virginity."

The words slam into me.

For a second I can't breathe. Maybe I misheard. Maybe the music twisted the sound. But Jared laughs again. Hunter's mouth twists into a serious expression that makes it clear he meant it.

"I don't know. She's definitely charming, if you know what I mean." Jared holds his hands in front of his chest, miming big breasts. "I'd like to see some more of her qualifications."

Hunter shoots him an icy look. "She's too much of a goody two shoes for that. I'd focus on somebody who's worth defrosting."

Jared laughs, slapping Hunter's shoulder. Hunter gives him an irritated glance. "Good one. Maybe you can give me a list, huh?"

Hunter grunts, sipping his drink. He opens his mouth to say something else, but at that moment, a group of drunk girls bursts out of the frat's back door, laughing and singing along to a Halsey song that's piped through the house's speakers. Hunter turns to look at them and misses me entirely.

Not that I really needed him to see me. I'm about three seconds away from sobbing.

My face burns. My throat tightens. Tears sting my eyes, hot and humiliating. I knew Hunter was mean. Everyone knew that. But I didn't know he'd ever waste that meanness on me. I thought… stupidly… I thought maybe he'd noticed me.

I step back, my shoes scraping the stone. More people pour out of the back door, the party swells, devouring the quiet in the backyard. Neither of them look my way. They don't even notice I'm there. My chest aches as I turn, pushing through the crowd at the edge of the yard. I shove past a couple making out against the wall, stumble against the gate, and spill out onto the side street.

That's when I run straight into Patrick.

He looks polished as always, his shirt crisp, hair styled, smile practiced. He steadies me with one hand on my arm, grinning. "There you are. I thought you stood me up."

Hunter's words echo in my head, cruel and sharp. Control freak. No sex appeal. Spreadsheet virgin. My stomach twists. I blink fast and force a smile. "I was looking for you."

Patrick slides his hand down my arm until our fingers link. "Want to get out of here? Somewhere quieter?"

I hesitate only a second before nodding. Anything to get away. Anything to silence Hunter's voice replaying in my skull. I squeeze Patrick's hand and tug him down the sidewalk. The October air is chilly, but my skin burns hotter with every step.

Patrick laughs, smug and careless. "Guess you're finally ready to fuck me, huh?"

The last fragile thread inside me snaps. I glare at him, my voice sharp. "Shut up, Patrick."

He laughs again, but I don't let go. I hold tighter because right now, I'd rather deal with Patrick's arrogance than spend another second in that backyard, listening to Hunter Huxley tear me apart.

And under all the shame and anger, something settles deep in my chest. A promise. If Hunter thinks I'm nothing more than a stuck-up prude with a spreadsheet, then I'll prove him wrong.

Present Day

I walk into my apartment ready to scream into a pillow for twenty minutes. It's been that kind of day at Foxies, the hell-hole that keeps on giving.

Foxies birthdays mean me dancing on the bar. Today? Six rounds. Add the usual: finger snaps, guys tugging my shorts asking if they come in a smaller size…

Yeah, I'm absolutely done with bullshit today. I've had my fill. But I come home to find Jessa practically vibrating with excitement, bouncing on her toes like she's about to burst.

"Oh my God, Juliet, you won't believe this," she says before I even get my Foxies sweatshirt off. "I talked to Ivy, the team's crisis communications director, and she wants to meet with you about the fake fiancée plan."

I freeze with one arm still in my sleeve. "Wait. What plan?"

Jessa's excitement falters slightly, and she suddenly looks sheepish. "The one you came up with last night? About Hunter needing a fake fiancée to fix his image? I told Ivy that you would do it. I thought you were serious."

The blazer hits the floor. "I hate Hunter Huxley. I told you that. When did I volunteer to fake an engagement to him?"

"Well, you didn't exactly, but you had the plan worked out, and you seemed so passionate about it. I thought…" Jessa's voice gets smaller with each word. "Oh God. I already pitched the idea. The team loved it. If you back out now, I'm going to look like a complete idiot."

"The fuck?" I stare at her as if she's speaking Mandarin all of a sudden. "Jessa!! You didn't just throw me under the bus. You backed the damn thing over my corpse!"

Of course they want me for this.

Not because I'm qualified. Not because I'm brilliant. But because I look good next to a six-foot-six tantrum.

"I know! I'm sorry! But think about it as doing the team a favor. A favor that might help you land your next actual job. You want to work in PR, right? Maybe someone on the team will owe you one. Maybe they'll throw you a client referral. Who knows what could come of this? Besides, they would pay you very well."

My brain is spinning. On the one hand, I want to strangle my roommate for volunteering me for this insanity without asking. She's not wrong about the opportunity. I desperately want to show the team that I'm competent and PR-savvy. This could be my chance to prove myself in the industry I've been trying to break into.

And if it paid well enough? Maybe I could finally ditch the crop top and launch my damn PR company for real.

But fake dating Hunter Huxley? The man who ruined my college internship with one thoughtless quote? The walking anger management case who punched a fan last night?

"Please," Jessa begs. "Just go to the meeting. You can explain the misunderstanding and fix this whole thing. You're amazing at talking your way out of situations."

I close my eyes and take a deep breath. "When's the meeting?"

Jessa cringes. "Right now."

"Right now?" My voice comes out as a shriek. "Jessa!"

"I'm sorry! I'm so sorry! But you have to go. Please? I

talked about your plan like it was going to happen... and now, it might be."

"Girrrrrrl." I glare at her. "You're lucky you're adorable, you know that?"

Jessa gives me a guilty grin. "Thank you, Juliet. You're saving my ass."

I have exactly twenty minutes to get dressed and drive to the arena. I race to my closet and pull out my usual conservative armor. Black blazer, black slacks, white blouse buttoned to my throat. I make sure that there's not even a hint of sexuality; this is the outfit that I want the team managers to meet me in. I want my qualifications to speak for themselves and have absolutely nothing to do with my tits or my ass.

It'll be the opposite of my interview to work at Foxies, which was less than a minute long. The manager took one look at me and practically threw a uniform at my head.

As I'm plotting revenge, Jessa intercepts me at the bedroom door.

"Wait. That makes you look like you're going to a funeral. What about this?" She holds up a black dress that actually shows some shape, with a neckline that hints at cleavage without being inappropriate.

"Absolutely not." I cross my arms.

"Juliet, you're supposed to be convincing them you could be someone's fiancée. At least look like you've heard of romance. You've gotta sell it a little."

I heave a sigh. Against my better judgment, I put on the dress and top it with the blazer for safety. I tell myself I can take the blazer off if I need to look more approachable. More wifely.

The drive to the arena is a blur of panic and half-formed strategies. When we arrive, I'm thrilled to be walking through the team offices. It feels like being close to magic, like I'm finally where I belong instead of serving wings in a glorified bikini.

That feeling lasts about thirty seconds.

When we walk into the conference room, Hunter Huxley is already there. He's sitting at the far end of the table looking like I kicked his puppy and then set his truck on fire. His stormy gray eyes lock onto mine with an expression that clearly says this is all my fault somehow.

I'm introduced to a room full of powerful people. Jimbo Greene, the team owner, is a paunchy man who looks like he eats smaller businesses for breakfast. Ivy Prescott, an icy blonde who introduces herself as the crisis communications director, and who's eyeing me like I'm an interesting specimen.

Coach Damian Cross towers in his black Havoc windbreaker, tall, Black, and built like he could still drop gloves if he had to. He obviously won some old fight that broke his nose.

The room carries a restless energy. Every man here knows last season was a disaster. Half the roster is gone, management burned the place down to the studs, and nobody is sure if what's left will hold together.

Cross crosses his arms and glares at the table. "We are not repeating last year. I don't care who's still shell-shocked about the roster cuts. We fix this now or we're all out of jobs."

Jimbo leans back in his chair, expression carved from stone. "The locker room is thin. Guys are second-guessing every shift."

Ivy clears her throat. "The rookies look terrified. It seems like everyone has serious whiplash from half the team being let go last year."

"We had to clean house." Jimbo looks around the room.

"The Havoc was on a losing streak for the last four years. Jared and I made the hard decision to fire most of the vets and bring in a bunch of rookies. It allows Coach Cross to rebuild the team from scratch."

"Not completely from scratch." Coach Cross fidgets. "We kept Huxley because he has a proven track record of winning games. But damn it, Huxley, you can't be fighting fans. We have to figure something out, stat."

Am I the *something* that he needs? I wait for Jimbo to address me, anxiety creeping in.

Hunter doesn't say a word. He sits in the corner like a coiled spring, jaw tight, every inch of him daring someone to tell him he's the problem. More than anyone else, people have blamed him for the team's collapse and rebirth.

I open my mouth to explain that this is all a misunderstanding, that I never actually volunteered for anything, but Jimbo cuts me off before I can get a word out.

"Now, Ms. Monroe. The hockey league is already calling, talking about a ten-game suspension for Hunter. Sponsors are calling, complaining," he says, showing the people in the room. "So we all had a meeting about last night's incident. And when Ivy told us your idea..."

"It wasn't–" I try to interject.

"Let me finish," Jimbo cuts in, his voice booming even though he isn't intentionally yelling. "If Hunter was defending someone he cared about, the league might treat it differently. There's already chatter online. People are wondering if something's going on between the two of you. Why not lean into it?"

"But–" I try again to correct them, but Jimbo talks right over me like I'm background noise.

"Ivy tells me you two went to college together," he says, directing the question at me like I'm being interviewed for a job I didn't apply for. "Did you know each other back then?"

"We did," I admit reluctantly, because lying seems like a bad way to start this conversation. My cheeks heat even though I have no reason to be embarrassed.

"Perfect!" Ivy claps her hands together like I just solved world hunger. "You're absolutely perfect for this role, Juliet. And of course, we'd employ you as a PR consultant during the arrangement. Jessa says you're interested in the field."

Oh. If I'm employed by the team, that would mean I could no-call no-show for my next shift at Foxies. That's a tantalizing idea. It's too bad that the opportunity is with Hunter Huxley, who absolutely hates my guts for no reason I can figure out.

He always has, as far as I can tell.

I look at Hunter for support. Surely he knows that this is the worst idea possible. Hunter, however, is glaring fixedly at a spot on the shiny conference room table.

I want to scream. Not just because it's the worst plan in the world, but because of how easily everyone assumes I'll go along with it.

They see curves and lipstick and assume I'll smile and say yes. They don't see the years I spent building a career nobody takes seriously because I didn't show up in a suit and a dowdy haircut.

Fake a relationship with a man who humiliated me in college? Sure, why not! Be charming, agreeable, helpful? Of course!

I swallow the resentment and let it simmer. It tastes familiar. Like every room I've ever walked into with a résumé.

Ivy looks at me. "You are interested in working in PR, aren't you?"

The mention of actual employment, of a job in PR, makes

my pulse quicken. I glance at Hunter, who's now glaring daggers at me, silently begging me not to say yes. But this could be my chance. My way out of the Foxies crop top and into an opportunity for advancement.

"The relationship needs to be public, visible," Ivy continues, warming to her theme. "It has to last long enough to sell the illusion. Long enough to make Hunter look like a changed man who's found love and settled down. Only six months."

"I'm not sure I want this," I say, but even I can hear that my voice lacks conviction.

That's when Ivy slides a tablet across the table. It's a still frame from last night, captured right before Hunter threw that punch. But he's not looking at the fan he's about to hit. His eyes lock on me and his expression is fierce and protective in a way that makes my breath catch.

He looks like a man defending his woman. The narrative has already started writing itself. I swallow.

"No," Hunter growls from across the table. "Absolutely fucking not."

I want to protest too, but my heart isn't really in it anymore. I'm staring at that image, at the way Hunter looked at me last night. Something warm is unfurling in my chest and I absolutely don't want to examine it.

Jimbo drops the hammer. "It's this, or you get traded, Hunter. Period."

The words hit the room like a physical blow. Hunter actually flinches, and for a second he looks less like the terrifying enforcer and more like a lost kid.

"I want to stay," he mutters, his voice less sure than I've ever heard it. "My brothers play here. I've played my entire career here. If I get a choice, I'll play here until I retire."

The admission hangs in the air, raw and vulnerable. This team isn't just his job. It's his family. And they're threatening to rip him away from it unless he plays along with this charade.

I'm furious and humiliated, but I'm also calculating. If I'm stuck in this situation, if there's no way out that doesn't hurt him and do me no favors, then I'm going to control the terms.

"Fine," I say suddenly, sitting up straighter. "Two bedrooms, one shared address. Five months. I'll handle the optics. He can sulk in the background, looking moody and misunderstood." I pause, drumming my fingers against my lips. "The PR team can soft-launch us the day after tomorrow with some carefully staged photos. And I will get a really massive diamond ring. I'm talking about the size that rock stars buy their girlfriends."

The words come out steady and professional, even though my pulse is racing fast enough to power a small city. I look up at Hunter, my gaze clashing with his. I'm pinned in place by his eyes, a violent swirl of blue-gray that makes me dizzy.

God, what am I doing?

Hunter's eyes narrow on my face for a long moment. He looks conflicted. It's a surprise to me as much as anyone else when he grunts, "Deal." Something electric slides between us across the table.

I've made a deal with the devil.

"Excellent!" Jimbo declares. He snaps his fingers at Ivy, who is already pulling out paperwork. "Ivy will set you up with the details. Welcome to the team, Juliet."

Ivy slides a short-term employment contract across to me. My eyes bug out at the dollar amount: one hundred thousand dollars. Holy god. That's a life-changing amount of money. I sign the contract without looking at Hunter, my signature quick and decisive.

And just like that, I'm fake engaged to Hunter Huxley.

Hunter and I leave the office together in complete silence. The hallway feels endless. By the time we reach the parking garage, the weight of what just happened is settling over me like a lead blanket.

God, this is going to be an awkward five months.

"Hunter," I start, turning to face him.

"You just trapped me in a fucking cage and threw away the key," he snarls. "I'm not a zoo animal, Juliet."

My name comes out of his mouth as if he's spitting poison. It sounds almost ugly. I shove a finger into his chest. "I saved your caveman ass. You're welcome."

We're standing too close, close enough that I can smell his cologne. Something woody and clean that makes me want to lean closer, which is absolutely the last thing I should think about right now.

That's when I catch him staring at me. But he's not looking at my chest like every other guy I meet. His gaze drops to my mouth, slow and deliberate. Like that's the part of me that might actually be dangerous to him.

For a second, I forget how to breathe. The realization that Hunter Huxley, the man who barely tolerated me in college, is looking at me like I'm suddenly on his menu short-circuits my brain completely.

"You're such a jerk," bursts past my lips. "Honestly, Huxley."

"Better than being all high and mighty," he sneers. "You were always holier than thou, weren't you, Ace?"

I bristle at the nickname. It's been years since I've heard him say it, making fun of my being on the school newspaper. And I hate it every bit as much now as I did back then.

"Grow the fuck up, Huxley."

We glare at each other in the fluorescent lighting of the parking garage. The moment stretches for several seconds until the silence grows unbearable. Am I going to be the one to break this tension?

"Five months," he husks out.

I arch a brow. He looks at me, those blue-gray eyes alight with resentment.

He looks at my mouth again. It's not subtle. My pulse does a stupid little stutter. He says, "That's the agreement. Five months, and then I can go back to pretending that you don't exist."

Finally. There is some give in his steely personality. I incline my head. "Five months. Then we call it quits."

I stick out my hand, offering it for him to shake. Hunter makes a face, because he's a prick, and then engulfs my hand in his giant mitt. His palm is hot to the touch and makes me nervous.

Guys like Hunter get praised for rage. Girls like me get told to smile more.

God, I can't stand him. Even things he can't control, like the fact that he runs hot, annoy the bejeezus out of me. I turn and walk toward my car, my heels clicking on the concrete. Hunter calls after me.

"Where the fuck are you going, Ace?"

I slow, turning, that nickname making me grit my teeth. "Home."

"Nah." He jerks his head toward his car. "You're riding with me, Ace. You started this blaze. Now you burn with me."

I should say no. I should walk away and slam the door for dramatic effect. Instead, I follow him like a moth straight into the roaring fire.

Chapter 4

Hunter

I dangle my keys in front of the face of the one woman that I truly loathe, just because I know it will make her cheeks grow pink with anger. Juliet screws up her face, her dark chocolate eyes flashing with something dangerous.

"Don't push me, Huxley."

"You're awfully self-righteous for someone who just hitched her wagon to my star."

"I did no such thing!" Her mouth bunches up, and she looks like she's about to explode. "You know what? This was a bad idea. I'll call Jimbo and tell him I'm not interested because you're a douche."

Like hell she will. I roll my eyes. "Calm down."

She points at me, serious as a concussion. "Don't tell me to calm down. I won't stand here and have you make sexist remarks to me."

"Sexist remarks?" I put my hands up. "Whoa, whoa. Let's back up. Can we just go somewhere to talk about this like we're fucking human?"

"You know what?" Juliet puts a hand on her hip, grinding

her teeth. "I need a drink. And you're buying. Consider it your thank you for not destroying your career."

I snort. "Please. I would've been fine."

It's half a joke, but also not really. I'm still running hot from that meeting, adrenaline tightening every muscle in my body like I just finished a fight.

"Do me a favor and just don't talk until you get me a drink."

I drive while she stares out the passenger window like she wants to break it with her mind. I tell myself to focus on the road, not on the tension rolling off her like heat waves. Not on her crossed arms or her clenched jaw or those ridiculous heels that are so impractical it's almost offensive.

Those same heels she always wore in college. Those dresses, pretty little floral wrap dresses that emphasized her innocence somehow, made her dark hair and olive skin pop. She's too polished, too composed, too everything. It pisses me off how tightly she keeps herself wound, like she's afraid of what might happen if she lets go for even a second.

I don't know either, but I bet it'd be entertaining.

I drive us to The Secret History, a noisy bar that's in my building. Living in the Sinclair, the team-owned luxury apartment building, puts me only a few minutes from the arena. I like The Secret History because not only is it close to home, but it has an excellent selection on tap and they highly discourage looky-loos by providing the Seattle Havoc players with a private back room.

Juliet strides inside like she owns the place and orders a gin and tonic with four limes. I get whatever's on tap and then lead her to a booth in the back room. It's almost empty, as it's a Wednesday night. Perfect for working out the terms of the ridiculous agreement that she's backed me into.

We sit across from each other, sipping our drinks, and it

feels like a standoff. Her arms folded on the table, my jaw tight enough to crack teeth.

She shrugs out of her blazer, and my eyes practically bug out of my head. That dress underneath is a fucking landmine. Tight across her chest, hugging every curve. I've been trying not to look at her mouth all night, but now I can't stop picturing the rest of her under me. I'm not even a tits guy, but suddenly I want to live and die by that neckline.

She catches me looking and turns red. "Really? That's where your brain goes?"

"What, it's my fault for noticing?" I mutter, taking a long drink of beer. "You're the one who wore the damn dress."

She rolls her eyes and pulls out her phone, then writes on cocktail napkins. Fast and aggressive, like she's solving a hostage negotiation instead of planning a fake relationship.

"Do you think we should be one of those couples that are saving themselves for marriage? Would that fly?"

I snort. "No way. Who would believe that?"

Juliet's mouth drops open. "What are you implying? That people think I'm a slut?"

"Jesus! No." I shake my head. "Honestly? I thought people would think that I'm too much of a slut."

"Oh." She sits back, the tension easing from her shoulders. "Hm."

"You know what will make this conversation go more smoothly? If you just assume that I'm not trying to slut-shame you with every comment I make. I may be an asshole, but I'm not that kind of asshole. I have never thought you were easy. If anything, I think the opposite."

She sniffs and adjusts the neckline of her dress so that I can see less of her cleavage. "I think it would be better if you keep your mouth shut about how you see me."

"Done." I sip my beer, trying to give myself a moment to collect my thoughts.

"So, about my apartment–" She pokes out her bottom lip, drawing my attention. Damn her and her bright red lipstick. "Frankly, I can't afford to split rent on a fancy condo when I'm already stretched thin financially."

Flipping my hand out, I brush off her concern.

"I'm paying the mortgage upstairs. I'll pay yours, too. For the next five months, I'm paying for everything and a fat fucking stipend on top of that."

She presses her lips together. "I don't own my apartment. Jessa and I pay rent. But… thanks. It'll help me get the rent taken care of for the next five months."

I don't want her to know that I have monitored her whereabouts since college. I checked on her every six months when she was living in Houston with that arrogant asshole Patrick Delacroix. And when she moved back to Seattle… I follow her Instagram through a Finsta, so I knew as soon as she moved back.

Why do I follow her? That much is unclear. Something about hating her fuckhole boyfriend, I guess.

Juliet takes a long sip of her drink, squeezing one lime into her glass and then nibbling on the leftover bits of lime clinging to the rind. Then she draws a deep breath and reaches for a stack of cocktail napkins.

"We're going to need house rules."

I'm not stupid. I know exactly what this is. Juliet doesn't trust me to behave like a normal human being. She's setting rules like I'm a rabid dog that needs a muzzle, and she's the handler making sure I don't bite anyone.

I feel like I'm being managed instead of respected. The worst part is I probably deserve it after last night. But that doesn't mean I have to like her rules or the way she looks at me like I'm a loaded gun someone forgot to lock up.

I'm not sure what to say, so I shrug a shoulder. "Yeah, maybe rules could be good."

She clears her throat. "First rule. Five-month engagement. Ends after the playoffs."

I grunt. "Agreed."

She purses her lips, tapping the end of the pen on the napkin. "I keep the ring until the end. You'll need to buy me one. Something big."

She says it with a straight face, but I catch the way she fiddles with the edge of her napkin. Like she's pretending this is all a joke. Like she's not a little curious about what a ring from me would look like on her hand.

My brain short-circuits at the image. Juliet in my jersey, bare legs tucked under her, that diamond flashing while she flips through papers and bosses me around like she owns me.

Ungh.

I shoot her a look. "Do you want diamonds or cubic zirconia?"

Juliet doesn't want just a ring. She wants proof. A trophy. Something that screams he's mine and you don't get to question it. And hell, maybe she deserves that.

Not with me, of course. But I have absolutely no doubt that some guy will buy her the biggest rock possible and love making her wear it. Some extremely lucky guy.

Her lips twitch. "Depends. Are you trying to look like you make the league minimum?"

I flip her off. She scribbles down the rule.

"Tons of content," she says. "We need Instagram posts. Couple-y, cute, believable stuff. I'll run the account. You'll act like you care."

"It already sounds fake as hell."

"Good. It is."

I lean in. "No touching my gear, my blender, my gym bag, my sticks, whatever."

"Gladly. I want nothing to do with your… stuff."

Thinking for a moment, I add:

"No hookups. Not with me, not with anyone. Don't make headlines. Don't embarrass me."

She stares at me. "Same to you."

"Never said I wouldn't be classy." I say it with a hint of a tease.

"Yeah, right." She snorts. "You've got the subtlety of a nuclear bomb."

It's weird, because we know each other. There's a history between us. Or at least, we know each other's reputations. Which is a toss-up.

I smirk at her. "I'm still hot, though."

Juliet looks away, biting back something. Could be a smile. Could be anger.

"Fine."

"Fine," I parry. "You'll move in tomorrow."

Juliet stares at me across the table as she stacks up the cocktail napkins and jogs them. Her second drink arrives, and she doesn't break eye contact while she takes a sip. I barely touch my beer. My stomach's too tight, too twisted up with whatever this feeling is.

"This is going to be hellish," I finally mutter. "And we haven't even been fake engaged for three hours."

She drinks, her throat bobbing gracefully. Doesn't say a word.

When Juliet disappears down the hall toward the bathroom, I finally exhale.

The teasing scent of whatever perfume she wears lingers after she's gone. It's citrus and heat and something that makes my whole body tense up. Like a memory I can't quite place but know I'd kill to relive. It makes my brain stall.

I can still feel her waist under my hand from earlier. Still remember the way she leaned into me when she slipped, like she trusted I'd catch her. Even if it was just for a second.

She's so small. I always forget how small she is until I see her and wonder how the world hasn't devoured her completely.

I shouldn't care. I definitely shouldn't be thinking about how good she felt pressed up against me. How easy it would be to press her harder. Pin her down. Slide my hand up that tempting little dress and see what else she's hiding behind that perfect mouth and terrifying brain.

I take a long drink of my beer and force myself to think about hockey. About press obligations. About anything that isn't the way she looked at me like she didn't hate me for once.

This is going to be hell.

Once she returns with the loud click of her expensive heels on the concrete floor, I say, "Are you planning on driving yourself home?"

"Yes." She crosses her arms. "Why?"

I flag down the waitress and hand her Juliet's unfinished drink. "She's done."

Juliet's eyes flash dangerously. "Excuse me?"

"You're five feet tall and maybe a hundred pounds soaking wet," I tell her. "You've had enough. We have a big day tomorrow. I'm not risking it."

She takes a long, deliberately defiant sip of her drink, then flashes me a sugar-sweet smile. "Get fucked."

I stand up and toss cash on the table. "I'm leaving."

"So leave. I'll get an Uber."

I lean in close, lowering my voice. "Like hell I'm leaving

you here alone. Look around. You think people haven't noticed us sitting together? They've been gossiping about us, no doubt. So act like you actually like me and let's go."

I thrust Juliet's blazer at her while she glares at me. Her spine straightens and some of the fight goes out of her. She doesn't argue. That tells me everything I need to know about how much this job opportunity really means to her.

Outside, she walks stiffly beside me. No words, just her heels clicking on the sidewalk and her jaw tight with suppressed anger.

"What's your address?" I ask.

She grinds her teeth. "Just take me to my car, Huxley."

"No. Stop being a brat and give me your damn address."

She blows out a breath like I'm the one being difficult. Me.

"11532 Rainier Place, Unit 112."

I key the address into my car's navigation system, pulling away from the curb. "Put your seatbelt on, future Mrs. Huxley."

"You're the worst," she bites back. But she pulls the belt across her body and fastens it with a click. "Now I'm going to have to get up early and go get my car from the arena."

"I'll take you."

"You're going to take me? Do you know how out of your way that is?"

"Just let me fucking take you, okay?"

"So damn bossy." She tsks.

"Pick a lane," I mutter as I start the engine. "Do you want to act like you're my fiancée or not?"

The idea of getting close to her feels like walking straight into a trap. She's too sharp, too smart, too everything I've never been good at dealing with.

The drive to her apartment is silent except for my navigation system reading the directions aloud. Her apartment is in Capitol Hill, a few blocks off Broadway. When I pull up to her building, I study it with a frown. It's not terrible, but it's not great either. A place where the locks might not work and the security cameras are just for show.

She gets out and I watch her summon that fake breezy confidence, the mask she wears when she wants people to think everything's under control. She struts to her door as if she doesn't have a care in the world. But when she thinks I'm not looking, her shoulders curl in. Just for a second.

I stare at her legs as she goes. She's tiny, but her bare legs below that short black dress are killer. That she can walk with as much sass as she does is honestly pretty impressive.

"What time tomorrow?" I call out the window.

She doesn't even look back. "We'll get it after we move."

Then she slams the door as though it insulted her mother.

I sit there for a minute, just breathing. My hands are tight on the steering wheel. Pushing out a breath, I shake my head.

Five months. One fake relationship. One tiny woman with ridiculous red lipstick that she wears like armor.

I've made a deal with the devil… and she wears red lipstick and heels sharp enough to sever a carotid artery.

Chapter 5

Juliet

I nibble on my lower lip as I stare down at the text conversation I'm having with Derek, my manager from Foxies. Apparently texting him I QUIT is not the way to actually quit working at his sleazy restaurant.

Juliet: I QUIT

Derek: You had better show up today for your shift.

Juliet: Or what?

Derek: Or you won't get a reference out of me for your next job.

Juliet: I don't like bullies, Derek. And I hated working for you. Don't contact me again.

Derek: Bitch

Blocking his number, I take a deep breath. That went about as well as could be expected. While I don't like drama, I am glad that I'll never hear from him again.

At ten a.m. on the dot, the moving company arrives at my old building. I greet them at the front desk in full armor. Red lipstick applied with military precision, hair piled high on my head and held with a clip, heels that say don't test me, and a pair of high-waisted wide-leg sailor pants.

"You're the Monroe move?" the lead guy asks, checking his paperwork.

"That's me. Everything's labeled and inventoried. Handle the boxes marked 'fragile' like they contain nuclear material."

The movers take one look at me and don't question a single instruction. They just move. Exactly like I need them to.

Jessa is here helping, which means she's hovering around the edges making anxious commentary while I orchestrate this entire operation like a general commanding troops.

"Are you sure you want to do this?" she asks for the fifth time this morning. "I mean, it's not too late to back out. We could say you got food poisoning or something."

"Jessa." I give her a look. "Is this about me paying rent? Because I already promised I would pay to keep my bedroom open for when I return in a few months."

She shakes her head. "It's not about that. I just feel terrible about getting you into this mess."

"You feel terrible? I'm the one who has to live with him."

She winces. "Maybe it won't be that bad. Maybe he's different now."

"He's fucking late." I give her a prim look. "I'll bet he's exactly the same."

I tell myself this is strategic, nothing more. A carefully calculated PR move to salvage Hunter's reputation and prove my own worth to the team management. But the real reason my stomach keeps twisting into knots isn't the cameras or the inevitable media attention we'll get. It's him.

He just rubs me the wrong way. I can't forget for one second that Hunter Huxley is the same man who once humiliated me at a college party in front of half the journalism department. The one who changed the trajectory of my career, of my entire life, by telling a journalist his inner thoughts about me.

Juliet Monroe? She's not really my type. Probably not anyone's.

Two days later, I found out I had been passed over for an internship position that I was all but guaranteed to get. And my face splashed across the "Interviews With Student Athletes" section, coupled with his hurtful statement, sealed my decision about him.

It's not Hunter's fault that Jared decided to print what would obviously in retrospect be off the record conversation. But Jared didn't trick him into saying those awful things about me. He's a fucking asshole.

Everything is perfectly in place by the time Hunter arrives. An hour late, of course. Because why would he respect the schedule he asked for when he can just show up whenever he feels like it?

He strolls in wearing aviator sunglasses, gray sweatpants that hang low on his hips, and the smug indifference of a man who knows he can get away with murder. His dirty blond hair is still messy from sleep, and he's got that just-rolled-out-of-bed look that somehow works on him in ways that deeply annoy me. There's stubble along his jaw that suggests he couldn't even be bothered to shave for moving day.

Jerk.

"You're late," I say, crossing my arms and giving him my best disapproving stare.

He pulls off his sunglasses and gives me a slow once-over, his gaze traveling from my heels to my face with deliberate slowness. "Traffic."

"It's Sunday morning."

"Church traffic."

"You don't go to church."

"How would you know?"

I gesture at his entire appearance. "Lucky guess."

He smirks like he finds my entire existence amusing. "Do you sleep in slacks?"

I'm wearing perfectly appropriate but dressy pants and a crisp white blouse, thank you very much. Nothing about my outfit warrants that kind of commentary. But I refuse to rise to the bait. I have better things to do than get into a fashion argument with someone wearing sweatpants to his own fake engagement.

Then he mutters, just loud enough for me to hear, "Let me guess. You get dressed in your room. With the door locked. Even when you're home alone and there's no one else to see."

I turn sharply, heat flashing up my neck. "Excuse me?"

He shrugs like he didn't just say something completely inappropriate. "Nothing."

He's teasing. I know that. But there's heat buried in the jab, something that suggests he's been thinking about my morning routine in ways that make my skin prickle. It throws me completely off balance. I'm sure that was exactly his intention.

That's when it hits me, in a sickening wave of realization. I won't have a single moment to myself while living with him. No lazy Saturday mornings in oversized t-shirts and messy hair. No wandering around in pajama pants with yesterday's makeup still smudged under my eyes. No breaks from being perfectly composed and camera-ready.

This version of me, the polished and unbothered profes-sional, is the only one he'll ever see. And I'll have to wear it like a second skin for the next five months. Jessa already teases me for wearing lipstick twenty four hours a day. Now

I'll have to deal with Hunter's snide little remarks, too. The thought is exhausting.

Can I back out of the deal now? Sure, the movers have already taken half the boxes out of my apartment. But it's probably not over till I've moved in with him…

Hunter jerks his head, motioning for me to follow him inside my now-empty room. The last of the boxes disappear down the hall. I rub my temples, a headache starting to bloom behind my eyes, and crouch to pick up a stack of loose hangers I forgot under the bed.

Before I can reach them, Hunter steps past me and grabs them first. No comment. No snide remark. Just picks them up, loops them on one finger, and sets them in the hallway.

I blink at him. "Thanks."

He shrugs. "Didn't want you to break a nail. You look like the kind of person who'd sue."

It's said with a smirk, but not a mean one. Which is maybe why I don't immediately snap back.

Instead, I glance over at him. He's reaching to adjust a stack of boxes, arm flexed, shirt riding up just enough to flash a sliver of skin. Just a hint of the V-cut under his abs. I look away immediately, like I've been caught doing something I shouldn't.

God. No.

No, no, no. I am not that girl. I don't care how hot he is, or how good he looks when he lifts heavy things like it's nothing. I do not get flustered over sweatpants and biceps and a hint of hip bone.

I'm just tired. That's all. Tired and overwhelmed and overly aware of the fact that I'm about to live with a man I can't stand in an apartment that isn't mine.

A man who just picked up my hangers without making it feel like a favor.

I don't say anything. I don't look again. But I feel the shift in the air like static before a storm. I follow him like he's a puppet master, pulling at my strings. I feel so helpless around him. Only him. Why is that?

He closes the door and looks at me. My breath stills.

"What?" I prompt.

"Before we do anything else," he says, suddenly serious. He pulls a small velvet box from his pocket. "We need to make this look real."

My heart does something stupid when I see the ring box. It's ridiculous. This is fake. A business arrangement. But there's something about the moment that feels bigger than it should, more significant than I want it to be.

As stupid and trite as it sounds, I have always imagined someone that really loved me and wanted to commit to me being the one to propose. Most little girls have the same fantasy, I think.

He opens the box and my breath catches in my throat. The ring is absolutely stunning, almost otherworldly. A huge marquise-cut emerald sits at the center like a sliver of green fire. Sharp, vivid, impossibly clear. The color shifts between deep forest green and brilliant emerald depending on how the light hits it. It's held in place by delicate tulip-shaped prongs that give the whole piece an almost vintage, fairy-tale feel. The band itself glitters with tiny white diamonds, tapering gently toward the center stone like a secret drawing your eye to the main event.

It doesn't shout for attention. It beckons. Regal, romantic, and just a little dangerous. Like a promise wrapped in velvet and thorns. I'm literally rendered speechless.

When he takes my left hand and slides it onto my finger, I suck in a breath. The fit is perfect, like he somehow knew my exact ring size. Which makes me irrationally angry. I don't want him getting things right. I don't want to feel chosen by someone who's only pretending to care.

The weight of it feels substantial, real, important. It's exactly the sort of ring I pictured in my mind's eye when I was dreaming about fairy-tale weddings and happily ever after endings.

How could he possibly know that? How could he pick something so perfectly suited to tastes I've never shared with anyone?

In the midst of a very unspecial moment, there's a bit of magic tucked inside. And I frankly don't know how to handle it.

The romantic part of my brain, the part I've been trying to silence since Patrick, whispers that maybe this means something. Maybe he put thought into this choice. Maybe he sees me as more than just a convenient solution to his PR problems.

I touch the ring gently with my thumb, trying to keep the awe off my face. I'll never receive another ring like this, not in ten lifetimes. This is utterly unique, a piece of art as much as jewelry. Damn him for making this harder than it needs to be.

Hunter is a bad idea wrapped in a perfect moment. That's all this is. A moment. He's not asking me to fall for him. He's asking me to get out of trouble. Anyway, I refuse to be that stupid with a guy again, especially not this guy.

I've definitely learned my lesson where attractive, virile hockey players are concerned.

Hunter doesn't say anything about the ring choice. Neither do I. I wonder if he picked the ring out or if someone with taste did. Probably some nameless, faceless young woman who works at the jeweler's shop.

We just stand there for a beat, both of us staring at my hand like we're not sure what just happened.

"So?" Hunter arches a brow. "I've never proposed to anyone before, but I think you have to say something."

I narrow my eyes. "You didn't ask me anything. You just shoved the box into my hand."

"I didn't shove it." He rolls his eyes. "Will this work for your engagement ring?"

I gaze at the ring again. It sparkles on my finger. I admit, "This will work, I guess."

"All right." Hunter nods, his expression relaxing a hair. "I went with the ring that I could imagine you wearing. I'm glad you don't hate it."

My eyebrows rise. So he did pick it out. Interesting.

"I don't hate it," I affirm. I check my watch. "But I think we should get going. We have a lot of stuff to do. Including getting my car."

He flaps his hand. "Don't worry about your car. Give me the keys and I'll have it moved to the parking deck under the Sinclair."

"Have it moved? What if–" I start.

He cuts me off. "Come on, Ace. You can't give me shit about everything. Pick your battles."

I hate to say it, but he's kind of right. I don't have time to run any additional errands today. Not if I plan to get things unpacked at my temporary residence. I want as little interruption to my schedule as possible, so that's my ambitious plan.

"Fine. I'll get the keys," I say. Walking out into the living room, I realize that the movers have finished taking my boxes and now the apartment looks oddly empty.

We leave, stopping for an early afternoon coffee and a bagel with schmear. I get a quad-shot Americano with a hint of oatmilk and an everything bagel with a sun-dried tomato cream cheese. Hunter looks a little disgusted by my food choices, which warms me up inside.

Hunter can go *fuck* himself.

We arrive at the Sinclair, parking in the lot below the building. We take the elevator to the tenth floor, which has a total of four apartments. Hunter's is the one closest to the door on the right. Then he opens the door for me, pushing me inside when I dawdle to check out the finished concrete hallway.

"I'm going, I'm going," I mutter under my breath. "God, you're so bossy."

"You like it." Hunter smirks. "Now get inside."

I head in and instantly, I'm struck by what I see. Clean lines, glass walls, and a view that punches you in the chest. It has a sweeping wraparound deck that looks out over the Belltown waterfront. The windows stretch from floor to ceiling, all sharp edges and reflected sky, with the kind of sunset glow that makes real estate agents salivate.

It's obviously a luxury apartment, but it has that funny habit of trait completely without warmth. Three bedrooms, three bathrooms, everything expensive and impersonal. Designed by someone with taste, clearly not Hunter, and that person had insight into the man who lives there. The furniture is minimal and modern, all steel, stone, and leather. Not a throw pillow in sight. The kitchen's pristine, barely used, with an espresso machine he doesn't know how to work and a fridge that's eighty percent protein shakes and bottled water, twenty percent prepared high-protein meals from a service.

There's no art on the walls. No photos. Nothing personal except maybe a pair of scuffed skates tossed by the front door and a dented hockey bag parked by the mudroom bench.

"You live here?" I burst into a fit of laughter when I step

into the living room and open up the door that leads onto the terrace. "It looks like a billionaire's Airbnb, not a home."

Hunter sends me a glare. "You're sounding awfully judgy for someone whose old apartment doesn't have a working elevator, but does have a green carpet the exact color of baby puke."

"Hey!" My mouth falls open. "That place is economical. All those things were there before we even got there."

"No shit." He shrugs. "I'm just pointing out that you probably shouldn't be feeling too picky. This place is incredibly expensive."

"I never said otherwise."

He glares at me. "Welcome home, future wife."

My cheeks color. "Is my bedroom down this way?"

He nods, turning to look down the hallway. "Mine is the one at the end. Yours is the first room on the right. There's one bedroom on the other side of the hall that's my home gym."

Trailing down the hall, I open the door to my room. It's been set up as a guest room, as bland as can be. A large, beige bed. A beige rug under my feet. Famous hockey players' photos on two of the walls. A large window that looks out on another apartment building. I open the walk-in closet to find a surprising amount of space in here, too.

Stacked against the walls are my boxes, stacked two or three high. The room will do just fine, but if this were actually my space, I would make some very different design choices. I sip my latte and have a bite of my bagel as I plan my unpacking.

I start putting things where I judge they should go. First a new purple silk comforter and pearly silk sheets on the bed. Throw pillows, a soft plush gray rug in the ensuite bathroom.

My desk gets placed precisely in front of the living room

window where the light is best for working. My flamingo lamp, a vintage find from last year that cost me a week's worth of tips, stands proud beside my desk. My bar cart, inherited from my grandmother and restored with love and several YouTube tutorials, gleams in the corner of the living room like a promise of future coping mechanisms.

I'm standing on my tiptoes trying to reach the top shelf in one of the hallway cabinets when I feel him behind me.

Close. Too close.

"Let me get it," he says, voice low and much too near my ear.

I flinch as his arm reaches past me, the warmth of his chest brushing my back. He's not even touching me, not really, but I feel the heat of him everywhere. His hand wraps around the box I was struggling with. His fingers are long, steady, casually powerful. I have literally the worst thought imaginable.

I wonder what those hands would feel like on my hips.

I step away fast. Too fast. The box tips slightly. I lose my balance on the balls of my feet. I stumble backward and crash into him.

Hunter catches me without hesitation. One arm around my waist, the other gripping my wrist. His body is solid behind mine. Hard muscle. Bare forearms. He smells like soap and skin and something faintly woodsy, and I want to die.

My breath comes out sharp. His hand doesn't move.

Neither does mine.

We stay like that for a second too long. Maybe two.

Then he lets go.

"You good?" he says, already stepping back like he didn't just short-circuit every nerve ending in my body.

"Fine," I lie, because the truth is not an option.

I smooth my shirt, grab the box from where it landed and bolt for the bedroom like I'm not thinking about the size of his hands or the way his breath hit the back of my neck.

God, I hate him.

I really, really hate him.

Lastly, I unpack my clothes and shoes into the closet. Because I moved so recently, I knew just how to pack and unpack with a precise economy of movement. Dresses, skirts, pants, and tops are already on their hangers. Shoes are packed in the order of which they should be lined up. I'm done with my closet in under twenty minutes.

I take a breath, trying to ground myself in the familiar ritual of organizing my space. Creating order from chaos has always been my way of maintaining control when everything else feels uncertain. It *almost* works.

The movers were efficient and careful with my belongings, which is more than I can say for Hunter, who's now wandering around the condo like he's conducting some kind of inspection. He touches things without asking, opens cabinets that don't belong to him, and generally makes his presence known in ways that set my teeth on edge.

It's surreal being here. Rehearsing a proposal I never got, setting up house with a man I barely tolerate, faking a love story I never asked to be part of. The longer I stand next to him, the more the lines blur between performance and punishment. I'm not here to fall in love. I'm here to protect a man who's never protected me, and every time I'll have to smile for the cameras, it's going to feel like selling a piece of myself I can't afford to lose.

That's when Hunter opens a kitchen cabinet and starts laughing. Actually laughing, like something is genuinely hilarious.

"Did you actually label the spice bins?"

I don't look up from carrying my coffee maker into the kitchen, a French press that's one of my most prized possessions. "Touch anything and I'll stab you with the label maker."

He almost smiles. For a second, he looks less like the intimidating enforcer and more like a regular guy who finds my organizational habits amusing rather than annoying. "You're terrifying."

"Good. I like when I'm in charge."

He wanders into the living room and lifts one of my mid-century table lamps, examining it like it's some kind of alien artifact. His hands look enormous around the delicate crystal base. "Is this supposed to be art?"

I snatch it from his hands before he can drop it and ruin months of thrift store hunting. "That's vintage. Mid-century modern. If you break it, I will break you."

"Copy that," he says, backing away with his hands raised in mock surrender. "Death by lighting fixture. Got it."

"Har har har, so funny. You're a real comedian."

The smirk he shoots me is dripping with irony.

The afternoon passes in a series of small territorial disputes. Hunter treats the shared spaces like his personal dumping ground, leaving things wherever he happens to set them down. I follow behind him, rearranging and organizing, creating systems he immediately ignores.

Figures. Typical male bullshit.

Later, in my bedroom, I'm arranging my perfume tray on top of the beige dresser when I hear him lean against the doorframe. I can feel his presence without looking up. Bottles lined up by size, glass trays angled just so, everything in its perfect place. It's a ritual that calms me, this careful arrangement of beautiful things.

"You've got a whole tray just for smells?"

His voice carries a note of genuine curiosity rather than mockery, which surprises me. I ignore him and keep arranging, hoping he'll take the hint and leave me to finish unpacking in peace.

But Hunter has never been good at taking hints. He walks into my room anyway, which violates about three of our freshly laminated house rules. His presence makes the space feel smaller, more intimate than it should.

"What's this one?" He picks up a tiny crystal vial, one of my more expensive purchases.

I hesitate, my mouth puckering, not sure why I'm about to be honest with him. "The scent Patrick hated."

Patrick, my ex-boyfriend of five years. The hockey player who had opinions about everything I wore, everything I bought, everything I did. The one who slowly chipped away at my confidence until I wasn't sure what I liked anymore.

Hunter sets the bottle down carefully, more gently than I expected. "And now you wear it?"

"Out of spite."

He makes a humming sound, unreadable, and starts to walk away. But when he glances back at me from the doorway, there's something in his expression I can't place. Not mockery. Not quite curiosity either.

Something that looks almost like understanding. Like maybe he gets what it means to reclaim pieces of yourself that someone else tried to take away.

Either that or he is just trying to figure out how to move my delicate art deco lamp back into my bedroom when I'm not looking. Probably that.

He moves into the living room, following me, and I hand him a laminated sheet of paper. The house rules, typed up in professional font and protected by plastic for durability.

"You laminated the house rules," he says flatly, holding the paper like it might bite him.

"I did."

He grunts, reading through the list with what I can only describe as resigned acceptance. Then he drops his gym bag directly in front of my carefully positioned bar cart, completely blocking access to my grandmother's crystal decanters.

I don't hesitate. I drag the bag across the hardwood floor, not caring if I scuff the polished oak, and dump it outside his bedroom door with more force than strictly necessary.

"Petty," he mutters, but he doesn't move the bag back.

"Basic hygiene. Learn about it."

We immediately get into our first real fight over the thermostat. I turn it up to a reasonable seventy-five degrees, a temperature that will suit us both. He turns it back down to a subarctic sixty five.

"Seventy-five is not hot," I say, adjusting it again while giving him a frosty glare. "I think better when I'm not freezing."

"I don't want to die of heat exhaustion in my own living room," he fires back without a trace of embarrassment.

"You're being dramatic."

"You can put on more clothes. I can't wear any less. Buy a hoodie."

"I'm not going to wear a coat in my own living space. Get a life."

The back and forth continues for several minutes, each of us adjusting the temperature when the other isn't looking. It's petty and ridiculous, but also strangely familiar.

If he doesn't wise up though, I'm going to kneecap him. Then he'll have real problems to worry about instead of whining about being hot.

Later, I open the hallway closet to hang up my coat and find his rank hockey skates shoved on top of my carefully organized coat bins. The smell hits me immediately. Leather and sweat and something that might be athletic tape, all mixed together in a cocktail that makes my eyes water.

"HUNTER!"

He sticks his head out of his room, toothbrush hanging out of his mouth and toothpaste foam at the corners of his lips. "What?"

"I need you to move your hockey crap out of the hall closet. It's foul. And I want to store my coats there."

"It's shared space," he argues.

"So is the trash chute," I snap, dragging his gear bag out and dropping it with a loud thud that probably violates our lease agreement. "Guess where this is going if you don't handle it?"

"You're a terrorist. A five foot tall terrorist in heels."

"Huxleyyyy," I purr, imitating a valley girl. I put my hands and my hips and give him a saccharine smile. "At least this time your comments won't get printed in the campus paper."

That hits home. His jaw tightens and for a second, something flickers across his face that looks almost like regret. The reference to college, to the interview that cost me my internship, hangs between us like a weight. But then it's gone, replaced by that familiar smirk that says he's not going to apologize for anything.

"You agreed to this, Ace. Actually, it was *your* idea."

"As if I could ever forget," I fire back. "And don't call me Ace."

"I think it suits you."

Eyeing him, I cock my head. "Are you telling your brothers about the fake engagement?"

His expression is perplexed for a moment.

"I haven't really thought about it. I guess I could, but Jett has a big fucking mouth. It's probably better if I don't give him a secret to keep."

"I'm just trying to decide if I should tell my parents about it."

He shrugs. "That's up to you. Would your parents care?"

"Mm." I screw my face up. "They'll judge me. They hate hockey players, especially after Patrick and I broke up." Her lips twitch. "Mom thinks you're all complete idiots for playing a sport with such a high concussion rate."

"Well, can't argue with that logic. It sounds like whether you tell them or not, you're screwed."

With that, he heads to his room. I stare after him, knowing he's right. Since I don't want to follow in my mom's footsteps, my parents aren't really supportive of any choice I make. It's better to have them in the dark than to try and get them on my side by sharing the truth.

I spend most of the day unpacking boxes. By evening, I am more than ready for a shower and a relaxing evening. Maybe I'll read a nice cowboy romance on my Kindle. I change into silk pajamas that feel like luxury against my skin. Then I stare at the ceiling, trying to process the day.

My body's exhausted from the physical work of moving, but my mind is completely wired. His presence is too close, just down the hall. His energy is loud even through a closed door and probably decent soundproofing. My skin itches with irritation. Or maybe anticipation. I honestly can't tell anymore.

This was supposed to be a professional arrangement. Strategic. Clean. A business transaction that would benefit both of our careers and nothing more. I had it all mapped out in my head. We'd coexist politely, put on a good show for the cameras, and go our separate ways when the contract was up.

But I'm not sleeping. And I'm definitely not calm. I'm an engaged woman now, technically speaking. Mrs. Hunter Huxley-to-be. The thought is completely overwhelming. It's like wearing a pair of pants that are several sizes too big and that you keep tripping over. And I definitely didn't plan on feeling anything when he watched me arrange my perfume bottles like the ritual actually meant something to him.

I mean, I didn't. Just… being here, in his space, is not as terrible as I would've thought. I'm not sure what I imagined before I stepped in the door, but it wasn't a space that could be so easily spruced up. A bar cart, a few vintage lamps. I could probably find some throw pillows for the black leather couch and sleek metal loveseat.

I could almost feel at home here.

I touch the ring on my finger, twisting it slightly. The emerald catches the candlelight and throws tiny rainbows across the ceiling. It's beautiful. Perfect, even. The kind of ring that makes a statement about forever and happily ever after and all the things I stopped believing in when Patrick left.

Too bad this is all fake. And for a guy that's probably my worst fucking enemy.

Tomorrow, we'll go to our first charity event as a couple. We'll smile for the cameras and hold hands and pretend we're the next great love story of the NHL. I'll wear something appropriately fiancée-ish. He'll clean up nice in a suit that probably costs more than my rent. And we'll convince everyone that the Chainsaw has been tamed by love.

The thing is, Hunter has always been good at getting under my skin. Even in college, when we barely spoke except to argue, he had this way of looking at me like he could see right through whatever mask I was wearing. Like he knew something about me that I didn't want him to know.

And now I'm going to be living with him for five months. Sleeping down the hall from him. Kissing him in front of the cameras. Pretending to be in love with him. Acting like the woman who tamed the beast and lived to tell about it.

Picking up a purple satin pillow, I cover my face and moan my pain into it. This is going to be a tough road, no matter how I've managed to make the guest room my own.

Chapter 6

Hunter

God damn. I'd rather take a puck to the teeth than walk into this ballroom.

Before I step through the hotel ballroom doors, I'm dreading this gala. Fake smiles, forced chatter, media flashbulbs. Nothing about tonight feels real.

But by far the worst thing about tonight is my fake fiancée. Juliet grips my arm, looking like a cool, collected, confident woman. Sky high heels. Raven hair bobbing around her shoulders, styled to emphasize her curls. Emerald dress poured over her curves, bare shoulders catching the lights from the hotel entrance, lipstick dark and dangerous. With her slightly olive skin, the woman looks devastating in jewel tones.

Juliet grips my arm like she owns me, a dangerous glint in her eye. A huge, sparkling ring on that finger. She's trouble wrapped in silk.

"Can you pose for me?" She holds up her phone, angling it just so to snap a photo. She frowns. "Oh my god. Come on. Pretend I'm the love of your life."

I try not to choke. Easing my arm around Juliet, I try not

to look like I want to strangle her. The camera flashes a few times, with Juliet adjusting to make each photo something new. Her hand comes to rest on my chest, her engagement ring glinting in the lights. She leans her head back a little and I instinctively cup her lower back to keep her standing upright.

Our bodies press together in a way that alarms me. I want nothing more than to take Juliet's shoulders, give her a shake, and put distance between us. What is the saying? Good fences make good neighbors?

I would prefer it if the little vixen moved to the damn moon.

She heaves a sigh. "I'm giving this everything I've got, Huxley. Do something better with your face."

I roll my eyes and then give her phone the same expression I give the camera at a sponsored photoshoot. No matter what I'm selling, I want to give the viewer a sense of debonair mystery. Juliet snaps more pictures, moving a little each time, and then looks at her phone.

"Oh my god." She shows me the last one. I look stiff and uncomfortable, my eyes narrowed, my head tilted as if I am trying to figure out where a foul smell is coming from. She giggles. "As expected, you're terrible at faking this."

"I think that speaks volumes about what kind of person I am."

She giggles again, the sound impish. "You keep telling yourself that, Hux."

I like the sound of my name on her lips. Ryan warned me earlier, "You don't have to like a plan, you only have to survive it." He was talking about something else, but I would do well to remember it and bite my damn tongue.

Juliet flutters her long, thick lashes. "Are you ready for this, honey?"

"Not even remotely, darling," I fire back.

She grins and tightens her grip on my arm. "Perfect."

She drags me forward. I exhale like I'm a warrior seeking the precise focus he needs to head into battle. My pulse's already climbing, and we haven't even crossed the threshold.

She always paints her lips the same deep red. Too precise, too deliberate. I've always hated that lipstick. It screams, look at me in a way that sets my teeth on edge.

I'm looking. Every man is looking.

My jaw ticks. I tell myself it's not jealousy, just annoyance. She's playing a part. That's all this is.

But when she bends toward the camera later, touching my arm and smiling with that perfect mouth, all I can think about is how that lipstick's going to end up on someone else's collar if she keeps tempting the wrong people. The thought makes me want to break something.

I recover by needling her. "Didn't know you owned anything that wasn't stitched up to your throat."

She pivots, giving me a glare sharp enough to leave a scar. "Didn't know you owned anything that wasn't covered in sweat stains."

I feel the familiar rush. Annoyance, attraction, pure adrenaline. Provoking her and hearing her whip-smart retaliations is addictive in ways I probably shouldn't examine too closely.

She walks into a room and owns it. I walk in, and people brace for impact.

That's why I need to stay away. When someone like her lets someone like me in, all I do is wreck the place.

I enjoy making her angry, though. She's like a little five-foot firecracker, all contained energy and sharp edges. During one pose, I bend her backward slightly, liking how stiff her body gets. She's fighting me tooth and nail, and I like the challenge.

I have to lean down every time I talk to her. Makes me feel like I'm handling a toy dynamite stick. She's tiny, dangerous, and always one wrong move from exploding.

Then I catch myself. This isn't a challenge. I don't need to win anything here. And I definitely shouldn't get any closer to Juliet than I already am.

Inside the ballroom, we circulate. Black and gold drape the entire room. Round tables draped in white linens and centerpieces that probably cost more than most people make in a month. It's an event where everyone's here to see and be seen, where the actual charity work is secondary to the networking.

Decker, Moose, and Shane spot us first and approach with open shock written all over their faces.

Moose nudges Juliet with his elbow. "How much are you paying him to behave tonight?"

"Not nearly enough," she shoots back without missing a beat. It gets a laugh from all of them.

Earlier today, Ryan had tried to run a new drill with the defensive line and ended up barking at Shane, who couldn't keep his spacing right. I had to grit my teeth not to intervene. It wasn't my job to coach the rookies. Still, watching the kid fumble beside Jett made me itch all over.

"I always knew Juliet and I would get together eventual-ly," I say, wrapping my arm around her waist and pulling her closer. "She's always been the most beautiful girl in every room. She kicks everybody's ass intellectually too."

It's not untrue, but Juliet turns hot pink at the compliment. I decide to rub it in. "Isn't that right, baby?"

When I nuzzle her neck, her eyes go wide and the alarm I see registered there is nothing short of hilarious.

She elbows me in the ribs, hard enough to make her point.

"Hunter's always been such a romantic," she murmurs

sweetly. "Just last week he compared my eyes to... what was it, my love? Fresh-pulled espresso. Practically poetry from his lips."

God, I don't mind a feisty Juliet. The guys are eating this up.

Shane and Decker stick around for proper introductions. I watch Juliet work her magic. She grins at them, lighting up the entire space, and jokes with them easily. They're completely charmed within minutes.

Where is that ease with me? Why am I the special case who only gets her sharp edges and careful distance?

I know the answer, unfortunately. We have history. And it's not flattering to me. I might have told a reporter once that she was stuck up and asked why anyone would even like her. The back of my neck heats just thinking about it. Definitely not my finest moment.

My brother Silas appears like a ghost, raises one eyebrow at our performance, and says nothing. Thorne, captain of the team, watches us like we're a live experiment he's conducting.

Grayson deadpans, "Did I miss a press release?"

Juliet probably remembers Silas from our college days, but she hasn't met Thorne or Grayson. Silas asks how she's been, and she frowns.

"Uhh, fine?" She looks to me for help in navigating whatever weird dynamic this is.

I just shrug and make proper introductions. "Juliet, meet Thorne and Grayson. Center and left wing. Guys, this is my fiancée."

The word feels strange in my mouth. Foreign. Like trying to speak a language I don't actually know. Silas has a coughing fit because he's so surprised. I shoot him a glare.

Juliet mentions she loves being at galas, then immediately

starts picking apart this one. "Though this one isn't really up to my standards." She scans the room with a critical eye.

"What's wrong with it?" I ask, genuinely curious.

She barely pauses before launching into it, all brisk and focused like she's presenting to a boardroom.

'The branding's off,' she says, pointing behind us. 'The sponsor logos don't match between the welcome banner and the press wall. One company's massive on the entrance signage, like front and center, then practically invisible once you get to the red carpet. That's not a minor mistake. It's a visibility issue. It makes the event look worse than slapdash.'

I blink at her. I was expecting a yes or no. Maybe a meh. Not a TED Talk.

She doesn't notice my surprise, as she's still in go-mode. "It's like if Nike paid to sponsor the Super Bowl and you forgot to put the swoosh on half the jerseys. Someone's gonna get pissed, and they'll take it out on whoever was in charge of optics."

Then she sweeps her hand at all the guests, starting with the dress code confusion. "The invitation said black tie, but half the people here are in cocktail dresses. And look at this décor. String lights and rustic table settings? It screams garden party, not luxury gala. The tonal dissonance cheapens everything."

She's right. I wouldn't have noticed any of it, but now that she's pointed it out, I can't unsee the problems.

"And don't get me started on the silent auction. Shoved over there with no signage, terrible lighting, and handwritten bid sheets instead of tablets. They'll be lucky to raise half their projected total if nobody can even find where to bid."

I find myself impressed, though I'd never tell her that. I don't have the eye for detail that she does. Everything looks fine to me, but she sees all the ways it could be better. That's worth something, sure.

"It's okay to compliment me," she says with a quick smile. "Just once. I won't tell anyone."

I scowl. Of course, she has to have the last word.

"Ah, shit." Her phone buzzes, and she checks it with a frown. "An interview with your mom just went live on ESPN4."

I tense immediately. My mom? God knows what kind of poison is going to gush from her lying mouth. "Why would you even get that alert?"

Juliet gives me an odd look. "I set up a Google tracker on your name. Professional courtesy. Plus, for the time being, our fates are entwined."

"She stole my playoff bonus, Juliet. You don't come back from that."

Speak of the devil, Jett shows up right then, smug as ever in his perfectly tailored suit. "Don't you two look nice."

"Jett!" Juliet greets him more warmly than she greeted Silas. Her excitement irritates me for reasons I don't want to examine. "Long time no see."

"Hey there, Juliet. You're a sight for sore eyes. I didn't think Hunter would ever make a move," Jett says.

Juliet jumps in smoothly. "Oh, he's been secretly obsessed with me for years. Haven't you, honey?"

"In your dreams," I mutter.

She purrs back, "No, sweetheart. In yours."

Jett laughs. "Feisty little thing, aren't you?" She fake-gags at the nickname, which makes him laugh harder.

"I love you two together," he announces before strolling off, looking way too pleased with himself.

I'm left seething, though I'm not entirely sure why.

Juliet spots the Seattle Havoc's crisis communications

expert, Ivy, across the room and rushes off to whisper something urgent in her ear. I've had tall, blond Ivy on my ass for the last few months, every time I get into a nasty fight on the ice. She's always saying something about trying to keep me off her radar. Now, she looks at me, her icy blue gaze piercing me.

She doesn't look happy to see me. Guess punching that fan in the face was the last straw for her.

I watch Juliet as she greets Ivy, noting the differences between them. Ivy is tall and willowy, dressed to kill in a short red dress that clings to her body. Juliet is almost her opposite. Short, stunning, wearing a knee-length dress with a low-cut neckline. She's got lush curves and they're on display tonight. Tits pushed high, hips wrapped in emerald fabric, ruby red lips pursed.

I can admit to myself that Juliet is as stunning as she's ever been as she laughs at something Ivy just said. She's just here because she's stuck playing my fiancée, but she looks like she belongs at this fancy gala.

At the bar, Jett approaches. "So. Fiancée, huh?"

"Yup." I scrub my hand over my mouth. "We were… uh… keeping things private until recently."

"Nice. I remember her from college."

I raise an eyebrow. "You were a couple of years above us."

"Yeah, but I definitely remember her being a hockey girlfriend. She was always on the arm of that dick. What's his name?"

I grunt. "Patrick."

Jett gives me a slow smile. "You liked Juliet back then. What are the chances that you two would reconnect?"

I want to murder him, but I just give him a tight smile.

"I doubt she even remembers me from U of W."

"Yeah, right." He snorts. "It's good to see you two together. She softens your whole I'm going to murder you in your sleep vibe."

I grunt. "Maybe that's the vibe I want to give off."

He arches a brow, shakes his head, then goes quiet for a moment. "Mom's been leaving voicemails again."

I go cold. "I don't want to hear anything Mom says. She's dead to me."

"I'm not planning to. Just thought you should know."

Fixing him with a stare, I make it clear. "Talking to her is like opening a vein."

I don't care how sorry Mom says she is. I'm not bleeding for her again.

Jett nods. "Fine. Just watch yourself."

When Juliet returns, I catch her fidgeting with her emerald engagement ring. Without thinking, I cover her hand with mine. Camera bait, but also something else I don't want to name.

Flashes go off. In the back of the room, I see Jimbo Greene and Coach Cross smiling at my little display of supposed affection. If fans had any idea what my relationship with Juliet was really like… the constant bickering, the stubbornness for no reason… they would stop showing up to my games with Chainsaws.

It would be one way to shake off the dreaded Chainsaw act.

"Smile for the cameras," Ivy calls, her grin smug. "You two get close now. Let's see a kiss."

"I hate you," she whispers under her breath, smiling for the photographers.

I lean in like I might kiss her and murmur, "Sure you do."

Then I lay a kiss right next to her mouth. She gasps for half a second before falling into step with me. Her fingers tense against my shoulder. She's playing along, but I can feel the uncertainty in her grip. We're off-script now.

I dip her back, my mouth against her cheek. We're pressed tightly together and I can't help but notice how neatly her small, sleek body fits against mine. She digs her fingers into my shoulder and smiles, showing her perfect white teeth.

This is our first genuine attempt at faking our relationship, and I'd be lying if I said I wasn't nervous. Not that I'd admit that to anyone, especially not her.

Juliet moves her hand closer to my neck, attempting to draw her ring into the picture. The emerald glints in the light.

When she first saw the ring yesterday, her breath hitched. That's how I knew I picked well. She isn't very flowery and dresses extremely modestly most of the time, but I just had a feeling she would like this antique ring.

Smug male satisfaction fills my chest thinking about her reaction to seeing the dazzling emerald.

I can't help but laugh. She smiles up at me with pure malice radiating from her every pore. "What's so funny?"

I stick out my tongue, staring down at my beautiful fake fiancée. That's right. I can admit that her dark curls, brown eyes, and olive skin make her a knockout.

Not that it should matter to me, I guess.

"Oh, that's the headline grabber!" Ivy crows. "Wow, you two have chemistry coming out of your asses, don't you?"

I cock a brow at Juliet. But she just rolls her lovely brown eyes at me.

"Cool it," she orders. "Let me go. The moment is over."

As I release her, she stumbles slightly on an ornate rug near the auction tables. I'm no goalie, but I have the reflexes of a pro athlete. I'm there instantly, crouching down, hugging her knees to my stomach and steadying her. My fingers brush against the bare skin at her ankle, and she goes perfectly still.

Interesting. Her response is… no response.

"You're good," I say, helping set her right.

Flashbulbs pop around us, capturing the moment. Ah yeah, our constant surveyors. The reason we're here. Juliet and I are hard-launching our engagement.

"It better not end up as a meme," she mutters.

"Too late, honey."

"You're the worst."

I arch a brow playfully. She tries to walk away, probably to escape to the bathroom or find Ivy again. But I follow her, not ready to let the moment go. Not tonight.

"Where are you going?" I ask.

"Away from you."

"That's not very convincing fiancée behavior."

"Good thing I'm not actually your fiancée."

Ouch. The reminder stings more than it should. For the rest of the night, I play it cool. I hang back, let Juliet talk to Jessa, watch Ivy dominate a sizeable chunk of her time. When it's time to go, I help her into her coat and walk her out.

On the way home, she barely says a word. Neither do I. But when she rubs her thumb across her ring like it means something, I wonder if maybe tonight worked a little too well.

Back at the condo, Juliet collapses on the couch with a groan. "I'm dead. Literally dead. And my feet are screaming."

I toss my keys in the bowl by the door. "Take off those torture devices you call shoes."

She straightens, prim now that we're alone. "No thanks. I'd rather die."

"You plan to be uncomfortable in your own home?"

"This isn't my home," she retorts. "It's a rental agreement until we break up."

That one lands harder than I expected. I head for the fridge, keeping my voice cool to mask the sting. "Suit yourself. I'm making this my castle."

I tell myself the public launch of our fake romance went well. She remained unflinching under pressure, tightly wound but professional. But I can't help feeling a flicker of respect when her eyes drift over me and her cheeks heat despite her best efforts.

The world is watching The Chainsaw with his so-called fiancée now. The pressure's on to make this believable.

But lying here in the dark, listening to her move around in her room, I'm wondering if I've already bitten off more than I can chew.

Chapter 7

Juliet

I'm working at the arena for the first time today, and it feels surreal. The title of Public Relations Coordinator has a beautiful ring to it. This morning I went upstairs and filled out more paperwork, got my official team ID badge, and now I'm here watching practice like I actually belong. I'm in full work mode. Heels, red lipstick, a short black skirt, and a blazer so sharp it could cut. The armor I wear when I need to feel untouchable.

Is it working? Not really.

I pull out my phone and record a bit of the practice, zooming in on my incredibly sweaty and somehow enticing fake fiancé. He keeps taking his helmet off and shaking his too-long hair out, damp pieces clinging to his neck in a way that makes me too aware of his hotness.

He glances at me and smirks. It makes me blush. Damn him.

I need new media content for Hunter's social accounts. I also need an excuse to burn off the nerves that have been eating at me since last night.

From the front row, I watch the team run drills. It's a blur of speed and sweat and controlled chaos. Hunter stands out immediately among his teammates. He's all aggression and raw power, but he's surprisingly graceful on skates. It reminds me a little of Patrick, who was the opposite. His skating was choppy and ever so slightly uncoordinated. He made it look like work.

Not Hunter. He glides across the ice before turning his blades to stop short, such a big guy moving with such ease. I can see him getting into it with another player mid-drill. Something about positioning, voices getting heated.

I brace for the explosion. I know him. He's a guaranteed meltdown in a jersey. I'm already cringing at what this will do to our carefully constructed narrative. Am I supposed to just sit here and support him when he's being a monster?

But then Hunter makes eye contact with me through the glass.

He scowls, that familiar furrow between his brows that usually means someone's about to get punched. But he doesn't snap. Doesn't throw hands at the other player. He breathes through it, shoulders tight, fists clenched, but he holds the line. No yelling. No shoving. He just skates away, slams his helmet down on the boards, and mutters something to himself that I can't hear.

I blink rapidly. That was not what I expected. And I hate that it makes me feel something like reluctant admiration.

You shouldn't admire someone just for not beating the shit out of someone else. That should be the bare minimum expected from a professional athlete. But I have a sinking feeling that he didn't escalate because of me. Because I was watching.

Because he's actually trying to change, at least when his so-called fiancée is watching.

That thought makes my stomach roll, uncertain.

My phone vibrates in my purse, and I swallow. There's also that; I'm on pins and needles today because our engagement announcement went viral last night. The comments poured in the second I posted to Hunter's Insta, and they're exactly what I expected.

People are speculating if I'm the next WAG, whether I got my job because I'm dating Hunter, saying how lucky he is because I'm so bangable. I am the next WAG, temporarily. But the rest of the gossip is just out-and-out offensive. One user reposted the image of Hunter and me, but they zoomed in on my chest like my boobs were the actual story here.

I wonder if people will ever see me as anything but a puck bunny in lipstick. My relationship with Patrick certainly didn't help matters.

I know this fake engagement is going to bring a lot of scrutiny. A lot of judgment. And undoubtedly, Patrick will have something to say as soon as he can get in front of a reporter. I flick through the comments on Hunter's Instagram account, bracing myself for the inevitable backlash.

My eyes skim the congratulatory comments and only stop at the sexist, body shaming assholes screaming their opinions at the top of their lungs.

This. This feeling that I'm so terribly familiar with. I finally left Patrick six months ago, after waiting oh so patiently for him for five years to propose. Five years of his family, the famous Delacroix clan, looking down on me and treating me like I wasn't good enough for their precious baby boy. Rubbing my arms, I shiver at the memory. I never should have gone with him to Houston. Never should have spent so many years on someone who, if I'm being honest, I never actually loved.

But it took me a lot of years to figure that out.

I watch the practice, pushing away thoughts of Patrick,

and grudgingly admire how Hunter controls himself on the ice. The team does several puck-handling drills, an exhausting-looking 20 minutes of bag skates, and then sets up for a controlled scrimmage.

Using only half the rink, they play their usual roles aggressively. Coach Ryan shouts out the rules. For the first five minutes, he wants to see only backhand goals. Next, players need to make three passes to other players before they shoot. Five minutes of no skating backward. Finally, one-touch shots only.

The rookies prove their status by going hard for the first ten minutes and drooping in the last ten. The vets have cooler heads, only pushing themselves when it's really necessary. Beck Tate seems like he's pushing himself diligently, ignoring the rest of his teammates. I watch Hunter and the co-captain, Alex Thorne, as they play aggressively but each selects their moments. That seems like the sweet spot between running themselves into the ground and playing a very lazy game.

By the end of practice, every single one of the hockey players is dripping with sweat and panting for breath. The rookies, especially Shane and… I think his name is Connor?? They make it off the ice and have to lean against the walls for a minute before they hobble toward the bench.

My lips lift at the corners. Poor guys. I remember when Patrick was in Houston his first year and he would come home with legs like Jell-O, bitching about how hard practices were. While I'm distracted, my phone buzzes again. I look down and find a text from Ivy.

It's a link to a gossip piece… and my blood runs cold when I see the headline.

#47's New Fiancée: From Houston Puck Bunny to Seattle Treasure?

Patrick gave an interview. Of course he did.

I click and immediately feel sick. He laced his words with fake concern about how he wished me well and how he was 'glad I'm finally learning how to work my way up'. The implication is disgusting. Everyone will read between the lines. I'm sleeping my way through the league. Supposedly, I used him for his connections. I'll never be anything but a puck bunny.

The words make me want to throw my phone across the room. God, I hate that phrase. It's used mostly by men to dismiss women who mostly just want to have unattached sex with athletes. There's nothing wrong with that, and if the genders were reversed, I'm willing to bet the world would be a lot nicer about it. It's just more sexism, and I loathe every bit.

But being labeled that way still guts me. It makes people think I'm only good because of who I'm dating, not because of my actual skills or intelligence. It's ridiculous and insulting.

I read the article as I wait for Hunter in the hall outside the locker room. Hunter finds me shortly after he's done with practice, freshly showered and smelling like soap and cedar. He takes one look at my face and immediately knows some-thing's wrong.

"What happened?" he asks, voice low.

I hold out my phone without a word, jaw tightening. Hunter reads Patrick's quotes and goes completely silent, his jaw ticking in that way that usually means violence is imminent.

We're alike in that way, I guess.

"That fucker. You want me to handle it?" he asks quietly.

I laugh, but there is no humor in the sound. "It's nice of you to offer, but really, what're you going to do? Houston is pretty far away, and the last thing I need is you starting a public feud with Patrick."

I shake my head, imagining Hunter and Patrick seeing each other in person. When we were all in college at U of W, they played hockey on the same team. But that doesn't mean they got along. Quite the opposite.

Now that I think about it, I'm not Hunter's archenemy. I'm more of an annoyance than someone Hunter wishes ill. Patrick would definitely qualify for that status, though.

I shake my head, my lips twitching at the idea of someone putting that douchebag Patrick in his place. It's not the worst idea. I sigh. "No. Unfortunately, I'm used to cleaning up after Patrick. I can handle this. I have to."

Hunter doesn't argue, but the heat in his eyes stays. He's a walking PR disaster, and yet I realize I trust him more than I ever trusted my ex-boyfriend. That thought alone makes me want to scream.

After practice, Hunter and I head home together. Hunter crashes for a few hours, exhausted from practice. I watch some foreign detective shows and scroll Instagram endlessly, switching from news of my fake engagement to Patrick's smarmy face next to quotes about how I "always look for someone to take care of me".

After an hour, I have to put my phone away and not look at the internet anymore because otherwise, I'll start crying.

When Hunter eventually wakes up, it's time for dinner. Our dinner. The one I've already planned as our next public appearance.

I get dressed carefully, choosing a soft blue floral wrap dress, showing off my collarbones and curves. It's sexier than my usual choices, designed to look effortless and romantic for the cameras.

But I regret it the second I step out of the guest bedroom

at Hunter's condo. It clings to all the places people already love to judge. Hunter straightens when he sees me, swallowing hard. But it's not my chest he's zeroed in on. It's my bare legs. And then his gaze travels up to my mouth, glossy and carefully painted.

I catch the way his eyes drag down my body, then snap back to my lips like he's trying not to think about them. It shocks me more than it should. Hunter Huxley, looking at me like he wants something he can't have.

I make sure I wear just a whiff of my favorite perfume and do my eye makeup perfectly. When Hunter sees me, he goes stiff and swallows audibly.

I smile slowly. "Eyes up, Chainsaw. Or you'll miss the best part."

He clears his throat. "You look... um… dressed."

"Wow," I say, adjusting my clutch. "Remind me to embroider that onto a pillow."

He scowls, watching me walk past. He is quiet as we ride to the restaurant. I think about the look on his face when I emerged. Surprised? Maybe slightly pleased? It was interesting.

When Hunter pulls up to the valet at the restaurant, I wait for him to come around to open my door. My heartbeat rises. I don't know why exactly; I did the hard part last night when I posted our fake engagement for the world to see. Hunter doesn't even look at me as he holds my door open, a fact that I don't miss. But I paste on a smile and grab his arm.

We probably look ridiculous next to each other. He's a towering beast and I'm… well, I stopped growing in seventh grade when everyone else was shooting up like a bunch of weeds. I've always been petite. We are quite a pair.

"Hunter! Hunter, over here!" I can hear camera shutters as Hunter puts his arm around me and pulls me toward the restaurant door. Just for the cameras, I lean into him and try to show some gratitude that he's sheltering me from the dogged press. Just for the show.

We make it into the restaurant, where someone whisks us to our table. I've asked for the table in the center of the dining room. It's definitely the spot to be seen. Paparazzi pictures from this restaurant fill the pages of every gossip column.

I picked well, if you ask me.

Clearing my throat, I tug at the hem of my dress, pulling down my neckline a quarter of an inch. I know what I'm doing; you don't spend nearly all of your adult life trying to downplay your boobs without knowing just how to make them highly visible. He gets an eyeful of cleavage and I don't miss the way his breathing changes.

Ugh, yes. I have breasts. Look your fill, I think. Hunter leans closer and whispers in my ear.

"You're doing this on purpose."

"Doing what?" I ask innocently.

He growls and his eyes drop to my chest. "That."

"That's not very specific," I say, smoothing my dress. "You'll have to be clearer."

His jaw tightens, and his glare intensifies. I lean in, brushing his arm, whispering, "You're staring so hard I might start charging admission."

He mutters something under his breath that I don't catch, but the flush creeping up his neck is reward enough. I hear camera shutters clicking; a few people who recognize Hunter have pulled out their cell phones to snap photos.

I've changed my mind. This dinner was actually a fabulous idea.

We sit at the fanciest sushi place in the city, all black marble and ambient lighting. Perfect for photos. I push his buttons throughout dinner, making him pose in increasingly intimate ways. Touching his hand, leaning into his shoulder, angling my ring so it catches the light just right.

Hunter growls warnings in my ear about behaving myself, which makes my stomach flip in ways I absolutely don't want to examine. I take selfies of the two of us. It's fun to make Hunter so deeply uncomfortable just by pretending to flirt with him.

At one point, I look at a picture I took and my breath catches. Wow. The way he's looking at me in the shot... if you didn't know us, you would think there was something real burning in that stare. His eyes are entrancing, intense in a way that makes my pulse quicken.

I order the most expensive sake on the menu and a dozen oysters. Hunter refuses to try even one, so I eat them all myself, slurping their juices and making a show of it. He seems riveted by my mouth, which reminds me I need to reapply my lipstick.

When some fans come over asking for autographs, he starts to say no, but I step in.

"Of course he'll sign," I say sweetly, nudging Hunter. "He loves meeting fans."

I take pictures with them, chat about the team, and act genuinely friendly. Hunter watches me work his fans with something that might be appreciation. At least he doesn't have to talk to them, I guess. Honestly, it's better for the fans that I'm here.

We head home afterward, settling into a silence that isn't as tense as usual. Thank god for that. I'm exhausted from performing all night, from being on every second we were in public. Still, it was successful. A good outing.

As we enter the Sinclair building, I'm about to tell him so when he gives me a long look.

"You sure you're not enjoying this a little too much? The lights, the looks, the attention. Kind of fits."

What? My jaw drops and my hands clench at my sides. The implication that I'm some kind of attention-seeking social climber makes me feel like a burned-out husk. I'm over here having a positive thought about Hunter for maybe the first time… and he has to douse me with cold water.

"You don't know what it costs me every time my name shows up next to my picture. I've spent years fighting to be taken seriously."

He goes still, his expression unreadable. I press the button for the elevator.

"I already had to survive Patrick," I add, keeping my tone light. "If I lose my credibility over this, over you, it's not just embarrassing. It's career-ending. You probably wouldn't get that though. I'd expect that kind of sexist thinking usually shows you in a more favorable light."

I step into the elevator when the doors open, furious.

Even Hunter doesn't see the real me. He sees what everyone else sees. Just a pretty face looking for an easy ride.

Shit. Now that I think about it, every public move we make could reinforce the wrong narrative about who I am and what I'm capable of.

"Ah, fuck." Hunter exhales slowly, but he doesn't look away. "I didn't mean it like that."

"No? Tell me. How did you mean it?"

His brow draws tight, and he looks at me as though working something through. "I was just trying to press your buttons, Ace."

I lose patience, growling. "Don't fucking call me that. Seriously, Huxley. You're on my last nerve tonight."

Lucky for both of us, the elevator dings and the doors

open. I stride out first, my heels clicking with every furious step down the hallway.

I don't say another word as we walk to our condo. I keep my shoulders square, my chin lifted, my expression locked in place. Every step feels like a battle not to let him see my hurt. That his casual dismissal of my struggles actually hurt.

Once the door shuts behind us, I go straight to my bedroom. I don't slam the door. Don't yell. Don't give him the satisfaction of seeing me lose control.

I wait.

Wait until I'm out of his sight, out of his reach.

Then I crumple onto the edge of my bed and bury my face in my hands.

My body is shaking. My throat burns with unshed tears.

I'm not crying over Hunter, I tell myself. Not really.

It's in the headlines. The whispers. The old fear that maybe Patrick was right about me. Maybe I am too cold, too ambitious, too much of a control freak to be loved for real. Maybe all I'm good for is playing a part in someone else's story.

I let myself cry for a few minutes, then I force myself to stop. Wiping my face roughly, I stand up. Fix my hair in the mirror. Reapply my lipstick with hands that only shake a little.

Even when I'm home, I'm performing. Protecting something fragile inside me, something I can't afford to let anyone see.

I'm Juliet Monroe. I don't fall apart. Not where anyone can see.

I walk to the kitchen and open a bottle of wine, pour exactly one glass, and leave it untouched on the counter. I stand there barefoot, staring at the clock on the microwave.

One night down. Months to go. And now the universe

thinks I'm in love with the one man who knows exactly how to unravel me with a single offhand comment.

Great. This is going really fucking great.

I lean against the kitchen counter and close my eyes. Tomorrow there will be more photos, more comments, more people dissecting every outfit choice and facial expression. More opportunities for Hunter to remind me he sees me the same way everyone else does.

Just another girl chasing the spotlight, willing to do whatever it takes to get ahead.

The worst part is that I think I'm caring what he thinks of me. And that's a complication I absolutely cannot afford.

Chapter 8

Hunter

It's halfway through November, the leaves have fallen off the trees, and the wet, chilly winter weather has set in. Personally, I love it. I can go for runs on some mornings in just a long-sleeve t-shirt and shorts without sweating my balls off. Most people miss the sun. I take a shit-load of vitamin D and exult in the dark, rainy skies that last from the middle of October until the middle of May.

Juliet and I have only been living together for a few days and we're already driving each other insane. I'm standing in the kitchen, mixing a protein shake in just a pair of low-slung gray sweatpants, when she struts out of the bedroom hallway and points at me like I committed a war crime.

"Did you mess with the thermostat again?"

I shrug. "Yeah, I did."

Her face gets hot, which is more attractive than it should be. "Hunter, I was freezing all night."

"You can put on layers. I can't make myself cooler."

She's wearing a short skirt, tank top, and heels at eight in the morning, which seems like overkill for hanging around the condo. But I'm not complaining about the view. If she were my fiancée for real, I'd find something better for her to do with that perfectly lipsticked mouth than harp on me for living the way I always have.

"And another thing," she continued, crossing her arms. "Your hockey gear is everywhere. It smells like death."

"It needs to air out."

"There are protein shaker bottles piling up in the sink."

"The maid comes twice a week."

"And you walk around naked after every shower."

I grin. "Problem?"

Her cheeks go pink. "Yes, it's a problem. I have to live here too."

"For four and a half more months. That's what you're being paid for."

She goes rigid. "That is not what I'm being paid for. I'm being paid to fix your image, not to live in a disgusting trash pit. I want the maid to come twice as often."

I step closer because pushing her buttons has become my new favorite hobby. "Anything else, princess?"

She looks at my chest and swallows nervously. I'm close enough now to smell that expensive perfume she wears, close enough to see the way her pupils dilate when she's trying not to look at me.

"You think I'm hot," I tease.

"I absolutely do not."

"You're looking at my chest right now."

"I'm looking at you because you're in my personal space."

"Oh yeah? Well, you drive me nuts too." I gesture around the living room. "What's up with all the furniture moving? You keep shifting everything around a little each day."

She straightens her shoulders. "I'm trying to find the optimal placement for everything."

"You're trying to make me crazy. I tripped over that random ottoman that appeared by the couch and almost died."

She rolls her eyes. "For a hockey player, you're surprisingly clumsy."

That's when she makes her mistake. She pokes a finger right in the middle of my chest, probably trying to emphasize her point. I'm amused but try not to show it.

"I think you just like seeing what buttons you can push," I say. "If you want me to fuck you and get the stick out of your ass, just ask."

"Fuck you!" she snaps, but her face is burning red now.

A little later, my phone buzzes with the team group chat. The guys are bugging me to hang out, and honestly, it sounds like a good way to blow off steam. I get dressed, figuring I'll head down to Secret History for a few beers.

Juliet knocks on my bedroom door just as I'm pulling on jeans.

"Get dressed," she demands through the door. "We're going out."

"I am getting dressed."

"Good. Ivy suggested that we appear in public more. Team bonding night is perfect for visibility and PR."

I was already planning to go to the team hangout, so I reluctantly agree. "Fine. But I'm not holding your hand the whole time."

"Just don't embarrass me."

She disappears to change, and when she comes back, she's wearing a tight little crop top that shows off her stomach. I liked the tank top better because I could see her nipples through it, but I keep that observation to myself. Actually, no, I don't.

"I liked your tank top more," I tell her as we head toward the elevator. "I could see your nipples in it."

She gapes at me, then hits my arm. "You're disgusting."

"Funny that you think that's going to correct my behavior."

Privately, I hate that I notice what she's wearing. Hate that my teammates are going to notice too. Anyone else getting to see Juliet look hot better keep their comments to themselves, or I'm going to cut out their tongues.

She takes my hand as we approach the bar, and I try not to think about how small her fingers feel wrapped around mine.

The Secret History is tucked into the bottom floor of The Sinclair, half-hidden behind an unmarked door like it's daring you to find it. All dim lighting, walnut paneling, and mismatched leather booths that look like they've soaked up decades of secrets. The place walks the line between exclusive and chaotic with perfect balance.

The bar hums with something low and sexy. Etta James or some moody cover of a Top 40 hit. The copper bar top gleams under candlelight, and there's a fireplace surrounded by velvet armchairs that the team has basically claimed as our territory.

Drinks here are pretentious in the best way. They have cocktails with names like The Scandal and The Home-wrecker. Juliet orders a gin and tonic with four limes like it's a religious ritual. I stick with beer, always the same brand, and never look at the menu.

The place is co-owned by Étienne, who's flamboyant and flirtatious and prone to wearing cravats or kilts depending on his mood, and his husband Olivier, who runs the bar with an iron fist and a permanent scowl. He knows everyone's secrets and keeps them locked away for top-shelf bourbon and minimal bullshit.

People look our way as we make our way through the main bar. I slide my arm around Juliet, thinking about the dicks that hang out here hoping to get close to team members or their girlfriends.

"Remember," she murmurs, "our rules say no flirting with anyone else. So there's no need to be all possessive or growl at every other man you see."

"No promises."

I push her straight into the back room, which is always reserved for the team since we live in the building. Everyone's already there. Jett's brooding against the wall like he's auditioning for a vampire movie. No idea what crawled up his ass today. That's what makes him the Wildcard, I guess.

Connor and Shane are razzing the other rookies about something. Thorne's drinking a soda because he doesn't touch alcohol during the season. Grayson's half-asleep with a beer in front of him. Silas is sitting across from Jett, shooting everyone malicious looks like we offended him by existing.

There's a table of women too. Ivy and Jessa are sitting with Wren, Coach Ryan's fiancée. Ivy waves Juliet over immediately.

I hang back and watch Juliet switch into her public persona. She's suddenly relaxed, magnetic. Laughing easily, touching arms, tilting her head when she talks. Everyone loves her within minutes.

She's not like that with me. She introduces herself to Wren and hugs her like they're old friends. Not that I want that level of intimacy with Juliet, but how is it so easy for everyone else?

The girls' table and the guys' table get shoved together when we join the group. I slide into a seat with the team, and immediately the comments start.

Connor grins. "I'm shocked Hunter's been domesticated."

Shane adds, "Is it true that Juliet cooks?"

How the hell would I know if she cooks? We've been living together for less than a week.

Grayson raises an eyebrow. "How long have you two been together, anyway?"

I deadpan, "Too long," and Juliet gives a fake laugh that sounds too real.

Ivy slides in with a cocktail and a sharp reminder. "You have a wedding venue appointment tomorrow morning in Westlake at ten. No murder attempts before then, please."

I lean over toward my brothers. "Are we still on for dinner this week?"

Silas shrugs. "Maybe."

"Maybe? What the hell does that mean?"

"It means maybe." He takes a sip of his beer and goes back to brooding.

He's so moody and silent these days that he makes me look normal, which is saying something.

"I'm in," Jett says. "As long as Ivy doesn't schedule another crisis management meeting." He gestures at the thick binder she's got propped against her drink. "Jesus, what's in that thing? Nuclear launch codes?"

Ivy gives him a look that could cut glass. "It's called being prepared. You should try it sometime."

Jett shuts up immediately.

"So, just FYI, you two." Ivy points to Juliet and me. "The wedding Save the Dates went out this morning. We sent them to the VIP mailing list, sponsors, and media partners."

Juliet goes rigid. "The what?"

"Save the Dates. For your supposed wedding next June? The campaign software already queued them up from the rollout deck last week. I thought someone already signed off on that?"

I look at Juliet, who's gone pale under her perfect foundation. For a second, she looks like she might actually throw up.

"We didn't discuss that," she says, her voice too controlled. The kind of control that means she's about to murder someone. "That kind of news could reach our families. Who approved that?"

Ivy's cheeks turn a scarlet hue. "I thought we had cleared it with you. Julien swore up and down he had already talked with you about it."

I snort under my breath. "That guy is terrible at his job."

Juliet turns her laser focus on me, all fire and frost. "Are you laughing?"

I bite the inside of my cheek to keep from smiling. "No. Not laughing. Just thinking about how glad I am that you're the one who's going to get dragged into wedding planning hell. You'll have to send me a nice snapshot of you at the venue, *darling*."

"You think I'm going to do this on my own? Like hell."

I raise both hands in surrender. "Hey. I didn't send the invitations. I still don't even know what a Save the Date is."

"Then maybe don't talk," she mutters. "Or breathe."

We stare each other down. Juliet lifts her chin, irritated. Unfortunately for her, it only makes her red-lipsticked mouth that much closer. She's so fiery, with her raven hair and flashing chestnut eyes.

"You're trouble, you know that?"

Her lips quirk, but she doesn't respond. Ivy spreads her hands flat on the table, quickly pivots to safer territory.

"So! Next topic. Venue content. We thought that the two of you could visit a few wedding venues for a social media post series. Nothing too formal. Just candid shots of you looking at flowers and cake samples. Maybe arrange for a few paparazzi leaks. Really lean into the soft-focus engagement narrative."

"You want me to pose like I give a shit about florals?" I couldn't roll my eyes any harder if I tried.

Ivy nods enthusiastically. "Exactly! We'll leak the pictures, stir up speculation about when and where. Maybe let your moms know about the—"

"Don't," I snap, suddenly all ice. The temperature in the room drops about ten degrees. "I don't want my mom involved, period. I think Juliet can say the same."

Juliet shifts slightly in her chair, nudging her knee against mine under the table. A warning or maybe a question. I'm not sure which. She looks at me, changing the subject rather than letting the room stew on what I just said.

"Come with me to look at venues," she tells me, ignoring the tension. "That's the whole point of the pictures. Right?"

Ivy nods eagerly. "Exactly. Couple goals content. Very aspirational."

I mutter, "I'll show up. But if anyone hands me a boutonniere, I'm setting the place on fire."

Across the booth, Jessa pulls plastic containers out of her purse and hands them around the table. "Okay, everyone has to try these. They're a new oatmeal dessert bar I'm testing."

"Why are you testing dessert bars?" Connor asks.

"I like to bake," Jessa explains. "And now that Juliet has moved out, I have no one to test my recipes on. I'm going to die of sugar poisoning if I eat them all myself."

Juliet gladly takes two containers. "You're the best, Jess. Seriously."

Grayson reaches across the table and grabs five. "I'll take these off your hands."

Shane raises an eyebrow. "Five? Really?"

Grayson glares at him. "I love dessert. You got a problem with that?"

"Nope. No problem at all."

"I'll be right back," Juliet says, standing up. "Bathroom."

While she's gone, I check my phone. Missed call from my agent. There are two texts that make my stomach drop.

Enzo Morelli: Your mother reached out again. It's no big deal, something I have handled. But I just want you to know.

Enzo Morelli: She is demanding a retroactive percentage of your paychecks for the last two years and then she had the balls to ask for box seats to the Vancouver game. Someone already handled it.

Fuck. My agent is a shark, a cutthroat former hockey player with amazing business skills. He's not someone I would ever want to have a drink with, but I trust him to get me great brand sponsorship deals and contract renewals. I want him to focus on that stuff, not to have to bother with my crazy mother.

Hunter: Thanks.

I don't know how to express my gratitude without coming off as a pussy, so I just leave it at that. Enzo will get it. I toss my phone facedown on the table with a huff.

Jett sees the look on my face and asks, "What? Mom?"

I nod stiffly but say, "It's already handled."

I'm not in the mood to hold hands and braid each other's hair while getting into deep philosophical topics with my brother.

Across the room, a guy from the main bar rudely walks into our private room, wandering over to our table. He's got that sleazy confidence that comes from too much to drink and not enough sense.

I push up from the table, about to tell the guy to leave. He zeroes in on the girls like a homing beacon, heading straight to them.

"This is a private room," I growl. The dude doesn't even seem to notice me, which is weird because I'm six and a half feet of pure threat. I snarl, but he's already talking to Ivy.

"Hey there, beautiful. I saw you from the main bar. Can I buy you a drink?"

Ivy smiles sweetly, standing up. "I would love that. Lead the way."

She follows the stranger to the bar. I watch her go, fuming, and I see that Jett's jaw tightens.

"What the hell?" he mutters.

"What's your problem?" Shane asks. "She's single."

"It's about team loyalty," Jett grumbles, which makes no sense since Ivy doesn't owe any of us anything.

"Uh-uh," I intone. "I don't like people just invading our space. It's supposed to be a private room."

Jett shoots me the dirtiest look and says, "That's, uh, my objection too. I'm with you."

I cock an eyebrow at him but he ignores me. Is he *blushing?*

When Juliet comes back, she slides in next to me, sitting closer than before. I forget all about my anger. I keep looking at her legs, specifically her thighs, thinking that anybody could reach up her skirt if they wanted to. Not that I want to, but I can imagine how some asshole might try it. She catches me looking and pulls her skirt down.

"Eyes up here, Chainsaw," she whispers.

I clear my throat and push my beer away. I definitely don't need to be less inhibited around her. Already, I'm thinking about whether she would taste as sweet as she smells.

"Oh my God, Hunter, you should have seen this guy at practice today," Shane says, elbowing Connor in the ribs. He launching into a story about rookies and equipment malfunctions.

Juliet throws her head back, laughing. "Are you serious? He actually did that?"

"Swear to God. Ask anyone."

She leans in close to Shane, touches his arm. "You guys are insane."

It burns in my chest. I don't understand why it bothers me. She's playing a part, the same as me. Still, something tight wraps around my ribs.

She must sense my mood because she puts her hand on mine where everyone can see and scoots closer, pressing her thigh against mine. I glare down at her hand. It's too small and delicate. A big guy like me could crush someone like Juliet without even trying.

Thorne, who's been sitting on the very edge of the group like he's not sure he wants to be here, suddenly stands up.

"I'm out," he says.

"Already?" Connor asks. "It's barely ten."

"Dawn practice tomorrow." Thorne rolls down his sleeves, covering the ink that covers both arms. He puts even tattooed me to shame. Tattoos cover forty percent of his body.

The second he steps outside the private room, he's surrounded by puck bunnies who've been waiting for their chance.

"Thorne! Can we get a picture?"

"Just one selfie, please?"

"No," he says gruffly, pushing through them toward the exit.

Good idea. I stand up too. "I'm tired. Heading up."

"But it's still early," Juliet protests, though she's already grabbing her purse.

"Long day tomorrow."

She follows without arguing, which surprises me.

In the elevator, she asks, "Are you mad?"

"Not everything's about you."

She doesn't get it. Nothing's about her. Nothing's about anybody. I don't give a damn what most of the guys think of me. I don't like them and I don't have to pretend to.

"Good to know." She pauses. "Is it about your mom?"

I react as if she just slapped me. Juliet and my mom don't belong in the same conversation.

"No."

She pokes out her bottom lip but says nothing. I can see her holding in her thoughts, pushing them down. Juliet isn't very good at hiding her emotions from me.

"Just say it," I sigh as I open the door to our condo.

"Say what?" she asks, blushing.

"Whatever it is you're thinking. I can tell you're trying to hold something back and be polite. We will not make it five months in this..." I point between us. "You're bad at keeping secrets."

"I am not! What I want is to have my own PR company, for God's sake. I'm *great* at keeping secrets."

"Well, those people aren't me. So go ahead. Tell me what you're so desperate to say."

"Your mom is a vampire." She scrunches her nose. "You can't give her whatever she wants. That'll only make it worse."

"Worse how? She's already pretty damn bad."

"You can't let her bleed you dry every time she feels like it, Huxley. If you've gone through this before, and it sounds like you have, say no."

I glare at her. "You don't get it. She's an endless pit of need."

"I get enough," she says firmly. "And if you want this to go away, you need to control the narrative. You can't just give her hush money and hope she disappears. She's clarified that it doesn't work."

I dig my nails into my palms and say nothing. Juliet touches my shoulder, her hand small and warm through my shirt. "I'm sorry you're going through this."

The genuine sympathy in her tone catches me off guard. It makes me wonder if there's more to Juliet than I've been giving her credit for. More than just a sharp tongue and a banging body. I haven't quite figured her out yet, and that bothers me more than it should.

I don't know what to say, so I just nod and head toward my room. Anything to end this awkward moment of niceness.

Juliet disappears into her room without another word. I go into mine, close the door, lock it, and pull the dusty shoebox from the back of my closet. It's pathetic that I still do this, but old habits die hard.

I flip through old letters I've written but never sent. Some are angry rants directed at Darla. Some are just blank pages with her name scrawled at the top, like I wanted to say something but couldn't find the words. Tonight, I scribble out my feelings in angry, jagged handwriting. Then, I add it to the pile without reading it or signing it.

I open my nightstand drawer and find the old sketchpad buried underneath receipts and tangled earbuds. The last drawing is of Silas, half-finished. I haven't touched this thing since a fan caught me sketching in one of Jett's Instagram photos and made a big deal about it online. The comments were *brutal*.

Apparently, hockey players aren't supposed to draw. We're supposed to hit things and grunt.

I think about starting something new. Maybe sketching helps me process things I can't say out loud. But I snap the pad shut again and do nothing.

I lie on my bed fully clothed, staring at the ceiling and listening to Juliet move around in her room. Water running. Drawers opening and closing. The soft sound of her voice on a phone call, probably with Jessa or Ivy.

Emotionally, I'm wrecked but holding it all inside like always. My mother is dragging old wounds into the light, making me relive the worst period of my life. I'm angry and ashamed and raw.

I'm also noticing Juliet. Really noticing her. The way she handled the guys tonight, how she made everyone like her within minutes. The way she looked at me when we talked about my mom, like she could see something under the surface that most people miss.

It makes me question what exactly I was thinking when I agreed to this ridiculous fake engagement. It's already annoying to deal with. Then Juliet does something like touch me while asking if I'm okay in that soft voice, and I don't know what to do with that.

It means nothing, though. It couldn't. The thought terrifies me more than any lawsuit ever could.

Because people like Juliet don't stick around for people like me. They get smart and leave before the damage gets too deep.

And I can't blame them. I wouldn't stick around for me either.

I'm tired of fighting with my mother. Tired of being painted as the villain in a story where I was the victim. I am tired of pretending her betrayal didn't break something in me I'm not sure I can fix.

But tomorrow I'll get up and put on the mask again. I'll tour fake wedding venues with my fake fiancée and smile for cameras that will broadcast our fake happiness to the world.

And I'll get through another day.

Chapter 9

Hunter

The ice feels perfect under my blades tonight. Sharp, clean, unforgiving. Just the way I like it.

Unfortunately, we're up against the Sacramento Inferno. And though the Havoc comprises individual players who are way better, those guys have an edge. Their team plays well as a unit. They always kicked our asses when we played them in the past.

I try to push those thoughts out of my head and focus on the upcoming game, but it's hard.

I'm skating warm-ups when I spot their enforcer, Marcus Kane, giving me that look. The one that says he's been watching game tape, studying my penalties, figuring out exactly which buttons to push. He's a big bastard, maybe six-five, with hands like anvils and a reputation for getting under people's skin.

"You ready for this, Chainsaw?" Thorne mutters as he glides past me, his voice low enough that the refs won't hear.

I grunt in response, keeping my eyes on Kane. The asshole's already chirping at our rookies during warm-ups, trying to get them rattled before the game even starts. Classic move. Get the young guys nervous, and they'll make mistakes all night.

"Stay cool tonight," Beck calls out from center ice, loud enough for the entire line to hear. "We need you out on the ice, not in the sin bin."

He's right. We're three games into a five-game homestand. But there's something about Kane's smug face that makes my jaw clench. I can already smell the scent of blood on the ice.

The anthem plays. I stand between Silas and Jett on the blue line. My brothers. My anchors. Jett's bouncing on his skates like he's got electricity in his veins, all golden hair and nervous energy. Silas is statue-still beside me, focused on something only he can see.

"Let's fucking go," I mutter under my breath.

The puck drops and we're off.

First shift, I'm out there with Thorne and Grayson. We're forechecking hard, trying to set the tone. Their defenseman tries to make a pass up the boards, but I'm there to cut him off. The hit sends him into the glass with a satisfying crack, and the crowd roars.

"That's what I'm talking about!" Coach Cross yells.

Kane's watching, circling. Always waiting.

Second period, he makes his move.

I'm battling for a loose puck in the corner when he comes in late, way after the whistle. His elbow catches me in the ribs, just hard enough to sting.

"Oops," he says with a shit-eating grin. "I didn't see you there, princess."

Princess. The word hits something primal in my chest. I know he's baiting me. I know this is exactly what he wants. But my fists are already clenching.

"You got something to say to me?" I growl, getting in his face.

"Just that you're softer than I expected. Heard you were supposed to be some kind of badass."

The linesmen are already moving in, but Kane keeps talking.

"Guess having a pretty little PR girl has made you all domesticated. She keeping you on a short leash, Chainsaw?"

That's it. That's the line. No one talks about Juliet to me and gets away with it. I can't stand for it.

I drop my gloves before the ref can separate us. Kane's ready for it, grinning like he just won the lottery. We grab each other's jerseys and start throwing punches. His first one catches me in the jaw, snapping my head back. Mine finds his ribs, and he grunts. I feel the satisfaction of my fist connecting with flesh.

The crowd's going insane. Phones are out, recording every second. I can hear the announcer shouting over the noise. But it's static to me. All I care about is Kane's smug face and making it hurt.

We go down in a tangle of limbs and fury. He gets me in a headlock, but I land two more shots to his kidney before the linesmen finally pull us apart.

The refs don't even have to tell us we're in trouble. I scramble to my feet, wiping blood from my nose, and start skating toward the penalty box.

We each get five minutes for fighting. Kane's laughing as they escort him to the box, blood spouting from his nose and darkening his teeth. I'm sure I look much the same.

"Worth it," he calls out to me. "Your girlfriend's gonna love seeing that on the highlights."

"I'll fuck you up!" I growl. I lunge, going after him again, but Jett's there, pushing me toward our bench.

"Cool it," he hisses in my ear. "You gave him exactly what he wanted. Now, everybody who wants you to be mad knows all they have to do is shit-talk your fiancée."

I know Jett's right. I know I fucked up. But the rage is still burning in my chest, making it hard to think straight.

Coach Ryan doesn't even look at me when I sit down. That's worse than yelling. His eyes say he's disappointed. Disappointment cuts deeper than anger.

The game gets away from us after that. Kane's line takes liberties with our guys, knowing I'm stuck in the box. Thorne takes a late hit that leaves him slow getting up. One of their forwards runs Jett, leaving Silas to step in before it gets ugly.

By the time I'm back on the ice, we're down two goals. My fault. My stupid, predictable temper cost us momentum when we needed it most.

I try to make up for it. Hit everything that moves, I win every face-off. I screen their goalie so hard he slashes at my ankles. But the scoreboard doesn't lie.

Final score: 4-2. Loss.

In the locker room afterward, nobody says much. Guys strip out of their gear in silence, the weight of another missed opportunity hanging over everything.

Thorne's icing his shoulder where he took that cheap shot. His jaw's set in a way that means he's pissed but too professional to show it. Grayson's staring at his phone, probably reading the stats that tell him exactly how many scoring chances we gave up while I was acting like a caveman.

Silas finds me by my stall, pulling off his shoulder pads with methodical precision.

"You good?" he asks quietly.

"Peachy."

"Hunter."

I look up. My brother's gray eyes are serious, concerned. It makes my chest tight in a way I don't like.

"I'm fine, Si. Just pissed we lost."

He nods, but I can tell he doesn't buy it. Silas sees too much, always has. It's eerie when I think about the fact that my brother probably knows me better than I know myself.

Jett appears on my other side, toweling off his hair. Even after a loss, he looks like he's ready to hit the club. He's such a fuckboy, but he's also my big brother. He gets the privilege of being able to lecture me.

"Kane's an asshole," he says simply. "Don't let him get in your head."

"He didn't get into my head."

Both my brothers give me looks that say they know I'm lying.

"Right," Jett says. "That's why you went full Incredible Hulk in the second period."

I want to argue, but what's the point? The video doesn't lie. Kane said the magic words. And me? I took the bait like a fucking amateur.

Beck's voice cuts through the locker room chatter. "Bus leaves in twenty. Anyone not on it can find their own ride."

The threat's mostly for show, but the message is clear. We fucked up tonight. We let emotions get the better of us, and it cost us two points we couldn't afford to lose.

I'm still pissed when I walk out of the arena twenty minutes later. The Seattle air hits my face, cold and sharp, but it doesn't cool the fire in my chest.

That's when I see her.

Juliet's waiting by the players' exit, looking like she just stepped out of a fashion magazine. Navy coat, red lipstick, that expression she gets when she's about to tear me a new one. She's got her phone in her hand, probably already dealing with the social media fallout from my little tantrum.

"Well," she says as I approach. "That was a disaster."

"Nice to see you too, Monroe."

"Don't." She holds up a hand, those dark eyes flashing. "Just don't. I can't believe you let them bait you like that."

I stop walking. "We lost a hockey game. It happens."

"You made it easy for them, Hunter. Like a rookie. Like someone who's never played this game before." Her voice is controlled, professional, but I can hear the anger underneath. "Kane played you like a fiddle. Now I have to clean up the mess."

"So clean it up. That's what you're paid for."

The words are out before I can stop them, and I see her flinch like I slapped her.

"That's what I'm paid for?" she repeats, her voice dangerously quiet.

Shit. That came out wrong. But I'm too wound up to back down now, too angry at myself and the world to think clearly.

"You knew what you were signing up for when you took this job. I'm not some project you can fix with a few photo ops and a fake engagement ring."

Her mouth opens, then closes. For a second, she looks genuinely hurt, and something twists in my gut.

"You're right," she says finally. "You're not a project. You're a grown man who should know better than to let some mouth-breathing goon manipulate him into a penalty that cost his team the game."

"We lost because we couldn't score, not because of one fight."

"You lost because you gave them exactly what they wanted. You proved that Hunter Huxley is still the same out-of-control hothead he's always been. And now, instead of talking about how well Thorne played or how Jett crushed in the third period, everyone's going to be talking about your meltdown."

She's right and we both know it. That just makes me angrier. She walks toward the street, her heels clicking on the concrete.

"Where are you going?"

"I'm getting on the bus."

And then she's gone, disappearing around the corner while I stand here like an asshole, watching her go.

I think about following her, about apologizing, but my pride's still burning too hot. Instead, I just let her go.

Less than three weeks into this fake engagement, and I can't wait for it to be over.

Chapter 10

Juliet

I wake up early, already dreading the day. A message from my mother pings on my phone.

Mom: Juliet Eloise Monroe! I just read a news article that says you are engaged?? Is this true??

Mom: ????????????????

I sigh. My mom knows. She's a corporate lawyer, spending every spare hour at the office. My entire childhood consisted of being told to sit in her office and do my homework while she attended a very important client meeting. Even at home, she was always fielding calls and sending texts. She is always neck-deep in her latest case. Like my dad, she's a serious workaholic.

I guess part of me hoped that Melissa and Tom Monroe would just not notice. After all, they didn't know about my breakup with Patrick until two months later, when I called to let them know my plans to move back to Seattle. Only then did my mom even think to ask about my boyfriend of five years.

Mom: Tell me you didn't let your family find out on the internet. Your grandparents will kill me, Juliet.

Ah, so that's what she's worried about. Not me, but how my uptight grandparents will react.

Yes, it was probably inevitable that my mom would find out about Hunter and me being 'engaged'. We appeared in public together often enough, holding hands and staring into each other's eyes, which led to countless sports news articles about us. That, plus Patrick's mud-slinging contribution to the news cycle.

So what lie am I going to tell my mom? I think for a second before I type out my answer.

Juliet: Sorry. It was a spur-of-the-moment thing.

Mom: I think we should meet and talk about the engagement.

Juliet: We're talking right now.

Mom: I'll make us dinner reservations somewhere nice. I wanted to catch up with you, anyway. You know, your LSAT scores are still valid for another two years. It's not too late to pursue a law degree.

I roll my eyes. It wouldn't be a conversation with Melissa Monroe if she didn't bring up law school, how I'm running out of time, and how I just need to apply to Stanford, her Juris Doctorate alma mater.

Juliet:

That's it. No congratulations on my engagement, fake or otherwise. No mention of the fact that I'm currently the most talked-about woman in Pacific Northwest sports news. Just a reminder that Mom still doesn't think this path is good enough for me.

I stare at the text for a long moment. Then I slowly flip my phone face-down on the nightstand and try to breathe.

This isn't the future she wants for me. Not PR work. Not the sports industry. She wants me in law school, following the path she's laid out since I was in high school. But this is what

I want, even if it means fake engagement schemes and damage control meetings. I'm building something real here, something that matters to me. Even if no one else sees it that way.

I drag myself out of bed and into the kitchen, already bracing for whatever mood Hunter's in this morning.

He's leaning against the counter, shirtless and smirking, holding two mugs of coffee. His hair is still messy from sleep. There's something almost boyish about his expression that catches me off guard. He offers me one mug as though he's being charming.

"Sleep well, future Mrs. Chainsaw?"

I snatch the coffee mug. I'm not in the mood for his jokes this morning.

"Why are you so fucking cheerful?"

Hunter blinks, caught completely off guard by my tone. His smile fades as he takes in my expression.

"Damn. Who spit in your kale smoothie?"

I set the coffee down harder than necessary. He watches me closely now, all traces of humor gone.

"What's going on?"

I exhale, feeling all the tension from this morning bubbling up. "My mom texted. I guess she found out about our engagement."

Hunter's jaw tightens immediately. "Yeah? Is that… bad?"

I shake my head, not wanting to repeat the exact words. "It's just another thing for mom to pick on me about."

Hunter's eyes go dark in a way that would probably terrify most people. "You need me to straighten her out?"

Despite myself, I laugh. It's a little choked sound that surprises both of us. "Wow. Tempting offer. But the point of this whole PR stunt is to make you look less like a rage monster, remember?"

He grunts. "Might be worth the hit to my reputation. Your mom can't just bully you."

"She's just doing what moms do, I think." I screw up my face.

Hunter takes a beat before answering. "I don't have a very good frame of reference for how normal moms behave. But for what it's worth, I think your mom making you feel bad about anything at all is bullshit. Moms are supposed to be… supportive and shit."

I roll my eyes, but I'm smiling now. Not because I'm over my mom's latest text, but because, God help me, it feels good to have someone on my side. Even if it's just fake. Even if it's just for show.

"You're a menace," I tell him.

"Yeah, but I'm your menace. And your fiancé."

The words hang in the air between us and I pretend they don't make my chest feel tight.

What would it be like to have a guy who says that for real? Heavenly, I imagine.

A few hours later, we're in my car driving to a luxury wedding venue in downtown Seattle. I insisted on driving because Hunter treats every red light like a personal insult. I need to arrive at this thing with my nerves intact.

There's something infuriating about how casually he takes everything. I watch him in the passenger seat out of the corner of my eye. His long legs splay out, and he drapes one hand casually on the center console as if we are just two people on an actual date. He makes me feel completely off balance, like there's a tide inside me pulling me toward him.

It's too bad that he's equal parts hot and terrible. Falling for someone like Hunter would be the most irresponsible thing I've ever done. I know exactly how that story ends. With my reputation in pieces and my heart as the punchline.

The venue is right on the water, all glass railings and driftwood accents and curated elegance. The place that charges five figures just to look at their brochure. It's beautiful in that effortless way that actually takes enormous effort to achieve.

Julien, the team's PR executive, meets us at the entrance with a clipboard and forced cheer that makes my teeth ache.

"Try to act smitten," he whispers. Like we're children who need basic direction.

Hunter mutters under his breath, "Can't wait." I catch his eye and repress a smile. He holds out his hand to me and I lace my fingers through his. His hand is too warm. It's almost comical seeing how giant his hand is holding mine.

My thoughts wander off for a second, wondering at the difference in our sizes. Hunter is so much taller than I am. He's a great bear of a person who slams through his opponents on the ice without ever slowing down.

I wonder if he's big… *everywhere*. My ex was a 6' hockey player and I know he had a surprisingly small dick. But something about Hunter's growly don't-come-near-me persona hints at him having a massive one.

I mean, he has to. Just *look* at him.

Sensing my gaze, Hunter arches a brow. "Are you checking me out, Monroe?"

"What?" I avert my eyes, my cheeks growing hot. "God, in your dreams."

"So you've said." He tugs on my hand, pulling me against his body. "You're supposed to be deeply in love with me, remember?"

"I remember." I pinch my lips shut and look away. "Let's just get this over with, huh?"

We're ushered through a tour of the grand venue that feels more like a performance than actual venue shopping. I have to take the lead, pointing out floral arrangements and asking questions about catering for the content we're supposed to be creating. Hunter grumbles every time I pull out my phone to take pictures, but he cooperates. Barely.

"Could you smile a little? At least try to look like you're having fun?" I complain.

He rolls his eyes. "I'm not having fun. I wouldn't be having fun even if we were really engaged. This shit is boring."

"You're the surliest guy in every room," I tell him as we pause by a wall of windows overlooking Elliott Bay. "It's exhausting. You know you can just not pick a fight every five minutes, right?"

"I didn't pick a fight. I didn't say fuck-all."

"I know, but you're over my shoulder in every picture, just glowering. Can't you behave for one measly hour?"

He arches an eyebrow, and I can't read his expression. "Where's the fun in that?"

As we are walking out, I line up a shot of us with the Seattle skyline in the background, the Space Needle visible in the distance. "Smile like you're not heading to your own funeral."

He bares his teeth in what could generously be called a grin. "Is this close enough?"

I snap the photo. "Perfect. You look exactly like someone who's planning to murder me on our wedding day."

"Murder your pussy, maybe." He says it so casually, like it's something he's thought about. I inhale so sharply that I suck a teeny bit of saliva down my windpipe, then cough violently.

All I can think while I'm pounding my chest and trying to

recover is that Hunter just talked about my… my *pussy*. I'm one part repulsed, one part shocked, and part deeply curious if I'm living with some kind of pervert.

If so, I should know. I'm supposed to be his fiancée, after all. While I'm wheezing, Hunter claps me on the back, looking pretty amused.

"You okay there, Ace?"

"I'm fine," I rasp. I cough into my fist, eyeing him. "And don't call me that."

"Was it what I said about your–" he starts.

A photographer pops out from behind a row of manicured hedges like a paparazzi jack-in-the-box. Hunter stiffens and pushes me behind him, a growl bursting from deep in his chest. Then another paparazzo appears. And another. Camera lenses glinting in the afternoon sun.

"Hunter! Juliet! Over here!" one yells.

Another demands, "How long have you two been together?"

"Is the wedding next month?"

"Are you pregnant?"

That last question makes my blood boil. How dare he ask something so personal? Before I can even open my mouth to respond, Hunter turns around and pulls me away from the photographer. His arm slides around my waist, yanking me close against his side. His body shields mine as we're pushed back toward the doors of the venue. Someone tries to step into our path; Hunter lets out a loud growl that makes the guy think twice.

It's not just acting anymore. There's something protective and fierce in the way he positions himself between me and the cameras.

I try to keep my head down, my hand flying up before my face, and focus on. But my stupid heel catches on a crack in the sidewalk. For a second, I wobble, unable to move without losing a Louboutin heel.

I flail. My heels are from college, a time in my life when my parents still paid for designer things. If anything happens to them, they are irreplaceable. I stumble, arms flinging wide as I try to catch my balance.

Hunter immediately catches me, one arm sliding under my thighs and the other around my back, lifting me clean off the ground in one smooth motion.

The flashbulbs go absolutely wild. Oh *god*. I'm having a *The Bodyguard* moment right now in front of frenzied, frothing paparazzi. There will be photos of this moment *everywhere*.

Someone yells, "That's love, baby!"

My reaction is to hide my face, turning away from the photographers and burying my nose against Hunter's shoulder. The cedarwood and tobacco scent of his cologne hits me like a ton of bricks.

No man should smell this good. Especially not someone so grumpy.

My face flushes hot with embarrassment as I breathe him in for a moment. Then I writhe, protesting. Carefully of course, because I'm wearing a very short skirt. "Huxley, put me down."

He looks down at me, storm-gray eyes taking me in. "You tripped."

I push against his chest.

"I'm wearing five-inch heels. Of course I tripped. I didn't need a fireman's carry."

"Looked like you did from where I was standing."

I mutter, "You're a walking PR crisis."

He sets me down gently, but his hand lingers at my waist

for a moment longer than necessary. I hate how steady he feels. How safe.

I must be hormonal or something, because I feel like his pheromones follow me. For all his rough edges, he settles me. He makes the noise in my head vanish.

God, I'm really on something today.

As we make our escape to the parking garage, the photographers are still shouting questions and snapping pictures. By the time we reach my car, my hands are shaking slightly from the adrenaline.

Back in the car, I stare out at the Seattle skyline, my arms crossed over my chest. The city looks pretty from here, all glass and steel and possibility. But I can't shake the feeling that I'm in way over my head.

Hunter smells good. Too good. That cologne he wears, smoky cedar mixed with something dangerous, lingers in the enclosed space of my car. It's distracting in ways I absolutely don't need right now.

I'm going to throw that cologne in the trash when we get home. Or maybe just hide it somewhere he'll never find it.

Because the truth is, I don't hate the way he smells. I don't hate the way he automatically moved to protect me from those photographers. I don't hate the way he caught me when I fell, like it was the most natural thing in the world.

And that's a problem.

The drive home is quiet, both of us lost in our own thoughts. With the announcement in the papers that Hunter and I are engaged, there has been an explosion of gossip about our supposed relationship online. It seems like fans have all but forgotten about Hunter punching that fan in the face. I haven't heard about the fan being paid off, but I'm almost positive that someone cut him a check for his silence. Otherwise, Hunter's grumpy face would be everywhere.

Instead, there are just a lot of photos of the two of us looking at each other in what the media assumes is a loving way. Barf. At least it seems to work to draw the heat off of Hunter.

The league has either forgotten him completely or Jimbo Greene has dealt with them.

Hunter's phone keeps buzzing with what I assume are notifications about the most recent photos of us at the wedding venue that are probably already being posted online. My phone is mercifully silent, but I know that won't last long.

By tonight, those pictures will be everywhere. Hunter carrying me like some kind of romance novel hero. Me looking flustered and breathless in his arms. The perfect shot to sell our fake love story to the world.

"That went well," Hunter says finally, breaking the silence.

"You think?" I give him an irritated look.

He shrugs. "The photographers got their money shot. Julien will be thrilled. Your ring was visible in at least half of those pictures."

He's right. From a PR perspective, today was a complete success. We gave them exactly the content they wanted. Star-crossed lovers shopping for their dream wedding venue. The big, protective hockey player and his tiny fiancée.

Too bad none of it's real.

"Patrick's going to love this," I mutter.

"Fuck Patrick."

The vehemence in his voice surprises me. "That's a lot of hate for someone you haven't even seen in years."

"I know everything I need to know. I know he's trying to make you look bad because he can't handle that you're better off without him."

I glance over at Hunter, surprised by the certainty in his voice. "How can you be so sure?"

"Because I know you, Monroe. You're sweet and support-ive, smart and sexy. You're pretty much perfect wifey mater-ial. He's probably kicking himself for letting you go."

The compliment hits me unexpectedly hard. Coming from Hunter, who's never been one to hand out praise, it means more than it should.

"Umm… thanks," I whisper.

"Don't thank me for stating facts."

We pull into the parking garage of our building.

"Hunter," I start, then stop. I'm not sure what I was going to say.

He looks at me expectantly, those gray-blue eyes focused on my face.

"Nothing," I finish lamely. "Never mind."

But as we ride the elevator up to our floor, I can't stop thinking about the way he looked at me when those cameras were flashing. Like I was something worth protecting.

I want my eventual husband, whoever he might be, to look at me that way.

Chapter 11

Hunter

We have a built-in timeout after the events at the wedding venue. The entire Seattle Havoc team leaves town, and it's a relief of sorts to me. Things with Juliet were getting a little intense, and having some breathing room from that isn't really a bad thing.

The road trip itself was brutal. Three cities, one win, two losses that felt like getting punched in the gut repeatedly. Coming home, the plane was practically silent, everyone withdrawn and licking their wounds. I crashed hard the second I hit my bed, still in my clothes, too exhausted to care about anything except unconsciousness.

This morning, I wake up to an empty apartment.

There isn't a note. No coffee waiting. There aren't any wafts of citrus and musk perfume. And most importantly, no tiny Juliet bustling around in those ridiculous heels, getting ready for whatever she has scheduled today. I shouldn't expect any of these things from her, but I long for them, anyway.

I grumble, rub the back of my neck, and mutter, "Awesome. Left me here like a damn dog."

The silence feels different than it used to. Before Juliet moved in, I liked the quiet. Now it just feels lonely.

I've been making more of an effort to be nice lately, because I can't get her words out of my head. *You know you can just not pick a fight every five minutes, right?*

It's harder than it sounds, but I'm trying. Holding the elevator door instead of punching the close button repeatedly. Nodding at Thorne in the hallway instead of scowling. Even mumbling something to Connor that might have been an apology for snapping at him when he dropped my hockey stick.

You know, it's weird trying to be considerate of other people. For ages, all that mattered to me were my brothers. But I don't hate it as much as I thought I would.

It feels… not-unpleasant.

I head to the team facility, hoping a good lift will burn off whatever mood I'm in. I'm supposed to meet my brothers here soon, but I want a little extra time alone to get in extra reps. Inside the weight room, the air smells like chalk and testosterone and the lingering ghost of yesterday's protein shakes.

That's when Darla's message comes through.

I shouldn't check my email during workouts. I definitely shouldn't open any mail from her. But I do anyway, because apparently I enjoy psychological torture.

Subject: Re: Your "fiancée"

You're always so easy, Hunter. A pair of tits in a tight dress and you think it's love.

My grip tightens on the phone until the case creaks.

She's not subtle. Those outfits? That lipstick? I know what girls like her want. You're just a stepping stone.

I sneer. What the fuck business is it of hers? A second email pings in before I can even process the first one.

She's angling for your money, your name, your spotlight. Just like I warned you about everyone else. I told you that people are users.

I don't forward it to the team's lawyers like I should. Don't delete it either. I just stare at the screen, feeling a familiar doubt creep in. The one that whispers I'm only worth what I can give people. Money, muscle, attention, protection. That nobody would want me just for me.

That's what my mom has instilled in her sons. We're only as good as the service we provide for her. We never talk about it, but I know Jett and Silas are every bit as fucked up as me.

What a fucking clown show I am.

When I step into the weight room, Jett and Silas are already there. Jett nods at me. "Hey, man."

"I didn't realize you two were going to be early," I say. "I planned to be here to have some quiet lifting time."

"Sucks," Jett says, grinning. "You should know by now that Silas is almost always in the gym before anyone else."

Silas just grunts in response to me, which is pretty much our relationship these days. "Gotta stay fit."

Of the three Huxley brothers, Silas is the most slavishly devoted to diet and exercise. He spends all his free time either lifting weights, cycling endlessly, or running stats in his head. I can't say the last time I've seen him eat anything isn't salmon, broccoli, or rice.

Fun foods, drinking, and doing things that won't propel his career forward just aren't Silas's style. I clap him on the shoulder and drop my bag by the wall.

"You look like shit," Jett offers helpfully, curling a barbell that's probably heavier than most people.

I shrug. "Thanks, big brother. That's exactly the support I needed today."

"Engaged life not treating you well?" Silas deadpans,

eyes focused on his reflection in the mirror as he stacks some weights onto the leg press machine.

"Everything's *fine*." I grab a bar and load it with more weight than I probably should. "I've got it handled."

Jett snorts. "Sure you do. Is that why you were brooding on the bench all last week?"

"Fuck off." I ignore him and focus on my setup.

"Don't forget I was there in college," Jett says, resting his elbows on the bench press bar. "You couldn't shut up about her back then. Every time she walked into a party with Patrick, you looked like someone kicked your puppy."

The back of my neck heats and I grit my teeth. "I don't remember it quite like that."

"Christ," Silas mutters. "You have the girl. What's your issue?"

Before I can come up with a clever response, Moose and Shane burst into the weight room like a tornado of filthy jokes and terrible timing.

"Look who it is!" Moose hollers. "Mr. Happily Ever After!"

Shane doubles over laughing. "Yo, how's the wife-to-be? Is she waiting at home for you in nothing but your jersey?"

The image appears before my eyes, tempting. Juliet in bed, wearing my jersey, beckoning. I swallow roughly.

"I think that means she is," Shane jokes. "She's so hot."

I spin toward them, probably looking like I want to commit murder. "Do you want to get body-checked through a wall?"

The laughter dies immediately. The room goes tense, that kind of silence that happens when everyone realizes they've pushed too far.

I storm over to the squat rack, breathing hard and trying

to remember why assault charges would be bad for my fake relationship.

That's when Ryan walks in. He takes one look at the room and sighs as though he's aged ten years in the last thirty seconds.

"Walk with me," he says.

We step into the hallway. Ryan's voice is quiet, the quiet that means he's done playing games.

"You're scaring the rookies, man."

"I'm not doing anything."

"You're doing everything. I don't know if it's the road stress or this fake fiancée situation, but people are walking on eggshells around you."

"That's not true. I said I've got it handled."

Ryan doesn't argue. He just looks at me with an expression coaches get when they're deciding whether you're worth saving. "Then act like it."

He walks away, leaving me standing in the hallway feeling like I just got benched.

I come home later, exhausted and sore from taking my frustration out on the weight room, only to find Juliet curled on the couch with her arms crossed and her phone in her hand. Her mouth is tight. Her eyes are even tighter.

I glance over her shoulder and freeze.

The headline reads 'The Puck Bunny Playbook: From Hockey Lover to Hockey Wife?'

Underneath is another quote from Patrick, the gift that keeps on giving. "My ex-girlfriend is a real hockey god-chaser. She knows how to make a man feel like he's her universe, until you realize you're just a stepping stone to whatever she really wants. Then boom! Onto the next bed."

Red-hot anger builds in my chest. "He called you a puck bunny?"

"Jesus!" Juliet practically leaps out of the chair. Her eyes widen and she splays her free hand over her chest. "Give a girl a heart attack, why don't you."

I nod at her phone. "Patrick talked about you again in the press?"

"Yeah." She huffs out a breath and sags back onto the couch. "What an asshole. I want to hit back, but I know that'll only stoke the flames of public interest. It's hard, though."

"I'm telling you. You should let me shut him up for you." My hands form fists at the very tantalizing idea of punching Patrick Delacroix in his stupid, preppy face. I'd wipe that grin off for a good, long while.

"You're already almost kicked off the Havoc. Let's not put the nail in the coffin of your career, shall we?"

Juliet flashes a quick smile at me, and I hate it. I hate the way it makes my chest feel tight, like someone's squeezing my lungs.

Juliet isn't mine. She's just here to fix my mess, not to stay. Not to confess her undying love for me. And I can't blame her for that.

Girls like her don't fall for guys like me. Not without regretting it later. She's got ambition and polish and probably a perfect future planned out to the minute. I'm fists and chaos and a past I can't scrub clean no matter how hard I try.

But while she's here, we can at least be… I don't know, comfortable around each other. She's staring at her phone again, her teeth worrying her lush bottom lip. Thinking about her ex while I'm standing right here.

"Put shoes on," I say.

"What?"

"We're going to brunch."

It's my way of being helpful. Doing something instead of trying to find the right words, because comforting people with words feels impossible when you're better at breaking things than fixing them.

"I'm not in the mood."

"Tough. You need waffles and mimosas. Let's go."

She glares at me. "Your dragging me out won't fix anything."

"No, but sitting here stewing in asshole quotes won't either."

She sighs, the sigh that means she knows I'm right but doesn't want to admit it. "Fine. But I'm not smiling for anyone."

We head to a trendy brunch spot by the water, the place that charges twenty-five dollars for eggs and calls it *artisanal*. The second we walk in, we're swarmed.

We wade in line, looking up at the board before ordering at the counter. We're stuck in line for about ten minutes, not talking because fans keep coming up with near-endless requests for selfies and autographs. Fans shout my name, hold out phones, ask for selfies. One woman actually asks me to sign her cleavage, which makes Juliet cross her arms and look like she wants to commit murder. I plaster on a tight smile, sign a few napkins, pose for three photos, and try to get us to our table before things get completely out of hand.

We get our food astonishingly fast after we order and head out to find seats on the terrace. Once we're seated in a corner booth with a decent view of the water, Juliet stabs her fork into a biscuit like it offended her.

"You hate this," she says.

"What?"

"This. Being the Chainsaw. All the performing and the fans and the persona. You hate it."

I glance at her, surprised. "You noticed that?"

She shrugs. "Nobody else seems to."

I watch her for a beat, something uncomfortable shifting in my chest. She sees things other people miss. She always has, apparently. I feel a hard lump in my chest at that thought.

I nod toward the couple two tables over, the ones with a French bulldog in a baby stroller. "You think the dog picked that stroller out himself, or did they workshop it together on Pinterest?"

Juliet tries not to smile, but it cracks through. "You're ridiculous."

"That stroller has a sunshade and cup holders," I mutter. "I've seen players travel with worse setups."

She glances over. "I mean... the dog *looks* pretty comfortable."

"Comfortable?" I scoff. "That mutt is living better than I am. If it's got a skincare routine, I'm walking into traffic."

She snorts. "Jesus."

I can't stop looking at her. The lipstick, the bun, the dangerous heels. The way she's trying so hard not to enjoy this, like admitting she's having fun would be some kind of weakness.

Beside us, a kid at the next table over knocks over a glass of orange juice. I lean down fast, grabbing napkins and mopping up the mess before it can spread.

As she stands and stretches to help, the hem of her skirt rides just a little higher up her thigh. I don't even try to hide the way my eyes track the movement.

Juliet glances over her shoulder and catches me mid-stare. My expression is probably somewhere between guilty and tempted. It knocks something off-balance in both of us. For once, I'm not teasing or trying to get a rise out of her. I'm just looking. And she doesn't seem to hate it.

"Hey, little man," I say to the kid, distracting him with an eyebrow wiggle. "You just made brunch way more exciting."

Juliet watches me like she's seeing something brand new.

As we walk out, she murmurs, "As much as it pains me to admit this, I feel better now that I've eaten."

I nod. "Told you. Brunch solves everything."

"It's better than being cooped up in the condo for another three hours, torturing myself by rereading the article again and again."

"Same difference." I put my hand on the small of her back, enjoying the flush that spreads from her cheeks to her chest at my touch.

It makes me wonder if she's always so responsive. Would she make soft little sounds if I kissed her again? Would she gasp if I tugged her hair back and nipped her neck? God, I bet she would.

I'm in my bubble of horny thoughts as I touch her smooth, warm skin almost all the way home.

Back at the condo, the bubble stretches and pops almost immediately. We're only home for a couple of minutes when I catch her tinkering with the heat. Checking the temperature, I find it to be about seven degrees higher than I would ever keep my house.

I scowl at her. "Turn down the thermostat. I'm going to be sweating in my home."

She glares right back. "You're a giant. You generate your own heat. I'm freezing."

"Not my problem."

Juliet puts both fists on her hips and gives me an irritated look.

"You're such a cave troll. Also? Your music is too loud. Every night before I go to sleep, you blare the dumbest music. It's inappropriate."

She's hot when she's a little pissed off. "Aw, baby. I'm doing it for you."

"What do you mean, you're doing it for me? How does it help me exactly?" She cocks her hip.

I lean closer, invasion of personal space becoming a theme. "If I didn't play music, you'd hear me jerking off."

Juliet's cheeks turn a fiery red. She goes completely still. "That happens every day? You can't be that horny."

"I'm a professional athlete who's currently not getting any action. Masturbating once a day is barely taking the edge off." I step forward, close enough to see the flecks of gold in her brown eyes. "Why? Are you keeping track?"

Her breath catches. "No."

But she doesn't move away.

My hand brushes her arm. Her gaze drops to my mouth.

We move in the same orbit, drawn together like two bodies caught in the same tide. The air between us hums, thick and electric, a current thrumming between us until the only thing left is the pull of her mouth, the heat of her breath. When we collide, it is not gentle. It is heat and want, the sharp edge of something that has been building for years, a collision so inevitable it feels like the universe has been conspiring to bring us to this exact moment.

The kiss is messy, frenzied, uncoordinated, too much. Lips and teeth and desperation and years of unresolved tension.

I kiss her like I'm starving. Like she's air and I've been drowning without having her. Juliet kisses me like she forgot who she's supposed to be. Like all that careful control just evaporated.

Like she's desperate for my touch. Like she's *ravenous*.

She whimpers into my mouth and I slide my hand up her jaw, into her hair, hungry for more. More of her neediness, more of her desire.

I've kissed women before. Slept with plenty of them. But

none of them ever felt like this. No one has ever looked at me the way Juliet does. No one has ever tasted like heaven on my tongue and moaned, so soft and sweet, that I feel ruined by a kiss.

I'm going to fuck this up. Break her heart, crush her dreams. That's my track record. That's the pattern. People get close, and I ruin it. I disappoint them or hurt them or drive them away with my inability to be anything other than what I am.

But damn, at this moment, my lips move against hers, my tongue sweeping against her lips, seeking entrance. For a second, she makes a soft sound and nearly allows my tongue inside her mouth.

Then Juliet pulls back, breathing hard. She looks at me for several long seconds, her shoulders heaving, her face flushed. Those dark brown eyes of hers pin me in place.

"Huxley," she whispers. "This is a mistake. It can't mean anything."

I hate her for saying it, even though I know it's true.

"Yeah," I say, even though I want to drag her back and kiss her until neither of us can think straight. I clear my throat. "I agree."

She walks away toward her room. I stand there in the hallway, breathless, blood pounding in my ears.

She tasted of citrus, vanilla, and musk. Like danger wrapped in silk.

And now I want more. So much more.

What a terrible fucking idea to ever to kiss her.

Chapter 12

Juliet

That kiss. What was I thinking?

I don't even recognize myself at that moment. Leaning into Hunter like that. Letting his mouth find mine like I wanted it. Like I needed it.

I've never been the type to lose control, but Hunter has this infuriating way of peeling me open, one taunt at a time. He pokes at all my soft spots. Pushes me just far enough until I forget we're only pretending.

I keep telling myself it was just a strategy. Just part of the image we're selling. Two people caught up in the moment, playing our roles too well.

But I know better.

If I let it happen again, even once, I'll lose more than just a kiss. He'll take things I've spent years protecting. My image, my future, my carefully controlled detachment from men who think they can own me.

I should be worried about two things today.

One: that kiss. And I can't stop thinking about it.

Two: tonight's game. The Havoc's first big home match of the season.

Against the Houston Stars.

Which means Patrick Delacroix will be in the building.

I force a smile and adjust the lapels of my blazer as I enter the arena suite. Jessa's already there, feet up on the padded seat, sipping something way too sugary.

"There she is," she chirps, tossing me a protein bar. "You're late and you've got that 'swallowed a porcupine last night' expression."

"That's generous," I mutter, sinking into the seat beside her. "That would honestly be better than this."

Jessa frowns. "Is this about how Hunter carried you from the wedding venue like he was auditioning for a romance novel cover? Because I saw the photos. You looked hot. Like, two seconds from dragging him into a supply closet hot."

I open my mouth to argue, but Ivy walks in carrying a clipboard and looking exactly like a woman who has never made a single poor decision in her entire life. She sits on my other side without saying a word, just raises one eyebrow.

I exhale sharply. "Patrick's here."

That gets their attention.

Jessa's entire face twists. "Is this *the* Patrick? Like the ex?"

"The same. He plays for the Houston Stars."

"He's your ex! Shouldn't you get a reprieve?" Jessa asks, sounding irritated.

"The NHL doesn't exactly call us up and ask if we're avoiding any players on other teams," Ivy sighs. "In fact, I think that would make them schedule us to play Houston more often."

I wrinkle my nose. "I should've known that Patrick would show up with his smug little smirk and carefully edited sob story."

Ivy narrows her eyes, her tone flat. "Are you sure you're ready to see him?"

"Nope. Not at all."

I glance toward the ice, where the players are just starting warmups. Hunter is already out there, loose and powerful, his jersey hanging perfectly off his broad frame. Patrick skates by a few seconds later, catching my eye for just a moment. He gives me a subtle smirk like we're sharing a private joke.

I look away, nauseated.

"I hate him," I whisper.

Jessa leans in. "Tell us everything."

So I do.

I tell them how he used to tell me what to wear to team events. How his mother once called me 'decorative' to my face, and he didn't defend me. How he cheated and then had the audacity to spin it like I'd been the problem. And now, how he's giving interviews about how he's worried for me. Saying I've always struggled with 'boundaries and attention.'

"He's painting me as a gold digger," I finish. "Like I dated him for the clout and now I'm using Hunter to climb higher."

"Jesus," Jessa breathes. "That is next-level unhinged."

Ivy shakes her head. "He's a public relations nightmare. If he so much as breathes wrong tonight, I'll bury him in spin so fast he won't remember his own name."

That earns a laugh, shaky but real. "Thanks."

Down on the ice, Hunter slams a puck into the net with brutal precision. I see the moment he clocks Patrick. His whole body shifts. Less relaxed, more coiled.

Jessa follows my gaze. "Uh-oh. Hunter sees him."

"Yeah," I murmur. "He always sees him."

It feels reminiscent of college. Hunter and Patrick were on the same team then and they still got in an astounding number of fights with each other. They'd wait until a fight started and then jump in, hitting the other 'by accident'.

Patrick skates too close. Hunter's head snaps toward him like he's been waiting for the opportunity. They ram their shoulders as they skate past each other in a way that's definitely not accidental. Patrick is smaller than Hunter and takes the hit harder.

A dark part of me gets excited watching my fake fiancé demolish my terrible ex-boyfriend. I'm already wired to think hockey boys are hot, but now I'm doubly invested in what's going on.

Ivy whistles. "Patrick's about to get wrecked."

"I should be embarrassed by how satisfying that would be," I say with a wince.

"You shouldn't," Jessa says. "Let him suffer."

I look back at Hunter. He skates like he's angry at the world, like the ice owes him something. But when his eyes flick up to the suite and meet mine, it's like the chaos fades for one heartbeat. There's a moment of tangible connection.

And worse?

I like it.

Seattle Havoc rolls out in full force, and they are not fucking around. They snap into formation like muscle memory. It seems like every person on this team was born for this.

Patrick plays center for Houston and sidles up against Thorne, waiting for the puck drop. He keeps looking behind him though. I would be too if I were Patrick, because Hunter is hovering within a few feet of him, gliding lazy laps in the neutral zone like a predator biding his time.

The puck drops, and the first shift is brutal. Sticks clash, bodies crash, and nobody's playing nice. The forecheck is aggressive, the kind of hit-first, ask-later style they love to talk about in practice.

Thorne snags the puck and skates away toward the goal. Patrick trails behind him as he smoothly passes the puck to Grayson, who moves down the ice with the fierce motion of a hurricane. Tight turns. Hard strides. No hesitation.

When Patrick and Hunter draw even, Hunter checks him into the boards so hard that I suck in a breath. It isn't just a hit. It's a message.

"Damn."

Jessa's eyes sparkle. "That's your man down there."

"Jessa." My cheeks warm. "He's not my anything."

Hunter looks up and points at me, a dark grin on his face. Jessa squeals and grips my elbow.

"See?"

I can't help the small smile I give Hunter. Then there's a tussle farther down the ice, a full-on scrum behind the net, and Hunter's attention swings that way.

The game moves on, but my heartbeat is still racing.

Jessa elbows me. "He clearly did that for you."

"Huxley hates Patrick. Any excuse to fuck him up is more than enough."

I avoid Jessa's knowing gaze and focus on the game, watching as the Havoc cycle the puck deep in the offensive zone, relentless and hungry. Hunter goes after Patrick three more times, tripping him, slamming him into the boards. Hunter is so smooth that the refs never call him on it; he makes it seem like a part of gameplay. Patrick gets frustrated and tries to grab the back of Hunter's jersey. He shouts something at Hunter, which makes Hunter turn bright red.

Hunter waits until Patrick's head is down for half a second and absolutely *obliterates* him with a legal open-ice check. Textbook hit. Brutal timing. The entire crowd gasps.

Patrick trips and goes flying, stick falling by the wayside. Patrick sprawls and Hunter falls on top of him, putting his gloved hand to the back of Patrick's helmet and grinding his face down into the ice.

The fans go apeshit, screaming their heads off and waving their foam chainsaws. They love Hunter behaving badly. The refs pull Hunter off and the whole thing is over in less than two minutes. But when Hunter skates away, acting like it meant nothing, he points to me again.

This time, I grin. He earned it for making my ex look like a limp dishrag. Hunter heads to the penalty box for two minutes, but he doesn't seem to mind. He sticks his tongue out, clearly enjoying himself as he skates backward.

Why is it so hot when Hunter acts like a fucking caveman?

Between periods, I scroll through the latest Havoc press clippings on my phone. The team's trending, but not positively. Headlines use words like chaotic, penalty-heavy, and raw talent without a leash. One photo shows Hunter snarling at Patrick just before he checked him.

It was hot, but it's not exactly making Hunter seem even-keeled. I sigh.

After the game, which the Havoc win by two goals, I'm waiting outside the locker room. Jessa and Ivy are busy working. I'm propped against the wall, anticipation mounting. I know what's coming.

It's only a matter of time before Patrick makes his grand appearance. There's no avoiding him. If he doesn't get to make me miserable now, he might show up at my door in the Sinclair. I put nothing past him, the fucking asshole.

"Juliet." The sound of my name on Patrick's lips is like being doused with a bucket of ice water. I whirl, eyeing him.

He's still in his gear, helmet tucked under his arm,

looking exactly the same as he did when I left him six months ago. He shakes his sweaty blond hair out, a grin on his face, and he swaggers up to me like he has every right to be here.

Fucking asshole.

"Patrick." I shift and try to make it appear my heart isn't galloping a million miles an hour. "Oh *good*, you're here. I was just saying this hallway wasn't insufferable enough."

"Still snarky as always." He cocks his head at me, taking me in. "We need to talk."

"No, we don't." I try to push past him, but he blocks my way.

"This whole thing with Huxley is embarrassing. You're making yourself look desperate."

"If I'm desperate, what does that make the guy who's trapped his ex-girlfriend in a hallway?" I try to push him away, shuddering at having to actually touch him. "Get away from me, Patrick."

"I'm trying to help you," he continues, getting closer. "Everyone can see what you're doing. Using him for his money, his fame. It's pathetic."

My stomach lurches. I don't believe a word out of Patrick's lying mouth. But the thought that other people might see me as a user makes my heart stutter.

Is that what people think?

That's when Hunter appears from the locker room. He's still in his gear, but only half of it. Shoulder pads peeled off and dangling from one arm, chest damp with sweat beneath the thin compression shirt he never changed out of. His gloves are gone, exposing calloused hands and taped wrists, and his hockey pants hang low on his hips like they're only staying up out of spite. His dark blond hair is damp and curling at the edges.

Silas and Jett are right behind him, flanking him like

bodyguards, looking like two slightly smudged photocopies of the same big, angry man.

The temperature in the hallway drops about twenty degrees.

"Get the fuck away from her," Hunter growls. "Come here, Juliet."

He lifts his arm, and I flee to him like a stream to the ocean. Never in my life have I been so glad that I had someone bigger and far meaner in my corner. Hunter tucks me into his side, never breaking eye contact with my ex.

Before Patrick can respond, Coach Ryan cuts through the crowd. Ryan grabs Hunter's free arm, but his eyes lock on Patrick.

"Who the fuck do you think you are?" Ryan asks, his voice carrying absolute authority. "*No one* comes into my arena, into an area that's off-limits to non-Havoc personnel, and corners a woman who clearly doesn't want to talk to him."

He takes a step toward Patrick, who suddenly looks a lot less confident. He licks his lips, his lizard brain trying to come up with an excuse.

"This is a private matter between Juliet and myself."

"You want to start a fight with me instead?" Ryan asks. He steps up, bristling. He's got serious fuck around and find out energy going on right now. "Because I'd be happy to accommodate you."

An assistant coach from Houston's team walks by right then. Ryan calls out to him. "Hey, Martinez. Collect your player before he gets himself arrested for harassment."

The coach's eyes bug out when he sees the situation. He grabs Patrick by the arm and starts dragging him away.

"What the fuck is wrong with you?!" I hear him hissing as they disappear down the hallway.

Silas and Jett head back into the locker room and Coach Ryan follows them.

"Hey." Hunter looks down at me, concern clear in his gray eyes. He reaches up to touch my face with gentle fingers. "Are you okay, Monroe?"

Not even slightly. I'm still shaken from my run-in with Patrick. But I can't say that, so I go with, "Better now."

Hunter tips my face up, examining me. I hate how easily he does that. His hand spans half my face. I feel small next to him and not in the bad way Patrick used to make me feel.

"I should've known that vile piece of shit would come after you."

I shift, swallowing. I need to cry, badly, but I can't exactly let it out here in the hallway. Anyone could see. So I grab his hand, squeeze it, and exhale a shaky breath.

"I'm all right."

"Liar." Hunter drops his mouth to my ear, whispering, "I can feel you shaking."

Yup. I am definitely too close for comfort. I push against his chest and he lets me go, but his gaze is still intense. The man can make fucking eye contact, that's for sure.

"You should go," I tell him. "You have the press to deal with."

Hunter grunts. "They can do the press conference without me."

Jessa rushes into the hallway, her eyes wide. "Juliet!!"

I glance at my roommate and reach an arm out to her.

"See?" I say to Hunter. "Jessa's here. We're about to leave."

"Are you sure?" Hunter turns and looks toward the locker room, clearly torn.

Jessa pulls me into her arms. I flash him a half-smile. The

last thing I need right now is to deal with whatever complicated feelings I have about him defending me.

"Absolutely."

"Go right home," he orders, walking backward toward the door. "No detours. I mean it."

"So *bossy.*" I roll my eyes at that. "I'll go right home, dad."

I hate him. Hate the way he acts like he owns me. But the worst part is I can't stop thinking about him. *Asshole.*

His mouth twitches, not quite a grin. He can't seem to help himself when it's me mouthing off.

His eyes twinkle. "We can talk about you calling me Daddy at home."

Jessa bursts into giggles, and I shake my head. "In your dreams, Huxley."

He turns and heads into the locker room, leaving me with Jessa. She squeals and pinches my arm. "What was that?"

"Just Huxley being a brute."

"Yeah, a brute who scares away your bullies."

That's a little too accurate for my liking. Jessa walks me to the exit, leaving me there since she still has work to do as part of her housing and lifestyles coordinator position. We agree to have a girls' night soon and hug before I step out of the building.

If I can't keep myself from bursting into flames every time he looks my way, Hunter Huxley will be the death of me.

Chapter 13

Juliet

As I drive home, my head is spinning with Patrick's accusations, Hunter's protective anger, and the way my body still remembers last night's kiss. It's a lot, all considered.

Patrick is probably talking about me in the press, but I can't add that to my list of troubles. I feel this pressure building in the back of my skull and in my sinuses.

The condo is dark when I step inside. I won't have an audience for the epic emotional breakdown that's about to happen. My lungs feel tight. The sadness and panic I've been avoiding claw at the insides of my chest. I need to let it out.

I drop my tote bag, kick off my heels, and run straight to my bedroom, closing the door a second before I burst into sobs. I bury my face in the pillow, screaming, and let it all out.

My tears aren't dainty or cinematic. They're messy. Violent. Full-body sobs wrack my chest and leave my throat raw. This is how I fall apart.

Fast, hard, and *always* behind closed doors.

I've always cried like this. Too much. Too easily. It's not

a weakness, exactly. It's release. A ritual. It's like my body stores up everything I won't say, then forces it out in one awful wave.

I cry until I'm shaking, until my mascara's on the pillow more than my face and my lungs hurt from the effort. I cry like I'm trying to wring out my heart.

Then, my crying slows. I lie still, blinking up at the ceiling with eyes that feel scraped raw. The worst part isn't the crying. It's the emptiness that follows. I've emptied myself out and there's nothing left to feel.

I hate how familiar this is. The swollen eyes, the damp pillowcase, the hollow ache behind my ribs. I've done this enough times to know it fixes nothing. It just quiets the noise for a while.

Dragging myself upright, I see that mascara has streaked down my face. My throat burns, and I'm already bracing for the guilt that always comes next. I should be stronger. I *should* be more in control. But sometimes this is the only way I can breathe again.

I am desperately thirsty, so I get up, wipe the remnants of my mascara off, and head for the kitchen. Unfortunately, I glimpse myself in the hallway mirror. Messy hair, disheveled dress, barefoot, lipstick partly rubbed off from nervously chewing my bottom lip. Panic flickers through me. If Hunter walks in now, he'll see the version of me I never show. The version that's not perfectly put together.

I bolt to the bathroom, swipe on red lipstick with shaking hands, twist my hair into a half-tidy knot, and yank on an oversized hoodie over my dress. Half-hearted armor for when I'm too tired to put on the real thing.

As I sip a glass of water, I sit in the kitchen and calm down by degrees. My mind slips away from the painful breakdown and settles on Hunter instead.

Defending me, sheltering me with his body, growling at my ex? A knot of twisted emotion forms in my chest at the thought of Hunter doing these things *for me*. I'm one part miffed, one part grateful, and one part turned on.

It's Hunter, though. He has always been a complete asshole where I've been concerned. For him to act like Patrick had attacked his real fiancée was… I don't know, unexpected I guess.

I wander into the living room and sit on the couch, lost in thought.

It's silly that I'm even thinking about this. I tell myself what I'm feeling is just heat. Just hormones and proximity and that stupid smirk he gets when he's trying to get a rise out of me.

But the way he looks at me sometimes, like he sees straight through the armor I wear, like he's just waiting for me to crack, makes something shift in my chest. A tiny fracture. Small, but dangerous.

Being truly seen, beyond the image I've carefully constructed, is destabilizing. And I can't afford to crack. Not again. Not for someone who could break me in ways Patrick never did; Patrick never really knew me well enough to destroy the real me.

The front door clicks open. Hunter's heavy stride crosses the living room. Grocery bags thump on the counter. I force myself to stay calm and walk into the kitchen like I haven't been having a minor breakdown for the last hour.

He pulls out a stack of prepared meal containers and a tub of protein powder with mechanical efficiency. No wasted motion. No conversation. Just the quiet thud of Tupperware hitting the counter. Without looking up, he murmurs, "Nice outfit, Ace."

He means my dress, still wrinkled from the drive back.

The zipper is halfway down, one sleeve sliding off my shoulder, and I am pretty sure there is mascara under my eye. He's always smug, always pushing. And that nickname hits a nerve I hate having.

"Maybe you should worry less about my clothes and more about the headlines you keep generating."

He finally looks at me. His brow lifts. That slow, crooked smile spreads across his face like he is enjoying this way too much.

"I thought you enjoyed fixing my messes."

My skin goes hot. I cross my arms and let it rip.

"You mean the brawl you started after warmups? Or the stick you shattered mid-shift that almost hit a water boy? Or maybe when you walked out of a press event with a sponsor wall behind you like you were storming off a reality show?" I sputter. "By the way, Huxley, I hate that nickname. It doesn't even make sense now that I'm not on the school paper."

He shuts the refrigerator. His expression changes. Not cocky now. Just quiet.

"I didn't know Ace bothered you."

"Are you kidding me? I've told you like a thousand times!" I gesture wildly, my face heating. This shouldn't be a big deal, but now I've already overreacted.

Hunter leans against the counter and looks me up and down. His lips purse, considering. "All right. Juliet then. Or maybe Firecracker. I think it fits better, anyway."

My heart skips. Does he see me this way? Something about how he says my name so softly, like he actually means it, unravels something in my chest. I blink fast, trying not to let him see it.

He turns back to the counter and starts measuring protein powder like he did not just hit a nerve I have spent years trying to bury.

He turns away, changing into gray sweatpants right there in the kitchen, completely nonchalant about being half-naked in front of me. I whirl around and head back into the living room, my face flaming bright red. Then he stretches out on the couch with a protein shake like we didn't just have a fight.

I perch at the other end of the couch, still vibrating with leftover adrenaline. He absent-mindedly reaches down to pass me the TV remote, his knuckles brushing mine, like touching me is the most normal thing in the world.

I adjust the hem of my skirt for the third time and catch Hunter watching me from his end of the couch.

I straighten, cross my arms defensively. "You're staring at my chest again."

Hunter doesn't even blink. "No, I'm not."

My eyes narrow. "You always do it. Every time I wear something remotely fitted."

He smirks, and I know I'm about to regret asking. "If I were staring, it wasn't at your chest."

I blink. Yeah, *right*. "Oh, really?"

"Yeah." He takes a sip of his protein shake, gaze lazy and heavy. "It was your legs."

My mouth opens, but nothing comes out.

"And maybe your lips," he adds casually. "Not gonna lie, the tits are great. But they weren't what I was looking at."

Color explodes across my face. I huff, look away, then back, like I can't decide whether to slap him or run away.

Hunter grins, slowly and dangerously. "You blush easily."

"I do not," I snap.

"You do," he says, voice lower now. "And it looks good on you."

I glare at him, but I can feel my ears turning pink. The bastard notices everything.

I can't stop replaying last night's kiss. His mouth was hot against mine, the way my body just melted into his like it had been waiting for permission. Shame and craving coil together in my stomach. Suddenly my imagination is supplying images I absolutely don't need. His mouth on my breasts, on me, him pushing deep while whispering my name.

"You're such a *player*." I curse my traitorous brain and blurt out, "You'd better keep your hands off other women while we're fake engaged. I don't want to be embarrassed."

His head snaps toward me. "Never crossed my mind. I'm a one-woman guy, even if it's pretend."

The intensity in his eyes steals my breath. His lips twitch.

"I got you something," he says.

My heart slams against my chest as I feign a deep lack of concern. "Oh?"

Hunter disappears into his room and comes back with something I wasn't expecting. A jersey. His jersey, but in a smaller size that would actually fit me.

"You should wear this to games from now on," he says, holding it out. "You know, to keep up the facade. If you were really mine, you'd wear it."

The possessive way he says *mine* makes my heart skip, even though I know he doesn't mean it. Not really.

I take the jersey, feeling the soft fabric between my fingers. Number 47. Huxley. It smells like him, that cedar and danger scent that's been driving me crazy.

"Fine," I say. "For the cameras."

"Obviously," he grunts.

Hunter watches me hold his jersey, jaw flexing, something protective and dangerous in his gaze. My heart skids between fury at myself for caring and fierce, illicit delight at the way he's looking at me.

"Pack a bag for the weekend," he blurts.

"What?"

"The team rented a compound on Orcas Island for a bonding retreat. We'll show up, spend hours in close contact, and share a room. The whole couple experience."

I blush so hard I'm probably glowing. "Share a room?"

"That's what couples do, Firecracker."

I swallow. Is that what we do, though?

"We don't have anyone to fool on the team, though. Right? I thought we were just supposed to be seen out and about together in Seattle."

He arches a brow. "My brothers know that our engagement is fake. Jessa and Ivy know. I guess Coach Ryan, too. But otherwise, the team doesn't have a clue. I would never tell them something so personal."

"You don't mind lying to them?"

"That's not really how I see it. Besides, what's a little white lie if it means an entire weekend of relaxing and hanging out on the water?"

"I concede your point."

Hunter winks, picks up his shake, and heads off to his room, closing the door. I do the same, my mouth dry, sinking down onto my bed. My hands spread over his jersey pressed against my chest. I'm breathing hard, wondering why the idea of sharing a room with Hunter is making me feel so turned upside down.

We're absolutely fake. I'm just making this into something it's not.

I'm not falling for the enemy. I'm not. Just because he's occasionally thoughtful and defended me from Patrick and looks like sin in a button-down means nothing. He'll ruin me like all the others. That's what men like Hunter do. They burn things down and call it passion.

As if to prove my point, he plays loud music from his room, bass thumping through the walls.

Oh god. Does that mean he's… touching himself?

I should feel annoyed. I *am* annoyed.

But that doesn't stop my stupid heart from racing, thinking about him and what this weekend will be like.

Chapter 14

Hunter

I crowd onto the seaplane with the rest of the starting lineup and a couple of rookies: Thorne, Silas, Jett, Grayson, Beck, Shane, and Connor. Coach Ryan also enters at the last minute, hustling his flame-haired fiancée Wren with him. The salt wind sneaks through the open hatch. The team's packed in here like sardines.

The ladies who work for the team, Jessa, Ivy, and Juliet, stuff themselves in the very back of the plane. Connor claims the spot next to Juliet until I growl at him, making him move to the front of the plane.

I have eyes only for Juliet, who's gripping her seat like the plane might fall apart at any second. We take off without incident and she relaxes incrementally.

"Better?" I ask.

"Maybe." She arches her brow and leans close to my ear. "Think you can handle sharing one bed without making it weird?"

I fire back, "Adults have self-control, Firecracker."

Her cheeks warm. "That's a way better nickname than Ace."

I give her hand a squeeze. Under the banter sits an electric hum I'm not ready to name. Something that's been building since that kiss in our hallway, something that makes the air between us feel charged every time we're in the same room.

Going on this weekend will be interesting. It'll be a view of how Juliet acts around me, not just because cameras will watch, not because we have to pretend. I know I told her I'm trying to keep our fake relationship under wraps from my team, but it will be an interesting litmus test.

Orcas Island is part of the San Juan Islands, a cluster of rugged, forested gems tucked between the Washington coastline and the Canadian border. It's about a hundred miles northwest of Seattle, accessible only by ferry or seaplane. We skim over the Puget Sound in a tiny plane that buzzes like a dragonfly before landing with a splash in the harbor.

The island itself feels like another world. Everything is wild and green and cinematic. Towering firs crowd the shoreline. Jagged cliffs drop into the deep, inky water that somehow always looks cold, even when the sun hits it just right. The air smells of pine needles and salt and woodsmoke. It's nature in high definition, dramatic and moody and so beautiful it almost feels rude.

We hop on the golf cart shuttle to Orcas Point. The place that we're staying is absolutely obscene. A cedar and glass main lodge perched over slate cliffs, five guest cottages tucked into the fir trees, private docks stretching out into silver water that looks like a postcard. There's a heated pool and a hot tub steaming in the October chill, fire bowls already lit and crackling.

"How much does this weekend cost per person?" Juliet whispers as we put our things down in the main house.

I wave a dismissive hand. "Basically nothing. Greene's yacht club buddy basically comped the whole thing as a favor. As long as we don't break anything or set the place on fire, we're golden."

"It must be nice to be so rich you can just let a hockey team stay in one of your weekend vacation compounds."

"Right? I earn a lot of money, but I'll never have that billionaire yacht vacation estate kind of cash."

She wrinkles her nose at that, her dark eyes sparkling. She's in a good mood today. With the gorgeous Orcas Island surrounding us, who wouldn't be?

Our entire party cozies up in hoodies and fleece jackets and gathers on the lawn of the main house like we're at summer camp. The plan is to hike up the trail outlined in the binder for the estate. The party ambles, Ivy leading the charge, Jessa and Jett close on her heels. Grayson and Beck are right behind them, strolling more than hiking.

Silas hangs back to spot the rookies who are struggling with the incline. I end up in the middle beside Juliet, matching her shorter stride. She's wearing a dark gray Seattle Havoc hoodie that I've never seen her wear before, a pair of stretchy black yoga pants, and a pair of weird-looking high heel-slash-boots on her feet.

Her legs pump twice as fast as mine just to keep up. "You walk like a giant," she mutters.

I grin. "You're five feet tall, Juliet. You're tiny."

"I'm not tiny." She glares at me, breathing hard. "I should have stayed in the house with Ryan and Wren. This is way too much exercise for me."

"You're tough. You can do it." I smirk and pretend not to enjoy the flush creeping up her throat.

"You're enjoying this way too much," she pants.

"What? Watching you struggle up a hill? Never."

"Sadist."

"You're the one who packed heels for a camping trip."

"These are hiking boots," she protests. "I got them especially for this trip."

"They look extremely uncomfortable."

Juliet sticks her tongue out at me, and I let out a bark of laughter. She's usually all stiff and formal, but trudging uphill through the woods seems to strip away a layer of her starchiness.

She walks faster, intentionally leaving me behind. I don't complain though, because now I get to stare at her ass in those yoga pants. Damn, if Juliet were my real fiancée, I would count down the minutes until I got to strip those leggings off her and sink my teeth into that ass.

I'm never going to get to take her pants off, but it never hurt anyone to look.

When we get back to the house, Juliet devours a chicken caesar salad wrap that the estate's private chef makes for lunch. I quirk a brow as she puts down a plate of fruit salad, a huge brown butter cookie, and a bottle of electrolyte sports drink.

"What?" she says, glaring at me.

I shake my head, finishing my second wrap. "Nothing. It's just that girls rarely eat around me."

She rolls her eyes. "I just burned like a billion calories. Would you prefer I starve?"

I smirk. "With legs that short, I'm shocked you burned any at all." She kicks me under the table hard enough to make me laugh.

"I'm kidding." I reach out and touch her hand, getting her to look at me. "It's cute."

"You're being weird." She stands up and carries her plate into the kitchen.

I watch her go, considering. Am I being weird? Maybe.

I think this relaxed atmosphere is doing funny things to both of our personalities.

After lunch, we mark off end zones with pieces of driftwood and play touch football on the damp grass. Moose cheats constantly, Thorne trash-talks everyone, Jett keeps stealing the ball from Jessa, and Juliet keeps score while chirping me for being overly dramatic when I score a touchdown.

She has to jump to snatch the ball out of my hand when I tease her.

"Give it back, Sasquatch," she says, stretching uselessly. I hold it just high enough to make her glare.

Her laughter keeps finding me across the field. Every time it does, something tight in my chest loosens, like I've been holding my breath without realizing it.

What is going on between us exactly?

Juliet's eyes sparkle as everyone huddles up for the punch. She's having fun. Miss Stick-Up-Her-Ass is learning that life is more bearable when you don't treat everything as a task on an endless checklist.

"You know this is supposed to be touch football, right?" she calls out when I level Shane with what might have been excessive force. "Not murder ball."

"Tell Shane to run faster."

"Tell yourself to dial it back, Chainsaw."

The nickname should annoy me. Instead, it makes my lips twitch with humor.

Sunset bleeds orange over the water. Eventually, we circle around the fire pit wrapped in blankets, beers sweating in our gloved hands. Embers pop and spark; someone queues up music from the nineties. Ryan roasts me for losing some bet I don't remember making.

I lob back a dig about his questionable coaching decisions until Juliet nudges my knee under the blanket.

"Easy, Chainsaw," she murmurs. "PR is off duty this weekend."

The simple contact buzzes hotter than the flames. Her knee stays pressed against mine. I try my damnedest not to read too much into it.

Later, there's a night swim dare that has the rookies cannonballing into the heated pool. Almost everyone jumps in, beers in hand. Silas won't drink, so I don't even bother checking with him. He'll stay and watch the pack. He's a sheepdog like that.

After a couple of beers, I get antsy. I catch Juliet's gaze. "Hot tub?"

She bites her lower lip gently, some sort of decision-making process happening in her head. I have to say, I like that about her. At last, she shrugs. "Okay. Let me change into a bathing suit."

I hurry to change into my trunks, feeling a charge of anticipation. I haven't ever seen Juliet in a bikini and I have to admit, I'm looking forward to it. Grabbing a big, fluffy towel, I head into the private grotto where the hot tub is situated.

I climb into the steaming tub, instantly groaning. It feels amazing on my stiff right knee and my bruised right ribcage. Okay. When I eventually get a house, a hot tub is going to be on my list of must-haves.

Juliet makes an appearance a few minutes later, wrapped in a fluffy yellow beach towel. She sends an apprehensive look over her shoulder as she hands the towel over a deck chair, revealing a jaw-dropping little body in a navy high-waisted bikini. The structured and sleek top lifts and curves in all the right places without showing too much.

Which somehow makes it worse. The fabric clings like a second skin, hugging her waist and hips, dipping just enough at the neckline to short-circuit my brain. Juliet's legs look impossibly long. Her skin is smooth and flushed from the cool air. She pulled up her hair, which leaves her graceful neck bare, and all I can think about is pressing my mouth to the sweet curve where her shoulder meets her neck.

She looks as though she belongs in a photoshoot. Elegant. Immaculate. A little self-conscious, but trying not to show it. She crosses her arms for a second, then catches herself and lets her tits drop, chin lifted like she knows exactly what effect she's having.

I am already in the hot tub and barely keeping it together. I drop my gaze to the bubbles and force myself to breathe through my nose. Cold water probably would have been smarter. She's not even looking at me, but I can feel the burn of her skin near mine, the gravity of it pulling me in. I shift slightly, adjusting the angle of my hips beneath the surface before things get too obvious.

I'm getting hard over her, looking at my stunning fake fiancée.

Juliet steps in and slides beside me like nothing's happening. The water swirls, heat rising, steam wrapping around her bare shoulders and collarbones. Her thigh brushes mine, and she doesn't flinch. If anything, she leans in closer.

Keep my hands on the edge of the tub, I train my eyes on the water. I try not to imagine what would happen if I turned toward her and pulled her into my lap. The sounds she would make. The feeling of her heated skin under my palms.

Fuck. I have to stop. Beneath the surface of the water, I'm hard as stone, silently begging the water to hide it.

"This is nice," she says, leaning back against the edge.

"The hot tub or the company?"

"The hot tub. The company remains to be seen."

I splash her, and she shrieks. She splashes me back and I grab her hand, smirking.

"You wanna go, Monroe?"

"*Huxley*." She feigns innocence. "I don't know what you mean."

She follows her words with another splash. Suddenly we're having a water fight like actual children instead of two adults pretending to be engaged. I scoop water and dump it on her head. She returns the favor with smaller, more forceful splashes that nail me in the face every time. In the end, I grab her hands, pulling her close as I grin down at her.

"This is why I call you Firecracker." Holding both of her hands in one of mine, I tickle her ribs lightly. She reacts as if I just set her on fire, her body contorting.

She's extremely ticklish. That's good to know. I file that away, even though I have no use for the fact.

"Truce," she gasps, writhing out of my hold.

"Only if you admit I'm excellent company."

She wipes her face and cracks, "You're tolerable company."

"I'll take it."

She moves a little further away, which the caveman inside the back of my head doesn't like one bit. I reach for her feet, pulling them into my lap. She pulls them back an inch, brows drawn like she's debating whether it's worth the risk of letting me touch her like this. I don't push. I just wait, silent. Eventually, she sighs and slides her feet closer to me.

"Do *not* tickle me," she warns, her eyes on my face.

"I would never." That's... probably not a lie. I might, under the right circumstances. "Gimme."

Juliet's toes curl slightly like she's already bracing for something. I settle her ankle against my thigh and start slowly, letting my thumbs work into the arch of her foot with steady pressure.

She exhales, soft and shaky, and it shoots straight to my cock. Her other foot shifts under the water, brushing my calf like an accident. I keep my face neutral, my jaw tight, pretending this is no big deal, like I'm not completely wrecked just from the way she melts when I hit the right spot.

She makes a tiny, involuntary sound in the back of her throat, almost like a whimper, and I suppress a groan. That *noise*. Jesus. If this is how she sounds from a foot massage, I'd bet money she's fucking devastating when she's being touched the way she really wants to be. Pinned to a wall, mouth on my neck, legs wrapped around my waist while she makes those same breathy little sounds right into my ear.

I adjust her heel in my palm and keep going, fingers gliding over soft skin, thumbs pressing into all the tension she tries to hide. She's trying not to react. I can tell. But her body gives her away. Every tiny twitch, every shift in her breathing. She's not relaxed. She's lit up. Just like me.

At length, Juliet pulls her feet away and clears her throat.

"Thanks." Her mouth pulls to the side. "Uh, do you know when dinner is?"

"I think we're missing it," I say with a shrug. "I can't hear the football game going on anymore. That usually means food has been served."

"Want to go up?"

Yeah, I do want to follow her. But I also don't want Juliet to see the fact that my cock is still at half-mast over the sounds that she was making.

"Sure. You go ahead. I'll be right there."

She gives me a dubious look, like I'm up to something

nefarious, before getting out, water running down her ass and legs like some kind of porn video made just for me.

"Get dressed before dinner!" I call as she's disappearing upstairs. I'm not sure if she heard me, but if she doesn't put a lot of clothes on, my teammates are going to have trouble keeping their tongues in their mouths when they see her.

That thought gets me up and toweling off, eager to chase Juliet up the stairs. She gets dressed in a soft white sweater and dark jeans that make her ass look fantastic. No makeup, no jewelry but my ring on her finger.

I don't know why that's so sexy, but damn. Juliet is smoking hot, especially when she bends down to get her shoes on and I get a peek at her creamy tits. I'm hard for her in a heartbeat, imagining the taste of her pussy and the feel of her nails against my scalp.

She doesn't seem to notice that I'm a horny, brooding idiot. I'm thankful for that, at least. She looks up at me. "Ready?"

The private chef has laid out a feast for us. Cedar-plank salmon, truffle risotto, and lime gimlet cocktails strong enough to fell a tree. It's all incredibly delicious. Most of the team finished eating at the large dining room table before we arrived. I spot Shane yawning even though it's barely eight.

It's been a long, full day.

Juliet enjoys two cocktails, after which I put a can of bubbly water in front of her. Those cocktails were strong, and she's a tiny person. She gives me a mischievous look but sips the water without complaint.

Jessa and Ivy bail early, citing the long day. Moose herds the rookies toward their cottage, muttering something about bedtime stories. Juliet catches my eye across the table, taps her wrist, and mouths, *bedtime?*

I push back from my chair immediately, pulse already drumming. "We should probably head out too."

The walk to our house feels longer than it should. Every step makes this more real, more immediate. We're about to spend the night in the same bed and I'm trying not to think about what that means.

She deserves someone stable. Someone who doesn't flinch when the word mom comes up in conversation. Someone whose worst day doesn't end up on ESPN with slow-motion replays. I can fake it for the cameras, but she'll never *really* want a damaged defender like me.

Not if she ever sees the full picture of who I am underneath all the performance, anyway.

But damn if I don't want to take her to bed right now.

Our cottage smells like cedar and sea brine. It's cozy, with a king-size bed dominating the main room and floor-to-ceiling windows overlooking the water.

Juliet ducks into the bathroom and emerges in silk shorts and a camisole, her face scrubbed clean except for that lethal red lipstick she never seems to go without. I strip down to boxer briefs.

She catches sight of my body, her eyes sinking down to my abs and then briefly considering my dick. Then her face flames.

"Huxley! Put some clothes on!"

I knew that would get her going. "I run hot!"

Really, I just wanted her to look. She fans herself with her hand.

"You're the worst."

I look down at myself, as if considering her words. "I don't think you mean that. Look at these abs. Do you know how hard I've worked for these?"

She practically swallows her tongue, scowling, and climbs under the duvet. I watch as she immediately starts building a wall of pillows down the middle of the bed.

"Really?" I ask. "What is the pillow barrier for?"

"For… protection. So there are no *mistakes*."

Juliet says that pointedly, as if I would be the one to feel her up in my sleep. The joke's on her because I don't think I can sleep at all with her half-naked in my bed.

I get under the covers on my side, amused by her pillow fortress. "This is ridiculous. Two grown adults, playing sleepover like we're twelve."

"Pretty sure twelve-year-olds don't build pillow fortresses to avoid sexual tension," she mutters into the blanket.

I grin. "So you admit there's tension."

She kicks at the comforter. "There's no tension."

"You're lying through your teeth, Firecracker."

A beat of silence. I hear her shift, feel the mattress dip slightly as she moves closer to the pillow wall.

"You really run hot or is that just an excuse to show off your abs?"

"Busted."

She exhales what might be a laugh. "You're impossible."

"And you're blushing."

"I am not."

"You always get flustered when you picture me naked? Or is that a new thing?"

A pillow thumps against my side. "Go to sleep, Huxley."

I grin into the dark. "Not until you admit you've thought about it."

She goes quiet for long enough that I think maybe I pushed too far. Then I hear her swallow.

"I hate you."

"Sure you do."

She shifts on the bed. "Hunter?"

I look over at her. She's sleepy, which is adorable. "What is it, Monroe?"

"Thanks for this weekend." Her lips pucker for a moment. "We didn't have to come."

Turning onto my side, I consider her words.

"I'm glad we're here. It might be a shade awkward…" I motion to the wall of pillows between us. "But it's nice to be… friendly. Friend-*adjacent*."

"It's nice." A dreamy smile tugs at her lips. "A lot better than going on vacation with Patrick. He almost never took me anywhere. And on the few times he did, he made his mom and dad tag along. They loathed me."

"What? Why would they do that?"

She groans and stretches on her back, her camisole riding up, giving me a glimpse of her belly button.

"Apparently, I wasn't good enough for him. The Delacroix family is old money, you know. I wasn't blue-blooded enough for them. I wore the right clothes, went to all of Patrick's games, and was perfect wifey material. But because my mom worked for a living, Patrick's mom always made the most cutting remarks at my expense."

"And what did Patrick have to say about that?" I tense, already knowing that it's going to be awful.

"He blamed me for being oversensitive. He said she was just looking out for him." Juliet stares off into space, her lips parted. Seeing a memory, maybe. "You know, the first Christmas I spent at their house, she made me cry. *Twice*. And Patrick never said a word in my defense. I wish to hell I had headed for the hills right then and there."

I stare at her, the pillow barrier between us suddenly feeling like a wall I want to tear down. "You deserved better than that. Way better. I would *never* let anyone talk down to you. Especially not my mom."

She gives me a tiny shrug, pretending it doesn't matter anymore. But I can see the way her throat works as she swallows. It hurts more than she lets on.

I clear my throat, searching for something to say that won't sound clumsy. What do I say? That I wish she had dated me in college? That both of our lives would be completely different if I'd had the balls to ask her out?

That would be absurd. So instead of saying any of that, I reach for a bottle of water on the nightstand. My notebook is lying just beyond that. Of course, her eyes catch on it.

"What's that?" she asks, tilting her head toward it.

"Nothing." My hand shoots out to cover it, but she's already pushing up on an elbow, curious.

"Hunter…"

I take a sip of water. Are we both baring our souls tonight? I wish that having a fake fiancée came with an instruction manual.

"It's just sketching," I mutter. "And some journaling. I used to draw all the time back when I was a kid. Darla thought it was a waste. Told me it made me look weak. So I stopped." My jaw tightens. "She found some old sketchpads once and ripped them up in front of me. Said no son of hers was going to be a starving artist."

Juliet's eyes widen, glinting in the dim light. She doesn't laugh, doesn't make a joke. She just looks at me like she sees something I thought I'd buried. "You're good, aren't you?"

I shake my head. "Doesn't matter."

"It does," she says quietly. "That's… that's awful, Hunter. No wonder you're so hard on yourself."

"I think I chose my profession pretty well. I'm not missing out on anything." Putting my hands behind my head,

I shrug. "I don't know if you know this, but the Havoc pays very well."

Her lips twitch. "So I've heard."

She yawns, sinking back onto the bed. I let the silence fall between us, stretching. She closes her eyes, shifts, getting comfortable.

"All that hiking really…" She yawns again. "Took it out of me."

"Just relax, Monroe," I whisper. "I'll still be here when you wake up."

"Mmkay. Goodnight…"

Sixty seconds later, Juliet's asleep.

That was fast. I guess all this fresh air and exercise have really done a number on her. I lie still for a minute, watching her. The first thing she does is kick all the pillows she put up as a boundary straight onto the floor. Take that, anything in Juliet's way when she's trying to get *comfy*.

I smile at that. She's every bit as much of an ass-kicker and a name-taker when she's asleep as when she's awake. Gotta admire that.

But then she rolls over, wiggling until she's pressed up against me. My body stirs, as if it's been called into action. Which it *hasn't*. As much as I glorify having an enormous cock and knowing just how to use it, at this very moment, I would appreciate having a smooth, Ken-like bump on my groin instead of a penis.

What if Juliet wakes up and I'm this close to her, all fucking horny? I don't want to ruin the fragile maybe-peace we've found today.

She moves her head until it comes to rest on my biceps. Oh, this is double trouble. Her dark hair spills across my arm, her red-painted lips parting just so. I can feel heat brush against my skin as she draws gentle breaths.

I should move. Should rebuild the pillow wall and maintain some boundaries. Instead, I lie there listening to her breathe and trying not to think about how right this feels.

She fights me as if she's trying not to feel something. And maybe that's what pisses me off most about this whole situation. I feel it too. This pull between us that's bigger than our fake engagement, bigger than the PR strategy we're supposed to be executing.

It would be easier, safer, if I felt nothing. If I could just play my part, skate my games, fake a few smiles for the cameras and coast to the finish line when our contract expires.

But now she's in my head. In my space. In my fucking bed with her hair smelling like something expensive and her body warm against mine.

And I'm not sure I know how to come back from that.

I watch her sleep for longer than I should, memorizing the way her eyelashes cast shadows on her cheeks, the way her mouth relaxes when she's not guarding every expression. She looks younger like this, softer. Less like the polished professional who can command a room full of executives and more like… just *Juliet*.

I think about what it would be like if this were real. If she were really mine, if I could wake up next to her every morning without pretending it's just for show. If I could kiss her without it being a mistake that we both immediately regret.

But that's not what this is. This is a business arrangement with an expiration date. And girls like Juliet don't fall for guys like me, not without regretting it later when they realize what they've gotten themselves into.

Still, lying here with her curled against my side, I can

almost convince myself that maybe, just maybe, some part of this could be real.

Even if I know better.

Even if I know I'll probably ruin it, like I ruin everything else that matters to me.

But for now, in this cozy cottage by the sea, I let myself pretend. Just for tonight, as my eyes grow heavy with sleep.

Chapter 15

Hunter

Before dawn, I wake to find her thigh draped over my hip and the soft weight of her hand resting so low on my stomach it's not-quite touching my cock. I inhale sharply. Citrus and warm skin fill my head. I have to fight every instinct I have not to rock against her just to feel more.

Her breath is warm against my neck. One of her legs is hooked over my hip like she's claiming territory. My dick is hard, of course it is, and I lie stone-still with my heart hammering, unsure if moving would make things better or worse.

She stirs against me, making a soft sound that goes straight to my groin. "Hm?"

My mouth goes dry. I'm dying to answer her with a soft kiss. I would do anything that she asked at this moment.

Looking down at her lips, lipstick smudged and rubbed off, I bite my lower lip.

What the fuck is wrong with me all the sudden? Why can't I tear my eyes away from Juliet's mouth?

"Mmph... what the..."

Her eyes snap open. She takes a few moments to figure

out where she is and who she's touching. The second she realizes our position, she bolts upright like someone set her on fire.

"Shit!"

I look over at her, still groggy but definitely amused by her panic. "Morning, Monroe. Sleep okay? You seemed comfortable."

She scrambles backward, dragging the comforter with her and leaving me exposed to the cool morning air. "You didn't... I mean, we didn't..."

"Nah. You just crawled over here on your own and used me like a body pillow."

Her face flames red. "I did not."

"Pretty sure your leg was over mine. And your hand? Yeah. That was adventurous."

She makes a strangled noise that's somewhere between embarrassment and outrage, then dives off the bed, grabbing for her jeans like the cottage is on fire.

"Relax," I say, stretching deliberately so she gets a good look at what she was just pressed against. "I won't tell anybody that you had a moment of weakness."

"What?!" She launches a pillow at me, her cheeks still glowing pink. "You're the worst, Huxley. The. *Worst*."

I can't help but laugh.

"You keep saying that, but here you are... still thinking about my abs."

"I'm thinking about how fast I can get out of this cottage before you say something else that makes me want to drown myself."

I stretch again with a smirk, hands behind my head. "Race you to breakfast?"

She huffs and disappears into the bathroom, slamming the door harder than necessary.

I lie back, still smiling. "Still got it," I mutter to myself.

When she emerges, she's back in full armor. Jeans, a cream sweater, makeup perfectly applied. But I notice she's switched lipsticks from the deep red she wore last night to something lighter. And her eyes keep darting to my mouth when she thinks I'm not looking.

I want her. Of course I do. I've wanted her since college, if I'm being honest with myself.

The second I laid eyes on Juliet Monroe, my brain got rewired in some essential way. I've never thought that she was anything less than a perfect ten.

But it's more than that.

That's what makes this dangerous. Because want is one thing. I can handle want. It's straightforward, manageable. It's the need that messes me up. And lately, when she's not in the room, it feels like something's missing.

She hurries out of the room, leaving me to shower and get changed alone.

Morning chaos greets me when I finally make it to the main lodge. Someone's burning bacon in the chef's kitchen, filling the air with smoke and the sound of fire alarms. Moose is outside barefoot, punting a football across the lawn in what I assume is his version of a morning workout. Jessa's in the kitchen mixing hangover smoothies that are the color of algae and probably taste worse.

No way am I getting talked into tasting one of those.

I see Juliet looking sadly at a coffee urn. When I sidle up next to her, I look at the empty mug in her hands.

"No luck, huh?"

"No." She looks at me, her brows descending in a pout. "The chef said she was making more."

Oh. She usually has a pot of coffee brewing anytime she's at the house. She probably relies on the kick of caffeine to get her engine started. It's making a *lot* of sense right now.

Plucking the mug from her hands, I pick up the handle to the urn. "I'm going to go check on that. Hold on, Monroe."

She gives me a not-too-grateful glare, which makes me chuckle. She's a little surly this morning and I can't say that I dislike it.

I stride into the kitchen, where I find the chef frying bacon and cooking eggs. She spots the urn in my hands and shoots me an apologetic smile.

"Sorry. I have my hands full. If you could just wait, I can refill the coffee in a few minutes."

"Don't worry about it." I walk over to the industrial-size coffee machine. It's a familiar model, one that I remember from my days bussing tables at a steakhouse. "I've done this a million times before."

I pull out the basket, dump the coffee grounds, and replace the damp filter with a fresh one from a stack on top of the machine. The chef is watching, so I ask her for directions how much coffee I should pour in. Then I hit brew.

A minute later, the coffee maker is pumping out dark, fragrant liquid. I let it brew straight into the cup in my hands before setting up the urn with its lid open. Lifting the cup at the chef, I head back to Juliet.

She's standing in the dining room, looking mournful.

I corral her, hand her the fresh-brewed cup, and watch her eyes light up.

"You got coffee!" she says, voice sounding breathy. As if I'd conjured a miracle.

"I did."

I point to the several cream and sugar options and she falls all over herself to add plenty of oat milk and raw sugar to her coffee. Then she stirs it and takes a sip.

"Mmm. It's actually good."

"Anything for you, *honey*."

Juliet gives me side-eye as she has another sip. "Thanks, *baby*."

I like the teasing we've got going on. Wandering over to her, I slip an arm around her waist before I can overthink it. She doesn't pull away.

"Hm. Maybe the Chainsaw has a gentle setting after all." Her voice is soft, just like her skin under my hands.

"You are a Firecracker, aren't you?"

She rolls her eyes, but the smile stays. Until the chef announces that breakfast is served, she allows me to hold her for a few minutes. She sets up plates of eggs, scrambled tofu, bacon, hash browns, and fruit salad. I finally get a cup of coffee, a pile of eggs, and fruit.

No one is sitting at the dining room table. Everyone lounges in their own space, if they're here at all. Silas, Grayson, and Ivy haven't appeared at all yet.

I head out to the deck overlooking the rugged shore leading into the Salish Sea. Juliet is sitting outside on a deck chair and I grab the seat beside hers. For a minute we just eat and sip coffee; I put my eggs away in a very short amount of time and then look at Juliet.

"You switched lipsticks," I observe.

"So?" She brings a paper napkin to her lips. "I can wear different lipsticks. I change them all the time."

She's always a tiger on the attack. I smirk.

"Just surprised. I liked the one you had on in bed."

Her eyes sparkle, and she flicks her hair out of her face.

"I think you like whatever color my lips are, no matter what. You're basically captivated by them." She pauses, tilting her head. "Are you obsessed with me, Huxley?"

Isn't that obvious? I cough, covering my reaction with a

low laugh. "You know, you talk a big game, Firecracker, but you were real cozy this morning."

She spears a strawberry and points it at me. "I was asleep."

"Yeah. Real peacefully. Right on top of me. You snore, by the way."

Her eyes narrow to slits. "I do not."

"You definitely do. It's kinda cute, though."

"Do you wake up every morning this annoying or is this a special treat?"

I grin and lean in just a little, close enough to catch a whiff of the expensive perfume she wears. "Only for you, *sweetheart*."

Her breath catches, just for a second. Then she turns on her heel, muttering something I can't quite catch, and walks away. I watch her go, satisfied with myself.

I'm winning. Whatever game this is between us, I'm definitely winning.

The rest of the day slides into something warmer, slower, more intimate than either of us meant for it to be.

Around noon, we get dragged to the massage cabin by Ivy and Jessa, who claim it's a team bonding requirement. I scoff, saying there's no way I'm getting oiled up by some stranger, but Juliet smirks and calls me a coward.

That earns her a challenge I refuse to back down from.

"Fine," I say. "But if this is weird, I'm blaming you."

"Everything's weird with you," she shoots back.

Tucked in the trees is the cozy massage cabin. Juliet ends up on the table next to mine, separated by a gauzy curtain that doesn't quite reach the floor. When the massage therapist works on her, she lets out a groan so sinful it makes my fists clench.

"Jesus, Monroe. Those *sounds*," I mutter through the partition. "Are you trying to get me arrested?"

She hums, voice lazy and content. "You're the one who insisted on being here."

"I didn't insist. You challenged me."

"Same thing."

For the next hour, I have to listen to her make sounds that should be illegal while someone works knots out of muscles I didn't know I had. By the time we're done, I'm wound tighter than when we started.

Afterward, we both look thoroughly worked over. Hair mussed, faces flushed, clothes slightly rumpled. When we get back to the main cabin, everyone teases us about the afterglow. I nearly deck Silas when he makes a stupid comment about *couple's activities*.

Later, we wander back to the media room where a few players and some of the staff are playing cards. Shane pulls Juliet into a game of poker, declaring her his lucky charm. She leans over my shoulder during my hand, whispering strategy tips that are both terrible and probably meant to mess with me.

"You should fold," she murmurs in my ear. Her breath is warm against my neck and I can feel her body heat through the cream cashmere sweater she's wearing.

Down, boy. No letting my thoughts wander there. "I've got a good hand," I proclaim.

Juliet's eyes sparkle and she shakes her head at me like I'm a petulant two-year-old who won't listen.

"You've got nothing," she purrs. "Trust me, *honey*."

I know she's doing it on purpose. I also don't care. Having her this close, feeling the heat of her body pressed against my back, is worth losing a few hands of poker.

At one point, she laughs too hard at something Moose

says. She loses her balance, throwing her arms around my neck to catch herself. The hug should be brief, but... It isn't. My hands come up instinctively, one at her waist, one on her back, anchoring her there.

Neither of us says anything. The room continues around us, but we're in our own bubble. She drags herself away, eyes flicking to mine, cheeks pink.

"Sorry," she whispers. She bites that lush pink lip, sinking her teeth into it.

Would she like it if I kissed her right now? Would she moan?

"Don't be," I husk out.

Eventually, the card game fizzles out. People drift toward the fire pits or the hot tubs for the evening wind-down. We stay behind, alone in the quiet media room.

I stand behind her at the window, watching the sun drop lower over the water. The view is incredible, all gold light and lavender sky, but I'm more interested in watching her reflection in the glass.

"It's so beautiful here." She crosses her arms, gazing out with me. "I don't want to go back to real life."

Neither do I. Tomorrow we'll return to Seattle. Here, in this bubble we've created, things feel simple. Real.

Well, more real than they have been anyway.

I say nothing. Just slide my hand to the small of her back and leave it there, letting the warmth soak in. She doesn't pull away, doesn't tense up. Just leans back slightly into the contact.

We stand like that for a long time, watching the light change over the water. The silence isn't awkward or charged with the usual tension. It's peaceful in a way I'm not used to.

"This place is like a different world," she breathes.

"Yeah."

"No cameras. No reporters. There won't even be any stupid exes making statements to the press."

"No fake smiles or staged photos."

She turns slightly, still within the circle of my arms. "Is this what normal people feel like?"

"I wouldn't know. I've never been normal."

That gets a small smile. "Me neither."

I study her profile in the golden light. She looks younger here, softer. Less like the polished professional who can command a room full of executives and more like just Juliet. The woman who builds pillow walls and snores in her sleep and makes sounds during massages that drive me crazy.

"Do we have to go back?" she asks. "Can't we live here? Just move here?"

If I'm reading the room correctly, I think she's asking a loaded question. What happens to this thing between us when we return to our fake relationship and our real lives? What happens when the cameras are rolling again and every touch has to be calculated for maximum PR impact?

"It sounds nice," I admit. "But I don't know. I think the owners will probably come back eventually."

She smiles softly as she looks down at the shore below us.

I don't know what we are or what this is becoming. I only know that this part, the peace and the weight of her against me and the quiet way she breathes, is the kind of thing I shouldn't get used to.

Because it's going to end. In a few months, our contract will expire, and she'll move on to whatever comes next in her carefully planned career. And I'll go back to being the Chainsaw, the guy who fights more than he scores, the walking PR disaster who can't keep his mother from selling him out to the press.

But standing here with her in the fading light, I let myself pretend for a little while longer that maybe this could be real. Maybe someone like Juliet could actually want someone like me for more than just a business arrangement.

Even if I know better.

Even if I know I'll probably ruin it like I ruin everything else.

For now, at this moment, it's enough to just hold her and watch the sunset over the water and pretend that tomorrow doesn't exist.

Chapter 16

Juliet

There is really horrible traffic because of construction near the waterfront, so I'm already late as I run out of the cab and into the chrome and glass-fronted restaurant. Le Bernardin, exactly the upscale but sterile restaurant my mother prefers, is busy with the lunchtime crowd. I breeze past the hostess, headed for the table that Mom always insists on in the restaurant's front right by the plate-glass window. White linen tablecloths, low classical music, no warmth anywhere to be found.

When I see my mom, she is frowning at her watch. My cheeks burn; there is no excuse for being late to see Meredith Monroe. She's impeccably dressed as always, wearing a navy blazer and the same deep red lipstick that she always wears. Same dark hair as me, same dark eyes. That's where the resemblance ends, though.

"Hi Mom," I say, stepping close and offering her my cheek for a kiss.

"Hello, darling," she murmurs. She pecks the air by my cheek, making a kissing noise, then looks me up and down. "I was beginning to think something had happened to you. You're usually more respectful of others' time."

There it is. The condescension. I smile and sit down across from her, making my excuses. "Sorry, Mom. There was a lot of construction traffic."

"Isn't there always traffic?" She picks up her menu and calls the waiter over. "I'm starving, so get ready to order."

I don't even have to pick up the menu. We've been coming here to have lunch for years and the menu hasn't changed. I order the farmhouse salad, which has blackberries, chevre, and a steamed filet of salmon on top. My mom orders the roasted duck breast with baby Brussels sprouts, her usual. She also orders us both a glass of Pipcoul, a white wine varietal that's so dry it sucks all the moisture right out of my mouth.

It's certainly no gin and tonic with four limes.

Mom launches into thinly veiled criticism before I can even speak.

"You look exhausted, Juliet," she says, studying my face like she's cataloging flaws. "Are you getting enough sleep?"

"I'm fine, Mom."

"Hmm." She sips her sparkling water with the precision that makes everything feel like a performance. "You should really talk to your doctor. Have them check your thyroid and iron levels."

"Really, Mom. I'm fine."

Years of private schooling and pointed judgment taught my mom how to lift her wine glass with elegance. Her hairstylist styled her hair perfectly. Her blouse could undoubtedly pay my rent several times over.

Why did I say yes to our regular lunch date?

"I saw your name in that society column," she says casually, as if it doesn't cost her anything. "We should talk about your engagement."

She looks pointedly at my ring finger. I took my ring off on the way over here and it's now hiding in a zippered compartment of my purse. Now I feel like a soldier advancing on his enemy without a chain mail vest.

The diamond is protection, I realize. A way of telling people how they ought to interpret me. A way of saying that I belong to someone, even if it's just a convenient lie.

I reach for my water and nod like it's no big deal. "Yeah. Sorry, uh. It happened so fast that you and dad haven't had time to meet him."

This tracks. My mom is insanely busy practicing corporate law. Because he's busy, my dad is rarely present in my life. My parents met Patrick only three times, twice at my graduation and at the dinner they hosted for me afterward.

It's not so much that they're uninterested in their dutiful daughter. It's more that they are always busy with something more important. Business has always come first.

"We'll look at our schedule and get back to you with a time to meet this fiancé of yours." That idea makes me vaguely nauseous. Mom pins me with a look. "So? Who is he?"

I gulp. "Hunter Huxley. He plays for the Seattle Havoc."

"Another hockey player?" She blinks once. "I assume this is a publicity stunt." Then she smiles, like she's offering me an out. "Unless this is one of those opposites attract situations. A phase, maybe?"

"It's not a phase," I say, because that feels like the right answer. I take a sip of my wine. "He's a good man. You would approve."

I'm kidding myself if I think Meredith Monroe would

approve of Hunter. He's my opposite: arrogant, threatening, coarse. My mom would *hate* him.

Her brow lifts slightly, just enough to make the judgment known.

"You think so?"

No, I don't. "We're a power couple."

"Is that what you want now? To be seen? To be… visible?" Her eyes flick over my blouse, my curly hair, the bright red lipstick I knew would draw her ire. "You used to value subtlety, Juliet."

It's not possible for me to become a man. I can't somehow be less curvy. Hiding my body in clothes is impossible." Pressing my napkin into my lap, I bite my lip to keep from saying something I'll regret. "It's not that I don't value ambition, Mom. I just don't think it has to come in a navy pantsuit."

My mom tilts her head, her expression softening. "I know, sweetheart. It's hard to be a woman in this world. You have to fight tooth and nail to get an ounce of respect." The waiter arrives with our food, so she's quiet for a moment. But as soon as he leaves, she presses on. "That is why I'm trying to guide you to the path that I've forged. I will not lie and tell you that there are no misogynists in corporate law. But I'm a name partner, Juliet. I don't have to put up with anyone's bullshit."

Ducking my head, I nod. "I appreciate that, Mom. I know you are looking out for me. But I'm fine. Doing well."

She tilts her head and gives a closed-mouth smile, the kind she always uses before making a surgical strike. "Your LSAT scores expire in another year. It's a shame to let them rot."

I knew it was coming. The LSAT thing. She always circles back to it as though it's the only real measurement of my worth. I force myself to take a bite of salad, even though it tastes like ash.

"Going to law school doesn't interest me," I say carefully. "I never did. I just didn't know how to tell you that."

Her fingers glide along the rim of her wine glass. "You didn't have to tell me. It was obvious when you followed that boy to Houston instead of taking the interview I arranged for you." Her tone stays mild, but I hear it. The disdain. The memory she's never quite let go of.

I bristle. "Patrick was a mistake. We both know that."

"Hmm," she says, which means she agrees but won't give me the satisfaction. "I never liked how he spoke to you. Smug. Entitled. The way he used your ambition against you. No backbone."

That part surprises me. She's never said it outright before, not even when I came home sobbing the week I ended things. She'd only handed me tissues and changed the subject.

"I've moved on," I say, even though it feels like I'm saying it for myself as much as for her. "That relationship doesn't define me."

She sets down her fork and checks her watch, not because she needs to, but because she wants me to know she has somewhere better to be. "Then stop acting like it does."

"I know what I'm doing, Mom."

"Do you? Because this whole thing with dating a second hockey player seems..." She pauses, choosing her words carefully. "Impulsive. Beneath you."

I want to tell her that Hunter isn't beneath anyone, that he's actually more complex than she'd ever bother to discover. Instead, I just nod and smile and let her pay for lunch while she continues to discuss my life like it's a problem that needs solving.

This lunch just reinforces the fact that I shouldn't have

ever come back from vacation. My Jimmy Choos suck all the joy out of my life as I return to Hunter's apartment. These things *hurt*.

Back at the condo, I slump on the couch with my phone in hand, looking through the news for mentions of Hunter's name. Then, I get a text from a group.

Jessa: Hi! Ivy suggested I make a chat with all the girls so that we can talk about using witchcraft to control the Havoc team. What do you think?

A laugh bubbles out of my chest. I write: Do we think we have that kind of power?

Ivy: Ivy here. Speak for yourself, Juliet. I hexed my last three meetings.

Wren: Hi, it's Wren. I know I'm not part of the team, but Ivy said I could still be here. Here's my contribution:

Jessa: We should call ourselves The Coven. Let people know we're totally serious about using witchcraft to control our fate.

Ivy:

Me: Sounds wicked. I'm in.

Something about that name sticks in my chest. I don't say anything out loud, but it hits me that this might actually be a real circle of friends. Not networking contacts or professional acquaintances, but actual friends who text each other memes and make plans just because they want to spend time together.

Jessa: Coven meeting tonight?

I type: Yes. We'll do it here. Hunter's place is really fancy. Bring wine and takeout. I'll provide the couch.

Wren: *can't freaking wait* gif

Twenty minutes later, another message arrives on my phone. This one's from my mother. It includes the links to two law school applications.

Mom: Just in case you change your mind.

Something inside me buckles. I stare at the links for a long moment, then walk into my bedroom, close the door, and sink down onto the bare hardwood floor, hugging my knees to my chest.

The tears come hard and fast. I don't even try to stop them. Before I can control my emotions, I'm crying over the pressure, the constant judgment, the tightrope I'm always walking between who I am and who everyone else thinks I should be. I cry because my mother can't see that I can exist without her supervision.

That I've basically been in charge of my life since I was six years old.

That's when I hear footsteps outside the bathroom door. Hunter, back from dryland practice. I freeze, hoping Hunter will just walk past, but the footsteps stop.

"Juliet?" His voice is softer than I've ever heard it.

"I'm fine," I call out, but my voice cracks on the words.

The doorknob turns. *Damn.* I realize I forgot to lock it. Hunter appears in the doorway, takes one look at me on the floor with makeup streaked down my cheeks and trembling hands, and his expression changes completely.

"What happened?"

I try to brush it off, wiping my face with the back of my hand. "Nothing. I cry a lot. I'm always too much."

I expect mockery, or worse, awkward silence. Instead, he kneels beside me on the bedroom floor, his voice awkward. "You aren't too much, Juliet. You're just enough."

The laugh that I release is harder than I had intended. "Enough for whom? Who's going to put up with my crap every day?"

He touches the back of my hand, drawing my eyes to his face.

"Anyone would be lucky to get to put up with you. Okay? Patrick wasn't a good fit for you. But that's just because he was too weak. A real man would deal with you just fine."

My breath catches. It's too kind, too generous. I'm not actually upset about Patrick at this moment, but Hunter has no way of knowing that. I don't know how to process it, this version of Hunter who's careful with my feelings instead of trying to provoke me.

"Thank you," I manage stiffly. "Really. You can go now, Hux."

He hesitates for a moment, glancing back like he's memorizing the sight of me falling apart on the bedroom floor, then leaves me alone.

I sniffle, wiping my face.

I hate that he gets under my skin so easily. One comment and I'm off-kilter. One touch and I forget what I'm supposed to be doing. It's infuriating.

"I'm going to go out with the boys tonight," he says. "They just put in a new driving range by the Rainier Bank Center, so we're going to hit some balls and blow off some steam."

"Fine." It comes out huffy, like I'm upset with him. It's not that. I'm more upset that I wanted to spend the evening on the couch with him, watching Detective Saga hunt for clues. I heave a sigh. "The Coven wants to get together. Maybe I should invite them over."

"What the hell is the Coven?" He looks baffled, which makes me smirk.

"That's what we're calling the group of girls. You know, Jessa, Ivy, Wren. We decided that sounds as witchy as we want to be."

Hunter rolls his eyes. "What it sounds like is trouble."

"It's only trouble for the guys we hex." I flick my wrist at him. "Go play golf."

"You sure?"

"A thousand percent."

I watch as he heads out of my bedroom, closing the door behind him with a soft click. I fire off a text to the Coven, declaring this a girl's night and saying that I have a very comfy couch. The girls chime in enthusiastically, saying they'll be here in a couple of hours.

I sigh, putting my phone down. Hunter has been really nice lately. But there's no room for him in my life. No matter how good he smells or how gentle his voice is when he tries to talk me down.

I would do well to remember that.

After Hunter leaves for a guys' night, The Coven arrives right on schedule. Wren brings Thai takeout in enough containers to feed an army. Ivy has wine that definitely costs over twenty dollars a bottle. Jessa clutches a crime documentary playlist on her phone like it's a holy relic.

We crash onto my couch, tearing into pad Thai and gossip with equal enthusiasm.

"Okay, but seriously," Wren says, stabbing a piece of chicken with her fork, "I'm a reality tv producer and I'm looking for a new show idea to bring to my television network. Ryan mentioned this idea of, like, following the team around? I think we should push for it."

I perk up immediately. "That's brilliant. The behind-the-scenes content would be incredible. Think about the storytelling possibilities."

"Right?" Wren's face lights up. "You could help me pitch it."

"Absolutely. We should schedule a meeting."

"Really?" Wren blushes. "You'd really do that?"

"Of course. We're a coven now. We help each other."

"Wow." Wren grins. "I've never really had my own group of friends."

Jessa cuts in, "Well, now you have us."

Ivy, who's been unusually quiet, suddenly announces, "I had athletic sex this morning."

Jessa turns bright red. "Ivy! TMI!"

Ivy looks nonchalant. "What? I thought we were ready for a new topic."

"Athletic how?" Wren asks with scientific curiosity.

"Like CrossFit but naked," Ivy explains matter-of-factly.

"Oh god." Jessa puts her hands over her ears. "I'm not hearing this."

Wren cocks her head. "Part of being in a coven is promoting sexual freedom for women. I want to hear more, Ivy."

"I'll tell you everything. Including his dick size," Ivy announces.

"Please, no," Jessa begs. "Text Wren that stuff if you really have to tell someone."

Ivy arches a brow at Wren, who claps her hands. "Yes, please!"

I'm dying. Absolutely dying. This is exactly what I needed after the disaster lunch with my mother. I cackle.

Then they turn their attention to me. I know I'm in trouble.

"Speaking of athletic activities," Ivy says with a wicked grin. "You and Hunter looked *very* cozy during the team retreat."

"We did not."

"You totally did," Jessa agrees. "There were pictures."

"Staged pictures. For publicity."

"Uh-huh." Wren doesn't look convinced. "And what about when you thought no one was looking?"

I try to deny it, but eventually I cave. "Fine. He's attractive. Straight up hot. Too bad he opens his mouth and ruins everything with his words."

Ivy raises an eyebrow. "I bet you'd like his mouth just fine if it was too busy to talk."

My face burns. "Ivy."

She doesn't stop there. "Licking your clit, for example."

Jessa puts her hands over her ears again.

I shriek and throw a decorative pillow at Ivy's head. "Oh my God! Stop!"

The room explodes with laughter. Despite myself, I can't help but laugh too, even though I'm dying inside because now I'm definitely thinking about Hunter's mouth and what it might feel like.

Heavenly, I bet. But… I'm absolutely not going there.

"Your face right now," Jessa gasps between giggles.

"I hate all of you," I announce, but I'm still laughing.

"Not me!" Jessa stage whispers. "I didn't do anything!"

"You love us," Wren says confidently.

And the scary thing is, I think I actually do.

After they leave, I clean up the takeout containers and wine glasses, still smiling from the evening. It feels good to have friends who see me as more than just a professional contact or someone to network with. People who tease me about boys and bring me wine when I need it.

I'm walking past the dining area when I catch sight of Hunter at the table, sketchbook open in front of him. His pencil moves fast and surely across the page.

For a moment, I'm transfixed. I didn't know he could draw.

The second he senses my presence, he looks up, and our

eyes meet. He immediately slams the sketchbook shut like I caught him doing something illicit.

I freeze, stunned. I want to ask him what he was drawing, want to tell him he doesn't have to hide it from me. But before I can say anything, he mutters, "Goodnight," and disappears into his room.

A few minutes later, music blasts from behind his closed door.

I stand there in the hallway, my heartbeat loud in my ears. What did he say to me?

I have to play loud music, Juliet. Otherwise, you could hear me jerking off.

Electricity crackles through my body. Yes, I know exactly what Hunter's doing in there. Just like I know what I'm about to do in my room. The awareness sits between us like a live wire, sparking like an exposed wire we're both trying to ignore.

I tiptoe to my bedroom, close the door quietly, and lean against it for a moment, flushed and restless. I shouldn't be thinking about this. About him. About the way he looked at me in the bedroom earlier, like I was something precious instead of a mess crying on his floor.

But I am thinking about it. I'm thinking about *all of it.*

I'm picturing *him.*

I reach into my nightstand drawer and pull out my vibrator. In less than three minutes, I'm naked, spread wide on my bed, and whispering his name only once before biting my lip to stay quiet. My vibrator buzzes against my clit. I roll my head to the side and slide a pillow over my face. The way he knelt beside me in the bedroom is what I'm imagining, with the gentleness in his voice when he told me I wouldn't be too much for a real man. I can feel his heat, those rough hands, that mouth that probably knows exactly how to make me forget my name.

When I come, the waves of pleasure roll through my body, seemingly endless. I haven't orgasmed like that in I don't know how long.

I tell myself it's just a release. Just a passing craving that means nothing. But when it's over, my heart is still racing and my skin still burns with the memory of gray-blue eyes and careful fingers.

Living with Hunter Huxley for another four months is going to drive me completely insane.

Especially if he keeps being kind to me when I'm falling apart. I can't handle it if he keeps looking at me like I'm worth protecting instead of just tolerating. Kindness from Hunter is infinitely more dangerous than his usual antagonism.

At least when he's being an ass, I can maintain my defenses. But this version of him, the one who draws in secret and comforts me when I cry? This version could break me in ways that have nothing to do with business and everything to do with the heart I've been trying so hard to protect.

I pull the covers up over my head and try not to think about tomorrow, about pretending this is all fake when it's feeling more real than anything else in my carefully constructed life.

Four more months. I just have to survive four more months without doing something irreversibly stupid.

Like falling for my fake fiancé.

Too late, whispers a voice in my head that sounds suspiciously like Ivy. But I ignore it and close my eyes, hoping tomorrow will bring back the Hunter who annoys me instead of the one who makes me want things I can't afford to want.

Chapter 17

Hunter

I look up from my spot on the couch when Juliet breezes through the door. She carries a single shopping bag that says Ladybug Consignment on the side. I arch a brow.

If Juliet wanted something new, I could've bought it for her. She shouldn't be shopping at resale boutiques.

"I'm home," she calls.

Funny that she's calling my apartment home now. I can't say I hate it.

I arch a brow as she drops the bag on the counter. "You've been busy."

She grins. "Had to be prepared. You said we were going to a nightclub tonight."

"Consignment?"

Juliet shrugs a shoulder. "Some of us don't make hockey player money, Hunter."

"You should ask me for my credit card the next time you go shopping. It's better than having to bargain shop."

"I bought a Loewe skirt with the tags still on it for a fraction of the actual price. Relax. I need to be ready for my close-up, Mr. DeMille."

"It's just a photo op," I tell her.

"And?"

I flap a hand as if to say it's no big deal. "It's what hockey couples do. The photographers camp outside the clubs. Fans eat it up. Sponsors want those pictures everywhere by tomorrow morning." I lean back against the couch. "It's part of the image, part of the job. Whether or not we like it."

Her mouth twists. "Sounds like a circus."

"Yeah, but it's a circus that pays for my ice time. And the entire team will be there. If we skip it, it looks like we're hiding."

She narrows her eyes. "Hiding from what?"

I smirk. "From proving we can actually pull this off in public. Unless you don't think you can keep up."

Her jaw sets. "Oh, I can keep up. But I'm not staying late."

"We'll see."

She disappears into her room, and I hear the shuffle of hangers, drawers opening, the faint thump of heels on the hardwood. Twenty minutes later, she steps out in a conservative trench coat that covers her from throat to knees.

"Really?" I can't help it. "You look like you're going to a board meeting."

She adjusts the belt at her waist with surgical precision. "Is there a problem with my outfit?"

"You look like you're about to negotiate a hostile takeover."

Her smirk is pure trouble. "Wait until you see what's underneath."

That shuts me up. My brain is already supplying images I shouldn't be thinking about.

She moves to the entryway mirror, reapplying the same blood-red lipstick with practiced precision. Smooth application, blot, another coat. Our reflections meet in the glass, and she doesn't look away.

"Are you done?" I ask, my voice clipped because I need to get out of here before I do something I'll regret.

She blots one last time, then caps the tube. "Just about."

I fold my arms against the doorframe. "Why do you always wear that stuff?"

Her brow lifts. "Excuse me?"

"The lipstick. You don't need it. It's... obvious."

She stares at me as if I've grown a second head. "Obvious?"

"Yeah. Like a sign. Look at me. Look at my mouth."

She laughs, sharp and short, until she sees my face and factors in my earnest expression.

"Wait," she says slowly, her voice dropping to that dangerous tone she uses when she's about to eviscerate someone. "You're serious?"

I don't answer because anything I say right now is going to make this worse.

"You think I'm trying to tempt someone?"

"Men look at your mouth," I say flatly. It's true. I've watched it happen a hundred times. "I've seen it."

"And?"

"And maybe you shouldn't make it so easy for them."

Her whole body goes still, like I just slapped her. The air in the hallway crackles with tension.

"You are unbelievable."

"It's a distraction," I snap, digging myself deeper into this hole. "You wear it like a bright red flag that says, look at me."

"What, you think I'm trying to seduce the entire room every time I put on lipstick?"

"No. Just..." I run a hand through my hair, frustrated. "I notice."

She scoffs, shaking her head. "You're the only one who's ever complained about it. And definitely the only one who stares like you do."

That shuts me up completely because she's right. I stare.

I stare at her mouth way more than I should. Way more than is appropriate for a fake fiancé who's supposed to be keeping things professional.

She studies my face for a long moment. I can practically see the wheels turning in her head. "You're not mad about the lipstick. You're mad that you want to kiss it off."

The words hit like a physical blow. Because she's right and we both know it.

Now it's hanging between us like a live wire.

I'm hard the entire way to the club.

The team rented out the whole VIP section at Eden's Gate, one of the newer places downtown. I can feel the music in my chest and the bass thumps through the floor. The second we walk through the velvet ropes, Juliet stops to unbutton her trench coat. When she peels it off, I nearly swallow my tongue.

She's wearing a clingy black skirt that hugs every curve and a strappy crop top that shows off several inches of toned stomach. The top has intricate cutouts that reveal tantalizing glimpses of skin. My eyes bug out. Her ass looks incredible in that skirt and the fabric is so thin I can see the outline of her body underneath.

There's no way she's wearing underwear under that thing.

I hate that I noticed. Hate more that she's dressed like this in public, where every asshole with eyes is going to be looking at what's mine. Even if it's fake, even if it's temporary, for the next four months she's supposed to be mine.

"Jesus Christ, Juliet."

She looks over her shoulder at me, all innocence. "What?"

"That outfit."

The heels give her a couple of inches, but she's still so small I could toss her over my shoulder without breaking stride.

"What? You don't like it?" She flutters her lashes at me.

"I like it too much. That's the problem."

She gives me a naughty smile that undoes me. "Good to know."

I let her go join her friends, but I don't stray far. I stick close to her like a second skin. Like hell I'll let her strut around in that outfit without monitoring her.

Coach Ryan enters with his sweet fiancée Wren on his arm. She takes off when she sees the women, shyly saying hi to the group, who immediately welcome her with open arms.

Ryan strolls over to where I'm stationed at the bar, nodding hello. "Hope we're not crashing anything. Ivy told Wren to come. I feel a little like an interloper, dropping in and spying on the team when you're having a few drinks."

I wave him over. "You're more than welcome. Tonight seems to be more about what the ladies want than where I want to be."

"That tracks." Ryan grins. "I admit I'm wrapped around Wren's little finger. I go wherever she wants to go."

I order a beer and a gin and tonic with half a dozen limes, keeping one eye on the conversation as the rookies flood in. Shane's already loud, doing tequila shots with Connor and the other young guys, creating their own little chaos bubble in the corner.

"Yo, Hunter!" Shane calls out, waving a shot glass. "Come show these losers how it's done!"

"I'm good," I call back.

"Scared you can't keep up with the rookies?"

Connor snorts. "Dude, Hunter could drink you under the table."

I wave them off. I'm not getting into a pissing contest with a twenty-one-year-old. The established players cluster near the bar where Silas sits quietly, staring off into space. He looks creepy, but I know my brother well. He's running hockey stats in his head. It's what he does when he's bored or uncomfortable. Thorne and Grayson guard the VIP section like bouncers, watching everything with veteran awareness.

I take Juliet her drink, which she accepts with a coy smile that makes heat creep up my neck.

"Thanks, darling," she purrs.

The conversation flows around us, but I'm distracted by every movement she makes. She gestures in a certain way when she talks. The way she throws her head back when she laughs at something Wren says. Her fingers play with the rim of her glass and I can't stop noticing.

When Ivy shows up late in a short dress that makes half the team stop talking, the energy shifts. Shane immediately tries his luck and gets destroyed.

"Hey gorgeous, want to dance?" he sidles up with his signature cocky grin.

Ivy looks him up and down slowly. "Nice try, rookie. Maybe when you graduate kindergarten."

The entire rookies' table erupts in laughter. Shane takes it like a champ, raising his shot glass in defeat.

"Respect," he says, backing away. "I had to try."

I stretch out and put an arm around Juliet. To my surprise, she allows it, leaning into me slightly. Jett immediately starts giving me shit.

"Look at Hunter, all whipped already," he says loud enough for everyone to hear.

"Shut up, Jett."

"It turns out that our boy has feelings."

"Drop it."

"Never." Jett grins. "This is too entertaining. You should see your face right now."

Juliet turns toward me. "Are you two having a moment?"

"Jett's being an asshole."

"So, it's Tuesday?" she says dryly, making Jett sputter with laughter.

The girls decide it's time to dance. Ivy grabs Juliet's hand and drags her toward the dance floor with Wren and Jessa following.

"Time to hit the floor, ladies."

Jett begs them to stay in the VIP section. "Can't you just dance here? It's safer."

"Safer is boring," Ivy tells him.

"Fine, but we're coming with you," Jett says.

"Obviously," Juliet smirks. "You boys can't help yourselves."

Half the team follows them like puppies. I pull Juliet into my arms, her body warm against mine. The music pounds around us, bass thumping through my chest.

She moves against me, hips swaying, and I have to fight to keep my thoughts clean. Her skirt rides up slightly as she dances. I rest my hands on her waist, pulling her closer.

"You're staring," she says, lips close to my ear.

"Hard not to."

"Good." She spins in my arms, her back pressed against my chest now. "That's the point."

Some guy edges closer, clearly checking her out. I growl low in my throat and pull her tighter against me. She feels the vibration and tilts her head back to look at me.

"Possessive much?"

"Just playing the part," I say, but my voice comes out rougher than intended.

"Are you?" Her eyes sparkle with mischief. "Because I think you actually like this."

Another guy tries to cut in, tapping my shoulder. "Mind if I—"

"Yes, I mind." I don't even look at him, keeping my eyes on Juliet.

She bites her lip, suppressing a smile. "You know what?"

I look down at her. Always down. Her head barely reaches my chest, and it kills me she still squares up like she's taller than me. "What?"

"I like it when you get all growly and protective."

That admission hits me like a puck to the chest. "Juliet—"

"It's kind of hot," she continues, completely unaware of what her words are doing to me. "The way you look at other guys when they get too close. Like you want to murder them."

"Maybe I do."

She laughs, spinning to face me again. Her hands slide up my chest, fingers playing with the collar of my shirt. "My big, scary fake fiancé."

The way she says it, breathless and teasing, makes something snap inside me. I've been watching her dance for an hour, the way her body moves, the way she keeps looking at me with those dark eyes. She's been testing me, pushing my buttons, seeing how far she can go.

"You've been doing this on purpose," I say, backing her toward a slightly quieter corner of the dance floor.

"Doing what?"

"Teasing me. All night."

"I have no idea what you're talking about." But her smile says otherwise.

"The way you dance. The way you look at me. Pushing that guy toward Ivy just to see my reaction."

"And what if I were?"

Before I can second-guess myself, I cup her face and kiss her. She melts into me immediately, her hands fisting in my shirt. I want to fucking *devour* her.

When we break apart, we're both breathing hard.

"Hunter—"

"I know this is fake," I say against her lips. "But right now, I don't care."

She stares up at me, pupils dilated. "What are you saying?"

That I want to drag her out of this club. How desperately I want to find the nearest hallway and press her against the wall. I want to slide my hands under that tiny skirt and make her forget her own name.

"I'm saying—"

"Oh my God!" Wren's voice cuts through the music as she stumbles toward us, clearly hammered. "You two are so cute!"

The moment shatters. Juliet steps back, smoothing her dress, and I run a hand through my hair.

Ryan appears, looking apologetic. "Sorry, she got away from me."

"Did you see them kissing?" Wren asks loudly, pointing at us. "It was like a movie!"

"Okay, party animal," Ryan says, scooping her up. "Time to go home."

"But the night is young!" Wren protests as he throws her over his shoulder.

"I'm not a lightweight! I'm fun!"

"You're drunk."

"This is so embarrassing." Wren giggles. "But also kind of hot."

Ryan's face goes red as everyone laughs. "Thanks for including her tonight. She needed this."

"Anytime," Juliet says warmly. "Text when you get home safe."

As they leave, I look back at Juliet. Although the spell broke, the heat between us was still simmering under the surface.

"We should probably—" she starts.

"Yeah. We should."

But neither of us moves for a long moment, the music pounding around us, the tension thick enough to cut.

The night continues around us in a blur of music and laughter. Fans start flooding the VIP section despite security, and I get increasingly protective as random guys try to approach our group.

"How the hell did they get past security?" Thorne mutters.

"Social media," Grayson says grimly. "Someone posted our location."

One particularly aggressive fan pushes too close to me. "Hunter! You can chainsaw me anytime!" she shouts, grabbing at my arm.

I push away from her. "Back off, puck bunnies."

"Come on, just one picture!"

"I said back off." I step further away, disgusted.

Juliet grabs my arm, looking angry.

"Don't use that term."

"What term?"

She narrows her eyes and shakes a finger at me.

"*Puck bunny*. No one ever has shit to say about hockey players getting laid left and right. But the world is really eager to call any woman who so much as looks at one of you funny a puck bunny. It's fucked up and sexist."

Honestly, I had no idea that Juliet held that in. I practically swallow my tongue. "Right. Sorry."

She nods, satisfied. "They're just fans. Misguided, but fans."

Eventually, the rookies get too sloppy, and the veterans corral them toward the exits. Ivy vanishes with a random guy, and Juliet looks worried until I tell her I saw them leave together.

"I'm ready to go," Juliet finally says, leaning against me.

I practically bolt for the exit. "Let's go."

She makes sure The Coven gets into Ubers safely before we leave. She's always taking care of everyone else first.

We ride home together in the back of an Uber. Juliet's tipsy and leans against me, her head on my shoulder. I don't take advantage. I just let her rest against me and try not to think too hard about the warm feeling spreading through my chest.

"You smell good," she mumbles against my shirt.

"Thanks."

"Like danger and... wood?"

"It's called cologne, Firecracker."

"Mmm. I like it."

She curls up against me. I want to kiss her again, but I think she's falling asleep on top of me. When we get home, I help Juliet out of the Uber and up the elevator. She giggles; she's had too much to drink for me to get handsy, but that doesn't stop her from turning and kissing me at the door. Her mouth is heaven. Soft, warm, and sweet. For a second, I forget everything and kiss her back.

The world slows down, the moment narrowing. It's just the two of us right here, right now, and she tastes delicious.

She parts her lips and I dip her back a bit, growling as I sweep my tongue against hers.

Then I remember she's drunk and gently stop her.

"Juliet."

"What?"

"You're drunk."

"I'm tipsy. There's a difference."

I help her out of those ridiculous heels and walk her to her room. "Come on. Bedtime."

She strips down without hesitation, her skirt hitting the floor, her bra landing on my shoe. I immediately look away, focusing on turning down her sheets.

"You're no fun," she complains, but she's smiling.

I almost smile back.

I get her water and ibuprofen from the bathroom. "Drink the water. Take the pills in the morning."

"You're taking care of me."

"I'm making sure you don't die of dehydration."

"Same thing."

I make sure she's tucked in and leave her door cracked open in case she needs anything.

Later, in my room, I pull out my sketchpad. I try to draw her from memory. Her eyes when she laughed at something Wren said. The way she smirked when she caught that fan trying to flirt with me. The soft way she looked at me in the Uber.

I think about how fun the night was. How different she was out there. Loose, wild, magnetic. If she were anyone else, I'd say I was developing a little crush on my not-fiancée.

But she's not anyone else. She's Juliet Monroe. She's way too good for someone like me… even if tonight made me forget that for a few hours.

Chapter 18

Juliet

A few days later, I am still brooding about the events at the nightclub. My brain replays every moment in slow motion: the heat of the dance floor, the smell of his cologne when he leaned close to hear me, the way the lights caught on his jaw when he smiled.

Craving Hunter in a way that I shouldn't have. I crossed a line. I *know* better than this.

I keep thinking about how respectful he was. Not one wandering hand. Not one crude comment. He kept a careful distance, even when I leaned in. Even when I tilted my head so our faces were inches apart. I remember the way he looked at me at that moment. His eyes were dark and steady. His hand stayed on my waist, firm but not possessive. He acted like a man in control.

I acted as though I had absolutely none.

I'm embarrassed at how I threw myself at him. More than that, I'm irritated that I cannot stop thinking about it. A couple of cocktails do not explain the way I pressed against him during that last song.

The music was loud. My pulse was louder. I kissed him

hard, gripped his shirt, and would have taken it further if Wren had n't interrupted us.

God, I am a mess.

The team got back very late from an away game last night. When I got up this morning, Hunter was still asleep. That is probably for the best, because I'm not sure I could look at him without thinking about that kiss.

And I'm not sure I could look at him without wanting to try again. Which is exactly why I am still kicking myself.

Thankfully, I'm pulled from my contemplation when I get a text from The Coven asking me to join them at an SPCA charity event. It's technically a team thing, but… apparently I'm sort of part of the team now, which still feels surreal.

Being seen by the team management as someone who fits in and helps can only make my case for a future job in PR stronger. Hunter is still asleep when I leave the condo at eleven; I write him a note asking him to meet us if he feels up to it as I head out the door.

The event is at a local park, with adoption booths set up under white tents and adorable dogs everywhere. I find Jessa and Ivy picking out funny selling points to write on the adoption cards for the dogs.

"This one's name is Princess, but she clearly has anger management issues," Ivy says, scribbling on a card. "Perfect for someone who needs a guard dog with attitude."

"That won't help her get adopted," I laugh.

"Are you kidding? Honesty is refreshing. Plus, look at that face."

Princess is indeed adorable, despite apparently being a tiny terror.

Only a few team members are in attendance since they all had such a late night. Thorne's here with some rookies, all of them looking ragged and running on maybe four hours of sleep.

"Hey!" I say, greeting Thorne and Shane. Ivy put them in charge of the doggy kissing booth. For a cash donation, you can receive kisses from either a pit bull or a terrier. It's adorable.

"She lives!" Shane says, teasing. He holds up his terrier, talking to her. "Have you met Juliet? She's a party animal!"

Thorne coughs and nudges Shane in the ribs. I blush.

"Oh no. Did I misbehave?"

"Nope," Thorne says. "You were perfect. Right, Shane?"

Shane grins. "I was just kidding. You were an angel, Juliet."

"Uh huh." I give them both a knowing look. "I'm keeping an eye on you two."

I circle the adoption fair, then settle in with Jessa and Ivy, who are in a large circular pen with a few small dogs that are fiercely friendly. Jessa hands me a little packet of dog treats and I lead the dog up to a curious family standing to one side of the pen.

They enjoy meeting Piglet, a five-year-old Yorkipoo. The little girl gives Piglet a few scratches behind the ear and declares that she's perfect. Her mom smiles gently and tells her they have to look around a bit, but they can come back to Piglet if they want.

I pet Piglet, giving her a wink. "You hear that? You're perfect."

She gives me a doggy grin before barking twice and running off to sniff a mini schnauzer's butt.

I turn, scanning the rest of the pen for a new family. Ivy is telling an older man where to go to apply for an adoption. It makes me smile. We're a pretty good team!

That's when I see him. Patrick, walking toward our booth like he owns the place. What the hell is he doing here??

My stomach drops. "Shit."

"What?" Jessa follows my gaze. "Oh shit. Is that…?"

I nod. "That's my ex."

Ivy hears, immediately going into protective mode. "Want me to spill coffee on him? Or maybe I can get a dog to pee on his leg…"

I gulp, my hands balling into fists at my side. My body is ready to go to war, if that's what it takes. "No, I can handle this."

It's better if I draw him out, make him approach me. His plan is to stare at me and hope to make me stumble over my words. Hiding isn't how I'll win today. I know Patrick and just how he behaves.

I step out of the pen, walking toward the kissing booths. Drawing him out. Patrick corners me, a familiar smirk on his face that used to make me feel special.

Now, it makes me want to throw up.

"Well, well. If it isn't Juliet Monroe." He looks around the fair. "Where's your boyfriend?"

I straighten my spine. I hold up my hand, flashing my ring. "Hunter is actually my fiancé."

Patrick laughs, the sound sharp and condescending. "Fiancé? Really?"

He reaches for my hand before I can pull away, lifting it to examine my ring. His touch makes my skin crawl. I pull my hand out of his grip and shoot him a pained look.

"Could you please not touch me?" I say, hoping my tone is thoroughly dripping with disdain. "Why are you even here?"

"Your ring is tacky," he declares, loud enough for people

around us to hear. "But I suppose some women trade up, and some just settle for whatever they can get."

The words hit like a slap. I loathe Patrick with every fiber of my being. Just because he's from an old-money family, he thinks he's too good for everyone.

If I hadn't been so weak when we were dating, I would have left him years earlier. Instead, I let him and his snooty family push me around and make me feel less than. Never, ever again.

"You're an asshole."

"And you're a two-dollar hooker," he fires back.

I feel helpless and humiliated, rage burning in my chest, but before I can find my voice to tell him exactly where he can shove his opinions, my new friends come to my rescue.

"Is there a problem here?" Ivy asks sweetly, but there's steel in her voice.

Thorne appears too, looking exhausted but alert. "Everything okay, Juliet?"

"Fine," I manage, but my voice sounds shaky.

Patrick smirks. "Just peachy, right Jules?"

Uh, I *loathe* that nickname. It's a thousand times worse than Ace, the one I made Hunter quit calling me. At least Hunter *listens*. And he's not even my real fiancé!

Thorne steps in, looking menacing. "I think you'd better get lost, loser."

"Loser?" Patrick barks a laugh. "You'd better watch who you're calling names, Alex. At least I'm a hockey player. This bitch is just a wannabe puck bunny."

"Shut the fuck up! How about that?" Ivy jeers. "I need you to leave, stranger."

That's when Hunter walks in, which surprises me because he wasn't supposed to be here. He must have gotten four hours of sleep maximum, but he looks amazing in dark jeans and a fitted henley that shows off his arms. Even though I absolutely should not have been hoping for Huxley to save me, relief floods through me at the sight of him.

"Sorry I'm late, babe," he says. He walks straight to me and pulls me into a kiss that makes my knees weak.

"So, Hunter." Patrick smiles at Hunter. "Do you know any high-end consignment boutiques around here? I figure you must really love used goods. I mean, since you're set to marry Juliet and all."

Hunter goes absolutely still. I can feel the tension radiating off him as he lunges for Patrick's throat. I grab him by the shirt. He stops, but he's glaring daggers and lobbing f-bombs at Patrick like grenades.

"You want to say that again, fuckface?" Hunter snarls. Rage is rolling off him in waves.

"Hunter, don't," I hiss, still gripping his shirt. "Please."

"He just called you used goods." Hunter's voice is deadly quiet.

"Let it go."

"Like hell I will."

I realize cameras are appearing. Local news crews covering the charity event, phones coming out, people recognizing Hunter.

Hunter seems to realize it too because suddenly he's switching gears, wrapping his arm around me and speaking directly into a camera.

"Actually, I'm excited to announce a wedding date. Juliet agreed to marry me this February. We're getting married right after Valentine's Day. I can't wait for her to be *Mrs. Huxley*."

"You two are disgusting," Patrick spits.

"Disgustingly *in love*," Hunter says, needling Patrick. "Isn't that right, baby?"

"Yes?" My answer comes out as a question, but neither

man is really paying attention to me, anyway. My eyes widen as I stare holes into Hunter's face. Where does he come up with this shit? Announcing a wedding date that will never materialize? I dig my nails into his arm.

Hunter looks at me, smirking, and leans down to whisper in my ear. "Relax. It's just for show, Firecracker."

I shudder. Hunter's name for me coming from his mouth sounds sweet as pie. Too bad I want to throttle him right now.

Before I can process what's happening, the Havoc's social media guy and a cameraman materialize at my elbow like vultures scenting fresh drama.

"Juliet, perfect timing," he says, already waving the camera into position. "We'd love a quick clip about the engagement. You and Hunter have such amazing chemistry."

He glances toward Patrick, who's lingering far too close, then back to me with a smile that says he knows exactly what he's doing. The camera swings up, the ring light flares, and suddenly I'm trapped between Hunter at my side and Patrick watching from a few feet away.

The interviewer leans in, mic ready. "So, Juliet, tell us what it's like to be engaged to Hunter Huxley. Especially with such a history between the three of you."

My smile feels frozen in place as I hear myself say, "It's been… incredible. Hunter is amazing. I'm so lucky. We're, uh… going to get married this winter, like Hunter said. It's going to be a private ceremony, of course."

I nod, tilt my hand so the emerald catches the light, and keep talking while my heart pounds. Patrick's eyes are on me, unreadable. Hunter's palm settles low at my back, warm and steady, as if to remind me whose fiancée I'm supposed to be. The camera eats it up.

God, I hope my parents don't watch this clip. I like that

Hunter is sticking up for me, but I hate that I have no control over how this is going down.

"I think we're both ready to be an old married couple already," he says. He hugs me tightly against his body. "Isn't that right, baby?"

The smile I give Hunter is partially a *what the fuck are you talking about* look.

He's unpredictable, but not in the way I expected. Instead of completely losing it, he's holding it together and backing me up. That takes me by surprise. I didn't think he could control himself at all when pushed.

Patrick, not to be outdone, pulls out a pen. "Where do I donate? I want to pledge ten thousand dollars," he announces to the cameras.

My lips twitch. Patrick has a nasty habit of promising things on camera and never actually following through with them. He's done it with breast cancer research, orphans from Rwanda, and 9/11 survivors.

Hunter immediately outdoes him. "Make it twenty-five thousand from me."

"You know what? I think it would be great if you both went to the bank and paid the pledge in cash. *Today*. Before any of this airs on TV."

Hunter arches a brow. "Gladly."

Patrick hesitates too long. "That's… not a problem…"

Meaning that he didn't actually plan on fulfilling his pledge after all.

I turn to the camera, smiling widely. "I think that would make for some compelling TV. Right? Have both of them hold up their checks to the camera after they endorse them?"

"Absolutely!" the sportscaster agrees. "We'd love to put that on the news."

Patrick excuses himself to "move some money around",

his face nothing short of sulky. I grip Hunter's arm as the news crew moves on to film more of the adoption fair.

"That was a mess," I sigh. "Patrick turned up here out of left field. How could he even know that I was going to be here?"

Ivy waves, smiling sheepishly. "That might have been my doing. When I drew up a press release about the adoption fair last week, I may have added you to the list of VIPs we would have here without actually talking to you about it. So sorry about that. I didn't think about the fact that you are probably trying to stay out of sight."

"It's fine." I give her a reassuring glance. "Honestly, none of us could have predicted that Patrick would show up here. He's supposed to be in Texas!"

"He's a fucking creep," mutters Hunter. "He'd better keep away from you or I'm going to make his skull into a decorative ashtray."

My eyes widen. "Huxley!"

"What?" He looks at me, feigning innocence. "It'll be an improvement for everyone."

"That's enough," I tell Hunter firmly. "Behave yourself or you're getting kicked out of here."

To my amazement, he does. He dotes on me, kissing the top of my head, wrapping his arm around me, being good. But no one can miss his malevolent glares in Patrick's direction.

"Could you quit looking in Patrick's direction?" I ask sweetly.

"The only reason I'm not dragging him outside and beating him into the concrete is because you told me not to." Hunter smirks. "But you can't ask me not to glare at the guy. That's unfair."

Biting my lip, I can't hide my smile. I smooth my hands

out over his chest and tip my head up, peering at him. "You are being very well-behaved, aren't you?"

"Yes," he agrees. His gray eyes dance as he catches my hands. "I expect a reward later for remaining calm."

My pulse kicks like a horse. "I'll remember that," I whisper.

Hunter picks up a black lab puppy and carries it over to a cluster of fans, who are as excited to pet the puppy as they are to see Seattle Havoc's #47.

Oh no. Something is shifting. The person who I thought I agreed to be in a fake relationship with was the Chainsaw, this larger-than-life asshole without feelings that was utterly one-dimensional. But that's actually not who Hunter Huxley is at all.

It turns out, not very far beneath his rugged exterior, there's this whole other person who smiles, who is kind to puppies, who *listens* when I ask him not to get in a fight with my ex.

Is this real? Hunter Huxley just controlled his temper for my sake?

What does that mean for how I feel about him? Is this the beginning of a crush I feel building in my chest? I'm unsteady, like the ground beneath my feet has turned to sand, which is now crumbling beneath my feet.

Hunter and I take a few more Instagram-worthy pictures with some adoptable puppies, then escape as quickly as possible. Patrick glares at us as we leave; there's something undeniably fun about walking out of the building, my arm tucked in Hunter's, my eyes glued to his handsome face.

I think even if Hunter wasn't just here to protect me from my ex basically stalking me, I might like to look at him and squeeze his hard biceps.

"Coffee?" he asks as we walk to his truck.

"Please. I need caffeine and sugar and possibly alcohol."

He stops at my favorite coffee place, the one I mentioned once in passing. "Quad cappuccino, extra shot, oat milk, no foam," he tells the barista.

I stare at him. "You know my order?"

"I pay attention."

"Since when?"

"Since always. You just never noticed."

Never indeed. My face grows warm, but he just hands me my drink without saying another word.

We drive home in comfortable silence, and once we're back in the condo, we collapse on the couch. I leave my heels on but make sure the bottoms aren't touching the couch as I curl up against the oversized cushions.

Hunter heads into his room. I scroll through my notifications on my phone, stopping at the email I've been waiting for. It's directly from Jimbo, the Seattle Havoc's team owner, about how well I managed the potential PR crisis. I didn't really do much. The others helped. But upper management is praising me anyway.

For a moment, I actually believe I might be good enough at this job.

I keep reading, sucking in a breath when I read the next part. Jimbo asks me to step up and fill some of the void left by Julien, who he apparently fired.

I fire off an email agreeing without a moment's hesitation, my career ambitions overriding everything else.

My pulse pounds. On top of Hunter being a gentleman after rescuing me today, this is the deep red cherry perched on my sundae.

Hunter comes out of his room, looking nearly indecent as he throws himself on the couch beside me. The first thing I notice is the pair of dark gray Seattle Havoc-branded sweatpants that sit low on his hips. Next is his tight white tee, the sleeves pushed up to his shoulders to show off his powerfully-muscled arms. His tattoos jump out at me, a chaotic collection of tightly packed line drawings of tents, compass roses, and pine trees. I guess I never noticed his tattoos in particular before now.

But it's the look on his face that gets me. Hair brushed back, high cheekbones, expressive full lips… and the naughtiest sparkle in his stormy gray eyes.

"Are you going to change?" he asks.

"Me?" I look down at my short white wrap dress, shrugging. "I don't see why I would."

Hunter kicks his long legs out, reclining, and puts his hands behind his head. Like I need any more reason to ogle him, jeez.

"You can't be comfortable like that. At least take your shoes off."

I look at my heels, checking again that the bottoms aren't on the couch.

"My heels aren't getting the couch dirty!"

He rolls his eyes. "Did I say that? Heaven forbid Juliette Monroe should get a couch dirty."

"What's your problem then?"

He jerks his chin at my heels. "You're at home. Relax. Take off your shoes, let your hair down. You can even wear something comfortable. There are no cameras here. You don't have to perform, Juliet."

"I'm not!"

"You are. It's okay to let down your guard a little. I promise I won't tell."

"Hm." I toe off my heels, dropping them to the floor. "Happy?"

Hunter shrugs. "It's a start."

I study him for a moment, uncertain how to behave. A manual about living with your fake fiancé would go a long way right now.

"Thanks for showing up earlier," I say, my voice soft. "And for not getting into a brawl with Patrick."

"Your ex is a piece of shit," Hunter says bluntly.

"Tell me something I don't know."

"I don't get how you ever found him attractive."

I snort. "Have you seen him? He's objectively handsome."

"He's got nothing on me."

The cockiness in his voice makes me smile. "You're right. You're definitely hotter."

Something shifts in his expression. "Yeah?"

"Yeah." I take a sip of my perfect cappuccino. "Plus, you know how to order me coffee. Patrick never remembered what I liked in five years."

"Oh yeah? Just your coffee order, huh? What else didn't he remember?"

The question hangs between us, loaded with implication. Before I can stop myself, I blurt out, "He never made me come. Not once in five years. He said I took too long, whatever that means. I guess I'm broken."

Hunter immediately gets upset, leaning into my personal space. "What do you mean he never made you come?"

"Exactly what I said. I must be defective or something."

"Bullshit." His voice is a growl. "You're not broken. He's just a selfish asshole who didn't deserve you."

I shrug, aiming for casual even as my cheeks burn. "Or maybe it was me. Maybe I'm just… hard to figure out. Some kind of unsolvable puzzle. Not worth the effort." I try to tack on a quick laugh, like it's all a joke, but it lands flat in the air between us.

"Don't," he says fiercely. "Don't you dare talk about yourself like that. You're amazing. Patrick is lower than dirt."

Then Hunter kisses me. His mouth moves against mine with a kind of patience I didn't know he possessed. Each brush of his lips is deliberate, like he's memorizing the shape of me. His thumb keeps stroking over my cheekbone, slow and steady, as if grounding me at the moment.

I can feel the faint scrape of stubble against my skin, the heat of his palm, the subtle shift of his breath as he tilts my head to deepen the kiss.

The taste of him is warm and familiar. Coffee, yes, but also something darker, something that clings to the edges of my senses and makes me lean closer without meaning to. His scent wraps around me. Firewood, vanilla, and a trace of his natural masculine smell. It's dizzying in the best and worst ways.

Every nerve in my body feels awake, pulling me into him when I know I should pull back.

I'm half convinced he can feel my heartbeat against his chest. The steady weight of his hand on my face says he's not in any rush to stop. His other hand settles at my hip, fingers flexing like he's fighting the urge to drag me closer. I can sense the restraint in him, the way he's holding himself back when every line of his body tells me he wants more.

When he finally murmurs, "Firecracker," it isn't teasing. It's reverent, almost careful, like he's speaking to a part of me no one else has bothered to see. I know if I let him keep going, he'll burn through every wall I've built.

He should move away, make a joke, ruin the moment like he usually does. But for once, he doesn't. He pulls back just enough to look at me, his gray-blue eyes intense.

"Promise me something," he says.

"What?"

"If you ever doubt yourself again, if you ever think you're broken or not enough, you come to me. Let me show you just how un-broken you are. Over and over again, until you believe it."

My breath catches. "Hunter..."

But he's already pulling away, standing up abruptly. "I should go to my room."

"You don't have to."

"Yeah, I do."

He leaves me gaping at his retreating back. A few seconds later, I hear his bedroom door slam. Then the music blasts.

I sit there for a moment, touching my lips, still feeling the heat of his kiss. Is he… touching himself? Is it because of our kiss?

I sneak up to his door and listen. I can hear his moans over the music as he jerks off, my name falling from his lips like a prayer.

I did that to him? Jesus. That knowledge turns my entire body into a pillar of flame.

My maybe crush just turned definite.

I tiptoe back to my room, my heart racing and my skin burning. Everything has changed between us.

And I'm not sure there's any going back.

Four more months of this arrangement suddenly feel like both forever and not nearly long enough.

Chapter 19

Hunter

I pull up outside the youth hockey clinic and sit in my truck for a minute, preparing myself for the sheer controlled chaos that I'm about to walk into. It's one of those community outreach events we do a few times a year, but this one's high profile. Tons of local press, major league sponsors, a large crowd of parents in attendance with their phones out.

Walking up to the event, I can hear the noisy bleating of a whistle and the clatter of hundreds of pairs of skates. Through the glass doors, I can see Juliet already inside with her clipboard, talking to the rep from a sponsoring bank. She's dressed for the cold of the rink but still somehow looks expensive. Long black coat, hair sleek and pulled back, a pair of black boots with spike heels.

She spots me walking in and waves me down to where she stands in the bleachers. I trot down the metal bleachers. Juliet gives me a hug and a kiss on the cheek, squeezing me in the hug. A public display surely meant for the cameras, but she's almost friendly about it. Warmer than usual.

"You're late," she says, but she's smiling. It doesn't sound like much of a scold.

"Traffic."

"Sure it was."

If this is what it means for her to be taking a more active PR role with the team, I'm all for it. Ryan mentioned it to me yesterday. Otherwise, I wouldn't have even known about the change until now. I'm a little miffed that she didn't tell me herself, but I guess we're still figuring out how to communicate about work stuff.

Well, all stuff, to be perfectly fair. I feel like she's just now stopped walking on eggshells around me.

On the ice, chaos reigns. The kids are excited and loud, the parents even louder, and my teammates are only marginally more helpful than the children. Shane's trying to organize equipment while Connor argues with a ten-year-old about stick technique. A group of kids surrounds Moose, asking him if he really eats moose, which he's playing up for all it's worth.

"Let's get out there." She pats me on the butt playfully. "*Honey.*"

"You bet, *sweetheart.*" I grin at her. "Lead the way."

I watch as Juliet handles the event without breaking a sweat. Juliet runs point on every moving piece, directing press photographers to better angles, calming the overwhelmed volunteers, and smoothing over a minor incident with a sponsor whose banner had the wrong logo. Handholding and reassurance are not things she needs. She doesn't flinch when a reporter shoves a microphone in her face asking about her engagement to me.

Watching her work like that, watching her take control and stay calm and not once get flustered, I find myself impressed. The situation really impressed me.

We lead some basic drills on shooting, skating, and goal-keeping. The rookies have to chase down every stray puck. The kids have fun, laughing and shouting, running the rookies nearly into the ground trying to keep up.

Ryan skates up, his Havoc sweatshirt damp with perspiration.

"Juliet's fantastic at this," Ryan says. "She's definitely meant to run PR."

"Yeah, she is." I feel a little pride puffing out my chest. It's not earned, because this whole engagement is fake. But I'm proud anyway.

Ryan looks at me suspiciously. "You sound surprised."

"Maybe a little," I admit, shrugging.

He grins. "You thought she was just a pretty face?"

"I thought she was a pain in my ass."

"She's that too. But she's also smart as hell."

Juliet turns to look at me, arching her brows and waving us over.

"Come show them what an enforcer does!" she calls. "Coach Ryan, can you play someone on the rival team?"

Oh, *fuck* yeah. I skate over, showing the kids a very light version of what an enforcer does when someone takes liberties with his team. Ryan squares up in front of me, grinning like he's already planning payback.

I exaggerate the movements so the kids can see. Closing the gap fast, locking onto his jersey with one hand, and giving him a harmless but dramatic shove that sends him sliding back a few feet.

"That's how you let someone know they've messed with the wrong guy," I tell them, keeping it playful enough for the audience but still sharp enough that Ryan knows I could've dropped him if this were real. The kids laugh and cheer, and Ryan smirks like he's dying to go another round.

I notice Juliet gets this kind of pleased, pinched look on her face every time that I take a minute to show any of the kids something. What's running through her head? I can't be certain. But her cheeks gradually grow bright pink as she watches me interact with a ten-year-old, teaching her how to hold her hockey stick when she's moving across the ice at a clip.

When I look again, Juliet's face is glowing like a coal, her eyes glued to me. Is she getting all hot and bothered watching me? Or is it a bit of baby mania creeping in?

Something is making Juliet swoon. Whatever it is, I lean into it. I crouch down to fix a seven-year-old's skate that's coming loose.

"There you go, buddy. How's that feel?"

"Good! Can you teach me to fight like you?"

I laugh. "Let's stick to skating for now."

I give an older boy some gentle coaching on puck handling, showing him how to keep his head up while he moves the puck around cones. Even take a few deliberate falls just to make them laugh.

"Coach Hunter fell down!" a smaller kid shrieks with delight.

"I sure did. Good thing the ice is soft, right?"

Juliet watches all of it from the sidelines, her eyes soft in a way I've never seen before. She smiles at one point, unable to hide her actual genuine smile, and something unfamiliar twists in my chest.

I enjoy earning her approval. Having someone on the sidelines that not only sees me, but likes what I'm doing, feels indulgent somehow.

Of course, Juliet and I take a ton of pictures throughout the clinic. Holding hands while skating together reveals that she's actually a pretty graceful skater. Better than I expected.

"Where'd you learn to skate like that?" I ask as we glide around the rink.

"Lessons from when I was a kid. My mom thought it would be character building."

"Your mom was right."

"Don't tell her that. She'll never let me forget it. She still blames the lessons for getting me into hockey."

She looks at me for a long moment. "Can I ask you something personal?"

"You can ask. Doesn't mean I'll answer."

"It's about your mom." She purses her lips. "I know she was your agent. Why didn't your mom represent your brothers, too? Why just you?"

I sigh. "Jett straight up refused to have Mom as his agent. He said that he didn't trust her. It was a major source of tension between them, believe me. Jett told both of us that we should get other representation. Silas did. I didn't. I guess I just thought that she deserved to get her cut." Screwing up my face, I admit, "I never thought that she would steal from her own son."

Juliet moves closer and takes my hand, lacing her fingers through mine.

"She fucked up. You're a good man."

I snort. "I'm not a good man."

"Yes, you are." She tugs on my hand. "I know you, Hunter Huxley. Don't forget that."

"I remember everything." I look down at her, my lips tipping up. "Want to race?"

Her eyes light up. "Oh, you're on, hockey boy."

Juliet takes off without another word, leaving me to catch up. I don't put much effort into the race. It's more fun to watch her competitive side come out.

She's good at skating. I wonder what else she's surprisingly good at. What other skills she's hiding under that polished exterior. I'd bet my last dollar she's the woman who approaches everything with the same focused intensity, including sex.

The thought hits me out of nowhere and I have to concentrate on not tripping over a stray puck.

Should I be thinking about this? I glance at my pretty fake fiancée and shrug internally. As long as it's just me thinking about it and not acting on it, what harm does it do?

And yeah, just because the thought of her being baby crazy gives me all kinds of caveman-brain ideas about pretty little Juliet carrying my baby, doesn't mean it's ever going to happen.

We hate each other. Except when we don't.

I catch Juliet watching me with this confused expression, like she's seeing something she didn't expect.

This version of me, quiet and gentle and unguarded with these kids, probably isn't what she imagined when she agreed to this fake engagement. Hell, it's not even how I see myself most of the time.

Later, as we're packing up the equipment and the parents are herding their sugar-crashed kids toward the parking lot, Juliet approaches me.

"You're good at coaching," she says. Her tone is neutral, but her expression isn't. There's curiosity there, maybe even a little admiration.

I shrug, suddenly uncomfortable with the attention. "I'm just good with kids."

It sounds gruffer than I mean it to. Juliet doesn't push. She just nods, that quiet acknowledgment she's so good at giving.

"They loved you out there."

"Kids are easy. They don't care about your reputation or your penalty minutes. They just want to have fun."

"Is that why you like working with them?"

The question catches me off guard. "I guess. They're honest. No bullshit."

She studies my face for a moment. "You should do more of this."

"More what?"

"Community stuff. It's good for your image, but more than that, you're actually good at it."

Back in the locker room, Ryan tosses me a towel. "You looked less miserable than usual out there."

I grunt something noncommittal while I unlace my skates.

Ryan pauses, then adds, "You like her. That's the problem, isn't it?"

"Fuck off," I mutter under my breath.

Ryan just laughs and walks away, like he's solved some great mystery.

Shane bounces over, still high on adrenaline from skating with the kids. "Dude, that was awesome! Did you see the kid who tried to check me? Little savage."

I have the perfect opportunity to mock him for being a goofy rookie who got schooled by an eight-year-old, but I just shake my head.

"You did well out there."

Shane blinks at me like I've grown a second head. "Thanks, man."

"Who are you and what did you do with Huxley?" Jett asks, tossing a towel at me.

"Shut up," I say, but there's no edge to it.

Silas raises an eyebrow from his corner stall. "You didn't growl at the reporter. You didn't snarl at the fan asking for a selfie. Are you dying or something?"

I flip them off lazily. I'm not about to admit it, but their teasing doesn't land the way it used to. It just feels lighter somehow. It feels like something has smoothed the sharp edges.

I shower fast and get out of there before anyone else can comment on my apparent personality transplant. While I'm thinking about Juliet, I can admit something.

She isn't who I thought she was. Not the icy, career-obsessed robot I used to make fun of in college. She's steady and smart as hell. And when she smiled at me earlier while I was working with those kids, it felt like sunlight breaking through a crack in a concrete wall.

I don't know what to do with this feeling.

I head home, restless energy making it impossible to sit still. I toss my gear in the corner and turn on the TV, but I'm not really watching whatever hockey highlights are playing. My mind keeps drifting back to the way Juliet looked at me today.

Eventually, I drag out the old journal from where I keep it buried in the back of my closet. I haven't touched it in years. Not since my mom found one of my journals and read it to my brothers like it was a stand-up routine.

That was enough to make me burn the rest. But tonight my hands itch to do something that won't end with me punching a wall.

10/14

Told myself to stay away. Safer for her that way. Better she only ever sees the part of me built to push people back.

She should have someone who takes her to dinner without looking for a fight. Someone who sleeps through the night without waiting for bad news. Someone whose hands aren't always cleaning up the wreckage he caused.

But I keep seeing her at the clinic. Rinkside in that coat, laughing when the rookie made the kid smile again after the spill. Later, that same smile for me—when I was on my knees retying laces, talking stick handling like it was the only thing in the world.

At night she keeps me awake. When she moves around her room, I hear the faint creak of the floor. I picture her hair loose, her skin warm from sleep, her eyes finding mine in the dark. I turn over and try to shut it out, but she's everywhere. In my head. Under my skin. Close enough to touch if I were willing to cross the line.

I write it down so it can't slip away. That smile. The light in her eyes. For half a second, she looked past the temper and the ruin, like maybe she saw something worth keeping.

When I'm done, I shut the journal and shove it back in the closet. Lock it away like everything else that matters too much to risk losing.

I lie awake that night thinking about her. Not about sex, though that's definitely part of it. Not about the fake engagement or what the team might say if they knew how badly I want her. Just about the way she looked at me today.

Like maybe she saw something I didn't even know was still in there. Something that isn't just anger and hockey fights and family drama. Something that might actually be worth keeping around.

Maybe it wouldn't be the worst thing in the world if she knew the truth about who I am underneath all the performance.

Maybe.

The thought should terrify me. Usually when people get too close, when they see past the Chainsaw persona, they either get scared off or try to fix me. No one can fix me. Too many pieces are missing or broken beyond repair.

But Juliet doesn't seem like the type to run from a challenge. And she definitely doesn't seem like the type to waste time on lost causes.

So maybe, just maybe, there's a chance she could see the real me and stick around anyway.

If I'm not careful, this fake relationship is going to turn into something real. And once that happens, there's no going back to the safety of pretending I don't care.

Chapter 20

Juliet

I 've secured you an interview at Harver, Lansley, and Burnsfeld. They're one of the premier corporate law firms and they're willing to take you on as an intern while you finish law school–

Ugh. Not interested. Especially *now*.

My mom's text comes at an inopportune time, just as the usher guides me to the team box at the Rainier Bank Center. When I step inside, instantly the entire energy in the arena is absolutely electric tonight.

I'm wearing Hunter's jersey, like everybody else seems to be. The only difference is that he gave me mine. The memory makes me smile softly to myself.

It's louder than usual with the fans going wild for Hunter in ways that make my chest feel tight. There are chainsaw graphics flashing on the jumbotron every few minutes, chants erupting every time he gets near the puck. A group of fans in the lower bowl holds up foam chainsaws and waves them like weapons.

Then I see something that makes me flinch. A woman near the glass pulls up her shirt, revealing a phone number scrawled across her chest in black marker along with "Call me, Chainsaw" in bold letters.

I look toward Hunter just in time to see the way his shoulders tighten. He doesn't acknowledge the attention, doesn't even glance toward the woman who's basically throwing herself at him. His movements on the ice are aggressive and controlled, but there's no enjoyment in it. He's not soaking up the adoration like I'd expect. He's surviving it.

Not something I would have expected to see a month ago. Maybe I never noticed how it wears on him.

I study Hunter closely as the game goes on. He plays hard tonight. Harder than usual. He seems angry, like he's trying to prove something to someone. I get the Chainsaw thing now. The fans might have made up his nickname, but he has a mentality that goes with it. When the inevitable fight breaks out in the second period, Hunter throws off his gloves and goes toe-to-toe with a guy half a foot shorter than him. The crowd goes absolutely wild.

My heart races watching it, but not for the same reasons as everyone else. I'm not thrilled with the violence. I'm worried.

About his safety, I tell myself. Not about how crushed I'd feel if he got hurt. Just professional concern for the success of our arrangement.

After the final buzzer, I head down toward the tunnel for my first real post-game media coordination. I'm tingly with excitement, nervous energy making my hands shake slightly. It's the first time the Havoc organization has really trusted me with something like this, even if it's only to help Ivy with damage control.

I walk into the tunnel just as everything explodes.

"Hunter!" comes a woman's voice. "Hunter Alan Huxley! I know you can hear me!"

I whip my head around to identify the source of the voice, a woman's voice that swings between sweet and sharp, like honey with glass shards mixed in. Hunter freezes in the tunnel and I realize that something important is happening. As I watch, his entire body language changes. The confident swagger disappears, replaced by something that looks *almost* like fear.

That's when I see her. The woman is tall and scrawny, with bleached blond hair, deep blue eyes, and outstretched hands tipped with fake nails. I don't know who she is at first, but when Hunter backs away from her, I realize this is bad. *Very* bad.

She reaches toward Hux, a sneer on her lips, and something clicks into place. The similarity is uncanny.

This woman is Darla Huxley, Hunter's mother. She's gotten past security and into the player tunnel, which should be impossible. She's wearing a designer purse that probably cost more than most people's rent.

I've never seen Hunter backpedal to duck from someone's touch before.

"Hunter, baby, don't you want to talk to your mama?" Darla calls, reaching out to grab his arm before he can escape. The slightly terrified look on his face is enough to make me move.

Oh, *hell* no. This lady doesn't get to grab at Hunter, especially when he clearly wants nothing to do with her.

I rush forward to help, instinct overriding everything else. I try to put myself between them, to pull her back from him, but Darla reacts with surprising strength. She grabs a handful of my hair and yanks hard enough to bring tears to my eyes.

"Get your hands off me, you little slut," she snarls.

Hunter immediately shouts and moves to intervene, but not to protect himself. He's trying to distract his mother, to redirect her attention away from me. "Mom, let her go. She's not part of this."

Darla softens for a moment, loosening her grip on my hair. She seems enamored with her son. "How are you, Hunty? I miss you so much."

"Let go, Mom. Please." He carefully separates her from me, disentangling her from my hair with a ginger touch, and then pushing me behind him protectively. He growls, "You need to leave."

"I just want to talk to my son. Is that so wrong?"

"Fuck around and find out," he hisses. "You aren't welcome in my life anymore."

Her face changes again, like a switch has flipped. "You abandoned me," she shouts, her voice echoing off the concrete. "You used me and threw me away like garbage." I can feel eyes turning toward us, see the glint of phones being raised by fans and reporters at the tunnel's edge.

Then she turns her venom on me, jabbing a manicured finger in my direction. "And this is the little fiancée? The one you're using to replace your own mother?"

Hunter flinches as though she struck him, but he says nothing. Her smile twists with satisfaction. "That's what I thought."

Security finally arrives, pulling her away as she calls over her shoulder, "You'll come crawling back. They always do." The sound of it follows us down the tunnel like smoke that won't clear.

I turn my back on her, looking up at Hunter. He looks down at me, gripping my hips. On impulse, I press up on my tiptoes, dragging his jersey down until my mouth meets his.

The moment our mouths meet, the tunnel vanishes. Noise drains away to a faint hum, and all that's left is the bright heat of him pressed against me. His lips are sure yet searching, tasting faintly of sweat, Gatorade, and the metallic tang of blood. My hands fist in his jersey. I drag him closer until there's no space between us. His breath brushes my skin in slow, rough bursts, each one wound tight with restraint.

Fingers thread into my hair, curling just enough to tip my head back. The kiss deepens, pulling a sharp rush of heat down my spine that melts into something sweet. I breathe him in: firewood, salt, and male sweat. The crowd blurs. The phones vanish. Nothing exists except the weight of his palm, the solid press of his body, and the deliberate way his mouth moves over mine, like he's memorizing it.

He tears himself away so suddenly I have to steady my feet. His breathing is uneven, and his eyes hold mine in an unyielding stare.

"Don't mess with me," he whispers. "I can't take it right now."

I don't understand the warning, but it lingers between us, heavy and close, refusing to fade. Hunter brushes me off and storms down the hall without another word. I'm left stunned in the tunnel, everyone staring at me with a mixture of curiosity and pity.

Later that night, after making sure the footage hadn't leaked to social media and helping Ivy spin the narrative with the few reporters who witnessed it, I plunk myself down on the couch. It's naughty, I know, but the time has come for a little internet sleuthing.

If only to understand Hunter's words from earlier. *Don't mess with me. I can't take it right now.*

Context will help me bring the picture into focus. Grabbing a Stanley Cup full of Diet Dr. River for fortitude, I pull up old articles about Hunter's history with his mother.

One headline talks about a court case. Something about financial mismanagement and stolen funds. Another describes a violent outburst at a restaurant that ended with police being called. The Hunter I know, grumpy and difficult and unfiltered, suddenly feels layered.

Heavy. He's human in ways I'm not prepared for.

I hear noise from the kitchen and turn to find Hunter pouring whiskey from a bottle I've never seen before. The amber liquid splashes over ice cubes with a sound that seems too loud in the quiet condo.

I stand up and freeze in place like a deer in headlights. I've never seen him drink hard liquor, not even at the team retreat when everyone else was getting wasted. He's always been a beer guy. He controls his alcohol intake just like his daily macros.

"Is everything okay?" I ask quietly.

He doesn't answer. Doesn't even look at me, actually. He just drains the glass in one swallow and pours another.

"Hunter."

Still nothing. He guzzles the second drink, leaves the glass on the counter, and walks away. I'm left standing alone in the kitchen with the smell of expensive whiskey hanging in the air.

Wow. Hunter is more screwed up than I realized. What kind of number did his mom pull on him, exactly?

I give up trying to talk to him and go take a shower, hoping the hot water will wash away the lingering feeling of his mother's hands in my hair. Afterward, wrapped in just a towel with my hair dripping, I open the bathroom door and run directly into Hunter in the hallway.

He jerks as if I startled him, eyes dropping to the towel

wrapped around my body and then snapping away like he's not allowed to see me in a towel.

"Be more careful," he mutters.

I blink, offended by the tone. "Excuse me?"

"You heard me."

He disappears into his room without another word, leaving me standing there in my towel, agog. He might have had the shittiest day imaginable, but that's no reason to take his frustrations out on yours truly.

Miffed, I get dressed quickly, still fuming from the encounter. This whole situation is spiraling out of control.

Someone has to deal with it. It looks like I need to get ahead of it before it destroys everything we've worked for.

I find the original list of house rules pinned to the fridge with a magnet. I stare at it for a long moment. If we're struggling this much to maintain boundaries, fine.

We need new ones. Stricter guidelines. More distance.

No more walking around half-naked. The shared beds, even when we're exhausted from events, have to end. There can't be gray areas that leave room for misinterpretation.

If we want to make this work for the remaining months of our contract, we have to treat it like what it is. A business arrangement. Nothing more.

I head for my room, trying to reassure myself that this is what I wanted.

Boundaries. Professionalism. Clarity about our respective roles in this arrangement.

But when Hunter turns on loud music from his room, the same music I've learned to associate with him jerking off, I know exactly what he's doing. And it drives me absolutely crazy.

Maybe he is more affected by our proximity than he lets on. Or maybe this is just his normal routine and I'm reading too much into it. I don't know how often he got off before I moved in, but now it seems like it's happening twice a day.

Is that normal for men? Patrick only ever wanted to have sex maybe once a month. Even then, it felt like a chore he was performing grudgingly. Then again, he was probably having affairs the entire time we were together.

I lie in bed staring at the ceiling, feeling like everything is slipping through my fingers. Not for the first time, I wish I had another option than to have to talk to Hunter tomorrow. It sounds *hard*.

The music from his room stops abruptly, replaced by the sound of his shower running. I try not to think about what that means, try not to picture him washing away the evidence of whatever fantasy he just indulged in.

Try not to wonder if I played a role in that fantasy.

My phone buzzes with a text from Ivy: "Damage control worked. No footage leaked. You did well today."

I should feel relieved. Proud, even. I handled my first genuine crisis for the team without falling apart. But all I can think about is the look on Hunter's face when his mother grabbed my hair. The way he immediately moved to protect me, even though it meant giving her exactly what she wanted.

And the way he looked at me in that towel. His eyes said that I was something dangerous he needed to avoid.

Four more months of this arrangement suddenly feel impossible. How are we supposed to maintain professional distance when every interaction feels charged with electricity? When I catch myself listening for the sound of his breathing through the wall that separates our rooms?

When I'm caring more about his wellbeing than my own career advancement?

I pull the covers up to my chin and close my eyes, trying to block out the sound of his movements in the next room.

Trying not to think about how small and fragile his mother had seemed until she turned violent. Trying not to wonder what other secrets he's hiding behind that carefully constructed wall of indifference.

But sleep doesn't come easily. And when it finally does, I dream about gray-blue eyes and gentle hands and the way someone's voice sounds when they're trying not to wake the person sleeping next door.

I dream about things that can't happen and probably shouldn't. But feel more real than anything else in my carefully planned life.

Chapter 21

Hunter

Practice is brutal today. Coach is in rare form, running us into the ground with herbies, those suicide sprints that leave your lungs burning and your legs feeling like jelly. Skate from the goal line to the blue line and back, then to center ice and back. The far blue line and back, then to the far goal line and back. Repeat until someone pukes or passes out.

You'll get no complaints from me. I need the punishment. The noise in my head needs to be drowned out by physical exhaustion. My body has to hurt more than my brain does.

Thorne's been speaking up more during practices lately, directing lines mid-drill. As the new team captain, he's slowly growing more comfortable calling out what he sees and praising players when they do something right. It's not perfect, but I'm seeing flashes of the captain he might become. Coach Ryan too, snapping at guys about spacing and redirecting body position with clipped gestures that somehow work better than yelling.

I haven't thrown a punch all week. Not even once. Which is probably some kind of record for me.

During a water break, Thorne skates over, looking me up and down. "You're taking this engagement awfully seriously."

I grunt and squirt some water into my mouth. "What do you mean?"

"Living with Juliet is supposed to make your life easier, but all I see when I look at you is a man under stress." Then, after a pause, he adds, "You okay, Hux?"

I shrug it off. "Don't start getting feelings on me."

But the question digs in anyway, finds a soft spot I didn't know was there. Is this engagement taking up a larger portion of my mind than it should? Probably yes.

"Get out here and run the drill again or we're doing bag skates!" Coach Ryan barks from center ice. Groaning, we all get back to work.

Later, in the locker room, Jett and I are the last ones left. Everyone else has cleared out for lunch or whatever they do with their afternoons. I'm sitting in my stall, still in my gear, not ready to face the real world yet.

"Mom showed up again," I mutter, just loud enough for him to hear.

Jett sits down on the bench beside me, frowning. "Yeah?"

He doesn't push for more information. He just listens while he unlaces his skates.

"She grabbed Juliet," I add. "Pulled her hair."

That gets his attention. His hands hover over his laces. "Mom hurt her?"

"Not really. But she scared her. It made me see red."

"Mom's vile." Jett finishes with his skates and looks at me. "You're not alone in this. And you're not her."

"I know." I scrub a hand over my face. "Seeing Juliet scared by my mom doesn't make me feel good, though."

He claps me on the shoulder. "It doesn't matter what

Mom says or does. You know who you are. You know Juliet likes you."

I give him a skeptical look. "Juliet Monroe hates me."

"Is that what you call it when Juliet keeps sneaking looks at you when you're not paying attention, biting her lip like she's eyeballing some dessert she wants?"

"She doesn't do that," I snap. A prickle of irritation runs across my skin. "Mind your own business, Jett."

"Okay." His smirk speaks volumes, though. "Maybe she looks at all the men she agreed to pretend to be engaged to that way."

"Fuck off."

I leave the rink feeling unsettled. Grateful for my brother's support, but I don't need him poking his nose into my affairs.

Juliet hates me. I hate her right back. So why the hell do I catch myself thinking about her when I'm supposed to be focusing on the drive home?

Back at the condo, I walk in still damp from the shower, towel around my neck, hair wet and dripping onto my t-shirt. I expect silence, maybe Juliet buried in her laptop responding to emails and avoiding me like she has been since our encounter in the hallway.

Instead, the kitchen's warm and filled with music playing low. It smells incredible. Garlic, lemon, something roasting in the oven that makes my stomach remind me I haven't eaten since breakfast.

Juliet's barefoot, hair up in a messy twist that's falling apart, wearing one of my old Havoc shirts. It hangs off her shoulder, exposing her throat and collarbone. She's humming along to whatever song is playing, moving around the kitchen like she belongs there.

I'm caught off-guard, standing as still as a statue, staring at Juliet.

Sometimes I want to tell her everything. The letters I write but never send. I still see my mother's face when I close my eyes too long. Hear the echo of her voice making promises she never intended to keep.

But what would that do? Juliet would look at me differently. She'd see me like I'm fragile or broken. Or worse, like I'm someone she could fix if she just tried hard enough.

And that's not what I want. I want to be seen for who I really am and still be desired. And that's probably too much to ask from anyone, especially someone like Juliet, who has her whole life planned out.

I stand in the doorway and watch her. She bends to pull a pan from the oven, and the shirt rides up. She's wearing a short skirt underneath, and I glimpse bare skin that makes my mouth go dry.

For the umpteenth time, I hazard a guess that Juliet isn't wearing any panties. *Again.* It's obvious from the lack of panty lines.

My body goes tight, blood rushing south before I can stop it. God, she's so fucking hot.

Juliet looks over, notices me standing there, and blushes. "Oh. Hey. I figured you'd be hungry after practice."

She gestures to the counter where two plates are waiting. Salmon with an herb crust, salad, dressing on the side, roasted potatoes, even a small cupcake for dessert. It's too much. It's perfect.

"You made me lunch?"

She shrugs as though it's no big deal. "You've been going hard lately. Thought you might want something real before the guys drag you out tonight. The Coven mentioned you all have plans."

She turns back to the fridge, licking a smear of dressing off her fingertip, and something inside me snaps.

I cross the kitchen in three steps and kiss her. No warning, no buildup. Just my mouth on hers, hands curling around her waist to pull her closer.

Touching her, sweeping my tongue against hers, my body sings with *rightness*. As if this is what's *supposed* to happen.

At first, Juliet melts into it. Her hands come up to grip my shoulders, and she makes this quiet whimper when I lick into her mouth that nearly undoes me.

Fuck, she's so damn responsive. Immediately, images of her splayed out on the kitchen counter, legs parted as I lick her pussy, come into my head. The sounds she would make, guiding my movements, making me slow down or speed up, make me shudder with want.

I bet Juliet would come all over my chin, her citrus-scented perfume crowding the air around me, her muscles clenched and spasming. I could just push her up on the counter, right here and now, and claim her like I want to.

I think I'm starting to *need* her.

But Juliet soon pulls back, breathless. "We can't."

I press my forehead to hers, trying to catch my breath. "I know."

She's breathing fast, looking up at me, her pupils dilated. "This will blow up everything. My maybe-job with the team. Your reputation. We can't afford that kind of risk."

I nod, even though every part of me wants to argue. "Fake fiancée. PR stunt. I know."

"Also..." She closes her eyes like she's trying to gather herself. "You're you."

I huff out a laugh. "Yeah. I'm a fucking disaster."

"I'm trying to build something here, Hunter. Something that matters."

"I know."

But then our mouths crash together again anyway. This time it's hungrier, more desperate. My hand slides under the hem of her shirt, fingertips finding the warm skin of her hip. She gasps when I touch her, arching into me.

Needing to satisfy my curiosity, I skim my fingertips up her thigh, underneath her skirt. My fingers run across her outer hip and I'm right, of course. She's not wearing any panties.

Fuck *me*. My kisses turn possessive, needing to devour her.

She pulls back again, shaking. "Hunter—"

"I know." My voice comes out raw. "I know it's a mistake. I just... I've never had anyone do this before."

"Do what?"

"Make me food. Take the time to know what I want without my having to ask. Just be kind."

She blinks up at me, eyes wide and confused. "I wasn't trying to—"

"You didn't have to try. That's what makes it matter."

Her lips part like she wants to argue, but she doesn't. The way her fingers curl into my shirt leave it rumpled. Her eyes search mine, and for once I don't look away.

"You keep saying this will ruin everything," she whispers. "Why?"

I step back just enough to breathe. "Because I'm not good at this. Any of it. Relationships. Trust. Letting someone close."

She tilts her head. "You've had girlfriends before."

"Not really." My laugh is short and bitter. "A few women, here and there. It never sticks. I don't let it." I rake a hand through my damp hair, still tasting her on my lips. "Every time I let someone in, I end up on my ass. People leave, or they want more than I can give. I've gotten good at making sure no one sticks around long enough to hurt me."

Juliet studies me, her brow drawn tight. "That sounds exhausting."

"It's easier than the alternative," I say. "On the ice, I know who I am. Off it… I don't. If hockey disappeared tomorrow, I wouldn't know what the hell to do with myself. That terrifies me."

Her breath hitches. "You really think there's nothing else?"

"Nothing that matters the same way," I admit. My chest feels raw, scraped clean. "The game is all I've got."

Silence stretches, heavy but not uncomfortable. Then she lifts her chin. "So you stay where you know who you are. I get that."

I narrow my eyes. "What about you? Why'd you stay with a guy who didn't respect you?"

The words hit her like a slap. She stiffens, then forces herself not to look away.

"Because I was trying to be the person he wanted me to be." Her voice cracks but she pushes through. "I kept thinking if I was perfect enough, he'd finally see me. But then he cheated. And thank god he did, because it woke me up. It made me look at my life and realize I was wasting time."

I can't stop staring at her. "He cheated, and you still thought it was on you?"

"Not anymore." She swallows. "But yeah. Back then, I built everything around him. My days, my choices, my whole damn self-worth. And when it fell apart, I had nothing left except this drive to prove I mattered. I needed to prove it to everyone."

I grip the counter to steady myself. She's baring herself to me in a way I've never seen. It feels unfair that she trusts me with this when all I've done is push her away.

"You're not wasting time now," I say.

Her eyes glisten. "I hope not."

For a long moment, neither of us moves. The air between us is different now. Heavier, sharper. My body still aches to touch her, but my chest aches harder. I want to tell her she deserves more than scraps from assholes like Patrick. I want to tell her she deserves someone who sees her, all of her, even the parts she hides.

I whisper, "You matter, Juliet."

Her breath catches. She leans toward me, her fingers brushing my shirt again, but this time we don't kiss. Her lips part like she wants to say something else, but then her fingers curl in my shirt and she pulls me back in.

We kiss hard this time. Dirty. My hands slide under her shirt, mapping the curve of her waist, the soft skin just above her ribs. She's warm and perfect and everything I shouldn't want but can't stop thinking about.

I pick her up and set her on the counter. She wraps her legs around my hips immediately, pressing against me like she needs this just as badly as I do. The friction makes me groan into her mouth.

We both know this can't keep happening. We both know it's going to complicate everything we've worked for. But neither of us stops.

We're supposed to be enemies. So why can't I stop kissing her?

I hate that I can't walk away from her. Hate that I'll be replaying this all night when I should shut her out of my head.

Her hands tangle in my still-damp hair, pulling me closer.

I can taste the mint from her lip balm. I can feel the rapid beat of her pulse under my thumb where it rests against her throat.

"This is crazy," she whispers against my lips.

"Completely insane," I agree, then kiss her again.

Eventually, she pulls away, lips swollen and pupils blown wide. We're both still breathing hard, still touching, my hands on her thighs and hers gripping my shoulders.

But reality crashes back in. I step back, putting space between us before I do something we'll both regret.

She smooths her shirt down, doesn't meet my eyes. "Food's going cold."

I want to kiss her again. Every careful rule she's written to keep us apart? I want to ruin them all.

Instead, I grab a fork and force myself to sit at the counter. I try not to look at her thighs when she walks past to put things away.

She's pretending it didn't happen. Pretending I don't get under her skin the same way she's gotten under mine. Fine. If she wants to keep it fake, I'll keep it fake. I'm good at pretending. Good at keeping things bottled up until they rot.

It's not like I'm boyfriend material anyway. We both know that.

The salmon is incredible, perfectly cooked and seasoned. The meal that takes time and thought; it's not something you throw together on a whim.

"This is amazing," I tell her.

"Thanks. I used to cook for Patrick sometimes when he felt stressed about work.

The mention of her ex makes something ugly twist in my chest. "He was lucky."

"He never seemed to think so."

"There are a lot of things I would do differently if I were in his place."

She gulps, looking down at the table, the back of her neck growing pink.

"Thanks."

Later, when she disappears into her room, I blast music in mine and try not to picture her in my shirt, legs wrapped around me, eyes full of heat and want.

I fail miserably. I fist my cock and jerk off while I picture her spread out on my bed, still wearing that shirt but nothing else. Think about what she'd taste like, what sounds she'd make when I made her come. It's so hot that I blow my load after only a minute.

Fuck, she's driving me crazy.

The orgasm is unsatisfying, so I plow right through, fist working hard against my dick. The whole time, I'm promising myself that after this orgasm, I'll have had enough. My consuming crush on Juliet will end and we'll go back to being awkward, distant enemies.

We are supposed to be enemies, after all.

When I come the second time, still quicker than I'd like, I feel empty. If anything, I feel lonelier than I did before.

And Juliet is still on my mind. *Damn her.*

After everything's calmed down and I've gotten myself together, I'm in my room with the door cracked open, trying to cool off and pretend I have any self-control left.

I hear her padding down the hall in bare feet, then a light knock on my door.

"Sorry," she says, opening the door just a little without stepping inside. "I can't find my phone charger. It might be in your car."

"I have a few extra." I gesture toward my closet. "If one of those doesn't work, I can run downstairs soon."

I watch her cross the room carefully, like she doesn't want to intrude on my space. She opens the closet slowly and crouches down to a box filled with carefully spooled cables, sitting on the floor next to my hockey gear.

Shit. I glance at the shoebox that I keep pushed back behind my equipment bag. It's filled with my journals and my unsent letters. It usually has a lid on it to deter any prying eyes. But for some reason, the lid is askew and the contents are easy to reach.

Why didn't I just get the fucking phone charger for her?

Juliet doesn't see the box at first. But when she shifts the box of cables to get a better line of sight, the letter slips free from where I'd shoved it inside.

Handwritten envelope. My mother's name scrawled across the front in my messy handwriting.

I tense, my whole body locking up like I'm about to get hit.

Juliet freezes too. She picks up the envelope, but doesn't open it or try to read what's inside. She just studies it for a beat, taking in the careful way I've written "Darla" on the front.

Then she gently puts it back in the box like it's something fragile that might break if she's not careful. She closes the lid with the same care she'd use in handling glass. She doesn't look at me when she straightens up with her charger in hand.

"I didn't see anything," she whispers. Not flippant or dismissive. Not pitying either. Just soft and understanding.

She finds what she came for and leaves without another word, closing the door behind her with barely a sound.

I sit on the edge of my bed for a long time after she's gone, staring at the closet where that box sits with all my unsent letters and half-finished thoughts.

She didn't make it weird. I didn't ask questions about what those letters were or why I write to someone that I never want to see again. She didn't look at me as though I were broken or pathetic for keeping them.

And somehow, that kindness wrecks me more than if she'd just ignored it completely.

Because it means she sees me. The real me, not just the Chainsaw persona or the fake fiancé or the guy who loses his temper too easily. She sees the part of me that writes letters I'll never send and keeps them in a shoebox like they matter.

And she didn't run.

That terrifies me more than any fight I've ever been in.

Chapter 22

Juliet

I wake up to silence. Again.

It's been a week since Hunter left for the road trip, and I thought I'd love having the apartment to myself. For the first few days, I did. I could eat cereal for dinner without judgment, watch trashy reality TV without him making sarcastic comments, and work in complete quiet without the sound of him clanking around in the kitchen or grunting through his workouts.

But now? The silence feels heavy. Oppressive. Like it's pressing down on my chest every time I walk through the living room and see the couch where we've been spending our evenings, pretending to be a couple who actually likes each other.

I hate him. I hate the stupid way he invades my space, my life, my head. But somehow I hate the silence without him even more. *Ugh. He's the worst.*

I grab my phone from the nightstand, scrolling through the usual morning notifications. Three texts from my mom about LSAT prep courses, two emails about potential job interviews that probably won't pan out, and one Instagram notification that makes my stomach twist.

It's a photo of Hunter and some of the other Havoc players at dinner last night. He's laughing at something Silas is saying, his face relaxed in a way that makes something ache in my chest.

Oh, I definitely have a crush. And that thought *terrifies* me.

The caption is just a bunch of hockey stick emojis, but there are already dozens of comments from women telling him how hot he looks. Making a face, I screenshot it for our fake relationship Instagram account, then immediately feel pathetic for caring enough to do that.

My phone buzzes with another text from my mom: *Have you given any more thought to the December LSAT? Registration closes soon.*

I stare at the message, a familiar knot of anxiety forming in my stomach. Law school. The plan I've had since I was sixteen. The safe, respectable path that will prove I'm not just a hockey player's arm candy or some man's convenient girlfriend.

But sitting here in Hunter's apartment, wearing one of his old team shirts that I *definitely* didn't steal from his laundry, I can't shake the feeling that maybe I don't want to be safe anymore.

Maybe I want this. Whatever this is.

I type out a response to my mom about needing more time to think, then delete it. Instead, I scroll to Hunter's contact.

Me: How's the road trip going?

I hit send before I can second-guess myself, then immediately regret it. We don't text each other when he's away. We're not actually together. This is all fake, and I need to remember that.

My phone buzzes almost immediately.

Hunter: Exhausting. I can't wait to get home.

Home. He called it home.

I stare at the message, reading way too much into three simple words. He probably just meant home, not specifically here, not specifically to me.

Me: When do you get back?

Hunter: Tonight. The flight lands at 6.

Me: Cool. I'll probably be here.

It's not true. I have no plans except sitting on this couch and pretending I'm not waiting for him to walk through the door.

Hunter: I'll see you soon, Firecracker.

Firecracker. The nickname that should annoy me, but it makes my stomach flip-flop. I'm definitely losing my mind.

Wanting my day to be productive, I apply for three more jobs, none of which I actually want. I clean the apartment even though it's already spotless. Then I reorganize my closet and do laundry. Basically, anything to keep myself busy.

By five-thirty, I'm pacing.

By six, I'm refreshing the flight tracker app I definitely didn't download just to see when his plane landed.

By six-fifteen, I'm sitting on the couch pretending to read a book while listening for his key in the lock.

When I finally hear footsteps in the hallway, my heart does a stupid little jump. I force myself to stay on the couch, eyes on my book, like I'm not hanging on every sound.

The key turns in the lock. The door opens.

"Juliet?"

"In here," I call, not looking up from my book. Playing it cool. Totally normal and not at all pathetically excited that he's home.

I hear his bag hit the floor, his footsteps crossing the hardwood. Then he's standing at the back of the couch, hair messy from travel. I try not to seem like I'm checking him out while I pretend that I'm reading. He's still in his team tracksuit, looking tired but somehow still annoyingly attractive.

"Hey," he says. There's something soft in his voice that makes me actually look up.

I smile. "Hey yourself. How was the trip?"

He shrugs, moving into the room and dropping onto the other end of the couch. "Long. We lost two out of three, so everyone's in a shit mood."

"Sorry."

"Not your fault." He stretches his legs out. I try not to notice the way his tracksuit pants pull across his thighs. "What'd you do while I was gone? Paint your nails? Have a pillow fight with the girls?"

I roll my eyes. "Hilarious. I worked. Applied for a few PR gigs. You know, responsible adult things."

"Right. Any luck?"

"Define luck."

He studies my face. I hate how easily he seems to read me these days. "That bad, huh?"

I close my book with more force than necessary. "I don't want to talk about it."

"Okay." He doesn't push, which is worse than if he'd demanded details. It makes me want to tell him everything.

We sit in silence for a moment. I can feel the weird tension that's been building between us for weeks crackling in the air.

"I'm going out with the girls tonight," I say suddenly, remembering my lie from earlier.

His face does something subtle. A flicker of disappointment, maybe? "Where?"

"Just drinks. Probably start at Ivy's place, then hit a few bars."

"Want me to come? We should… uh… probably make an appearance together."

The offer catches me off guard. Hunter voluntarily spending time with my friends is not exactly his favorite activity. "You don't have to. You look exhausted."

"I am exhausted." He runs a hand through his hair. "But if you want company…"

There's something in his voice, something that makes me think he doesn't want to be alone tonight either. Like maybe he missed this too. Missed me.

"The girls would love that," I say, which is true. Not telling him my actual feelings, which are ecstatic.

"Give me twenty minutes to shower and change?"

I nod, and he pushes himself off the couch with a groan. As he passes behind me, his hand briefly touches my shoulder, and I have to fight not to lean into the contact.

"Juliet?"

I turn to look at him. "Yeah?"

"I'm glad to be back."

He disappears down the hallway before I can respond, leaving me staring after him and wondering what the hell that meant.

Twenty minutes later, he emerges from his room looking completely different. Gone is the travel-rumpled hockey player, replaced by Hunter in dark jeans and a black henley that fits him in ways that should be illegal. His hair is still damp from the shower. He smells like a combination of soap, pine scent, and something distinctly him that makes my brain go fuzzy.

"Ready?" he asks.

I am so not ready. For any of this.

We start at Ivy's apartment, where the Coven is already two drinks in and gossiping about a scandal involving a local influencer and a married city councilman. Hunter endures their interrogation about the road trip with surprising grace, even laughing when Jessa asks if he brought me back anything.

"Shit," he says, a smile on his lips. "I knew I forgot something."

"You were supposed to bring her a souvenir?" Ivy asks, clearly delighted by this development. "How romantic."

"No," I blurt. "He wasn't. We don't do that."

"Why not?" Wren demands. "Ryan always brings me something when he travels."

"Because we're not..." I catch myself before I say *actually together*. "Because we're not cheesy like that."

Hunter gives me a look I can't quite read. "I'll remember next time."

Somehow, the idea of there being a next time makes my chest tight. Three and a half more months. There should be plenty of opportunities, I guess.

We migrate to The Secret History around ten, claiming the back room like we own it. Most of the team is there, celebrating being home, and the energy is loose despite their recent losses. I end up in a corner with Silas and Jett, who are apparently determined to entertain me with increasingly ridiculous stories about their teammates.

"So there's Hunter," Jett is saying, gesturing wildly with his beer, "standing in the hotel lobby in nothing but a towel because Shane thought it would be funny to steal his room key and all his clothes while he was in the shower."

"What did he do?" I ask, genuinely curious.

"Walked right up to the front desk like nothing was wrong," Silas chimes in. "He was basically naked when he asked for a new key in the politest voice I've ever heard out of him. The poor desk clerk didn't know where to look."

I laugh, picturing Hunter's face in that situation. "He's got more confidence than shame, I'll give him that."

"That's Hunter in a nutshell," Jett agrees. "Zero shame, maximum chaos."

Across the room, I catch Hunter watching us, and there's something possessive in his frown that makes my skin buzz. It says that he doesn't love seeing me laugh with his teammates, even though they're just being friendly.

The thought shouldn't thrill me as much as it does.

Ivy appears at my elbow with a tray of shots. "Courtesy of Etienne," she announces. "He says they're called 'Havoc Bombs' and I'm not allowed to ask what's in them."

I take one of the small glasses, which contains something blue and ominous-looking. "This seems like a terrible idea."

"The best kind," Wren agrees, grabbing her own shot.

We count down from three and throw them back in unison. The liquid burns going down, but there's a sweet aftertaste that hits immediately. Whatever's in these things, it's strong and fast-acting.

I feel the buzz almost instantly, that warm, loose feeling spreading through my limbs. The room gets a little softer around the edges, and conversation flows more easily. I laugh and have another shot. What the hell, my week was dreadful enough to have earned it.

Hunter steps up beside me. "Are you ready to go?"

I blink because I have been staring at his mouth. "Sorry. Did you say something?"

His brows lift. "Yeah. Twice."

"Oh. Right. I was… distracted."

"By what?"

I glance away before he can read too much on my face. "Nothing important."

He leans closer, his voice low in my ear. "I said I'm beat. Do you mind if we head out?"

I should say no. If I were being proper, I would stay out with my friends and maintain some distance. But I want to go home with him. I want to sit on our couch and talk about nothing important and pretend this is real.

"Yeah, okay." I turn to say goodbye to the girls. Ivy slides me a little smile that says she knows exactly why I'm leaving early.

"Have fun," she says with a smirk. I huff, resisting the urge to flip her off.

The walk upstairs is quiet, but it's a comfortable quiet. Hunter keeps pace with me despite his longer stride. When I stumble slightly as we get in the elevator, his hand automatically goes to my lower back to steady me.

He doesn't move it right away either.

"Thanks," I murmur. I am all too aware of the warmth of his palm through my shirt.

"Always."

Upstairs, he heads straight for the kitchen and returns with two glasses of water. "Drink," he orders, handing me one.

The way his mouth quirks when I roll my eyes… it's not his usual scowl. It's softer. I think that maybe he saves those rare smiles just for me.

"I'm not that drunk," I say, smiling up at him. The edge of my vision is fuzzy.

"Humor me."

I drink the water mostly because I like when he takes care of me, even in small ways. It's not something I'm used to. Patrick never paid attention to things like whether I was hydrated or eating enough or too tired to make the best decisions.

Hunter settles on the couch, patting the cushion beside him. "Come here."

I should go to my room. Should maintain the boundaries we've somehow kept mostly intact for the past few weeks. Instead, I curl up next to him, close enough that I can feel the heat radiating from his body.

"Thanks for coming tonight," I say. "I know team bonding isn't really your thing when you're tired."

"It's fine. I came because you were there."

The honesty in his voice catches me off guard. "What?"

He looks at me, something vulnerable flickering across his face. "I'm too exhausted to party, but I wanted to see you. So I came."

My heart does something complicated in my chest. "Hunter..."

"I know. I know this is all fake and temporary and whatever. But I missed you this week. I missed coming home to you."

I should tell him to stop. Should remind him of the rules we set, the boundaries we agreed on. Instead, I lean closer, my hand finding his chest.

"I missed you too."

The admission hangs between us, heavy with implications we're both trying to ignore. His eyes drop to my mouth, and I know I should move away. I should go to my room and pretend this moment never happened.

Instead, I lean closer.

"Juliet." His voice is rough, warning.

"I know," I whisper. "I know this is a complicated situation. But I don't care right now."

When he moves to get up, probably to escape to his room and maintain what's left of our professional arrangement, I make a choice. I lean forward and kiss him.

It's supposed to be soft, testing. A question more than a statement. But the moment our lips touch, something ignites. He makes a soft moan in the base of his throat and his hands find my face, holding me like I might disappear.

We're kissing like we're drowning, like this is air and we've been holding our breath for weeks. His mouth is warm and demanding, and when his tongue slides against mine, I forget why this is a bad idea.

"Fuck yes, Hux. Oh, I love how you kiss me." I climb onto his lap without thinking and straddle him. My hands tremble as I kiss him the way I've wanted to for months. Hunter groans against my lips, his hands sliding down to grip my hips. I can feel how much he wants this, wants me, and it makes me dizzy with power.

"Fuck, Juliet," he breathes against my neck, his mouth hot on my skin. "You're going to kill me."

I thread my fingers through his hair, tugging slightly. "Good."

His laugh is rough. "You enjoy torturing me?"

"Definitely." I give him a cheeky smile.

We're pulling at each other's clothes, desperate and clumsy with want. His shirt hits the floor and I run my hands over his chest, marveling at the solid warmth of him. When he tugs my top over my head, I feel exposed but not vulnerable. Not with him looking at me like I'm something precious.

I'm wearing a lacy baby pink bra that I wore just on the off chance that he might see it tonight.

"Christ, you're beautiful," he murmurs, his hands skimming up my sides.

I want to deflect, to make a joke, but the way he's looking at me steals my words. He means it. Like he's been thinking about it for a while.

"I'm horny," I admit softly. "I thought about you a lot while you were gone."

"Oh yeah?" Hunter ghosts his fingers over my collarbone. "And just what was on your dirty little mind, Monroe?"

I laugh breathlessly. "You don't stop, do you? Your mouth is filthy."

His grin is pure sin. "Filthy enough to make you wet just listening."

My face heats but I don't look away from his smoldering blue-gray gaze. Before speaking, I bite my lip and say, "This." "I imagined the heat between us if we could ever shut the fuck up for ten seconds."

He sinks his fingers into my hair, tugging to expose my neck before he runs a trail of kisses from just below my ear to the joint of my shoulder. I close my eyes, tilting my head more, encouraging him with a sultry groan.

Hunter's hard cock presses against me. I can feel it through his thin pants. I drop my hand to brush the front of his package and he makes a pained sound.

He needs this as much as I do.

I cup his dick through his sweatpants, my fingers trailing over him. I stop when I feel something even harder. A piercing? Does Hunter have his cock pierced? Oh, my god.

I have to find out.

I grind against him, testing the friction, and his head falls back against the couch. "Jesus, Juliet."

I love the way he says my name when he's losing control. Love that I'm the one making him fall apart.

"Jules," he breathes. I freeze, going completely still.

Everything stops. The warmth in my chest turns to ice, and suddenly I'm somewhere else entirely.

Patrick's apartment, six months ago, his voice casual and cutting as he told me exactly why no man would ever choose me over his own comfort.

"Don't call me that," I say, my voice flat.

Hunter blinks, confusion replacing the heat in his eyes. "What?"

"Jules. Don't call me that."

"I... did I do something wrong?"

I'm already reaching for my shirt, pulling it over my head like armor. "It's just a name Patrick used to call me."

Understanding dawns on his face, followed immediately by something that looks like guilt. "Shit. I'm sorry, I didn't know."

"It's fine," I lie, even though it's not fine at all. Even though hearing that nickname in his voice just reminded me of every reason this is a terrible idea.

Hunter doesn't push, which somehow makes it worse. He just watches me retreat, probably wondering what the hell just happened.

I pull my legs up to my chest, suddenly cold despite the heat still radiating between us. The room feels too small, the air too thin. Like I can't get enough oxygen.

"Hey," Hunter says quietly, leaning closer. "What's wrong? And don't say anything, because you just went somewhere else entirely."

I shake my head, not trusting my voice.

"Talk to me, Juliet."

The gentle way he says my full name almost breaks me. Patrick never said it like that. Like it mattered. Like I mattered.

"You ruined everything for me in college," I hear myself saying. "You don't even remember, do you? That night at the Delta Tau Delta party."

His face goes blank, then careful. "What about it?"

"You said I wasn't your type. That I was a control freak with no sex appeal. That I probably had a spreadsheet for my virginity."

The words taste bitter in my mouth. "You thought it was funny. Someone printed it. I lost everything I'd worked for."

The color drains from his face. "Fuck. I didn't... I didn't think anyone was listening. I didn't know it got printed. It was... offhand."

The old anger rises in my throat. "You still said it. It's what drove me right into Patrick's arms."

He eyes me. "Do you think I didn't know everything you did in college? I was obsessed with you. I am obsessed with you, Monroe."

"What?" I shake my head vehemently. "You're just saying that."

He's quiet for a long moment, processing. Then he leans back, running both hands through his hair. "Why do you think I've never had a girlfriend?"

"I don't know. Your whole..." I wave at his face. "Big scowly hockey dude vibe?"

He grunts. "Like that scared off the jersey chasers. No, I always had the image of you in the back of my mind. How could any other girl possibly live up to you?"

My mouth hangs open. "You're full of shit."

"I'm dead serious. I didn't know that journalist was going to print that quote. But I'm still sorry, Juliet. If I could go back in time, I'd do it differently."

I believe him. I can see the regret written all over his face, the genuine remorse. But it doesn't change what happened. It doesn't change how small he made me feel, or how that feeling led me to spend five years with someone who made me feel even smaller.

"Patrick always made me feel like a transaction," I mumble. "Like love was something I had to earn by being small enough. Soft enough. Quiet enough. Less."

Hunter's jaw tightens. "He was wrong."

"Was he?" The question slips out before I can stop it, raw and vulnerable. "Because sometimes I think he was right. Sometimes I think I'm too much. Too ambitious, too intense, too..."

"Too what?"

"Too everything."

Hunter stares at me for a moment, then reaches out to touch my foot gently. "Whatever it is, you don't have to say it. Just... don't sit here alone with it."

His quiet comfort is everything. I look at his mouth, his hands, the soft place at his throat where I want to press my lips. When he moves like he's going to get up, probably to give me space, I make another choice.

I tug him closer and kiss him again.

He murmurs, "I'm going to ruin you. You realize that, right? Make it so no other man can ever please you."

I groan. "Hunter, your mouth. The things that come out of it are disgusting."

His chuckle vibrates through me. "You love my filthy mouth."

He bends down so far to reach me. Sometimes, I swear that kissing him feels like I am climbing a mountain, and my legs are not ready for the hike.

This time, our kiss is different. Slower, more intentional. Like we have all the time in the world instead of three months and a contract between us.

"Juliet," he murmurs against my lips, but I can hear the surrender in his voice.

"I know that our situation feels complicated," I whisper. "I know this thing ends. But right now, I don't want to think about that."

We're back to pulling at clothes, but it's less frantic now. More like exploration than desperation. When his mouth finds my breast, I arch into him, shocked by how sensitive I am, how every touch sends electricity straight through me.

"God, you're responsive," he breathes against my skin.

I should feel embarrassed, but I'm not. Not with him looking at me like I'm a gift he can't believe he gets to unwrap.

"Only for you," I groan. "Only you make me feel this way, Huxley."

I move against him again, seeking friction, and he reaches his hand between our bodies. I gasp as he pulls up my skirt and presses his fingers against the spreading damp spot on the front of my panties. It's exactly where I need him most. The touch is electric and I gasp, my hips jerking involuntarily.

"You're so wet," he marvels, his fingers moving in slow circles. "Fuck, Juliet."

I try to pull away, embarrassed by my body's obvious response, but he catches my wrist.

"Don't," he says urgently. "Don't hide from me. Let me make you feel good."

There's something desperate in his voice, like he needs this as much as I do. "It's all I want," he continues. "To be useful. To matter."

The vulnerability of those words undoes me completely. This giant man in front of me, begging to take care of me, is so different from the arrogant asshole I thought I knew.

I stay, sucking in a breath and nodding quickly.

Circling my clit, he touches me like he means it. As if he's memorizing every response, every sound I make.

When his mouth finds me, the sensation is so sharp and unexpected my knees almost give out. "Yes," I moan. "Harder. Right there, oh *goddd*."

Heat floods my body in a dizzy rush. His lips close around me, hot and wet. The scrape of his tongue sends a pulse of pleasure straight through my spine. Every nerve feels lit from the inside, so sensitive I can hardly stand still. My hands find his hair, twisting in the strands, holding on like he might vanish if I let go.

He moves with a slow, consuming purpose. Every stroke is unhurried but devastating. His tongue teases, then presses, falling into perfect rhythm with the slow circles of his fingers. My breath becomes ragged. Each touch opened me in ways I did not know I could be opened. My thighs tremble around his shoulders. He holds me steady, murmuring something I can't quite hear.

The words leave my mouth like a chant. "Oh my God, yes. Fuck me with your mouth, Huxley. Don't stop, please don't stop."

It builds within me, a wave gathering force. I feel like I might break apart if I try to hold it in. My hips shift without my permission, chasing the exact angle he's found. I need it. I can't stop. His grip tightens around my thigh, keeping me exactly where he wants me. The sounds he makes against me are low and hungry, curling deep in my belly. I bite down on a gasp and fail. The sound spills out anyway.

When release finally tears through me, it's raw and consuming. My whole body jerks against his mouth. Every muscle tightens. Pleasure rips through me in waves that feel endless.

"Fuck, Hunter! Yes. Oh, fuck, yes, yes." My voice is loud

and unrestrained. Heat rises in my cheeks even as I surrender to it. He doesn't pull away. He stays with me, steady and unrelenting, riding out each aftershock until I'm shivering from the intensity.

By the time I slump forward, I'm spent and shaking. My chest rises and falls in quick bursts. My hands slide from his hair to his shoulders, clinging without thought. He eases back just enough to look up at me. His lips are glistening. His eyes are dark and intense. The way he looks at me makes it clear he's not just touching my body. He's memorizing me. Every part of me.

When my breathing finally slows, I reach for him, wanting to return the favor. But he gently catches my hands.

"Not tonight," he says quietly. "Tonight is just for you."

"But you..." I gesture vaguely at the obvious evidence of his arousal.

"I'm fine."

I study his face, seeing the tension there, the careful control. "You're holding back."

He doesn't deny it. "I know you're scared."

I nod, because I am. Terrified of what this means, of how it changes everything.

"I'm scared too," he admits.

The silence that follows is heavy but full of meaning. We're both acknowledging something we can't take back, something that makes this fake relationship feel a lot more real than either of us expected.

Before I can make the mistake of asking for more, asking for promises he can't make, I gather what's left of my dignity and head toward my room.

"Goodnight, Hux."

"Goodnight, Monroe."

I close my bedroom door behind me and lean against it,

my whole body still shaking from what we shared. From what we almost shared.

Three months, I remind myself. *This ends in three months.*

But as I lie in bed, replaying every touch, every word, every look, I can't shake the feeling that three months will not be nearly enough.

Chapter 23

Hunter

I wake up to a generic hotel ceiling and the sound of someone knocking on my door. For a second, I think it's housekeeping, but then I remember I put the Do Not Disturb sign up last night.

The knocking stops for a second, and I close my eyes, drifting. Juliet is supposed to be flying in this morning with Ivy and the rest of the off-ice support team. I arrived with the team last night so that I could get a solid night's rest before we play against Boston, one of the toughest teams in the country. Thoughts of Juliet filled my dreams, and I slept fitfully at best.

It's been two weeks since I had to sleep in a hotel room, and the ache of loneliness is hitting me hard. Usually, I don't give a fuck if I'm on the road. But knowing the Juliet is at my house, probably wearing those silky little sleep shorts and no fucking bra… sitting on the couch, watching foreign detective dramas. Not missing me at all while I fucking wallow in my hotel room.

Fuck, I hate this. Do I even *like* Juliet? I'm not supposed to. But she's the first thing in my head when I wake and the last thing when I finally pass out. Why can't I just be a normal fucking human?

"Mr. Huxley? Room service!" a voice calls. The person outside starts banging on the door again, growing impatient. I drag myself out of bed, still half-asleep, and open the door to find a guy in a hotel uniform holding a breakfast tray. "Room service for Mr. Huxley?"

I frown. "I didn't order anything."

"Says here it's from your fiancée." He hands me the tray with a grin that suggests he thinks he's delivering something romantic. There's a paper bag on the tray with a note written in Juliet's neat handwriting, complete with a smug little heart drawn next to it.

I can't help it. I grin like an idiot at the stupid little heart. No one else in the world could make me do that. I tip the guy and shut the door, shaking my head.

Plucking the note off, I read it.

Wanted to make sure you're treating yourself right on the road. Good luck in your game today. I'll see you tonight.

XO, Monroe

My lips twitch. This is exactly what a real fiancée would do for her hockey player husband-to-be.

Inside the bag is my exact go-to breakfast order. Scrambled eggs, hot sauce packets, crispy turkey bacon, fresh fruit, and black coffee so dark it could strip paint. She got my order down to the specific brand of hot sauce I always ask for.

How? I'm not sure. I haven't ordered it in front of her. She must have gotten my order from the team's chef or something. I can't help but smirk. Juliet's not even in the room and she's already controlling my day.

The coffee is perfect, rich and dark, which pisses me off because I don't want to be impressed by her attention to detail. But I am. Because most people don't pay attention to shit like this. Most people don't care if I eat breakfast or survive on energy drinks and spite.

I text her: *How did you know my exact order?*

She writes back quickly.

Juliet: *To quote you, I pay attention. It's my doting fiancée impression. You like?*

Yes, I do like it. More than I should. Classic Juliet. Do something thoughtful, then respond to my questions with a joke.

Me: *For a PR nightmare, I feel very well taken care of.*

Juliet: *I'm very good at my job, Hux.*

Hux. The nickname slides against me, pleasantly slick.

I can see that she's good at what she does. Eating quickly and dressing, then catch the team shuttle over to the stadium. I don't see Juliet for over an hour while the team runs through puck-handling drills, line rushes, and two-on-two scrimmages. It's a relatively light day with a press scrum after practice.

It's time for Juliet to show us what she's made of.

I'm at the arena watching her glide around in those ridiculous heels like a tiny dictator. She's running point in the press pool, telling a pack of reporters where to stand, what video to shoot, and when to shut up. Her voice has a firm, velvet quality that makes grown men listen without questioning why.

I'm standing off to the side, catching my breath, watching her work with interest.

"Let's go over topics that are and are not appropriate for the press to ask the Seattle Havoc players." Juliet's brown eyes take in the press pool. She looks perfectly groomed in her navy skirt suit, paired as always with that sexy-ass red lipstick. "Anyone who asks anything outside the parameters we're about to establish will be kicked out of the pool… permanently."

Atta girl. You teach those bloodthirsty journalists how to heel.

The reporter, some middle-aged dickhead from a sports blog, says something about a pretty little thing playing dress-up. I can't hear exactly what he says, but Juliet's spine goes rigid.

Everyone straightens up, curious about how she will respond. Her eyes narrow; the temperature in the room drops by ten degrees.

She doesn't even blink. She snaps her fingers, points at him, and says, "I'm so glad that you brought that up. The number one rule for being in this room is that *you will* respect the team. That means the players, the managers, the coaches, and even off-ice talent… like me. This is your only warning. The next infraction will mean you to call your boss and explaining to him how the Havoc's PR just banned your entire channel from the press pool *forever*."

The man gapes at Juliet while she looks at him expectantly.

"I'm sorry, did you have anything you wanted to say in response?"

He swallows and shakes his head. "No…"

"You can address me as Ms. Monroe." She cocks her head, waiting. "Don't you want to be on my good side?"

"Uhh, yes, Ms. Monroe," the man says. His head bobs. "I do."

"I assumed so." Juliet claps her hands and turns to address the press pool. "I think you'll find today's focus is on the team's performance metrics and playoff positioning. Unless anyone else would prefer to discuss something as unimportant as my looks?"

The guy flushes red and fumbles with his notepad. The other reporters snicker, and I have to bite back a grin.

She's *terrifying*. Against my will, I'm impressed.

Juliet catches my eye across the media scrum and lifts her chin like she's daring me to cause trouble. I smirk back at her. Something passes between us. Some kind of challenge or acknowledgment that we're both enjoying this game.

"Okay. With that rule in mind, let's bring out a few players to talk to you. We have Alexander Thorne and Beck Tate, the team captains. Jett Huxley, goalie. And Hunter Huxley, right wing."

We file out dutifully, sitting at a long table set up with mics. Each of us takes turns fielding questions about the game: Thorne gets asked about managing ice time and keeping the forecheck aggressive. Beck fields a question about locker room morale after a rough first period. Reporters asked Jett how he handled the high shot volume in the second and whether a screen affected the tying goal.

Then the mic comes to me. A reporter asks if my line is finally finding chemistry and whether I was gunning for a Gordie Howe hat trick when I dropped the gloves.

I get in and out with the bare minimum number of words. Juliet is watching me, ready to jump in if there is even a whiff of a journalist asking a bullshit personal question about my life. But maybe because of her apparent readiness, there is not a single question that crosses the line. I would love it if I didn't have to answer journalists at all.

But in a world where that's not possible, I'll accept having Juliet standing nearby, ready to pounce. I feel protected.

Huh. That's a first, for sure. No one has ever whipped reporters into line for me before.

"All right." Juliet cuts in before anyone asks another

question. "I think that's enough. We should really let the Havoc go change. Have a great game, guys."

A warm feeling glows in the pit of my stomach at her words, especially when she makes eye contact with me. Her eyes sparkle.

Juliet is changing the PR game, here. The team has never received public support like this before.

"Hunter!" the photographer calls out. "Can we get you and Juliet for some shots?"

I look at Juliet, arching a brow to ask whether that's okay with her. She beckons to me. Damn if I don't rush over to where she's standing, quick as anything. She slides into position next to me like we've done this a thousand times. Her hand finds my arm. Even through my shirt, I can feel the warmth of her palm. I slide my arm around her waist and pull her against my body.

"Smile like you're not plotting my murder," she murmurs under her breath.

"Who says I'm not?" I tease.

"You're the worst."

"I'm the best and you know it."

Her cheeks glow pink, which is as much recognition as I'm going to get. The cameras click and we pose, answering a few questions about our supposed upcoming wedding. Okay, Juliet answers them, lying smoothly. She's rehearsed this.

Afterward, as we're walking away from the media area, Juliet says, "You didn't scowl once."

"I could've killed that reporter from KCPZ," I say, my eyes burning into hers. "No one talks shit to you."

"Except you, apparently."

"Except for me," I agree. "You did a good job of dressing him down, but I'd be more than happy to wait outside his house and break every one of his fingers for you."

She laughs, a little shocked. "I don't think that's necessary. Honestly, I'm just pleased you didn't implode. I'm impressed."

I huff, but there's something warm in my chest at her approval. It's ridiculous, but her saying she's impressed hits harder than any crowd applause ever could.

Breaking the journalist's fingers still sounds appealing, though.

We're heading toward the locker room when Connor comes barreling around the corner, not watching where he's going, and crashes straight into me. His coffee goes flying, splashing all over my shirt and the floor.

"Shit, sorry, Hunt. I'm so sorry, man. I wasn't looking where I was..." He's already scrambling to grab napkins, his face flushed with panic.

The rage hits me like a physical force. Hot and immediate and completely disproportionate to what just happened. My hands clench into fists, and I can feel my whole body going tight with the need to yell, to lash out, to make someone else feel as shitty as I do at this moment.

"Watch where you're fucking going," I snap, my voice louder than it needs to be. "Jesus Christ, Connor. Use your eyes."

The kid freezes, his face going white. A few other guys in the hallway turn to look. I can see the way they're all holding their breath, waiting to see how bad this is going to get.

"Hunter." Juliet's voice cuts through the haze of anger. Sharp and warning.

I look at her. Her expression is carefully neutral, but there's something disappointed in her eyes that makes my stomach twist.

"It was an accident," she says quietly. "The rookie made a mistake. He didn't kill your dog."

Connor looks like he wants to disappear into the floor. The other guys are still watching, waiting to see if I'm going to explode completely or if this is as bad as it gets.

I want to keep yelling. I want to make Connor understand that this isn't just about coffee; it's about everything. It's about feeling like I'm always one wrong move away from screwing everything up. About being tired of having to hold myself together all the fucking time.

But Juliet is looking at me like she's cataloging this moment for later reference. Maybe she's remembering why she thought I was a lost cause.

I clench my jaw and force myself to step back. "Just... be more careful."

It's not an apology, but it's not the explosion it could have been. Connor nods frantically and disappears toward the locker room. The hallway slowly empties until it's just me and Juliet standing there.

"Better?" I ask, my voice tight.

"Not really." She studies my face for a moment. "It's a start."

That night, after we've finished another round of media obligations and I've somehow managed not to alienate anyone else, I'm lying in my hotel room scrolling through my phone when I remember Connor's face earlier. The way he looked so panicked, so young.

I open the team group chat and scroll through a few stupid memes until I find one about faceoffs that's actually kind of funny. Something about how they're like awkward first dates but with more violence.

I send it to the chat without really thinking about it.

Hunter: *[sends meme about faceoffs being like awkward first dates but with more violence]*

Connor:

Grayson: If faceoffs are first dates, Connor's ghosted before the puck even drops.

Thorne: More like he's the guy stuck paying the bill while the other center skates away with the puck.

Jett: Nah, I figured it out. They're not dates for him. They're breakups. Every single time.

Connor: wtf guys 😩

Grayson: Don't worry, bud. One day you'll win one.

Thorne: Not today. Not tomorrow either.

Jett: Should we start a GoFundMe for his self-esteem?

Connor: I hate you all.

Hunter: *[sends gif of someone getting demolished in a faceoff]*

At the next practice, Connor gives me a fist bump when we're lining up for drills.

Maybe that counts for something.

The game itself is everything I needed it to be. Two goals, an assist, clean hits, no penalties. The performance that makes the coaching staff remember why they keep me around despite all the headaches.

I can see Juliet in the VIP section throughout the game, arms crossed but watching intently. Every time I make a play, I look for her reaction. Which is stupid, because this is supposed to be about hockey, not about impressing my fake fiancée.

But when I score the second goal, a beauty of a wrist shot that finds the top corner, I swear I see her smile before she catches herself and goes back to looking professional.

After the game, after all the interviews and handshakes and bullshit, I make my way back to the hotel. I'm exhausted in a way that only comes after a perfect game, when you've left everything on the ice and your body is finally coming down from the adrenaline.

I kick the door shut with my foot and collapse onto the bed, still in my post-game suit. I'm too tired to move, too tired to think about getting undressed. That's when I notice Juliet is already there.

She's kicked off her shoes and changed into sweats. There's another room-service tray on the desk. She looks comfortable in a way that catches me off guard. She acts like she belongs here.

"I figured you'd be hungry after your little hero routine," she says, pulling the tray lid off dramatically.

I peer over at what she's ordered, and my brain short-circuits a little. "Is that... chicken parm?"

"With garlic bread. And a protein shake that doesn't taste like chalk."

I stare at her. "How do you know all this?"

She shrugs, not meeting my eyes. "I pay attention. You always order like 5 chicken parms from the performance kitchen. You must like it."

She's right. Chicken parm is my go-to comfort food, the thing I always crave after a good game. And that protein shake is the exact brand I've been trying to find in hotel gyms for the past five years.

"Uh, thanks," I say awkwardly.

She gives me a funny expression. "Don't be weird, Hux."

She got the same thing minus the protein shake, so we end up eating on the bed with the TV playing some muted baking competition show. It's domestic in a way that should make me uncomfortable, but doesn't. At some point, I nudge her shoulder with mine.

"You were a menace out there today."

Juliet shrugs, stealing a piece of my garlic bread. "Someone has to make sure you don't ruin your fake life."

"Right," I say. "Fake life. Fake fiancée. Real garlic bread."

She snorts. Something about the sound makes my chest feel warm. We fall into a conversation that shouldn't feel easy but does. Maybe it's the post-game endorphins, or maybe it's because we're both too tired to maintain our usual walls.

"My brothers and I used to fight over rink time," I say. "Our dad said we all played or nobody did. So we rotated shifts like a prison schedule."

"Sounds weirdly wholesome."

"We still fought. Just not about ice time." I think about those early mornings, the three of us taking turns, always trying to prove we deserved more time than the others. "My younger brother Silas was the talent. Natural everything. Made the rest of us look like we were playing in concrete boots."

"What about your older brother?"

"Jett was the smart one. Captain of everything, straight As, full ride to Seattle U. Hockey was just another thing he was good at. He's an amazing goalie."

"And you were...?"

"The angry one." Before I can stop them, the words flood out. "The grinder. The one who had to work twice as hard for half the recognition."

She's quiet for a moment, processing that. "Sounds lonely."

It was. But I don't say that out loud.

Instead, I turn it back on her. "What about you? Any siblings to compete with?"

"Only child. But I had plenty of competition anyway." She sets down her fork and wipes her hands on a napkin.

"They forbade me to swear. Or dye my hair. Or look at boys. My parents weren't really around, but they still expected me to be their buttoned-up, emotionally repressed princess."

I raise an eyebrow. Thinking back to the girl I knew in college, it doesn't really track. "You made up for it later."

She gives me a look that's half amusement, half warning. "It wasn't a rebellion. It was survival. Have you seen my body? I'm five feet tall and have big boobs. From the second I turned thirteen, everyone treated me like a full-grown seductress."

That makes me go quiet. There's something in her voice, something sharp and painful that I recognize. The sound of someone who learned early that the world wasn't going to be kind.

"You think that made you guarded?"

"How could I not be?"

She sets her food down completely now, looking at me, sucking in her lower lip. I can tell we've shifted into deeper territory. The conversation that usually makes me want to run.

"Patrick told me once that ambition makes women ugly," she breathes.

My stomach knots up at the mention of her ex. I've heard enough about him to know he was a piece of shit, but hearing the specifics still makes me want to punch something.

"He said that I focused too much on my career and that I was too driven. That men want someone who makes them feel important, not someone who's always trying to prove herself." Her voice gets smaller. "I believed him. For years, I felt that if no one respected me, at least I could make myself lovable. Until I walked into Patrick's hotel room to surprise him and found him with a nineteen-year-old blonde. Then I realized he didn't love me. He kept me, which is different."

I shift toward her on the bed, every instinct telling me to

say something, to fix it somehow. But she's not looking at me, staring at her hands like she's remembering her bitterest moments. I get the feeling that interrupting would break whatever spell is letting her talk about this.

"You know what the worst part was?" she continues. "The first time he cheated, I took him back. I started believing his lies. He had me thinking that maybe if I were smaller, quieter, less… then he might actually want to stick around."

The pain in her voice is like a physical hit. I want to tell her that Patrick was wrong, that any man who can't handle her ambition is a fucking idiot who doesn't deserve her. But I also know that's not what she needs right now.

So I just stay there, silent, grounded, letting her know I'm listening. She goes quiet for a moment, then her attention shifts to me.

"You're not who I thought you were. I mean, you're still awful. But not how I thought. You're… something else."

I don't know what to say about that. Part of me wants to ask what ways do matter, to dig deeper into what she thinks of me now versus what she thought before. But mostly I'm just grateful that she doesn't think I'm a complete waste of space anymore.

"Thanks?" I say finally. She gives a brittle little laugh.

"That wasn't really a compliment."

I shrug. "I'll take what I can get."

We lapse into comfortable silence after that. The TV keeps playing its muted baking show. I watch her more than the screen. The way she absently touches her hair when she's thinking. The way her entire face softens when she's not actively managing something.

Eventually, exhaustion catches up with her. Her eyes drift closed, and she lies back on the bed without really meaning to. Still in her sweats, still on top of the covers, lipstick still firmly in place, but clearly done for the night.

I should probably go to my bed. Or at least move to the chair. But I gently pull off her socks, trying not to wake her. She stirs slightly but doesn't open her eyes.

I tug the blanket over her, then lie down next to her, fully clothed and staring at the ceiling.

I tell myself it's just pretend. That I'm being decent. That it's not real.

But that's bullshit, and I know it.

Juliet acts like this is just another job, just another box to check off her list. She's professional and efficient and keeps everything neat and compartmentalized. But the way she leans into me when we're in public, the way her breath catches when I brush her waist during photo ops? That's not nothing.

She's not as immune as she pretends to be. And neither am I.

She keeps playing it off like none of it means anything. Like I'm just a client. A puppet to be cleaned up and repackaged for public consumption. A project with a deadline.

If she knew who I really was, the things I needed to fulfill my fantasies, she'd run. They always do. The moment people see past the surface, see the mess underneath, they decide it's not worth the effort.

She shifts in her sleep. Her hand lands lightly on my chest, right above my heart. And I think, *God help me, I might be in trouble.*

This isn't supposed to feel real. It's supposed to be five months of playing house, helping each other get what we need, then walking away clean.

But lying here in this hotel bed, listening to her breathe,

feeling the weight of her hand on my chest, I'm starting to think clean might not be an option anymore.

Juliet makes a small sound in her sleep and shifts closer. I know I'm already fucked.

Three months left on our contract. Three months to figure out how to walk away from this without destroying both of us.

I should plan my exit strategy. Instead, I'm lying here thinking about room service breakfasts and the way she says my name when she's trying not to smile.

Yeah. I'm definitely in trouble.

Chapter 24

Juliet

On the plane the next day, Connor fist-bumps Hunter like nothing ever happened. I watch it from across the aisle and something slides loose in my chest. Maybe that's progress. Maybe Hunter's actually learning that not every mistake requires a nuclear response.

The flight back feels endless. Three days away shouldn't feel like a lifetime, but somehow it does. I'm exhausted in that bone-deep way that comes from being *on* for seventy-two hours straight. Smiling for cameras, managing reporters, making sure Hunter doesn't accidentally start a riot with an ill-timed comment.

Hunter just shuts his eyes and goes to sleep for the entire flight. Mind-blogging, considering how on edge I've been this whole trip. Babysitting him, making sure he doesn't murder someone.

By the time we get back to the apartment, I'm done. Completely and utterly done with being professional and polished and perfect. I'm not in charge of anyone but me and so fucking glad for it.

I disappear into my room and change into a camisole

and shorts. A comfortable outfit that doesn't require a bra or shapewear or any of the other crap I've been wearing for days. But I still put my lipstick on. Some habits die hard.

Red lipstick has been my uniform for so many years that I feel naked without it.

I park myself in front of the TV and flip to PBS, hunting for my Swedish detective show. It's my guilty pleasure, this slow-burn crime drama where nothing happens quickly and everyone speaks in hushed, meaningful tones. The exact opposite of my real life.

Hunter emerges from his room a few minutes later, wearing a t-shirt and gray sweatpants that should be illegal. Seriously. The fabric clings in ways that make it impossible not to notice... everything. And Jesus Christ, Ivy wasn't kidding when she whispered that she heard about Hunter's massive dick.

I can basically see the outline through the soft cotton. It makes me break out in a sweat and I have to force myself to look at the TV screen instead.

"What are we watching?" he asks, dropping onto the couch next to me.

"We?" I ask. More to fuck with him than anything.

He kicks out his long legs with a smug little grin. I side-eye him. He is so much taller than me, it should be illegal. "Yeah, *sweetheart*. It's my downtime, too. Not to mention my TV."

I don't push it. "Swedish crime drama. A woman gets murdered in the first episode, and Detective Saga spends the next six episodes drinking coffee and having philosophical conversations about justice."

"Detective Saga? Sounds riveting."

"Don't mock it. It's very atmospheric."

He settles back into the cushions, close enough that I can smell his shower gel. "Does anything actually happen?"

"Lots of things happen. They're just... subtle."

"Right. Subtle." But he doesn't change the channel, just watches with what appears to be genuine interest.

We're about twenty minutes into the episode when Detective Saga has a hookup with her informant in an abandoned warehouse. He's a very handsome dirtbag, and she falls for his lines, even though he'll almost certainly turn out to be a bad guy. Once they kiss, it becomes nothing but shadows and tension and barely contained desperation.

I feel the hair on my arms rise.

"Well," Hunter says, his voice slightly rough. "That wasn't subtle."

"It's character development," I say. My voice comes out breathier than I intended.

He glances at me, something sharp and knowing in his expression. "Character development. Right."

Neither of us says anything in the following silence, which is loaded with unspoken thoughts. I can feel the heat radiating off him. I can sense the way his attention has shifted from the TV to me.

"You've been... nicer lately," I say, observing him. "Less Chainsaw, more actual human man."

He snorts. "It's because you threatened to beat me with a clipboard."

"Or," I say with a smirk, "because you're trying. And I see it."

He grunts, but I can tell he's kind of proud of himself. There's been something different about him in the last few days. Looser. More comfortable in his own skin.

This is dangerous territory.

See, this whole fake dating thing is still just a game that I excel at. But if I let Hunter touch me, let this go a little further, it might get harder.

I can keep the upper hand. I can compartmentalize it like I do everything else. It'll just take some real sticking to my own boundaries.

I adjust the hem of my tank top, suddenly aware of how much skin I'm showing. The movement draws his attention. When I look up, he's watching me with an intensity that makes my stomach flip.

"You're staring at my tits again," I say, folding my arms across my chest.

Hunter blinks, slow and unbothered. "Not really."

I glare at him. "Want to try that again?"

"Look, tits are great. Yours seem spectacular." He shrugs, completely unrepentant. "But I've always been an ass man."

I open my mouth, then close it. That... was not the answer I expected. I was prepared for denial or deflection or even shameless admission, not this casual redirection.

Hunter tilts his head, watching me like I'm something he's trying to solve. His voice is rougher when he says, "Lately, I think I'm becoming a lip guy. That lipstick you always wear haunts my fucking dreams, Monroe."

The flush creeps up my neck before I can stop it. It's the way he says it, like he's been thinking about my mouth. Like he's been wanting to do things to it.

He catches the blush, of course he does, and smiles like a man who just won something important.

"You're impossible," I mutter.

"And you're blushing."

"I am not."

"You are," he says, leaning closer. "And it's still a good look on you."

The space between us feels vast and yet too narrow. I lick

my lips and glance at him, trying to feel him out. Suddenly, it's like we're balanced on the edge of something that will change everything once we cross it.

"Hunter," I start, but I don't know how to finish the sentence.

He's the one who moves first, closing the space between us without a word. One second I'm staring at the hard line of his jaw, the next his mouth is on mine. The kiss steals my breath. It isn't cautious or questioning. It's fierce and certain, like he's been holding back too long and finally snapped.

The taste hits me instantly. Toothpaste lingers in his mouth. A hint of salt clings to his skin, and I nip at him, curious. There's something sharp tasting to our kiss, like adrenaline. It makes me shiver.

His lips are hot against mine, rough and demanding, moving with a hunger that makes me ache. I make a sound, a whimper, and he devours it, licking the seam of my lips. My body answers before my brain can catch up. I lean in, parting for him, chasing every flick of his tongue like I'll starve without it.

Heat rushes through me, climbing from my chest into my throat. I catch a faint trace of his cologne, cedar and spice mixed with the clean bite of a fresh shower. His stubble scrapes my chin and I tremble. Everything about it is raw and overwhelming, like I've stepped straight into a fire.

I've waited for this moment for far too long and now I'm gluttonous.

The more I give, the more he takes. His hand knots in my hair and pulls just enough to tilt my head back. The kiss deepens and I gasp against his mouth. This sound gets swallowed instantly too, and he growls like it sets him off.

My hands clutch his shoulders, nails digging through the fabric, desperate for something to hold.

Every sense is lit up at once. The solid weight of his chest pressed against mine. The heat of his breath on my cheek. He kisses me like he can't decide if he wants to worship me or ruin me, and maybe it's both.

I'm not just kissing him back. I'm unraveling.

"Fuck, Juliet," he breathes against my neck. The sound of my name, raw on his lips like that, makes something deep in my chest crack open.

I think about Patrick suddenly, unbidden. Think about how he never made me feel like this. How he made me feel lucky to be wanted, but never truly desired. Sex with him was pleasant and predictable and completely forgettable. He never really saw me, not like this.

But Hunter is looking at me like I'm something he wants to *ruin*, like I'm the most fascinating thing he's ever encountered. It's in my head, I know, but it seems like he's been waiting his whole life for permission to touch me this way.

The fear hits me hard and sudden.

It's not just that Hunter's good at this. It's that I feel seen. Too seen.

It's been a long time since someone wanted me for me and I've been aching for this kind of connection on such a soul-deep level.

I *need* to be needed. Not desired, but wanted for something other than my great tits. Hunter barely notices them. I can feel myself getting lost in the kiss, in him, and that terrifies me more than anything.

But then his hand slides between us, sweeping down my body, parting my thighs. His hot fingers press against the fabric of my shorts, seeking and quickly finding the little wet spot. He rubs hard circles just above it, pressing against my clit, and all rational thought flies out the window.

I gasp, arching my body, eager for more. I'm greedy,

seeking friction, seeking more of whatever he's offering. He barely touches me and I pant for him. It's embarrassing, but I'm about five seconds from straddling him, ripping off my clothes, and demanding he finish what he started.

He kisses along my neck, nudging my thighs open a bit more. "Let me touch you, Monroe. Let me feel you."

"Fuck it," I gasp. Pushing his hands away, I straddle his lap. Hunter's hands find my hips, encouraging me to roll them against him. It's not work to spread my legs wide, bury my hands in his hair, and buck my pussy against his steely length.

Something impossibly hard and cool brushes against my clit. My eyes bug out as I look down between us. "What was that?"

"This?" Hunter bites his lip and thrusts against my pussy again. I feel metal brush me again, but I can't see it.

"Yes!" I splay my hands against his muscular chest. "Hunter, are you… pierced?"

"Yes, sweetheart." He rocks his hips slowly, pressing his hand between our bodies to make sure that I feel the mysterious piercing with each thrust. I can't see his cock, but I can feel it, his hot, impossibly hard length teasing my slit. "That's not a problem, is it?"

I groan. One part of me wants to know when he got the piercing and if it hurt. The other part of my brain is tuning out, narrowing to the feeling of my clit pulsing and the heat between our bodies.

Am I drooling? God, I hope not. My orgasm face might be humiliating. The thought slows my hips again.

"You're thinking too much." Hunter tugs my head back and growls in my ear, "Let me make you come, Monroe."

God, he's killing me. I'm fucking *needy* and my face is on

fire. Nodding to him, I relax an inch. He moves his hips faster, his eyes on me.

"Are you going to come just from me touching you like this?" He seems curious. His stormy blue-gray eyes probe me. "How does my cock feel, Juliet?"

"Good," I gasp. "So fucking good. Don't stop."

He's playing me like a fucking fiddle. How embarrassing. My breath hitches as he snaps his hips, his clothed cock brushing against my clit. Every thrust brings a brush of hard metal. My whole body shudders, knotting.

"I wouldn't dare." Hunter smirks. "Do you have a very sensitive trigger, baby? Is that it?"

I swallow. I'm very close to the edge, hanging on the precipice by my fingernails. "Uh-uh."

He grips my hips harder, thrusting against me more forcefully. My eyes roll back in my head. "I'm–I'm going to–"

"That's it." His hips move faster now, rolling against me, his hands the only thing tying me down to earth. "You're so fucking hot. So perfect. I can feel how wet your pussy is getting, sweetheart. I want you to come on my cock."

I seize up somewhere just before he tells me to come, exploding, shaking, my fingers digging into his shoulders hard enough to leave marks. Hunter keeps thrusting while I ride the wave, washing up and over me like a tidal wave and then leaving me a gasping mess.

I remind myself to chill out a bit. Hunter has barely touched me. I need to slow my roll down a little. Brushing the hair out of my face, I look at him, breathing hard.

"Can I touch you?" I ask, feeling silly.

His lips twitch. "Juliet, you just came on my lap. I think you can touch me if you want to."

I bite my lip, smiling shyly. My palm finds the hard length

of him through those sinful sweatpants, shaping his massive cock, and he groans like I've hurt him in the best possible way. When I explore his pierced tip with my thumb, he groans.

"Jesus Christ, Juliet."

I slip my hand into his waistband, exploring his cock. Hunter's fingers cover mine as he sets a fast tempo. I want to pull his cock out so I can see the damn thing, especially the metal piercing that runs through the head of his dick. But I'm not sure he'd be into my scientific curiosity, so I move my hand in the rhythm he's set.

"Talk to me, Monroe," Hunter whispers. He knots his fingers in my hair, dragging his top teeth across his full bottom lip. "Tell me what you think about when you're in bed, all alone and horny."

"Lately?" I suck in a breath. "You. How you smell. How big your hands are. The feeling of kissing you. How big your cock probably is…" I smile sheepishly. "I spend a lot of time imagining how it would feel if you fucked me."

"Fuck, Juliet."

I kiss him hard, my hand moving faster, flicking the metal barbell each time I work my hand along his cock. "Mmm, you're so hard. Is that for me?"

"Fucking right it is," he growls. His breathing gets ragged; his control slips. There's something intoxicating about being the one to reduce him to this.

When he comes, he says my name like a prayer, and I feel powerful in a way I never have before.

After, we sit there breathing hard, trying to process what just happened. His lips had my lipstick smeared across them. My hair is a mess.

I should feel embarrassed or regretful or something. Shouldn't I?

Instead, I feel electric. Alive in a way I haven't been in years.

Hunter doesn't say much, but I can tell by the way he looks at me, steady and possessive and almost proud, that he knows he gave me something no one else ever has.

I have only been with Patrick, and he never got me off. Not with my shorts on, not buck naked, not in five long, lonely years.

Hunter seems proud that my ex couldn't make me come the way he just did. That he could. He's not gloating exactly, but it's there in the way he watches me. Quiet satisfaction mixed with something deeper.

"That was the hottest thing I've ever seen," he says, sweeping my dark curls from my temple. "Juliet? Look at me."

Face red as a beet, I peek up at him. "I got kind of carried away."

"Are you kidding?"

I squint at him. "No?"

"Monroe." He grips my hips again. "I think we've both wanted this since college."

That's news to me. My eyes narrow. "I thought you said I wasn't the type of girl guys went for. I was *too uptight*."

"I said that, didn't I?" A low laugh snakes from his throat. "That's what you tell anyone who's sniffing around the girl you like. You tell them she's not the hottest thing you've ever laid eyes on and hope that your lying tongue doesn't rot out of your mouth."

My mouth drops open. I'm flustered, not just that he said it, but that it wasn't even how he really felt. I ball up a fist and pound it on his chest.

"You are horrible! You know that the guy you said it to ended up publishing your hateful words in the newspaper?" I smack him again for good measure. "One of my internship offers got pulled because the boss read your words and decided that your opinion meant more than my several-weeks-long interview process."

"What?" Hunter has the decency to look a little chagrined. "I'm sorry, Juliet. I was just trying to keep that dude from figuring out that you were…"

He trails off. I smack him again. "I was what?"

"You were perfect." He rubs the back of his neck. "Again, I'm really sorry."

What the hell am I supposed to say to that? I look at him, not really knowing what the proper thing to say is.

Thanks? I still hate you? I thought you were dreamy in college, too?

And that's when the panic sets in.

Because this isn't supposed to be real. This is supposed to be a business arrangement with some convenient chemistry on the side. It's not supposed to feel like this. Sometimes it's like he's seeing straight through all my carefully constructed walls to the messy, needy person underneath.

There's a version of this where I lean in. I could kiss him back like I mean it. I could let myself want something more than just survival.

But that version of me? She doesn't exist anymore. Five years of Patrick telling me I was too much, too ambitious, too everything kneecapped her. That version of me got suffocated by the realization that love is just another way to lose yourself.

Juliet Monroe doesn't get to fall. She gets to win. Or she gets to disappear. Not this complicated… whatever this is between us.

I move away, to put some distance between us before I do something stupid like tell him how I really feel.

"I should..." I start, my voice clipped and shaky. "I should probably get some sleep."

But Hunter catches my wrist before I can stand up completely.

"Don't."

I freeze, not sure what he's asking.

"Don't run," he clarifies. "Not tonight."

There's something vulnerable in his voice, something that makes my chest tight. It seems like he's asking for more than just my physical presence.

"Stay with me."

Staring at him, my heart still pounding, my body hums from his touch. I don't know what to say. I don't know if staying would make this better or worse.

All I know is that I'm terrified of how good this felt and how much I want it to happen again. I'm scared shitless of how easy it would be to let myself believe this could be real.

"Hunter," I whisper, but I still don't know how to finish the sentence.

He doesn't push or demand an explanation or try to convince me of anything. He just looks at me with those steady blue-gray eyes and waits for me to decide.

And for the first time in a long time, I don't know what the smart choice is.

The safe choice would be to go to my room. Lock the door. Pretend this never happened and go back to treating this like the business arrangement it's supposed to be.

But sitting here on this couch, looking at Hunter's face in the blue glow of the TV, feeling the warmth of his hand still wrapped around my wrist, I'm not sure I want to be safe anymore.

I'm not sure I want to be smart.

Maybe I want to be reckless. Maybe I want to see what happens when I stop running from things that scare me.

"Okay," I say finally, my voice barely above a whisper. "I'll stay."

Something shifts in his expression. Relief, maybe. Or gratitude. He doesn't say a word. He just pulls me back down onto the couch next to him.

For a moment we sit in silence, the TV murmuring in the background. My heart's still racing, but not from the kiss. From the way he's still holding me, like the doesn't plan to let go.

"I wasn't supposed to be reckless," I hear myself say, surprising us both. My voice is soft but steady. "Not growing up. My mom had this whole blueprint for me. Perfect posture, perfect grades, perfect internships. I was supposed to be polished and professional. Not loud. Not messy. Definitely not reckless."

Hunter glances over, brows pulling together, but he doesn't interrupt. He just waits.

"I tried," I go on, my throat tightening. "God, I tried. But it was never enough. She'd always find something to criticize. My laugh was unprofessional. My hair wasn't right. I wasn't ambitious or cutthroat enough. I was never the daughter she wanted me to be."

The words hang in the dim light between us. My throat aches. I rarely admit this to myself, much less anyone else.

Hunter's jaw flexes. "Sounds like she's the one who wasn't enough. Not you."

I blink hard, not trusting myself to answer.

"What about your dad?" he asks gently.

"He checked out a long time ago," I whisper. "He hides behind his work and lets my mom call the shots. When I'd cry in my room, he'd say she just wanted the best for me. That I'd thank her someday. I'm still waiting for that day."

For a while, neither of us speaks. His hand finds mine and rubs gentle circles into the back of it with his thumb. After the silence stretches for a good long while, I ask, "What about you? What was your childhood like?"

Hunter shifts, eyes on the flickering TV. I'm not sure he even heard me.

"Lonely," he says finally. "After my dad died, it felt like the house went quiet. Everyone was grieving in their own way. My mom… she couldn't look at us without seeing him. So she looked away. A lot."

"I'm sorry about your dad," I whisper. "Being lonely when you're a kid is the absolute worst."

He shrugs. "I had my brothers, but they were just kids too. Hockey was the only place that made sense. The rink was loud, physical, and you could understand the rules. Out there, you either scored or you didn't. You won or you didn't. It was the one place I felt like I had control again."

"Ah. So you dedicated your life to it."

Huxley looks over at me. "Yeah. I guess I haven't really thought about it that way, but I like to be in control. Everything feels better when I'm the one pulling the strings."

I study the hard lines of his face. There's no self-pity in his voice, only fact. But underneath it, I hear the boy who lost his dad too young and had to build armor to survive.

"I'm sorry," I say again. "Can I… give you a hug?"

He shrugs, but his eyes flick to mine. "I would never turn down a hug from you."

I scoot over, slipping my arms around his waist and burying my nose in his t-shirt, hugging him and inhaling his woodsy scent. His smell and the feel of his colossal body pressed against me do something complicated to my brain chemistry. My mouth waters, my skin feels hot, but my mind tries to relax.

This man is turning me into a fucking turnip and I'm trying to get closer. At this moment, if I could crawl inside his chest, I would. He seems to feel similarly because he presses his nose into the crown of my head and breathes me in.

So we're both a little weird, I guess.

We just sit here, watching Swedish Detective Saga piece together clues in her methodical way, pretending we're not both hyperaware of every place our bodies are touching.

But I can feel something has changed between us. We crossed some line we can't uncross. And as much as that terrifies me, there's a part of me that's relieved.

Because pretending not to want him was exhausting. Pretending this was all just fake was becoming impossible.

Now I just have to figure out what the hell I'm going to do about it.

Chapter 25

Hunter

I wake up early to find Juliet still curled against me on the couch. Her face is soft in the morning light filtering through the windows. We fell asleep watching that Swedish show, tangled together like we've been doing this for years instead of just pretending for a few months.

She looks smaller when she's sleeping and vulnerable in a way she never lets herself be when she's awake. Her red lipstick is mostly gone, smeared somewhere between the couch cushions and my mouth. Without it, she looks younger. More real.

I should wake her up. Untangle myself and go make coffee and pretend last night was just another step in our fake relationship playbook. Instead, I carefully lift her into my arms.

She stirs slightly as I carry her to my bedroom, making this soft sound that goes straight through me. But she doesn't wake up, just settles deeper into my chest like she belongs there.

I tell myself it's just the setup. Just two people playing pretend, maintaining the illusion in case anyone checks our social media or asks invasive questions about our living situation. But then I see her curled up in my bed, wearing my old hoodie she must have grabbed at some point, her mouth parted slightly.

And I feel something I don't have a name for. Something I don't want to feel.

Because if I let this become real, if I let myself actually want her, I know I'll screw it up. I always do. I'm amazing at hockey and I suck at everything else, especially for people who matter. And this time, I wouldn't just lose her. I'd *ruin* her.

She wakes up an hour later, blinking slowly in the dim light of my bedroom. For a second, she looks confused, like she's trying to remember how she got here. Then her eyes find mine, and something shifts in her expression.

"Morning," she says. Her voice is still rough with sleep.

"Morning."

We're both acutely aware of the fact that she's in my bed, wearing my clothes, looking like she belongs here. The tension that's been building between us for weeks feels like a live wire now, crackling in the space between us.

I tip her chin up with a finger, kissing her gently. Her breath hitches and she presses forward, deepening the kiss. Her eyes flutter closed for a moment, enjoying the way I run my mouth down the column of her throat. I keep my touches light, avoiding her breasts and hips and ass. She throws her leg over me, her soft gasps driving straight into my fucking cerebellum.

My cock, already hard when I woke up, is painfully aware of every single sound that leaves her perfect mouth. I bite my lip and smooth my hand up her thigh. Juliet Monroe is going to kill me.

But when I don't push for more, just continue kissing her

neck and ears, she opens her eyes and levels me with a gaze. "You're playing with me."

"Maybe a little." My lips twitch. "I'm enjoying getting you worked up."

"I want you to take control, Hux. I think you like to dominate. Show me. Show me what it's like when you get rough."

God *damn*. Does she even have the faintest idea of what her words do to me?

"Monroe." I shake my head. "You don't know what you're asking for."

"Maybe not." She sounds breathless. "But I won't know unless I try. Maybe I'll like it rough."

She's serious as an open grave, tempting me to do the dark, wicked things that I want to do to her. She's tiny and fragile. I could snap her bones by accident just by putting my full weight on them.

"Juliet…" I grab her chin, pinning her with my gaze.

She rakes her nails down my chest, giving me chills. "Yes?"

"I can't do this halfway. If I take control, it's mine until you say stop." My eyes bore into hers, trying to make sure she understands.

She smirks. "Like a… secret code?"

Sliding my hand into her hair, I tug her head back, running my nose along her exposed throat. "A safe word. How about Firecracker?"

Juliet's eyes sparkle, and she grins. "Sounds good."

I draw my finger in a line down her collarbone and between her breasts.

"Until I hear your safe word, Monroe, everything is on the table. Spanking, sex toys, restraints, spitting, edging, anal…"

"I want to walk on the wild side for once." She licks her plump lips. "Bring it on, Huxley."

Gripping her hair harder, I kiss her fiercely. She takes everything I have to give her and returns it to me, hips bucking against me, her mouth opening to let me in. It's a little hard for me to take in for a second.

Could Juliet actually like this fucked up, kinky shit? That's impossible to wrap my head around.

"Juliet." I mean to keep it low and casual, but my voice comes out a hungry rasp. "Come here."

She slides over without a word, practically in my lap before I can reach for her. I wind a hand in her hair and pull, just hard enough to make her gasp, and she climbs onto me, straddling my thighs. It's not a test of wills anymore. It's need, pure and simple.

I run my hands up her calves, skimming over the soft skin. I pause when I get to her thighs and squeeze. She shivers.

"Is this what you want?" I ask. "You want me to take what I need from you?"

She answers with a kiss, messy and too hard, lipstick dragging over my lips. "Stop asking. *Take it.*"

I laugh, my tone a little mean. "You trying to run the show? That's not how this works, Monroe."

Her eyes go wide and then narrow, as if she's weighing whether to bite my head off or just give in. I'm rooting for the latter.

"Maybe I like it better when you're not in control," I whisper, my mouth at her ear.

"Then show me," she dares, voice shaking a little. "Prove it."

That's all I need. I grip her ass and lift her. Her legs lock around my waist. She's so tiny it's ridiculous, but the way she presses her hips into me makes me feel like I'm the one being devoured.

If I ever doubted how badly she craves my cock, now I'm certain. I push her away, my heated gaze on her body.

"Strip," I tell her. Instantly she nods, wriggling out of her oversized hoodie, tank top, and silky sleep shorts with zero pretense.

She's fucking beautiful. Incredible tits, perfect hips, toned legs, and an unstoppable ass. The hottest girl I've ever seen, bar none. And she's looking at me like she's parched and I'm the cool drink of water that she's been praying for. *Fuck.*

I take off my shirt slowly, just to watch her squirm, then drop my sweats and climb onto the bed.

Her jaw drops. "It *is* huge. I knew it was big, but… *damn*, Hunter."

I love the surprised tone of her voice. I arch a brow. "Were you under the mistaken impression that my cock might not match the rest of my body?"

"*No.*" She flushes. "Just saying. I'm not even sure how you and I are supposed to fit together."

"We'll make it fit," I say with a smug little grin. "But not right now. First… I want to lick your pussy. I've been dreaming about how good your cum tastes, Firecracker."

"Such a filthy mouth," she chides.

I drop a kiss on her collarbone. "You love it."

Juliet looks up at me, naked before me, arms above her head, lips a bright red slash against her flushed skin. Her nipples harden, and the sight of her tits, full, perfect, tipped with dusky-pink nipples poking out at me, makes me stop and stare.

"You're obsessed," she says, rolling her eyes.

"I like your tits," I admit, not bothering to hide it. "I'd be an idiot not to be a little obsessed. Look at you. I'm obsessed with every part of you. Tits, ass, and especially this soft, pink pussy. I could eat this pussy all goddamn day. I would die a fortunate man if you were my last fucking meal."

"*Hux.*" The way she moans my name makes me so goddamn hard. "You're killing me."

"Am I? Let's see."

I run my thumb over her nipple, circling lazily, then drag my palm down her ribs, mapping every inch like I'm memorizing her. I stop at her hips, digging in with my hands, kneading until she arches.

She tries to touch me, reaching for my shoulders, but I catch her wrists and pin them together above her head. She moans, the sound low and breathy, and it makes my cock twitch.

"Stay," I command. Juliet does, her arms straining but not pulling away.

I grab her discarded tank top, looping it around her wrists and tying a loose knot. She could wriggle out if she wanted, but the point isn't the restraint. It's the surrender. She tests it, pulling once, and then lies still, eyes locked on mine.

"Are you still okay with this?" I ask, softening just for a second. If she even has a moment of hesitation, I'll stop. I've chased off half a dozen meaningless hookups with my need for dominance.

I won't risk Juliet Monroe getting cold feet when she's naked in my bed. Having her soft and willing is more important than fucking her exactly how I want to.

"I'm sure." She nods her head, the movement impatient. "Don't you dare stop."

I give her a slick grin. "Didn't plan on it."

I lean in and kiss her, starting slow, tasting her mouth and the faint tang of her lipstick. She kisses back with teeth, nipping at my lower lip, then opening for me, letting me take over.

I move down, lips trailing along her jaw, her throat, her collarbone. I bite the spot where her shoulder curves, sucking until I know it will bruise. She groans, pushing up into my mouth, and I reward her by dragging my tongue lower.

Her tits are next. I take one in my hand, squeezing, then close my mouth over her nipple, sucking hard enough that she whimpers. I flick it with my tongue, then bite, and she bucks against me, thighs squeezing my hips.

"Jesus, Hunter—"

"Yeah?" I ask, switching to the other nipple. "You like that?"

She gasps, then lets out a full-bodied moan. It echoes around the room, dirty and desperate. It heats my blood.

"You are such a tits guy," she accuses, breathless.

I look up at her and smirk, mouth still wrapped around her nipple. "Not true. I'm an everything guy."

She laughs, but it dissolves into another moan as I move down, kissing her sternum, her ribs, the delicate skin of her stomach. I stop at her bellybutton and swirl my tongue around it, feeling her shudder.

When I get to her hip bones, I pause, hands planted on her thighs to hold her in place.

"Want me to stop?" I tease.

"Don't stop," she pants. "Please."

I spread her legs and look down at her pussy, just to torture her. She's soaking, folds slick and glistening. I drag my fingers through her wetness, circling her clit, then spreading her wider so I can see everything. She tries to close her legs but I hold her open, loving the way it makes her blush.

"Look at you," I marvel. "You're pussy is a goddamn masterpiece. So fucking wet and ready for me."

"Oh *god*." She moans as I lick her inner thigh. "You're killing me, Huxley."

I lower my mouth and lick, starting slow, just the tip of my tongue flicking at her clit. She jerks, every muscle going tight. I hold her down, licking harder, then sucking her clit between my lips and letting it go with a pop.

"Fuck—" she gasps, hips rolling, trying to chase the sensation.

I bring my hand up, pressing two fingers against her entrance, teasing just a little before sliding them inside. She's hot and so fucking tight I have to work my way in, curling my fingers to find the spot that will drive her insane.

The second I touch her g-spot, she goes rigid, back arching off the mattress.

"That's it," I murmur. I work her clit with my tongue for a moment. "Let go, Monroe. Come for me like a good fucking girl."

She does. Her whole body clenches. She comes hard, noise raw and guttural. I keep going, licking and stroking, not stopping even as she trembles beneath my hands.

She pants. I look up at her. "You like me telling you that you've been good, don't you?"

Juliet sucks in a breath, turning pink, and nods slowly. I reward her by humming against her flesh, burying my face against her hot pussy. She groans and bucks her hips, unable to move her arms.

She's not just tolerating my being a fucking caveman. She *likes* this. That stirs something deep inside me.

I grin, fingers still moving inside her, and go back down. This time I fuck her channel with my tongue, spearing in and out, savoring the taste of her. She claws at the sheets, hands bound and trembling, making desperate little noises.

"Mmm. You taste so fucking good, Firecracker."

The second orgasm hits her even harder. She screams, actually screams, and I'm pretty sure my neighbors are going to hate me forever.

Fuck them. They're not Juliet Monroe, with the glorious, golden pussy. I want to live in this moment for fucking *ever*.

Her legs go limp, but I'm not done. I give her a minute, kissing her inner thighs, then start again, this time with just my mouth. I circle her clit, slow and steady, and her whole body shakes.

"Hunter—" she warns, voice already breaking.

"Tell me to stop," I say. I kiss her clit, my face messy, unable to smell anything but delicate citrus and heady sex. "Say firecracker."

She doesn't stop me, just moans again. I forge ahead, focusing solely on her clit this time. She's already trembling, quaking, after the first two rounds. She slides her hands into my hair and whines.

"I can't." Her breath comes in gasps. "Hux, I–"

I just hum against her, the vibrations passing from my mouth to her glistening clit. She contorts and bucks against my mouth. I glance up and see Juliet with her mouth open, eyes clenched shut, a groan rattling from her chest.

This is what I want. What I *need*. She's so fucking sexy right now when she's unable to pull her shields into place.

"Are you going to come again?" I ask.

She nods, feverish, eyes clenched hard. "I'm so close."

"I want to hear it." I rear back, spit on her clit, and murmur, "I want to hear my name on your lips when you come for me like a good fucking girl."

As soon as I dive back in, my lips encircling and sucking

on her clit, she shakes violently, falling apart. Her third orgasm rips through her like a live wire, back arching, thighs crushing my head. I keep licking, determined to wring every drop of pleasure out of her. Only when she collapses fully, hair plastered to her face, breathing like she just ran a marathon, do I finally let up.

I crawl up her body and untie her wrists, massaging the marks left by her straining at the knotted camisole. She looks at me, eyes glazed, lips parted, like she's forgotten how to speak.

"Are you alive?" I prompt.

She nods, limp as a rag doll, and then giggles, high and delirious.

"That was…" she says, but can't finish the sentence.

I kiss her, long and deep, letting her taste herself on my tongue. She moans into my mouth, greedy for it. When I break away, she chases my lips, hands scrabbling for any part of me she can reach.

She tries to slide her hand down to my cock, but I stop her.

"No," I say, voice going dark. "You're not in charge right now."

She grins, then pouts, batting her eyelashes. "So what happens now?"

I kneel over her, cock in my hand, already leaking pre-come. She watches, transfixed, as I stroke myself. I brace one hand against the headboard and jerk my cock, slow and rough, never looking away from her face. My piercing catches the light and I bite my lip.

It increases the pleasure for both of us. Or it will as soon as I fuck her. That'll have to happen *soon*.

She watches me with huge, blown pupils, chest still heaving. Looking at her naked body, still flushed from orgasm, makes me groan. Her citrus and musk scent is in my nose and I huff a breath, trying to get more of it.

My cock throbs, my balls tensing already. I'm on the precipice. When I come, I shoot all over her stomach, hot and messy, painting her skin with it. I watch the realization hit her. She enjoys being marked up, loves knowing she did this to me.

I smear my cum across her belly, rubbing it into her skin with my palm. She groans, writhing a little. I dip my fingers into the mess and bring them to her lips. She opens, tongue flicking out, tasting me without hesitation.

"Good girl," I whisper. "That's perfect, Monroe."

She glows, eyes closing. I flop down beside her and gather her in my arms. She's soft and melty, all the fight gone out of her, and I like it more than I should.

We're supposed to be enemies. But enemies don't do what we just did so very well. Unless hate sex counts… that could be something.

We lie together, trying to catch our breath, defenseless for just these few moments. She moves a little, and her arm catches my cum, which is still smeared across her stomach. Seeing her discomfort, I roll out of bed, grab a warm washcloth from the bathroom, and return to wipe her clean. She lets me, quiet and content, eyes watching me with something that looks a hell of a lot like trust.

What do I do to earn that? And how do I keep it?

When she's cleaned up, I tuck her under the covers and slide in next to her. She says nothing, just curls into me, her hand pressed over my heart.

She's glowing in the soft light, with a faint smile on her lips, like she's holding onto a secret. But I'm already in my head, already withdrawing, already pretending like it didn't mean everything.

Because it meant everything. And that's the problem.

Not only did Juliet just let me dominate her. But she liked it. She *asked* for it. What am I supposed to do with the information that my fake fiancée might be just as kinky as me?

"You okay?" she asks quietly.

"Yeah. Fine."

It's a lie and we both know it. But she doesn't push, just watches me with those dark eyes like she's trying to solve a puzzle with missing pieces.

I should feel satisfied. Mission accomplished, fake relationship believably consummated, whatever.

Instead, I feel exposed. Stripped bare in a way that has nothing to do with the fact that we're both naked.

The silence stretches between us until it becomes unbearable.

"Why don't you ever talk about your mom?" she asks suddenly.

The question hits me like a punch to the gut. Of all the things she could have asked, that's the one I'm least prepared for.

"What do you mean?"

"You talk about your brothers sometimes. But never your mom."

I sit up, running both hands through my hair. This conversation is dangerous territory, but something about the way she's looking at me makes it impossible to deflect.

"There's not much to say."

"Hunter."

My name in her voice like that, gentle but insistent, breaks something loose in my chest. I roll onto my side facing Juliet and prop my hand on my head.

"She used to manage my money. She stopped being just my mom then; she was my agent too. When I got drafted, she had me convinced that she would look out for me. Keep it in the family, she said. Trust the people who love you."

Juliet doesn't interrupt, doesn't fill the silence with platitudes or advice. She just listens. I pick my next words carefully.

"Mom stole from me. Millions over years. She set up accounts I didn't know about, moved money around, told me the investments were performing badly, when really she was just taking it." The words taste bitter in my mouth. "When it all came out, she didn't even deny it. Just blamed me for making it easy."

"Jesus, Hunter."

"Yeah." I laugh, but there's no humor in it. "Best part? She told me I was ungrateful. She said everything she did was for the family. It sounded like stealing from me was some kind of *sacrifice* that she made. It all got twisted and turned and convoluted."

I can feel Juliet watching me, processing this information. She's probably wondering what kind of person lets their own mother rob them blind. My not seeing it coming and that it went on for years, unchecked, still shames me on the deepest level.

There's a reason I never talk about my mom.

"I'm sorry," she says finally.

"Don't be. I should have known better."

She touches my forearm, etching the tattoos I have there. "No, you shouldn't have. She was your mom. You should've been able to trust her."

The simple certainty in her voice does something to me. Because she's right, but I've spent so long blaming myself for being naïve that I'd forgotten that.

The weight in my chest eases for the first time all day. She makes the noise in my head vanish.

"Do you ever miss your dad?" she asks gently, shifting the subject slightly but not completely.

I shrug. "Not really."

It's automatic, the response I always give when people ask about him. Clean. Simple. Final.

But lying here next to Juliet, still feeling raw and exposed from everything we just shared, it doesn't feel true anymore.

Because sometimes, I miss him. I miss the dad he was before the drinking got bad. Before the gambling consumed everything. Before he became someone I didn't recognize.

I miss fishing trips and hockey lessons in the backyard. He used to ruffle my hair and say he was proud, and I miss it. I thought that he'd always be there, that he'd always choose us over whatever demons were chasing him.

I miss having a father.

But I don't say any of that. Some things are still too raw, too complicated to put into words.

Later, after Juliet has gone to take a shower and I can hear the water running through the walls, I pull out my journal. It's filled with practice notes and play diagrams and random thoughts I don't know what else to do with. It also has letters to my mom, to my brothers, and to my old coaches.

Anybody that I wanted to scream at, but couldn't.

I flip past the lists and sketches and scrawled observations about weak spots in opposing teams' defenses. I land on a blank page and pick up a pen.

Dear Dad, I write, then stare at the words for a long time.

What do you say to a dead man? How do you start a conversation that should have happened years ago?

I'm playing the best hockey of my life. You'd probably be proud. Or maybe you'd find something to criticize. Hard to know.

I met someone. She's... complicated. Smart. Way too good for me. She makes me want things I didn't think I could want.

I wish you were here to meet her. See how I've grown up. I wish you were here to tell me how to navigate this minefield I've trapped myself in.

I close the journal before I can write anything else. Some conversations are better left unfinished.

When Juliet comes back, hair damp and smelling like my shower gel, she finds me on the couch flipping through my sketchbook. It's another old habit, something that keeps my hands busy when my brain won't shut up.

She settles next to me, close enough that I can feel the heat radiating from her skin.

"What are you drawing?"

I look up at her. Normally, I would hide my notepad and make a sarcastic comment. That's my go-to. But since I just painted her with my cum, I'm feeling a little soft. Lying to her seems wrong.

"I *sketch*," I clarify. "And I write. Sometimes when I can't sleep, it helps me to get out whatever's bothering me."

She peers over my shoulder as I flip through the pages. There are rough sketches of plays, a few landscapes from road trips, random observations of teammates in unguarded moments.

And then I flip to a page I forgot was there.

It's her.

Not sexy or romantic or posed. Just Juliet reading on this same couch, feet tucked under her, hair tied up in a messy bun. Soft. Still. Safe.

I drew it weeks ago, some night when I couldn't sleep and she'd fallen asleep with a book open on her chest. I didn't intend it to be anything. Just my hands working while my brain processed things I didn't want to think about.

She says nothing about it.

But her silence makes it worse.

That sketch wasn't for her. Wasn't part of the game or the PR plan or anything I know how to explain. It was just for me. I wanted to remember what she looked like when she didn't know I was watching.

Now it's out in the open, and I feel like I've been gutted.

"That's..." she starts, then stops.

"It's nothing," I say quickly, flipping the page. "Just something to do with my hands."

"Hunter."

"Really, it's not a big deal."

But it is a big deal. It's the biggest deal. Because that sketch proves what I've been trying not to admit even to myself.

My feelings for her have morphed from fake and ridiculous to… something else.

And caring about people is dangerous for someone like me. People who care about me get hurt. Get disappointed. Get stolen from or lied to or abandoned.

"I should probably get moving," I say, closing the notebook and standing up. "I have a team meeting this afternoon."

She watches me retreat. I can see the wheels turning in her head. She knows I'm running from this conversation, from the implications of that sketch, from whatever this thing between us is becoming.

But she doesn't call me on it. She just nods and sits up. "I'll let you get ready."

After she leaves the room, I sit back down and stare at the closed notebook in my hands.

Five months. That was the deal. Five months of fake engagement, then we go our separate ways.

I'm sitting here in my bedroom, still smelling her perfume

on my clothes, still tasting her kiss on my lips. I'm thinking the remaining two and a half months are going to go by in the blink of an eye.

And that terrifies me more than any opponent I've ever faced on the ice.

Because this time, when I inevitably screw it up, it's not just going to hurt me.

It's going to destroy us both.

Chapter 26

Juliet

I'm in the kitchen before eight in the morning, standing on tiptoes in a short black skirt and thigh high socks. Currently, my arms are elbow-deep in a bag of Pillsbury flour. I'm not even sure where the flour came from. This apartment had never had real groceries before I moved in.

But last night's sex left me feeling restless and sugar-starved, so I impulse-bought chocolate chips, brown sugar, Tahitian vanilla, and eggs. The flour puffs in a slow-motion mushroom cloud as I pour, dusting the dark countertops and sticking to my arms, the dark gray sleeve of Hunter's old hockey hoodie rolled up over my elbow. The place smells like cinnamon and butter, the way I always dreamed my home would smell one day when I grew up.

My childhood kitchen was spacious and even more luxurious than this one, but I can't recall anyone ever using it. My mom and dad took me out to dinner a lot, or when left to my own devices, I ate pizza or Chinese. I don't think a tray of cookies ever made it into my oven at my parent's house.

That's what you get when your parents work really long hours and leave you to fend for yourself. But today, I woke up wanting fresh-baked cookies. And the easiest way to get them seemed to be… this. I look around at the flour and eggshells scattered across the counter.

I'm trying something *new*.

I have to stop and check the recipe at every step. My hands move clunkily. Crack the eggs, whisk the sugar, add too much vanilla, mess up the order of the steps and pretend it doesn't matter. All the while, my brain is running a slow-motion reel of every second spent with Hunter in the hours before dawn.

The way he took me apart, piece by piece. He acted like I was the first beautiful thing he ever touched and he wanted to learn how I worked. The way he called me a good girl, over and over, like no one else had ever been good for him. Plus, he made me come so hard my vision went white, then cleaned me up with a hot rag and tucked me in like I was his.

If there is a heaven, I'm pretty sure that was it. I've never felt so delightfully boneless before.

It's embarrassing how badly I want to replay it. My entire body hums when I think about him calling me Monroe in that gruff voice. His hands gripped my waist, guiding and steady, even when I tried to act like I was in control. He made me come three times and never once called me the wrong name.

Something that I must admit was a regular occurrence with Patrick. I figured all guys just had terrible memories when their dicks were hard. I think Hunter broke that illusion, but I'm not mad.

Is it a problem that I can't think of Hunter Huxley today without a secret little smile?

I slide the first tray of cookies into the oven and set a timer, leaning against the counter. The kitchen is warm, and the city outside the window is all wet light and noise, early morning delivery trucks echoing off glass towers. My phone is face-down on the counter, vibrating every few minutes with notifications I'm ignoring.

Probably Ivy texting a million fire emojis or Jessa sending the latest photoshopped meme of me and Hunter. I don't check. I want this domestic bubble to last five more minutes before the world calls bullshit.

The oven ticks. The smell gets sweeter, richer. It almost drowns out the low-grade dread building in my stomach.

When the cookies are finally done, I pull the tray out with my bare hands, hissing as I remember too late that I'm not immune to heat. I drop the pan back on the rack and pick up a kitchen towel, cursing. I set them down on the stove and blow on my fingertips, watching the chocolate chips bubble and settle.

The cookies are irregular, mutant, nothing like the Insta-gram-perfect plates on my feed, but they look good. Maybe even good enough to eat with someone else.

Before I can psych myself out, my phone pings again, this time with a distinct vibration pattern. A news alert. I fumble for it, my thumb leaving a crescent of chocolate on the home button. The headline is already trending.

"HAVOC STAR'S FIANCÉE BLINDSIDES EX WITH NEW 'ENGAGEMENT'," the push notification screams. My stomach drops. There's a subhead: "Patrick Delacroix Breaks His Silence on Juliet Monroe's Wedding-to-Be." I scroll through, seeing that it links to Patrick being interviewed by some bro-dude for his podcast.

Hesitating, I push play.

"She was always driven," Patrick says in the clip. "But never through love. I think the only thing she ever really cared about was winning. Her dreams were huge, her ambi-tion even bigger."

A sick feeling swirls in my stomach.

"If you know Juliet, you know she was born for the podium, not the altar. She doesn't know how to make space for another person in her life. Never has."

My cheeks go hot. *Is this real?* I keep listening against my better judgment:

"Juliet Monroe was so focused on her own image, her own hustle, that she never made room for anything else. Not even me."

There's a photo below the interview, a candid from the year we dated. Me in a very demure blue ballgown, arms folded, standing next to Patrick's trophy wife mom at a charity gala. I glare at the camera like the person taking my picture spat in my drink.

My phone grows heavy in my hand, and I turn it off. I want to be furious, but the truth is I don't have the energy. Because Patrick's not wrong, not really, not about the core. I'm cold. Sometimes, I'm obsessed with image and control. I have never, not once, let myself need another person so badly that I can't survive without them.

My parents taught me that and Patrick drove the lesson home. If you let people see your weak and vulnerable sides, they can decide that they don't want you. Don't want to deal with you. You're too much, too loud, too *everything*.

I can't let that happen again. Not after Patrick.

A door creaks open. Heavy footsteps pad down the hallway. I freeze halfway to the table, and try to look like someone who isn't coming apart at the seams.

Hunter emerges, shirtless, hair damp from the shower, sweatpants hanging low on his hips. His eyes are sleepy, but when they land on me, there's a flash of something. Concern maybe, or just his usual predatory awareness.

"Hey," he says, voice raspy. "Smells good in here."

"Don't get too excited," I say, forcing a smile. "I may have forgotten the salt."

He glances at the cookies, then at my face. His mouth twitches, almost a smile, then he goes to the cabinet and pulls out mugs, setting them next to the stove. Whether I want coffee is never a question. He just makes it, black for him and, without looking, a splash of oat milk for me. He slides my mug across the counter. The cookie tray is still between us, steaming.

"Rough morning?" he asks. His question is casual enough that it doesn't sound like he's fishing.

"I didn't sleep well," I lie. Taking a sip of coffee, I let the taste ground me. I want to tell him about the podcast, about the way Patrick's words still sting, but the idea of saying them out loud makes my tongue feel impossibly large in my mouth.

Hunter doesn't push. He leans on the counter, biceps flexed, watching me in that way he does when he's trying to read the scoreboard before the first period even starts.

I break the silence by sliding a cookie toward him. "They're not exactly grandma quality, but—"

He grabs one, still hot, and takes a giant bite, almost burning himself. Chocolate smears the corner of his mouth, but he doesn't notice. He opens his mouth and groans.

"These are fucking incredible," he says, voice thick. He swallows. "You should open a bakery."

I snort. "No one involved would like that, Hux."

He shakes his head, chewing. "No, I'm serious. Best cookies I've had in years."

He says it so earnestly that my face goes warm again. He's obviously insane. That, or he doesn't have many cookies. It's probably that one, seeing as how he's a professional athlete with a team performance kitchen and dietician. I look down at the counter, resisting the urge to fidget with my hair.

The silence grows. It isn't awkward exactly, but it's charged in a way that makes my skin prickle. I can feel him watching me, not just my body, but the way my fingers drum the side of the mug, the way my eyes keep darting to the phone screen. He knows something's off, and the longer I sit here, the more I want to tell him.

But before I can, his own phone buzzes. He checks the notifications, reads something, and grimaces.

"Looks like Silas got in a brawl at a bar last night," he says, passing me his phone. There's a photo of Silas, hair soaked in beer, face-to-face with some massive asshole, fists cocked. "Matthew Wallen, that douchebag from the Vancouver Vipers. Why they were in the same bar, I have no idea. They hate each other."

I scan the article, muscle memory taking over as I make mental notes. I'm thinking about what angle to play in the press release, whether we should paint Silas as a victim or a hero, and how to control the narrative before it gets out of hand.

"Do you want me to call Coach Cross?" I ask, already drafting an email in my head. "Or should we wait for the league to weigh in before we start damage control?"

Hunter shrugs, muscles rippling. "Up to you. If it were me, I'd want you in my corner. But Silas might prefer to handle it himself."

I nod, thinking about how different the three Huxley brothers are. Silas with his quiet discipline, Jett with his cocky bravado, Hunter with the walls he builds and the fists he throws. I like that he trusts me enough to let me take charge, even if it's only for a minute.

"Maybe we wait," I say finally. "Give it a chance to blow

over first. Something else might happen in the next few hours that sucks the oxygen away from the story."

Hunter grins, a real one this time. "Good call, Firecracker."

I roll my eyes. "Don't start with the nicknames again."

He laughs, the sound low and unguarded. I feel the sound low in my stomach, for a second remembering the events of yesterday. The way his mouth felt on my skin, the way his hands gripped my thighs like he never wanted to let go.

I think about telling him. Genuinely, I do. I imagine saying the words.

Hey, I saw what Patrick said about me, and it gutted me. I need you to tell me I'm not cold or impossible to love. I want you to say that I'm not just a placeholder for the real thing.

But I don't. I can't. I don't have the guts to ask my worst enemy to comfort me.

Instead, I finish my coffee and busy myself cleaning the kitchen, wiping flour from the counter and stacking the dirty bowls in the sink. Hunter watches for a moment, then stands and moves behind me, crowding me against the counter.

He rests a hand on my hip, the touch light but grounding.

I turn around, and he's there. From here, it's impossible to miss the stormy gray of his eyes, the faint pink scar under his left cheekbone, the place where his hair refuses to behave no matter how often he brushes it down.

"Jesus," I whisper, startled.

He grins. "You always get this flustered around me, Monroe?"

I roll my eyes, but my heart rate spikes anyway. "Only when you sneak up on me. Do you want another cookie?"

He ignores the cookies. "Do you want another orgasm?"

My hands tighten on the edge of the counter. My face

goes instantly hot, blood rushing in all the places he made it rush last night.

"You liked it," he says, voice velvet-rough. "When I made you come."

I can't look at him, so I stare at the kitchen tile. I want to deny it, joke, or brush him off, but everyone can see the truth on my face.

"I liked it," I admit, the words small and hot.

"Just liked it?" He moves closer. I swear I feel heat radiating off his skin. His hand is heavy on the counter beside mine, boxing me in. "Because I can't stop thinking about it. You. The sounds you made. The way you looked at me when I made you come all over my face."

I'm speechless. For once in my over-scheduled, over-articulated life, I have nothing to say.

He leans down, his breath hot at my ear. "I bet you're already wet, thinking about it."

My pulse jumps. He's right. It's humiliating how fast my body betrays me. My nipples harden, my lower body knots, and heat gathers between my thighs. God, I'm so easy. I toss back my head, staring up at him, a challenge.

"Is that what you wanted to ask me?" I shoot back, desperate to reclaim an inch of high ground.

"No," he says. "I wanted to see if you'd beg for it."

He kisses me before I can answer. Not gently. There's nothing gentle about Hunter Huxley when he wants something. It's open-mouthed, greedy, and it steals the oxygen right out of my lungs. I kiss him back, frantic, my hands on his bare skin, scrabbling to pull him closer.

He makes a sound deep in his chest, almost a growl. In the next second he's lifting me onto the counter, cookies rattling behind me as he crowds my knees apart and slots himself between my thighs. He's already hard, pressing against me through both our layers of clothing, and my body answers before my brain can catch up.

It's chaos. His mouth on my neck, his teeth grazing my jaw, my hands clawing under his shirt to feel the perfect abs I've been dying to touch since the day I saw them glisten with sweat at training camp. My legs wrap around him, heels digging into his back. He palms my ass, squeezing, and I gasp.

"We're supposed to be fake dating," I gasp, biting down on the word fake like it's the last defense I have.

He bites my shoulder in retaliation, just enough to leave a mark. "This doesn't feel fake."

It doesn't. It feels terrifyingly, deliciously real. I slide my hands lower, under the waistband of his sweats, finding skin, muscle, the ridge of his cock straining under thin cotton.

"You're perfect," he growls, staring at my tits like he's seeing something rare and precious. "I want you. Right now."

I want him too. But I'm terrified of how much it means. I think about what Patrick said about how I'm exhausting to love.

Distracted by Hunter nibbling at my neck, I wonder if this is all just a fever dream that will end poorly.

He senses the hesitation. His hands soften, brushing a strand of hair behind my ear. "Tell me to stop," he whispers. "Use your safe word, Monroe."

I shake my head. "I don't want you to stop."

I grind against him, rubbing myself on his cock, desperate for friction. He moans, hands everywhere. Tugging my hair, gripping my hips, squeezing my tits like he can't get enough.

He never asks for permission. He just takes it. Every time he takes, he gives back double. He kisses me until my lips are swollen, then drags his mouth down my neck, biting and sucking, leaving a trail of heat behind.

"In the bedroom," he commands, picking me up as he carries me through the apartment. He grunts as he sets me down on the mattress.

I claw at his sweatpants, yanking them down just enough to free his cock. His cock is massive, bigger than any I've ever seen. I'm not sure whether to be impressed or afraid. And his piercing… I can't wait to find out exactly how that feels inside me.

Orgasmic, I'm willing to bet. My pussy gets wetter every fucking time I think about him filling me and stretching me out.

Hunter slides my panties off, the movement slow and deliberate. He takes a second to look at me, splayed out on his bed, hair a mess, cheeks flushed, breasts high and proud. The admiration in his eyes makes me feel like art.

His mouth is hot and hungry. He licks up the inside of my leg, then bites down hard enough to leave a mark. I yelp, the sound ricocheting off the bedroom walls, but he doesn't stop. He spreads my legs with both hands, rough and urgent. His tongue finds my clit, circling, flicking, then sucking it into his mouth with the precision of a man who has spent years perfecting this exact skill.

I don't want to think about how fucking good he is at this.

Grabbing the back of his head, I anchor myself so I don't float out of my body. I can feel him smirking against my skin when I try to squirm away. He just pins my hips down and goes harder.

"Oh my god," I gasp. I make an inarticulate noise of pleasure.

He looks up at me, eyes full of pride and predatory intent, and then grips my thighs hand enough to leave a mark. "Say my name."

"Hunter," I pant. I say it again when he plunges his tongue inside me. "Hunter, oh god, don't stop."

He grins, stubble scratching my thighs. He drives me over the edge with a final, devastating flick. I come so hard I nearly black out, the world narrowing to nothing but the vibration of his tongue, the press of his hands, and endless, throbbing, mindless pleasure.

He chuckles as I descend back to earth from whatever plane he sent me to. "Ready to use your safe word, Monroe?"

"Not a fucking chance," I rasp. "Not even close."

"Good, because I want to thrust my cock so deep into your pussy that it kills us both."

Before I can come up with a suitable answer to his ridiculous words, he flips me onto my stomach, yanks my hips up, and bumps his cock up against my pussy lips. My lower muscles clench in anticipation.

"God damn," he mutters. "You're so pretty here."

I breathe out a shaky breath. I feel his fingers spreading my pussy, exploring my wetness. "You're so wet for me, Monroe. Your body knows that I'm going to need extra lubrication, huh?"

"Just shut up and fuck me, Huxley," I order. I'm glad I'm facing the mattress because my cheeks are scarlet.

"Yes, ma'am." There's a moment of hesitation where I feel him slip from the bed and grab something from his bedside drawer. A condom, I realize, when I hear the scratching crinkle of Hunter ripping open the wrapper.

I should've thought of that. Hunter's got me so fucking worked up that I can't think straight. He rolls it on, spits on his cock, lines it up with my aching pussy, and buries himself inside me in one savage thrust.

My mouth opens in a silent scream. His cock is so big that it *hurts*.

It's too much. It's not enough. I want to cry from how good he feels, from how unprepared I am to be taken this way. I'm stretched from the inside out by his enormous cock, my walls trembling, my pussy twitching.

"Good girl," he coaxes. "You're fucking strangling my cock, Firecracker. Relax for me."

At the sound of his praise, my cheeks heat. I bite my lip, craning my neck to look back at him. He makes eye contact with me, grabbing my hips, his eyes sparkling with a dark light. I lick my lips and try to relax.

As soon as Hunter moves in earnest, he doesn't go gentle for even one moment. He fucks me with single-minded ferocity, every stroke threatening to split me in two. The breath leaves me with each thrust.

"You're so wet for me, Monroe. Did I do this to you?"

My pussy clenches at that. "Yes," I whisper. "Fuck yes, Hux."

My eyes roll up into my head. It's nearly violent, and yet… It's the hottest thing anyone has ever done to me.

And make no mistake, Hunter is doing this to me. He's Chopin and I'm his piano, helpless as he plays his "Revolutionary" étude.

"Fuck, you're so tight. So perfect for me," he mutters.

His hands roam my body, up my ribs, over my back, tangled in my hair, like he's mapping every inch, claiming it. He leans forward, weight braced on my shoulders, and pounds into me until the bed frame actually breaks, the entire structure collapsing with a groan and a spectacular crash.

I shriek, half-laughing, half-horrified. "Oh my god, you animal."

Hunter stops, chuckles, and pulls me down onto the floor. He lies down and encourages me to straddle him. "Come on, Firecracker."

I blush. "You want me to be on top? Don't guys have trouble staying hard like that?"

"What?" He looks genuinely puzzled. Then he fists his hard cock. "Does this answer your question, sweetheart?"

God. Patrick hated me being the one in control. He could only come when he was on top and I was silent. I guess it's time to unlearn some lessons he taught me.

I climb onto Hunter's lap, straddling him, and meet the tip of his fat cock as I sink down on it. I can feel his piercing touching the wall of my pussy as he thrusts upward gently. *Oh. Oh, wow.*

"Talk to me, Juliet. Tell me what you're thinking."

"I'm thinking about what your piercing is going to do to me." Biting my lip, I squirm. "I can feel it when I…"

I rock forward and back, my eyes rolling up in my head a little as I do.

"I love watching you enjoy my body, Monroe. You feel it on your g-spot?"

I nod, already on fire.

Hunter's chuckle does wicked things to me. His hands shape my tits, plucking at my nipples. A surge of heat runs through me, and I moan, rocking my hips in a slow rhythm.

My secret is that I love having my nipples touched. I could come from that alone, I think. But I refuse to let men ogle my tits because I won't be a blow-up doll for anyone.

Grabbing Hunter's hands, I slide them down to bracket my hips again. If he notices my discomfort, he says nothing. He just slips one hand between us to play with my hypersensitive clit.

"Not stopping till you come again," he growls. He thrusts up, meeting my movements, encouraging me to speed up. "You can take it, Monroe. Take it for me."

And I do. I meet his thrusts, greedy for it, hungry to be filled again and again. "It feels so good, Hux."

"What does?" he grunts. "Be explicit for me, baby."

I'm too focused in the moment to be ashamed of my answer. "Your… your cock. I love the feeling of riding you."

He slaps my ass, grinning.

"You're such a good girl. My good fucking girl. Taking every inch like you were made for it." Praise mixed with filth, all of it laser-calibrated to set me on fire.

Nobody has ever said these things to me before. I can't explain why it feels so good. Like every time he praises me, I get a little less hollow, a little more real.

He circles my clit with his thumb, pressing hard. When my inner muscles tremble, he senses it, slamming harder. "You gonna come for me, Monroe?"

I'm already there. I come again, mouth open in a silent scream, my body shaking so hard I nearly lose my grip on the sheets.

He finishes with a grunt, spilling into the condom and pulling me down beside him, all heat and sweat and ragged breathing. We're a mess, tangled in broken furniture and each other's limbs, neither one of us willing to move for a long minute.

He eventually props himself on his elbows, looking down at me with a crooked, exhausted smile. "You okay?"

I nod, unable to speak.

He kisses my cheek, then slides out and yanks off the condom, tossing it toward the trash. He flops back onto the floor, pulls me on top of him, and just holds me there, my head on his chest, his heartbeat pounding like a drum line.

I feel drunk. Boneless. Every nerve in my body is singing. I can't stop fucking smiling.

Eventually he stirs, but it's only to go down on me again,

this time with even more focus. His tongue is relentless, his fingers steady and firm, finding a spot inside me that makes my entire body clench. He doesn't stop, even when I beg him to, even when I'm shaking and oversensitive and on the verge of tears.

"Safe word?" he mutters into my flesh.

I open my mouth, knowing that I won't say it. Shaking my head vehemently, I let out an incomprehensible string of vowels.

He keeps going until I shatter, a bolt of hot pleasure tearing through me. My body gives a hard, involuntary spasm. I feel a rush of wetness soaking his face and the ruined mattress beneath us.

My entire body heats. "What– what was–?"

Hunter puts his mouth on my pussy and makes a horrifying slurping noise, burying his face against my skin until I squirm. He groans again when he lets me go. "Fuck, Monroe. Do you usually squirt?"

"No!" I reach for the blanket, needing some sort of cover. "Oh my *god*, Hunter. I'm so humiliated!"

"Really? You shouldn't be." He grabs my thighs and licks my slit again. "I've never been so hard in my fucking life."

"You're insane!" I gasp, trying to get away. "It's… gross!"

"Nah. Watch how much I love it." He groans in satisfaction, licks me clean, then kisses me hard, letting me taste myself on his lips. I shiver.

"I can't believe you like that." I cover my face, mortified. "And I think I broke your bed. I'm the worst fake fiancée ever."

He laughs, low and proud. "This is the best fucking morning of my life. Cookies *and* Juliet fucking Monroe came so hard she squirted on my damn face? Hashtag blessed."

"You're awful." I wrinkle my nose, pushing at his chest.

"You like it," Hunter says easily. "I'm pretty sure that I'm close to getting you hooked."

I should feel embarrassed, or at least cautious. But all I feel is high. I bury my face against his neck and drag in his burnt vanilla and tobacco leaf scent.

No one has had me like this. Not Patrick, not anyone. I have never even let myself have me like this.

Maybe Hunter will tire of me eventually, like everyone else. Probably. But right now, I am alive. Right now, I am wanted.

Right now, I feel like I am enough.

Chapter 27

———

Hunter

The ice feels different tonight. Not the surface itself, that's perfect as always, but something in the air. Electric. Like the building knows this game matters more than the others.

We're facing Sacramento again, the same team that made me lose my shit before. The same enforcer, Marcus Kane, who knows exactly which buttons to push. I can see him warming up on the other end of the rink, throwing glances my way like he's already planning his next psychological warfare campaign.

Asshole.

The difference is, I'm not the same player I was the last time we played. I'm better. Stronger. The team knows I have their back, and I'm going to have to trust that they have mine.

I promise myself that this game will be different.

I glide through warm-ups, my mind clear and focused. The anger's still there; it always will be, but it's controlled now. Channeled. I'm not a bomb waiting to explode anymore. I'm a weapon that knows when and how to strike.

"You good?" Jett asks as he skates past, his golden hair catching the arena lights.

"Yeah," I tell him, and I mean it. "I'm good."

Silas appears on my other side, silent as always, but I can feel his presence like an anchor. My brothers. My constants. No matter how fucked up everything else gets, they're there.

"Kane's been chirping our rookies during warm-ups," Silas says quietly.

I look over at the other team's bench. Sure enough, Kane's running his mouth at Connor and some of the other young guys. Their faces are tight, nervous.

If this were the last month, I would have skated over there and introduced Kane's face to the glass. Tonight, I have an alternate plan. I'm gonna trust my boys more to protect themselves. Not to jump the fucking gun and come in slinging fists.

"Let him chirp," I say. "We'll answer on the scoreboard."

Silas gives me a look that might be surprise, might be approval. With my brother, it's always been hard to tell what he's thinking.

The anthem plays and we line up on the blue line. I stand between my brothers, feeling that familiar pre-game buzz building in my chest. Not rage this time. Anticipation.

Coach Cross and Coach Ryan have been working us hard, drilling the same systems over and over until they become instinct. Pass, support, move. Trust your line mates. Play as a team.

It's clicking. Finally.

The puck drops and we're off.

First shift, I'm out there with Thorne and Grayson. We forecheck hard but smart, forcing turnovers without taking stupid penalties. When their defenseman tries to clear the puck up the boards, I'm there to cut him off. But instead of crushing him into the glass like I normally would, I just take the puck away and feed it to Thorne for a quick shot.

No unnecessary contact. No wasted energy. Just hockey.

"Nice play," Thorne mutters as we skate back for the line change.

I grunt in acknowledgment. It was a nice play. Clean and effective.

Kane tries his first move eight minutes into the period. A late hit after the whistle, nothing the refs will call but enough to get my attention. He grins at me, waiting for the explosion.

I just skate away.

His face twists with confusion and annoyance. Good. Let him wonder what's changed.

We're outshooting them two to one by the midway point of the first. Our forechecking is relentless but disciplined. When they try to make plays, we're there to break them up. When we have the puck, we're flying, making them chase.

We're going to crush this game and grind them into dust.

Grayson scores first on a beautiful feed from Thorne, burying a one-timer that the goalie never sees. The crowd explodes; I genuinely smile as we celebrate. Not the savage grin of violence, but actual joy.

Playing well feels *good*. I'd almost forgotten.

By the end of the first period, we're up 2-0. Jett added another goal on a power play where our puck movement was so crisp it looked choreographed. Even Beck's barking orders with something that sounds like pride in his voice.

"That's hockey!" Coach Cross shouts in the locker room during intermission. "That's what happens when you trust each other! When you play as a team!"

He's right. This feels different from our usual wins. Those were grinding affairs, ugly victories built on individual efforts and lucky bounces. This feels earned. Collective.

In the second period is where Kane gets desperate.

He tries everything. Slashing Grayson behind the play. Crosschecking Thorne in front of the net. Running his mouth at anyone within earshot about their mothers, their girlfriends, their hockey skills.

Each time, our guys handle it themselves. Grayson just skates away, letting Kane waste energy chasing him. Thorne gives Kane a look that could freeze the Niagara Falls and goes back to screening the goalie. The rookies ignore the chirping as best they can and keep playing their systems.

I'm fucking *proud* of them. That shit's hard.

Kane scores midway through the period on a lucky bounce off Jett's pad. It's their first real scoring chance of the game. You can see the frustration boiling over on their bench. They're being outplayed by a team they thought they could intimidate.

That's when Kane targets Silas.

It starts small. A little crosscheck here, an elbow there. Nothing the refs will call, but enough to throw my brother off his timing. Silas is a huge guy, taller even than me. Because of his size, anyone can trip him up more easily.

Which makes him a perfect target for someone like Kane.

I watch it happen from the bench, my hands gripping my stick tighter with each cheap shot. The old Hunter would have hopped over the boards already. But I need to make my violence count when it matters most.

Then Kane goes too far.

Silas is chasing a loose puck in the corner when Kane comes in late and low, catching him flush in the ribs with his shoulder. It's a dirty hit, the kind that can break bones or worse. Silas goes down hard, gasping for breath and cursing. Kane just skates away laughing.

That's when I see red.

I'm over the boards before my brain catches up to my body, but I'm not alone this time. Thorne's right behind me, then Jett from the crease, then half the team. We converge on Kane like a pack of wolves who've found something threatening their den.

"You got a problem with my brother?" I ask, getting right in Kane's face.

He grins that same shit-eating grin from last time. "Just playing hockey, princess. Maybe your brother should toughen up."

But this time, he's not just facing me. Thorne's on my right, all six-foot-four of controlled menace. Jett's on my left, golden hair and dangerous smiles. Even Beck's here, our captain backing his players. The rookies are behind us, no longer looking nervous or intimidated.

For the first time in my career, I'm not fighting alone.

"Here's the thing," I tell Kane, loud enough for everyone to hear. "You want to go after someone, you go after me. But you touch Silas again, and you'll answer to all of us."

Kane looks around, suddenly realizing he's outnumbered. His teammates are there, but they don't look as eager for this fight as they did when it was just me alone and stupid with rage.

"What, you need your full bench to fight your battles now?" Kane sneers, but there's uncertainty in his voice.

"Nah," I say, and I can feel my grin turning savage. "I just wanted them to see this."

That's when I drop my gloves.

The fight is brutal but quick. Kane's tough, I'll give him that, but he's not ready for the version of me that's been channeling anger into my training for weeks. Every punch lands clean and calculated. Every move has a purpose behind it.

I catch him with a right cross that snaps his head back. He

tries to tie me up, but I break free and land two more shots to his ribs. When he goes down, I don't keep hitting. The job's done.

The linesmen pull us apart, Kane's nose streaming blood, his jersey torn. He won't meet my eyes as they escort us both to the penalty boxes.

"Anyone else got something to say?" I call out to their bench.

A quiet, "Fuck you, Huxley!" comes from one of their rookies. Somebody looking to get their ass beat the next time we're on the ice at the same time. I flip the bird as I hit the sin bin.

For the rest of the game, Sacramento is toast. With Kane nursing his wounded pride in the penalty box, our guys play with complete freedom. Grayson scores twice more, both goals coming off beautiful passing plays that showcase everything we've been working on in practice. Thorne adds another on a power play, a laser from the point that beats the goalie clean.

Even the fourth line gets in on it. Connor, who's been struggling with confidence all season, buries a rebound for his first NHL goal. The celebration is worth the price of admission, guys mobbing him like he just won the Cup.

Jett's perfect in net, turning aside everything they throw at him. He's not just making saves, he's controlling rebounds, starting breakouts. Beck's everywhere, blocking shots, winning faceoffs, leading by example. When one of their forwards tries to run at him, Thorne steps in immediately. No fighting, just a hard, clean hit that sends a message.

We protect each other now. That's what teams do.

Final score: 6-1. It's not even close.

In the locker room afterward, the energy is electric. Guys

are laughing, sharing stories from the game, celebrating like we just accomplished something special. And maybe we did.

"That's what I'm talking about!" Beck shouts, still buzzing with adrenaline. "This is how we protect each other! How we play as a team!"

Silas finds me by my stall, working the kinks out of his shoulder where Kane caught him.

"Thanks," he mutters.

"Don't mention it."

"No, I'm serious. You could have just fought him right away, like you usually do. But you waited. You made it about the team, not just your temper."

I look at my brother, this thoughtful guy who sees everything and says little. His approval means more than any highlight or stat sheet.

"You're my brother," I tell him. "Nobody fucks with family. Nobody fucks with my team."

He nods. Jett appears, still in full gear except for his mask. "Did you see Kane's face when he realized the team was ready to go? Beautiful."

"We're getting better at this," I say.

"Yeah. We are."

We come off the ice, stripping down and debriefing with the trainers. The mood in the locker room is jubilant. It's contagious. I pad into the media area, and they want to talk about the fight, of course. They always do. They cluster around me, microphones waiting impatiently.

"Hunter, you showed a lot of restraint tonight before that altercation. Can you talk about your mindset?"

"Just playing hockey," I tell them. "Protecting my teammates when I need to. That's what this team's about."

"Do you feel you're finding your role within this group?"

I think about it for a second. "Yeah. I think I am."

Thorne and Beck come in, relieving me and attracting scrums. I move away, spotting Juliet tucked away just outside the press pit. I head toward her eagerly. Even though I know it's bad, I'm hungry for her after my team's big win.

I'm still sweaty in my base layers. I know I fucking reek. Waving a hand to stop her, I smirk. "Keep your distance if you don't want to smell–"

She ignores me, flinging her arms around my neck and kissing me with an intensity that surprises me. When she pulls back half an inch, she looks up at me. "Hell of a game, Hux."

Holy hell. If I wasn't hard for her when she kissed me, I was fully erect now. It's more than a little uncomfortable because I'm wearing a cup, but I ignore that. I cup her face, wanting to drink her in, consume her, any way I could get her.

"You're so fucking hot," I breathe. "I'm going to fuck you so hard tonight you won't walk right for a week."

Juliet laughs. "Is that a threat, Hunter Huxley?"

"Nope." I kiss her lips again because she's so mouth-watering. "A promise. I can't wait to find out what color panties you're wearing."

She flushes. "Who says I'm wearing any?"

Fuck me. "Don't toy with me, Firecracker."

"You'll just have to wait and see if I'm telling the truth." She hesitates, then changes the subject. "You didn't take the bait tonight. Kane was all over you for two periods and you just... played hockey. Until he went after Silas."

"He's my brother."

"I know." She reaches up, her small hands smoothing over my chest. "That's what made it perfect. You weren't fighting because you lost control. You were fighting to protect someone you care about."

Before I can respond, she pulls me down and kisses me. Fast, intense, full of passion. This is real, hungry, like she didn't get enough of me a minute ago. When we break apart, I'm breathing harder than I was after the fight.

"What was that for?" I ask.

"Because I wanted to."

I glance around the tunnel. It's mostly empty now, just a few equipment guys wheeling carts toward the loading dock. No photographers lurking in corners. There won't be reporters with their phones out. No reason for her to be here except that she wanted it.

That hits me harder than Kane's best shot ever could.

"There's nobody watching," I say, the realization making my chest tight.

"No," she agrees, her thumb brushing across my bottom lip. "There isn't."

She kisses me again, softer this time. I pull her closer and taste something that might be a promise.

Chapter 28

Hunter

"Do I have to go?" I whine as Juliet practically shoves me through the doors of the Ketten Club.

"If I have to go, you're coming with me," she shoots back, not slowing down for a second.

The place is exactly what I expected of Ivy's idea of *team morale*. Neon lights buzzing like dying bugs, complementing floors so sticky they could rip the soles off your shoes. Mirrored walls reflect the disco ball hanging over a tiny stage. The whole place smells of stale beer and sweat.

Not exactly my idea of a good night.

"Oh my god. This is ridiculous," I mutter, taking in the chaos. Half the team is already here, crowded around tables with pitchers of beer. I can hear Grayson's voice booming over the sound system as he butchers some classic rock song.

"You *love* ridiculous," Juliet corrects me, steering me toward an empty table. "You just pretend you don't."

"I do not." I shoot her a pouting glance.

"Please. You're the king of ridiculous. If I recall now, you once got into a fight with a mascot."

"That's not fair. That mascot started it!"

She rolls her eyes, but I catch the smile she's trying to hide. Truth is, she's only here because Ivy and Jessa bullied her into it, same as me. The difference is, she looks good doing it. Too good, actually, in that little crop top and skirt that's making every guy in this place take a second look. Possessiveness grips me.

I *dare* anyone to give Monroe a hard time.

I fold my arms and lean back against the booth against the wall, making it clear I think this whole thing is stupid. But I also position myself so I've got a line of sight to anyone who might get ideas about approaching our table. I'm glad that Ivy rented the club out; the number of guys eyeballing Juliet dropped dramatically when we stepped inside the place.

"You know you're being obvious, right?" Juliet says, settling into the chair next to me.

"Obvious about what?"

"The whole protective caveman thing. *Very* subtle."

"I don't know what you're talking about." My lips twitch. "But I will gut anyone stupid enough to fuck with you."

The look she gives me would make me scowl at anyone else. With her, I almost laugh. Almost.

She just smirks, rolls her eyes, and turns her attention to the stage. Beck is up there now, attempting what I think might be Queen. He can't sing *at all*. The entire team is howling, doubled over while he screeches something that was probably supposed to be the chorus.

"Scabbagoosh! Scabbamooch!" he tries and fails to sing operatically.

The girls giggle. Ivy's got her phone out, probably documenting this disaster for posterity, while Jessa makes faces that suggest she's questioning every life choice that led her here. I agree with her.

"Oh my God, he's so bad," Juliet laughs. The sound makes something warm settle in my chest. "This is painful."

"You want pain? Wait until they drag you up there."

"They're not dragging me anywhere. I don't sing in public."

"We'll see about that."

She shoots me a look. "What's that supposed to mean?"

Before I can answer, Connor gets shoved up on stage next. The poor kid tries to muddle through a Harry Styles song, his face turning redder with every line while the rest of us heckle him with catcalls and completely unhelpful advice.

"Louder, Connor!" Thorne shouts. "Project from your diaphragm!"

"What diaphragm?" Jett yells back. "Kid's got no diaphragm!"

"He's dying up there," Beck says. "Do you need help?"

Several people answer at once. "No!"

Tate pouts. "Just an offer."

Connor flips them both off without missing a beat, which gets him a round of applause that has nothing to do with his singing ability.

Juliet's got her phone out now, taking pictures and recording videos. She keeps trying to get me to pose with her, telling me to smile, which I hate.

"Come on, just one perfect picture," she says, holding the phone up. She has to stretch her arm all the way up just to frame us both. "You're like a skyscraper."

I grin. "You're like a fire hydrant."

"Ha ha. Now smile like you're having fun."

I repress the urge to smile. "I'm not having fun."

When Juliet keeps shoving her phone in my face, I feel the corner of my mouth give. She's the only one who's ever dragged a smile out of me against my will.

"Fake it. Your fans want to see you being human."

"I don't want them to see me being human. The Chainsaw isn't a person. He's a machine. I should scare fans off, not invite them to karaoke night."

"That's exactly why you should do it. Show them you're more than just the angry guy who fights everyone."

I glare at her, but she just keeps snapping pictures. Eventually I give her what she wants... sort of. My version of a smile probably looks more like a grimace, but she seems satisfied.

"There," she says, checking the photos. "See? You look almost approachable."

"Almost approachable is my limit."

She laughs and bobs her head. She's evil.

Silas appears with a fresh pitcher of beer, doing his best to blend into the wall. My brother's never been much for crowds, but he's here because the team expects it. Same reason we're all here, really.

"How long do we have to stay?" he asks, settling into the chair across from me.

"Until Ivy gets bored or someone gets arrested," I tell him. "Whichever comes first."

"Smart money's on Beck getting arrested," Juliet adds. "He's been eyeing that disco ball like he wants to take it home."

The genuine shock comes when Thorne steps forward and grabs the mic. I'm expecting another train wreck, but he sings "Rolling in the Deep" low and steady, smooth as hell. The bar actually goes quiet. I realize our captain has been holding out on us.

"Holy shit," I mutter.

"Right?" Juliet's got that look on her face like she's seeing Thorne for the first time. "Who knew?"

When he finishes, the place explodes. Everyone's clapping and pounding on tables like they've just discovered their captain moonlights on Broadway. Thorne takes a bow, grinning like he planned this all along.

"Show off," I call out, but even I have to admit it was impressive.

The room eats it up, but it grates on me. Everyone acts like we're one big happy family. We're not. I don't trust half of these guys. I don't like most of the other half.

It only gets worse from there. Ivy and Jessa hijack the stage next for some pop song I've never heard, throwing themselves into it with dance moves so dramatic that half the room's got their phones out for blackmail material. They are actually good, which is annoying, because now they have set the bar.

Ryan and Wren, after arriving last, get pushed forward to the mics. They do "Endless Love" while pretending to hate every second. Wren seems shy, but Ryan holds her in place, refusing to let her retreat. But by the end, even I have to admit it's kind of sweet. They look good up there together, like they belong.

"Aw," Juliet says, watching them. "They're cute."

"They're ridiculous."

"This again? You love ridiculous things, remember?"

I mutter something under my breath about how this night is ridiculous, but Juliet's sharp enough to notice the smirk I'm trying to hide. I'd rather be anywhere else. Trapped in a bar with guys I can't relax around isn't my idea of bonding.

She scoots closer, putting her arm around her and leaning into me. "See? You're having fun."

"I'm tolerating this for the team."

"Sure you are."

She's got that teasing look in her eyes, the one that makes

my pulse kick up even when I'm annoyed with her. Which is most of the time, if I'm being honest. Her bright red lipstick is *doing* things to me.

That's when Thorne gets his revenge.

"Juliet!" he calls out, grinning like the devil. "You're up!"

She freezes. "Oh no. Absolutely not."

"Come on!" Beck joins in. "Don't be shy!"

"I'm not shy; I'm smart. There's a difference."

But the guys don't let up. They chant her name. I can see the exact moment she realizes she's not getting out of this. Her face goes pale, then red, then back to pale again.

"I hate all of you," she announces, but she's already standing up.

And of course, as soon as she's cornered, the chanting shifts to me.

"Hunter! Hunter! Hunter!"

"Fuck off," I tell them, but the noise just gets louder. I bare my teeth. "You want a show? Go find another clown. I'm not here to sing. And I'm sure as hell not here to make any of you like me."

"Come on, man!" Jett shouts. "Don't leave your girl hanging!"

Your girl. The words hit differently than they should. If only that were the truth. I drag my ass up onto the stage before I can think too hard about why.

"I'm going to kill you all," I mutter as I join Juliet at the mic.

"Get in line," she shoots back.

We bicker before the music even hits, Juliet snapping that I'm dragging my feet, me firing back that she's the one who let this circus happen. The guys are eating it up, hooting and hollering like we're putting on a show.

Which I guess we are.

The track kicks in and I immediately want to die. "Call Me Maybe." Of course. All hearts and flowers, the thing I'd rather eat glass than sing.

"I hate you," I tell Juliet as the opening notes play.

"Sing the damn song," she mutters back.

We stumble through the first verse with nothing but sarcasm and rolled eyes, and I'm pretty sure we sound nothing like the original. But then something shifts. I lean closer, put my mouth to her mic so our voices blend, and suddenly it doesn't feel so terrible.

The team's going crazy, shouting encouragement and probably recording everything for future blackmail. But I'm not really paying attention to them anymore. I'm watching Juliet, the way she's getting into it despite herself, the way her eyes light up when she hits a note just right.

I catch our reflection in the mirrored wall behind the bar and see what everyone else sees. A real couple, touching, singing together, grinning like idiots. Is that really how we look to other people?

Juliet's flushed red, biting her lip between lines. For once, I don't bother hiding how much I'm enjoying myself. Because the truth is, I am enjoying myself. More than I had in a long time.

When the song ends, the room explodes in cheers and wolf whistles. Someone shouts "get a room!" from the back, which gets a round of laughter.

Without thinking, I pull Juliet close and kiss her, dipping her back like we're in some cheesy movie. The crowd goes wild, and when I straighten us up, she's staring at me with wide eyes and flushed cheeks.

"What was that for?" she asks as I guide her off the stage.

I lean close enough that only she can hear me. "Because you looked like you needed kissing."

She stumbles slightly, her pulse kicking against her throat. I have to bite back a grin. Two can play this game.

Back at our table, the guys are still giving us shit, making exaggerated kissing noises and being as mature as a pack of twelve-year-olds. But I don't care. I'm too busy watching Juliet try to compose herself. The way she keeps touching her lips like she can still feel my kiss is making my stomach knot up.

"Not bad, Huxley," Thorne says, raising his beer. "Didn't know you had it in you."

"I'm full of surprises."

"Apparently so is your girl."

There it is again. *Your girl.* I should correct him, remind him this is all fake, but the words stick in my throat.

Because sitting here, watching Juliet laugh at something Ivy's saying, still flushed from our performance, I'm thinking maybe it doesn't feel so fake anymore.

Maybe it hasn't felt fake for a while.

"You're staring," Silas observes, appearing at my elbow.

"No, I'm not."

"You're definitely staring. And smiling. It's disturbing."

"Shut up."

He just shrugs and goes back to his beer, but I catch him watching me with that knowing look he gets when he thinks he's figured something out.

The night continues with more performances, each one somehow worse and better than the last. Jett attempts rap and fails spectacularly. Three rookies do a group number that sounds like cats being murdered. Ivy forces Wren into a solo that actually makes people cry.

Through it all, Juliet stays close, taking pictures and videos, laughing at the worst performances and cheering for the good ones. She fits in with this group in a way that surprises me, like she's always been part of it.

"Having fun yet?" she asks during a brief lull in the chaos.

"It's tolerable."

"High praise from Hunter Huxley."

"Don't let it go to your head."

She grins and leans into me, and I don't pull away. Because the truth is, I am having fun. More fun than I've had in months, and it's mostly because she's here.

Which is a problem, because this is supposed to be temporary. A business arrangement with an expiration date. I shouldn't be forming attachments.

But watching her sing along to whatever train wreck is happening on stage, seeing her laugh until tears stream down her face, feeling the way she relaxes against me like she belongs there...

I'm pretty sure I passed *attached* about three songs ago.

And I have no idea what I'm going to do about it.

Chapter 29

Hunter

I can't keep my hands off Juliet. Last weekend, after karaoke. This morning when I was already late for my early morning practice. Anytime that I can make her moan, I'm game.

After all, she's Juliet Monroe, the most perfect girl ever to graduate from U of W. If you'd told me back then that I'd ever get her in bed, let alone that she'd like being dominated as much as I like it, I'd have told you to go fuck yourself.

We have sex in the shower, water running cold while I press her against the tile and she wraps her legs around my waist like she's afraid I'll disappear. Against the kitchen counter last night when she was trying to make dinner, and I came up behind her, pushing her skirt up and forgetting all about food.

In my car after team drinks, parked in the shadows of the arena garage because we couldn't wait the fifteen minutes it would take to get home. At the arena itself, tucked away in a storage room where we barely locked the door before I had her pressed against the wall, both of us trying to stay quiet while the rest of the team was just down the hall.

Every time it happens, it gets rougher, messier, more desperate. Like we're both chasing something we can't quite catch.

I'm addicted. Obsessed. Every kiss tastes like hunger, like I'm starving for something I didn't know I needed until I had it.

The last time is in the foyer of our apartment. We barely make it inside before I lose what's left of my control. Juliet drops her bag, keys scattering across the hardwood, and I grab her by the hips, spinning her around to face me.

"Hunter," she breathes, but whatever she was going to say gets lost when my mouth finds hers.

We don't even get out of our clothes all the way. Her skirt shoved up, my jeans pushed down just enough, frantic, against the front door like we're teenagers who can't wait another second.

She wrecks me. Destroys every defense I've ever built, every wall I've put up to keep people from getting too close. And I keep coming back for more.

I tell myself not to touch her when we're not actively fucking. Not to look at her the way I do when she's reading on the couch, unconsciously tucking her hair behind her ear. Not to memorize the sound of her laugh or the shape of her mouth when she's trying not to smile at something stupid I've said.

Because when this ends, and it will end, she'll go on like none of it mattered. She'll pack up her life and move on to the next job, the next opportunity, the next carefully considered step in her career.

And I'll still be standing here, fists clenched, pretending I didn't want more.

When we're finally still, curled together on my bed with

the sheets tangled around us, Juliet says something I don't expect.

"Patrick's words are stuck in my brain today." Her voice is quiet, careful. "No man will ever want to come second to my ambition. That's a quote."

The words hit me like a physical blow. Not because they're true, but because I can hear in her voice that she believes they might be.

I go still beneath her, every muscle in my body tensing. My jaw locks so tight I'm surprised my teeth don't crack.

"That guy's a fucking idiot," I say, flat and certain. "You already know that. Why are you taking his word on this one subject?"

Juliet flinches like she expected me to agree. It was almost as if she was waiting for me to confirm what that piece of shit drilled into her head. I'm unmoored by it.

I watch her for a long beat, taking in the way she's pulled back slightly, the careful blankness that's settled over her features. The same mask she wears when she's managing difficult reporters.

"Have you ever thought about replacing him?" I ask, quieter this time.

"What do you mean?" She gives me a puzzled look.

"You know the Houston Stars team management, right?"

"Yeah, I guess. I've never worked for them. But I was Patrick's girlfriend for five years. I've met the owner and their head coach a bunch of times."

I lick my upper lip. "Patrick has a big mouth. But he's also a pretty shitty player. And that's considering Houston recruited him, and it's a terrible team."

Juliet smothers a laugh. "Tell me how you really feel about him, Hux."

Her nickname warms the hard knot in my chest, tempting it to ease.

"It's true." I snicker. "I'm saying that I bet there's a rookie out there who'd kill for a shot to take his place. Someone quiet but talented, who needs somebody to hype him up. Someone who'd let you be the one to give it to him."

She blinks, her expression shifting. "I... what?"

"If you chose one or two graduating seniors from college who aren't already first or second draft picks, and you hyped them up to teams that you thought they would fit with, you'd make a killing off the deal. Plus, one of those rookies could replace your shitbag ex in the Stars lineup. See what I'm saying?"

"Maybe?" Her nose wrinkles. "That sounds like being an agent. I'm a PR girl."

"It's less about being an agent and more about making the right introductions, helping rookie players get in rooms that they wouldn't normally be invited into." I say it like it's obvious, because it seems like it is. "I'm just saying if I had the time and connections, that's what I would do."

"And what about my PR dreams?"

"You're great at PR. This would just be a little *bonus*. You don't even see how good you've got it, Juliet. Most people spend their whole lives looking for something they care about enough to fight for. You've got that, and you're good at it." I pause, hesitating. "Anyone who can't see that doesn't deserve you."

I watch her process this, see the exact moment something cracks open in her chest. Because I'm not trying to tame her ambition or convince her to want smaller things. I'm encouraging her to want *more*. I'm talking about her ambition like it's part of what makes her worth knowing.

She looks at me like she can't believe I mean it.

But I do. Every word.

"You think I should go after Patrick's spot?" she asks. There's something sharp and interested in her voice now.

"I think you should go after whoever you want. Build your own empire. Show the whole fucking league what they have been missing out on. PR and talent, all in one package."

Her mouth parts like she's going to say something, then closes again. Instead of speaking, she slides closer to me, close enough that I can feel her heartbeat against my ribs.

I reach for her without thinking, my hand finding her face, thumb brushing across her cheekbone.

When I kiss her this time, it's different. Slower. I feel like I'm trying to say something with my mouth that I don't have words for.

It won't be the last time. We both know that now. This thing between us has moved past the point of pretending it's just convenient chemistry, just two people scratching an itch.

But I'll never get enough of her. Never tire of the way she looks at me afterward, like I've given her something precious. I'll stop wanting to be the reason she smiles.

It's not just that I want her. I want her to look at me like I'm worth something. Maybe I want her to see past my flaws and see my strengths instead. I want her to see that maybe there's something underneath all the anger and the reputation that's worth keeping around.

"What are you thinking about?" she asks, her voice soft with exhaustion.

I flick a few strands of her wavy hair out of her eyes. Her hair is dark as a raven's wing and soft as silk to the touch.

"Nothing important," I lie.

Because how do I tell her she's rewired my entire brain? I used to think I was only good for hockey and breaking things. Now I catch myself wondering what it would be like to wake up next to her every morning for the rest of my life?

How do I tell her that when she talks about her career ambitions, I don't feel threatened or competitive? I feel proud. I want to clear the path for her, want to be the one standing behind her when she takes over the fucking world.

How do I tell her that Patrick was wrong about everything, but especially about the man who could handle being with her?

Because the right man wouldn't want to come first. He'd want to be her partner. Her backup. The person she comes home to after conquering whatever she set out to conquer that day.

He'd want to be worthy of someone that fucking magnificent.

I'm not there yet. Maybe I'll never be. But lying here with her curled against my chest, feeling the weight of her trust in the way she lets herself be vulnerable with me, I think I might want to try.

"Hunter?" she murmurs against my throat.

"Yeah?"

"Thank you. For what you said about Patrick. About my ambition."

I tighten my arms around her. "I meant every word."

"I know," she says, and there's something soft and surprised in her voice. "That's what makes it matter."

She falls asleep first, her breathing evening out against my neck. I lie here awake, staring at the ceiling and trying to process the magnitude of what's happening to me.

Five months. That was supposed to be it. Five months of fake engagement, mutually beneficial arrangement, clean break at the end. We're at the halfway point and my entire brain is screaming at me to make it more permanent somehow.

There's nothing fake about the way my chest tightens when she smiles, or the way I plan my days around the moments when I'll see her again.

There's nothing fake about wanting to tear apart anyone who's ever made her feel like she was too much, too ambitious, too everything.

There's nothing fake about the way I'm falling for her so hard it feels like hitting the ice at full speed.

The smart thing would be to pump the brakes. To remember that this ends whether or not I want it to. To protect what's left of my sanity before she walks away and takes half my heart with her.

Chapter 30

Juliet

Tonight is a Havoc game night event, the buzzing, high-energy gathering where sponsors write checks and players smile for photos and everyone pretends hockey is just a fun game instead of a multimillion-dollar business.

I'm doing my new job, following Ivy as she makes the rounds, staying visible but professional. She's good at this, better than I expected. Natural with people in a way that makes sponsors feel special without being obvious about it.

"The Hendersons are here," Ivy murmurs, nodding toward a couple near the bar. "Tech money. They've been thinking about a naming rights deal."

"Oh, I know the Hendersons. Fancie, the wife, was one of my tennis partners back in Houston." They're from Texas, although I think I heard something about them moving to Seattle to be closer to Jared's business headquarters. "Want me to introduce you?"

She eyes me. "Wow, I had no idea you were so connected!"

"Oh, well." I flush, smiling. "I met everybody and their sister when I was a Houston WAG."

"I'll just bet you did. I think we're okay right now, but keep an eye on them during the second period. If we're winning, I'll circle back."

"They were a good sponsor for the Stars. I know that a team like the Havoc will blow their minds."

"God." Ivy grins at me. "It's really nice to have a woman working with me who vibes on my level."

I wink at her, my face heating under her knowing gaze.

"Oh, no." Ivy frowns, looking at Jimbo Greene being practically assaulted by a young blonde. He looks a little uncomfortable as the blonde lays a hand on his arm and leans in, a smile on her face. "Shit, that's my sister Opal. God knows what she's saying to Mr. Greene. I have to go rescue him."

As she scurries away, I smile and shake my head. It feels good to be here tonight. I'm thinking about how nice it is to be working with Ivy when I spot my parents, standing near the VIP entrance like they own the place. Which, knowing my mother, she probably thinks she does.

My mom is wearing an elegant white blouse and a tight black pencil skirt. My dad is more casual, wearing jeans and a dark gray Seattle Havoc hockey shirt over his white button up. This is their usual getup when going to an event: my mom looks ready to pull out a law book and start lecturing anybody who gets in her way; my dad embraces the spirit a little more but is obviously pretty uncomfortable.

Classic Melissa and Tom Monroe. "Shit," I mutter.

My parents weren't supposed to come tonight. I've barely kept in touch with them over the last couple of months, even though I just moved back into the same city. And yet here they are, my mother in her perfectly tailored skirt and my father sipping a foamy beer like he's never tried one before. Just *perfect*.

"Hey mom," I say, waving awkwardly.

"What?" She tenses for a moment and then smiles. "Sorry, darling. This arena is loud! I can't believe how many people are here to see *hockey*."

I suppress an eye roll and hug her, then turn to give my dad a hug too.

"Hiya, Jujube." He gives me a one handed hug, trying not to dump his still-overflowing beer on me. God, with parents as dorky as these two, it's a wonder that I didn't come out with a pair of wire-rim glasses and a permanent wedgie. "We came to surprise you. Surprise!"

"I am," I say, nodding. I herd them out of the main hallway and toward the elevator. "You should've called ahead. But it doesn't matter. I'm sure that we can squeeze you into the team box."

"Are there less…" My mom looks around, dropping her voice. "Hockey people in the box?"

"*Melissa*. This is an ice hockey arena. Come on. Get into the spirit!" My dad gives me an apologetic look. This is part of their schtick whenever they're dragged to sporting events. Dad plays the cool one who's in touch with the people. Mom tries to look like she's not dying of boredom. It's why I would've arranged for someone to escort them around and answer their questions if they had called ahead.

But I just grin and bear it. I hustle them up to the team box. The suite is a dream; it feels less like a box and more like a private lounge floating over the rink. A wall of glass gives a perfect view of the ice, while rows of leather stadium seats face the action. The team placed Havoc-branded glassware and napkins in team colors on pub tables behind them. A spread of food lines the back wall: steaming silver trays, sushi platters, charcuterie boards, and bite-sized cheesecakes beside bowls of fresh fruit. The bar glitters with top-shelf liquor and chilled bottles of wine and beer.

My mom takes a sharp breath. My dad whistles, his hand on my mom's back. "Now this is serious hockey viewing! Wow."

"It's nice." My mom looks around, her mouth pursing. "Spotless."

There are a few other people enjoying the accommodations, getting plates of food and having drinks made by the uniformed bartender. I nudge my parents toward a table. "You guys go sit down, or get a bite to eat. I'll get drinks."

"Ah!" My mom's eyes light up. "A very dry white wine for me. Grenache Blanc, maybe?"

"We're in a hockey stadium, Mom. I'll ask, but they probably don't have your favorite varietal."

My mom heaves a sigh and wanders toward the buffet. That woman loves sushi, so I'm sure she'll find something to nibble on. I can hear my dad as I walk to the bar. "Honey, they have fancy nachos!"

God help us all. I paste a smile on my face and order a round of drinks. Another beer for my dad, a white wine for mom, and a diet soda for me since I'm working. I take a sip of my soda as I wait for the bartender. It's certainly no gin and tonic with four limes.

When I slip into a seat at my parents' table, I cast an eye down at the ice. The players are out on the ice, stretching. I see Hunter in full gear, doing a stretch that very much looks like he's trying to fuck the ice. My cheeks color.

"Thank you, darling," my mom murmurs. "You know, it's freezing in here. They should turn up the heat!"

I try not to sound irritated when I say, "It's a building designed for hockey. Most fans know to bundle up." I pause, trying to find my smile. "But if you want, I'm sure I can hunt down a Seattle Havoc sweatshirt for you."

My mom looks mystified. "Surely not. I'm wearing Prada, Juliet."

My dad's attention is on the big screen tv as he sips his beer. He's checked out already. I'm alone with my mom. I sip my soda and look down at the rink again. The guys are skating back toward the tunnel. The game is about to begin.

"Well!" My mom pushes her plate with what is probably very expensive nigiri around and purses her lips. "So how is your fiancé? Is he… playing tonight?"

I was wondering just how long it would take her to get to mention my engagement. My smile is stiff. "Yes, he's the starting right wing, #47. They're about to call his name down on the ice."

"And how is all of that going? Well enough, I presume?"

"Yes, Mom." I clench my glass a little harder. "My engagement is speeding along just fine."

"Still no date for the wedding?"

I study her, but she plays her cards close to her chest. So I bluff, because I'm not holding jack shit.

"Nope. We've only been official for three months. Why do you ask?"

She gives me a delicate shrug. "Just catching up, darling."

My ass. She's fishing, trying to find weaknesses. Luckily, at that moment, the announcer lists off the starting lineup, who skate onto the ice. I've never felt such relief in my life.

My mom hates that I've found happiness doing something she considers low class. Can you imagine? The amount of money hockey players make, and no class.

I spend most of the first period watching them instead of the game, praying that Hunter doesn't make too much of a big deal that I'm here. He keeps looking up at the box, sending sizzling looks my way that make my toes curl in my heels. I can't keep the smile from my face.

He should pay attention to the ice, not whatever I'm doing.

"You seem distracted." My mother clears her throat during the first intermission, putting on that smile she uses when she's about to say something cutting.

"Just working, Mom. This is my job."

"Hmm." She surveys the crowd like she's cataloging everyone's net worth. "Well, I suppose it's better than nothing. Though you know, sweetheart, you're going to be too old to change careers someday. Everyone likes a feisty young lawyer. No one wants to hire a middle-aged washup just starting their second career."

"*Mom*." I bristle, my spine straightening. "I'm barely twenty-three. Besides, I'm not washing out of my public relations career."

"Be serious for a moment, Juliet." My mom grabs my chin, gazing at me. "This is not a stable career. And being engaged to another hockey player isn't exactly wise, either. This is all very…"

She trails off. A flash of heat licks the back of my neck.

"What? Spit it out, mom. Say that you think hockey is low class."

Her eyes narrow. "You said it, not me. And just so you know, your father feels that your fiancé hasn't gone through the proper steps to propose to you. Right, Tom?"

"Huh?" Dad looks over from the ice. "Sorry, what did you say?"

"I told her that her fiancé didn't even have the decency to ask you for her hand in marriage!" My mom sniffs as if this is the worst behavior she can think of.

"Can you two not fight right here?" he whispers. Dad

looks between us, his brows descending. "There are other people not fifteen feet away. We don't want to spread our private family business all over."

What a cop out. I fold my arms across my chest and look down onto the ice, furious. Hunter looks up into the box and points directly at me, that cocky grin spreading across his face.

My cheeks flush hot. He should definitely pay attention to the game, not flirting with me from the ice.

"Well," my mother says, sounding pleased. "He's certainly... athletic."

"You really have no idea." The words are out of my mouth before I realize it. I put my fingers against my lips, as if to stop more insane words from escaping my lips.

My mom glares at me, and I fix my gaze on the ice.

I watch the game, noticing things I might have missed before. The Havoc guys are still a little sloppy, but they're less scattered than they were a month ago. Passes are connecting. Jett actually chirps a rookie about his stick handling and gets chirped back, which is progress of a sort.

It's not pretty hockey, but it's looking like *team* hockey. I'm not a hockey announcer or anything, but even I can tell that they're playing better.

And Hunter? Hunter is downright magnificent. The better the team plays, the better he gets. He feeds off their energy and growing confidence. He's been in a better mood lately too, less likely to snap at reporters or glare at teammates who make mistakes.

So different from when I first laid eyes on him a few months ago.

Midway through the second period, Thorne gets into it with a player from the other team. It's not a big deal, just a shoving match after a dirty hit. But for once, Hunter doesn't go in fists first. Instead, he skates over and stands beside Thorne, backs him up without bulldozing through the situation.

Afterward, I watch on the big screen TV as Thorne mutters something that looks like *thanks* under his breath. Hunter nods. That's it. That's enough.

"Yes!" I clap. "That's right."

"Excuse me, dear," my mother says, standing abruptly. "I need to powder my nose."

She disappears toward the restrooms, leaving me alone with my father, who's been quietly nursing the same beer for the entire game.

"She means well," he says without looking at me.

"Does she?"

"In her way."

That's about as deep as conversations with my father get these days. Before I can figure out how to respond, a man in an expensive suit appears beside me.

"Juliet Monroe? Doug Kellerman, Pacific Sports Media."

I recognize the name. He's one of those media executives who thinks he runs Seattle sports from behind a desk, the guy who name-drops and schmoozes and probably has never actually watched a full game.

"Mr. Kellerman." I force a smile. "How can I help you?"

"I just wanted to introduce myself. It's always exciting to see fresh talent in the industry." His smile is too wide, too familiar. "Especially someone with your... connections."

There's something in the way he says connections that makes my skin crawl. My dad is literally sitting right across from me, though he focuses on the big screen TV.

I shift in my seat. "I'm not sure what you mean."

"Oh, come now. Patrick speaks highly of you. He says you two had quite the partnership."

I freeze. *Patrick.* Of course. Because apparently I can't escape him, even here.

"That was a long time ago," I manage.

"Was it? Because from what I hear, you two made quite the team. Shame it didn't work out. Though I suppose these hockey players can be... challenging."

He glances down at the ice where Hunter is lining up for a face-off, and there's something dismissive in his expression that makes my hands clench into fists.

I can't deflect fast enough. Can't come up with the right words to shut this down without causing a scene. That's the moment that Ivy pokes her head into the suite.

I give her a wide-eyed look and she rushes over, intentionally interrupting.

"Is everyone doing okay over here?" she asks. "The team likes me to keep on top of these things."

Mr. Kellerman looks her up and down like he's found a tasty snack.

"Doug Kellerman. Pacific Sports Media. I would love to meet the man who was smart enough to hire both of you."

Ivy's expression twitches. "What now?"

"You're both just so beautiful." He looks between us, pleased as punch. "Has anyone ever tried to put you two in front of a camera?"

Ugh. As if I would ever leave a job with an NHL team to work for this jackass. I open my mouth to tell him that, or a more polite version, but Ivy stumbles, tripping over absolutely nothing.

"Oh my God, I am so sorry!" she gasps, somehow spilling her entire soda down the front of Kellerman's expensive shoes. "These heels are impossible to walk in. Let me get you some napkins!"

Before he can respond, Jessa is there, linking her arm

through mine. "Juliet, we need you over here. Sponsor emergency."

She leads me away without another word.

They never speak about it afterward. Don't make a big production of it or wait for thanks. They just handle it, smooth and seamlessly, like they've been doing this kind of thing their whole lives.

But I realize deep in my bones that these women have closed ranks around me. I'm not alone anymore. Not like I was with Patrick, when his friends became my friends by default and disappeared the moment we broke up.

This is different. This is real.

I don't see Kellerman's face again after that, so I can only guess that a member of the group lured him away. Either way, he's not in the tunnel when I rush through it.

After the game, which we win by two goals, I'm standing in the hallway outside the media room when my mother reappears, looking refreshed and ready to interrogate me about my life choices.

Hunter emerges from the locker room still damp from his post-game shower, hair messy, wearing that satisfied look he gets after a good game. When he spots me, his whole face lights up.

"There's my girl," he says, loud enough for half the hallway to hear.

I blush, unable to hold in a smile. Grabbing his biceps, I direct him toward my mother. "Mom, this is Hunter Huxley. Hunter, this is my mother, Melissa Monroe."

He grins at me but doesn't say anything, just extends his hand to my mother with that effortless charm that probably worked on teachers and coaches for his entire life.

"Mrs. Monroe. Nice to meet you."

"Mr. Huxley." She shakes his hand, sizing him up like

she's considering what he might be worth. "Congratulations on the win."

As we're talking, a young staffer hurries past and drops her clipboard, papers scattering across the floor. Before she can bend down to collect them, Hunter steps forward and gathers everything up, handing it back to her with a quiet, *there you go.*

No scowl. No muttered complaints about people being careless. He just does it, like helping is the most natural thing in the world.

Something warm unfurls in my chest. I don't say anything, just give him a quiet, knowing smile when he looks my way. I feel like I've been waiting for exactly this moment. Waiting to see proof that the man I've been falling for is real, not just an act he puts on for me.

Instead, I smile too tightly and look at my mom. "Did you enjoy the game?"

"It was... energetic." The tension from her comment stays with me long after they leave, following me home and settling in my chest like a stone. "It's nice that you seem to have found some nice coworkers."

After my mom and dad leave, I'm exhausted. I lead the press conference, snapping a little more easily than usual. It's over before too long though, and I'm left cleaning up the water bottles left behind by the hockey players.

I'm in my head, wondering about my relationship.

It started as a fake arrangement. A clever PR play. But that's not what it is anymore.

It's not love. I'm never going to be ready to risk that kind of vulnerability again.

But it's not nothing either.

It's two damaged people clinging to each other. Mess, hunger, and fear are all tangled up together. It's the way he looks at me like I'm something precious and the way I let myself believe it, just for a moment, before reality crashes back in.

It's also the best sex of my life, which feels shallow to admit but is undeniably true. I've had five orgasms a day every day that I've seen him. No idea how things will be when he goes on the road again, but… a girl can hope that it won't kill this thing growing between Hunter and me.

I thought I'd feel ashamed about that. Guilty for letting my professional arrangement become something so physical, so consuming. Instead, I feel raw. Wanted. Real.

And that's what terrifies me.

Because what if this isn't just lust? What if this isn't just two people scratching an itch until they get bored and move on?

What if it's him? What if Hunter Huxley, with his terrible reputation and his gentle hands and his way of seeing straight through all my carefully constructed walls, is the person who finally makes me understand what all the fuss is about?

My control slips at the thought. The walls I've built around my heart shake.

Later that night, when we're curled up on his bed after another round of desperate, clinging-to-each-other sex, I confess things I never meant to say out loud.

"My mom doesn't approve of you."

Hunter goes still beside me. Then he says something kind. Simple. True. I don't even remember the exact words, only how they land like a punch that somehow doesn't hurt. Gentle and devastating at the same time.

"No offense, Juliet, but… who cares what she thinks? It didn't seem like you two were getting along all that well when I met you." He pulls back to look at me. "Do you approve?"

I bite my lip to hide a grin. "I think so. You'd better kiss me again so I can make sure."

"My pleasure." Hunter kisses me, soft and pliant. It makes me kiss him back, more aggressively, pursuing something that I can't quite name.

Hunter makes me feel things I haven't felt in years. Heat and defiance and thrill and hunger. But those aren't safe feelings. They're the kind that burned me before, that left me picking up pieces of myself I'm still trying to reassemble.

Much later, when Hunter is asleep and I'm lying awake staring at the ceiling, I get up to get some water. On my way back from the kitchen, I notice a piece of paper on his dresser that wasn't there before.

I shouldn't look. It's probably nothing, maybe just a grocery list or some team notes.

But curiosity wins, and I pick it up.

It's a letter. Not addressed to anyone, maybe not even meant to be read. But it's about survival. About trying. About the daily work of holding yourself together when everything in you wants to fall apart.

Some days are harder than others, it says in Hunter's messy handwriting. *Some days I wake up and the anger is right there, waiting. Like it never left, just went dormant for a while. I used to think that made me weak. Now, I think it just makes me human.*

The trick isn't to stop feeling it. The trick is to feel it and choose something else anyway. Choose to be better. Choose to try.

I'm trying.

I sit there in the dark, holding the letter, completely undone.

Because suddenly I see it. How hard he's working just to hold himself together. How much effort it takes for him to be the man he is with me, patient and gentle and kind, when his instincts probably tell him to run or fight or both.

He's not perfect. Neither am I. But maybe that's the point.

Maybe this fragile thing between us could take root and bloom. Maybe it's about finding someone worth the challenge. Someone worth trying for.

I fold the letter carefully and put it back where I found it, then slip back into bed beside him.

He stirs slightly when I settle against his chest, his arm tightening around me in his sleep.

"Juliet?" he murmurs, not quite awake.

"I'm here," I whisper back.

And for the first time in a long time, I think I might actually mean it.

Chapter 31

Hunter

I'm on the third leg of this six city tour, and I'm dying. We won our first two games against Montreal and Ottawa. We were skating better, our defense seemed like they were more motivated, and our offense was playing pretty aggressively. Coupled with the fact that Montreal was coming off a five game streak and Ottawa played like they had never put on ice skates before, we crushed.

Then today, against Toronto, that momentum promptly crumpled. Their team is more coordinated, practiced, and has more to lose. They kept punching holes in our defense and leaving Jett in the goal to block every attempt. Our offense was trailing behind the Maple Leafs, trying desperately to steal the puck. Jett worked his ass off, sweat pouring off him, but there's only so much a goalie can do when he's on his own.

I did my part. I checked members of the opposite team into the boards at every opportunity, generally acting rowdy as fuck. I did my best to defend Jett in the goal, shoving and cross-checking Toronto's center and left wing, who wouldn't stay the fuck out of the crease. Thorne picked up on my attitude. He chirped, slashed sticks, and whacked skates like he was a born enforcer.

With the rest of the team struggling, even starting fights and tossing gloves wasn't helpful. In the third period, I started scrums and chased Toronto's captain like I was his fucking shadow, bumping, slashing, and talking shit. But it didn't help.

Toronto won by a cringeworthy 4-2. After that crushing loss, the team gets screamed at by Coach Cross. We deserve it; the complete game was a fucking mess. I've never seen Coach's face so red as he finishes his rant.

"Tomorrow morning before we load onto the plane, I want every single one of you to wake up and work your ass off in dryland training. We are going to run until everyone collapses."

A dull headache throbs behind my eyes as I head back. I need to eat, hydrate, and focus on stretching before lactic acid sets in. I don't want to get up tomorrow and already hurt before dryland.

The team has set up a team dinner for us in a private room on the ground floor of the hotel. I'm not in the mood to see anyone's face, so I grab two plates and load up on grilled chicken, tortellini with pesto, broccoli, and fresh fruit. I grab a couple of bananas and a six-pack of Gatorade, then head up to my hotel room.

I collapse on my bed. Today really sucked all around. I'm glad that Juliet wasn't here to see us drag ass around the rink. My head throbs as I wolf down my food and guzzle Gatorade. All I want at this moment is a little foam roller time and a fucking nap.

My phone buzzes when I'm halfway through my food. I check who it is, expecting to silence the call. But to my surprise, it's Juliet. She didn't text me at all today, which irritated me for absolutely no reason.

She's not my actual fiancée. I can't expect her to text me all the time.

But now she's calling me. I'm a little taken aback because we don't really have a phone call sort of relationship. I pick up her call, feeling a strange mix of excitement and dread.

"Hey, Juliet."

"Hey. Do you… um… wanna FaceTime?"

I blink slowly. She wants to see me? "Sure."

Juliet switches to a video call. I can see her relaxing on the couch, wearing a gray Seattle Havoc hoodie. My hoodie, I'm pretty sure.

"You look exhausted. I watched your game." She wrinkles her nose.

I sigh heavily. "Yeah?"

"Yeah. It was a tough loss." She props her head on her hand. "It seemed like you and Thorne were the only players who were awake other than Jett. It was hard to watch you guys skate yourselves into the ground while everybody else seemed sort of…"

"Fucking clueless?" I supply. I take another bite of pasta because, no matter how much I like Juliet, my stomach is still growling.

"Are you eating? I don't want to interrupt. I can call back later…"

"Nah." I shake my head. "Seeing your face is making my day less of a waste."

Juliet hooks her hair behind her ear and gives me a sheepish smile.

"The apartment is too quiet without you here. There's no one to turn on the blender at 4:30 in the morning. It's weird," she teases.

Warmth fills my chest. "Not to mention there's no big tall man to help get things down from the kitchen shelves. What have you been doing without me there?"

She blushes. "Eating a lot of takeout. There are clean dishes in the dishwasher that are staying put till you return because they belong in the top cabinets."

"I expected as much." I chuckle. "Just don't get any of your other 6'6" fake fiancés to put the dishes up. I don't want to share the space."

"Oh, *ha ha*. You're the only impossible bear of a man in my life at this moment."

We share a look, part humor, part awkwardness. I bite my lower lip.

"So did you have a reason for calling? Is this a booty call?"

"What?" She sits up, looking alarmed. "Hunter!"

"What?" I smirk at her and open a new Gatorade. "A guy can hope."

Her brow furrows. "You don't actually do that, do you?"

"What, phone sex?" I consider her words. "No. But for you, I would. We're breaking all the rules already. What's a little video work, heavy breathing, and masturbation in the mix?"

She rolls her eyes. "Stop trying to get me all hot and bothered."

"You called me," I pointed out. "I can't control where my mind goes after that."

"You're awful." She pokes her cheek out with her tongue and then admits, "I miss you, though. You've been gone too long."

My first instinct is to tease her again, ask how long it's been since she's touched herself. But what comes out of my mouth next surprises even me.

"After my game in Vancouver, come meet me for a weekend away," I blurt out.

Her eyebrows rise. "A weekend away?"

"Yeah. No cameras, no team events, no reporters. Just... away."

I don't know where the idea came from, but suddenly I need it. Need to be somewhere with her that isn't tied to hockey or PR or any of the reasons we're supposed to be together. I *need* Juliet to say yes.

"Where were you thinking?"

"I know a place. A cabin up north. Nothing fancy, but it's quiet."

She studies my face for a moment, probably trying to figure out what brought this on. But all she says is, "Okay. That sounds nice."

The cabin is owned by Mr. Greene and up for grabs to any player who wants it. During the summer and the post-New Year's snow, it's busy. But now, reading into the Thanksgiving holiday, it will be available. It's simple, rustic, the place where you can hear yourself think. No wifi, no cell service, no distractions.

And most importantly, plenty of isolation. The idea of spending a few days holed up with Juliet, fucking her, teasing her, making her laugh... It sounds downright dreamy to me.

"I'll send you a plane ticket and pick you up at the airport in Vancouver. The team has a week off after, so maybe I can convince you to stay for a few days?"

She nods slowly. "If the team has downtime, I should be able to get away. It's not like I have an office to show up at or anything."

"True." I take a few more bites of food. "Tell me a story while I finish demolishing this food, Monroe."

She laughs. "I can tell you about hanging out with the

Coven at Ivy's house. Ivy has wild taste in furnishings and even wilder taste in men."

"Tell me all about it." Grinning, I pull my plate of fresh fruit closer. "I'm going to stuff my face."

"Wow. When you said this cabin wasn't fancy, you weren't kidding." Juliet looks at the small A-frame cabin as I set our suitcases down to unlock the front door. I open the door and step back with a grin.

"For the next three days, it's home sweet home."

She sticks her tongue out teasingly as she heads inside. The place is small, with a tiny kitchen and cozy living room on the bottom floor. Up a corkscrew set of metal steps is a tiny library wall and the cabin's only bed. A fire crackles as we make ourselves comfortable.

For me, that means three days of sweet, sweet sweatpants. For Juliet, it's more yoga pants and my stolen hoodie. She still wears her heels, which makes me want to roll my eyes. Even at this remote cabin, Juliet needs to be done up.

She wiggles her eyebrows and shows off my hoodie. "You like?"

I'm not even mad that she stole it; she looks so tiny with the bulky sleeves shoved up that it makes me smile. Yeah, seeing her in my gear definitely does something to me.

"I really do," I admit. "In a possessive, fucked up way, I don't want you to wear anything else, ever. I like this better than a tight little skirt."

"It smells like you." She inhales a whiff of my hoodie and blushes. "I don't hate it."

I love seeing her like this, warm and soft and real. She

doesn't need anything from me here. Doesn't expect me to perform or be on or manage my image.

She just wants to hang out with me.

We cook dinner together, something simple that doesn't require much skill. She tells me about her first job out of college, working for a sports agency that treated her like a glorified coffee fetcher until she proved she was smarter than half the men in the room.

"The managing partner called me into his office one day," she says, stealing a piece of the garlic bread I'm making. "He told me I had potential, but that I needed to be more collaborative. He said I was too aggressive in meetings." She points the bread at me. "I was the only girl there and definitely the only one under 5'8". It was humiliating."

"What did you do?"

"I asked him if he'd ever told a male colleague to be less aggressive. He said that was different. I need to learn how to talk to men, I guess." She shrugs. "I had a new job lined up by the end of the week."

I love watching her talk about work. The way her whole face lights up when she's describing a satisfying negotiation or the strategy behind a successful campaign is something to see. It's not ambition for its own sake. It's a passion and an art.

Later, we're sitting on the couch in front of the fire, a card game discarded on the table in front of us, and she laughs at something stupid I've said about the terrible movie we're half-watching. It's not a polite laugh or a professional laugh. It's real and unguarded. Completely hers.

I think, *I want to be the reason she keeps doing that.*

The truth guts me. This isn't supposed to be about what I *want*. This is supposed to be a business arrangement with convenient chemistry on the side.

But sitting here in this quiet cabin, watching Juliet curl up against my side like she belongs there, I can't pretend anymore.

I'm falling for her. I've been falling for her since that first night she let me hold her. Maybe I've been holding a torch for her since college.

We have sex that night, but it's slower than our usual pace. Reverent. Almost shy, like we're both afraid of breaking something precious.

"Hunter." There's something in her low, throaty voice I can't quite name.

"Yeah?"

But she doesn't finish the thought. She traces patterns on my chest with her finger, like she's trying to memorize the feeling of my skin under her hands.

I hope, just a little. Maybe this thing between us could be real. Could last beyond the five months we agreed to.

The thing is, I've been here before. I've let myself believe that someone cared about me, that I mattered to them beyond what I could provide. And every time, I've been wrong.

Every time, I've stood there wondering what I did wrong, why I wasn't enough, why love always seems to come with conditions I can't meet.

"You're thinking too loud," Juliet murmurs against my shoulder.

"Sorry."

"Don't be sorry. Come back to me."

The way she says it, like I'm somewhere she can reach if I just let her, makes my throat tight.

"I'm here," I say. I'll try my best to make it true.

The next morning, I wake up before her and spend a few minutes just watching her sleep. She is wearing my hoodie with the hood pulled up over her head, the long sleeves drowning her hands. It's cute.

I make coffee and sit on the porch, breathing in the crisp mountain air and trying to figure out what the hell I'm doing.

Five months. That was the deal. Five months of a fake engagement, then we both get what we need and go our separate ways.

But I don't want to go my separate way anymore. I want to wake up next to her every morning. I want to make her coffee and listen to her talk about work and be the reason she laughs.

I want to keep Juliet Monroe in my life.

And that terrifies me more than any opponent I've ever faced.

Wanting something this much means someone can take it away. It means I can lose it. *I could lose her.*

"Morning," Juliet says, appearing in the doorway with her own mug of coffee. She's wearing my sweatshirt and nothing else. The sight of her bare legs makes my brain short-circuit for a moment.

"Morning. Sleep okay?"

"Best I've had in weeks." She settles next to me on the porch swing, pulling her feet up under her. "This place is perfect. Thank you for bringing me here."

"Yeah?"

"Yeah." She looks out at the trees, at the mountains in the distance. "It's nice to be somewhere that's just ours. No cameras, no expectations. Just us."

Just us. Like we're a legitimate couple instead of two people playing pretend.

Maybe we are. Maybe somewhere along the way, the pretending became real.

"Juliet," I start, but she cuts me off, shaking her head.

"I know," she says quietly. "I know this is complicated. I know we have rules and contracts and expiration dates. But this weekend... can we just be here? Can we just be us without all the rest of it?"

I nod, not trusting my voice.

Because I want that more than I've ever wanted anything. I would like to exist in this bubble where she's mine and I'm hers and nothing else matters.

Even if it's only for a weekend.

Even if it's all I get.

We spend the day hiking, holding hands like teenagers. And I let myself pretend that this is real. I act like this is my life and push the rest of my thoughts away.

Chapter 32

Juliet

I'm still floating from our weekend at the cabin when I find the package outside our door Sunday morning. It's addressed to me, postmarked locally, but there's no return address. My name is on the package, but I don't recognize the handwriting.

Inside I find a handwritten note and a manila envelope that feels heavy with whatever's inside.

The note makes my blood run cold.

Dear Miss Monroe,

I hope this letter finds you well. My name is Darla Huxley and I believe you know my son. I've been following your relationship with great interest. I think it's time we had a conversation.

There are things about Hunter you should know. I could tell you stories that might help you understand why he is the way he is. My son always needs saving from himself.

I have some materials I think you'd find illuminating. Perhaps we could meet for coffee? I'm sure we have much to discuss regarding Hunter's future.

A mother knows her son best, after all.

Sincerely,

Darla Huxley

My hands are shaking by the time I finish reading. I can't believe any mother would do this to her own son. Would reach out to someone in his life to... what? Sabotage him? Control him?

The envelope contains photos, printouts, and what looks like documentation of every mistake Hunter's ever made. There are a few legal papers from the money situation he told me about. Screenshots of old social media posts, too. Plus some photos from college parties that paint him in the worst possible light.

It's blackmail material. Pure and simple.

There are notes in the margins, Darla's handwriting pointing out details, spinning narratives, building a case against her own child. It's methodical. Calculated. Devastating.

And it's clearly meant to scare me away.

I don't hesitate. I grab the envelope and march into the living room where Hunter is drinking coffee and scrolling through his phone.

"We need to talk," I say, dropping the package on the coffee table in front of him.

He looks up, confused, then sees his mother's handwriting on the note. For a moment, he doesn't react at all. He stares at it like it's a bomb that might go off.

I see it hit him. A flicker of shame crosses his face. His shoulders shift, curling inward like he's trying to make himself smaller. I recognize that movement; it's almost like looking in the mirror.

"*Fuck*. Juliet, I'm sorry. I'm so sorry you got dragged into this. I never wanted her anywhere near you."

I cut him off before he can keep apologizing. "Do you think I deserved it when Patrick said cruel things about me?"

He looks stunned. "What? No. Fuck no."

"Then why would you think I want you to deal with this alone? I mean, it's clearly bullshit."

He stares at me, something shifting in his expression.

"I may not be your real fiancée," I mumble. "But I'm your real something. Right?"

That's the moment everything changes. I can see the way his walls crumble. He stops trying to protect me from this and starts letting me in.

"Yeah," he says, his voice rough. "You're my real something, Monroe."

He opens up then. Quietly. Honestly.

"My mom would call me crying," he says, staring at his hands. "You know, after she got caught stealing from me. She'd tell me she was proud of me, and say that she just wanted to help manage my money so I could focus on hockey. Then she'd guilt me about not trusting my family. She was beyond hurt that I'd even question her motives."

There's no anger in his voice now. It's more of a deep grief. He shakes his head as though he still can't believe it. I grip his hand, trying to let him know that he's not alone.

"When it all came out, she didn't even deny it. She just said I made it easy by being so trusting. Like it was my fault for believing her." He looks up at me. "Part of me still thinks maybe she was right."

I'm devastated listening to this. I'm seeing this side of him I never imagined. Not the public version. Not the reckless, angry man.

Someone gentle, maybe wounded even. Someone who's still standing despite everything.

"She wasn't right," I say firmly. "What she did was unforgivable."

"But she's still my mom."

"Being someone's mother doesn't give you the right to destroy them. What your mom did was more than just stealing money from you." I take a deep breath. "She stole your ability to trust, Hux. Your ability to let strangers in, if it ever existed, was just nuked by her greed."

We sit in silence for a moment, processing. Then he laughs, but there's no humor in it.

"You know what's funny? I told you in college that you weren't the type guys go for. Too uptight."

"Yeah, I remember." The sting of those words, the way they confirmed every insecurity I had about myself. "And I told you that you were just another hockey player looking to get laid. That not every girl was going to fall at your feet."

"I deserved it."

I shrug. "We were both assholes. We were kids." I pause. "Though I wasn't wrong about the getting laid part."

He actually laughs at that, and some of the tension breaks. "Fair point. If you'd have even looked my way, I'd have made sure you knew I was more than a little interested."

"How? By giving me a noogie?" I tease.

He looks at me with a sparkle in his eye, like I'm the most interesting thing in the room. That's mildly terrifying. If Hunter ever sees the authentic version of me, he won't look at me like that anymore. I frown.

"What are you thinking about?" he asks.

"Nothing good."

"Tell me anyway."

I study his face, seeing genuine curiosity there. Not the polite interest people show when they're trying to be nice. He has a sincere desire to understand.

"I'm thinking about how you look at me. It seems like you actually want to know me. And that scares me, because the real me isn't always very nice."

"I've seen you not be nice, Juliet. You're ruthless when you need to be. It's one thing I like about you."

"You say that now."

"I'll say it later too."

"You are just saying things because you want to get in my pants later."

"Honestly, Monroe." His blue-gray eyes spear me. "I wouldn't do that. One of the best things about being around you is the complete lack of lying about who you are. I like that when I'm looking at you, you don't put up walls or make up stories."

He cups my jaw. I run my fingers along his hand, gulping.

"Do you think most people aren't real?" I ask gently.

"I don't know." He brushes a hair back behind my ear, being unbearably sweet. "If I were being truthful, I'd say that I haven't let anyone close to me in a very long time. But you've worked your way under my skin. It turns out it's not terrible. It's…" He pauses. "Pretty great. You're pretty great, Firecracker."

I swallow, gripping his hand, scanning his face. He seems to be completely honest at this moment. Sucking in a breath, I blow it out slowly.

I can feel something shifting between us. Some barrier that we both held up crumbles and falls away. Without really thinking about it, I reach down and slip off my heels. Then I go to the bathroom and wash off my lipstick, staring at my bare face in the mirror.

I'm ready to take this chance. Hunter may not like the real me, the Juliet with no lipstick and no heels. But… what if he does?

When I come back, Hunter is watching me with something soft and intense in his expression.

"This is how I want it to be between us," I say. "No artifice. Just skin against skin."

He stands and comes to me, his hands finding my face, thumbs brushing across my bare lips.

"You're beautiful like this," he says. "You're beautiful all the time, but like this... this is just for me."

I bite my lip, lead him by the hand, and lower him to the couch. We sink together into the crisp leather. His knee presses against my thigh for a moment, and I can feel the heat even through my skirt. I'm still humming with adrenaline. Not from the confrontation with his mother, but from the way we stripped ourselves bare in front of each other.

No more fucking walls up. No more pretense. Just two hurt animals licking each other's wounds. Hunter leans back. I savor the anticipation sitting heavy between us. He's watching me, wild and wary, like he's waiting for me to flinch or run.

Instead, I plant my knees on either side of his, straddling him, and slowly unzip his hoodie from my body. It pools behind me on the couch, leaving me in nothing but a thin black lace bra and my tight black skirt. He's seen me naked before, but not like this.

Not stripped of all my makeup, my heels kicked away, my hair still damp from the bathroom sink and falling wild around my face. I look down at him, waiting for a reaction. For any sign that he misses the polished, packaged version.

Hunter's eyes go impossibly dark. His jaw tightens and I can see the vein in his neck straining.

"Fuck, sweetheart," he says. His voice is barely above a whisper. "You're killing me."

It's my turn to shake. For all my bravado, I have no idea

how to be vulnerable like this. I climb off his lap and sink to my knees between his legs, my palms running up his thighs, tracing the heavy muscle and the faint ridges of old scars. I feel him shudder beneath my touch.

I lean in and kiss his lips once, almost chaste, a thank-you for letting me in. Then I move to his neck, kissing the rough stubble there, inhaling the scent of his skin, the burnt vanilla of his cologne mixed with sweat and something uniquely him.

I tug his Henley up and he shrugs it off smoothly, leaving his chest bare to the waist. He is so fucking beautiful it's unreal. I run my hands up his sides, marveling at the heat and the way his body tenses with every touch. He sits perfectly still, hands gripping the edge of the couch like I might disappear if he moves too fast. I take his hands and place them on my weighty breasts, guiding his palms to cup me. I want him to explore the difference between the world's version of Juliet Monroe and the one kneeling in front of him now.

He doesn't need instruction. He rolls my nipples between his rough fingers, pinching and tugging until the peaks go tight and achy, sending shockwaves of sensation straight to my core. I want him to touch me everywhere, but this is enough for now. This is about undoing all the years I spent being untouchable, unreachable, untouchable. I arch my back, head falling, and he laughs quietly, the sound low and reverent.

"Goddamn," he mutters. "You're so fucking perfect."

I look up at him. "I'm not perfect." My voice comes out smaller than I'd like. "No one's ever accused me of that before."

He grins. "They should have. Were you kneeling and looking up at them with those fuck-me eyes?"

I smirk and slide his sweatpants down, hooked on my

fingers. He lifts himself up to help, slipping his boxer briefs off too. Hunter's cock springs out, already flushed and straining. For a second I just stare at it, at him, at the contrast between the size of my hands and the sheer massiveness of his thick cock.

It's long, pink, thick, and I can't quite close my fingers around the tip. Metal winks at me from where he's pierced; his entire cock is a walking red flag. One that I'm *hungry* for.

His dick is intimidating. Not just that, but it's *absurd*. If this were any other moment, I'd try to make some cutting joke about overcompensation. But right now I just want to worship the fact that he's here, he's real, and for the moment, he's *mine*.

Chapter 33

Juliet

I wrap my hand around him, feeling the velvet heat and the slickness already leaking from the tip. He inhales sharply, and I marvel at the way his entire body responds, like a machine perfectly tuned to my touch. I stroke him, slow at first, letting my thumb glide over the head, watching as his eyes flutter closed and his head tips back. I play with his piercing and he hisses.

"Good?" I murmur.

"Good," he grits out. "Just very sensitive, Firecracker."

"Mm." I lean in and kiss the sensitive spot just beneath the crown, tasting salt and skin, feeling the tremor that ripples through him. "You taste like you smell."

"Is that a good thing?"

"It's the best thing," I assure him. "I'm obsessed with the way you smell."

I run my tongue along the underside of his cock, a flat, slow lick from base to tip. He groans, the sound raw and unfiltered. I thrill at the power, the way I can reduce this man to pure want. I take him into my mouth, just the head at first, swirling my tongue, tasting him. He fists his hands against the couch and mutters a curse, his whole body tensing.

I take him deeper, slow and methodical, letting myself adjust to the stretch, the slight burn at the edges of my mouth. He's almost too big for me, but I want the challenge, want to push myself for him, for us. I use my hand to stroke the base while my lips and tongue work the rest. The noises he makes are guttural, reverent, helpless. They send sparks of heat through my body.

I look up and see him staring down at me, eyes wild, jaw slack, breathing like he's run a marathon. He brushes my hair back, gentle despite his size, and cups my face with a hand.

"You're fucking incredible," he says. His voice is hoarse. "You know that, right?"

Not breaking rhythm, I hum an answer. I want to please him, to make him lose every ounce of composure. If only for a minute, I want to erase the pain his mother left him with. I take him deeper, tilting my chin and relaxing my throat. He lets out a strangled gasp, hands flying to my shoulders like he's afraid he might hurt me. Or worse, lose himself entirely.

I keep going, wanting to see him undone. I want to be the person who gets to do that for him, who gets to see all the parts he hides from everyone else.

He strokes my hair, running his fingers through it, and I sense the effort it's taking him not to just grab and fuck my mouth harder. But he's holding back, for me. It makes me want to give even more. I moan around him, letting the vibration travel through his cock. He bucks his hips involuntarily, almost losing it.

I pull off, gasping for air, and look up at him. "You can. I can take it."

He hesitates, eyes searching mine for sincerity. He's always unsure about going harder, being himself. Maybe he's afraid that he'll hurt me. I'm a big girl though. I can stand up for myself. Plus, I trust him to listen if I say no.

I hate that he holds himself eternally in check. The urge to drive it out of his head rides me. "Stand up," I implore, my voice breathy. "Use me, Hux."

His eyes going dark, he stands up, towering over me. With one hand on the back of my head, he guides himself back into my mouth. This time he sets the rhythm, slow at first, then building, always watching my face for the slightest sign of discomfort. He's careful, but he's also losing control, and I love it.

"Fuck, Juliet. Your mouth is so perfect." He groans. "I've been dreaming about you marking my cock with your pretty red lipstick for too long."

My knees dig into the rug, and my jaw aches. My eyes water as he hits the back of my throat, but I don't stop. I take it, again and again, until his voice turns desperate, until he's cursing and praising me in the same breath.

"Good girl. See how well you take my cock?" He fists my hair. "I can't wait to taste you, sweetheart."

I'm perfect, I'm a good girl, I'm his. I want all of it. Every word, sound, and piece of him.

I run my hand down his thigh, knowing he can feel my pulse through my fingertips. I'm aware of how much I crave the illusion of control. But I want just this once to surrender. I want to let him take and take and take until there's nothing left of me but raw nerves.

"Jesus, Monroe..." he starts, but he's helpless to finish the thought. I hollow my cheeks and take him deeper, working my tongue in slow, measured swipes beneath the ridge, then dragging my lips back up, teasing the tip. He says my name like a prayer, over and over, each syllable more desperate than the last.

I could draw this out forever, but my need is as sharp as a blade, impatient and greedy. I take him deeper, swallowing inch after impossible inch, until I bury my nose against the sharp heat of his hip bone and his cock fills my throat. He's too big for me, but I want to prove that I can handle it, that I can handle him.

I can handle Hunter Huxley *any* way he gives himself to me.

He's close, I can tell. His thighs tense, his hand trembles in my hair, and his voice turns frantic, spilling out confessions in a rush. "You're so perfect—fuck, I never—I can't—"

There's a panic in his pleasure, a vulnerability I've never seen in him before, as if he's terrified of what he might do or say if he really lets go.

I want to see him break. I want to be the reason for it. So I grip his hips and pull him in, all the way, until my nose is pressed to his belly and my throat is full. I gag, choke, cough, but I don't tap out. I dig my nails into his skin and moan, letting the vibration push him further.

He can't hold back anymore. A groan escapes him, perhaps my name, as hot, salty cum fills my throat. He holds himself there, just for a few seconds, then pulls out slowly so that I can gasp for air. He strokes my jaw, thumb brushing away a tear, and says, "You okay?"

Swallowing, I wipe my lips with the back of my hand. "Never better, baby."

Time to recover is overrated. He yanks me up off my knees and paws at my hips until my skirt and panties tangle around my ankles. He strips my flimsy bra off too, then leads me to his bedroom.

He's had his bedframe replaced, I note with some small amount of pride. We could just break this one again. It sounds *fun*.

Inside his room, Hunter turns and cages me against the wall, his mouth crashing down on mine. He tastes sharp and familiar. A hint of sweetness from my mouth, the faintest spice of vanilla, and the metallic tang of his cum. He kisses me until I'm dizzy and clutching at him for balance, until my legs threaten to collapse.

"Hux," I gasp. "I really need you to touch me."

Hunter tosses me onto the bed. I let out a squeak. It's fun being with a *giant*. He stands at the edge of the mattress, cock jutting against his thigh, watching me with a focus so intense it makes me self-conscious. For a moment I panic, hyper-aware of every exposed inch of skin, every imperfection, that my tits aren't perky and I have stretch marks on my thighs. But he just drinks me in, eyes greedy, smiling like I'm the first and last thing he'll ever want.

It's sinful the way his gaze follows my every curve.

He kneels on the bed and leans over me, his hands sliding up my calves, over my knees, prying my thighs apart. He kisses a trail from my knee to my hip bone, biting down gently, marking me. I shiver, and he laughs softly against my skin.

"Look at you," he murmurs. His voice is dark as molasses. "Messy already. Is this for me?"

"Y-yes," I groan, shifting, sensation pooling between my legs. "You make me so wet, Hux."

A groan leaves his lips, reverberating through my flesh. He's so fucking *hot*. Pressing his nose between my thighs, he inhales, and I can't help the mortifying sound that escapes me. Then he flattens his tongue against my clit, slow and deliberate. The shock of pleasure is so sharp I gasp. My hips buck and he pins me against the mattress with an enormous hand over my abdomen. He's unhurried, in control.

He licks me in slow, lazy strokes at first, savoring. I

squirm. I need more, way more, an endless amount. *Bury me with his tongue between my thighs.* He speeds up, flicking and circling, sucking until I'm writhing. I want to play coy, to arch away or make him work for it, but my body betrays me. Every nerve ending is tuned to him, desperate for what only he can give.

I've never been like this. Not with Patrick, not with anyone. Only Hunter has made me this damn needy. I clutch at the sheets, then at his hair, pulling him closer, grinding helplessly against his mouth.

He's meticulous, relentless. He alternates between feathery kisses and deep, obscene plunges of his tongue. It's like he's mapping every secret inside me. It's both intimate and humiliating how he devours me. I feel exposed in a way I never let myself be, like he can see every craving, every weakness. I want to hide, but I also never want him to stop.

He's bringing me to the brink of madness and I only want *more*.

Hunter brings two thick fingers to my pussy entrance and slides them inside. I gasp at the sensation. It's only been a day since he fucked me, but I feel like this is the very first time. He curls his fingers upward with that same athlete's precision I used to loathe on the ice. Now it's turned to devastating, humiliating use. Grinding down, I'm greedy for the stretch and fullness, for the friction. I *need* to come. I'm *desperate* for it. He pumps his fingers in tandem with his mouth, tongue flicking faster. Soon I'm blabbering nonsense, unable to hold back.

"Fuck—you're—oh my god—Hunter, I'm—" I break off as the orgasm hits, sudden and overwhelming. It's not the usual tidal wave, but a series of sharp, rolling aftershocks that leave me trembling and gasping, clutching at his arms and begging him not to stop.

He doesn't. He pushes me through the crest, then straight through another, coaxing every shudder from my body before he finally comes up for air. His chin and mouth are slick with my wetness. He grins like a cat who ate the fucking cream, unrepentant.

He hovers above me, bracing himself on his forearms. He kisses me, letting me taste myself on his lips. I feel raw and open, barely able to catch my breath. He watches me with that fierce, possessive look, like he wants to memorize me at my most undone.

The most crazy part is that *I want him to.*

"You good?" he asks. His voice is so low it's almost a growl.

I nod. I can't speak yet. He nestles down next to me, gathering me into his arms. He strokes my hair like I'm something fragile. The gentleness after such violence undoes me. It's like he's letting me know I'm safe, even after everything.

But I'm greedy. I feel empty without him inside me, a hollow ache that pulses between my hips. I want more, want all of him, want to see him lose control. Just the way he made me come. I recover just enough to roll over him, straddling his hips. His hands settle on my ass, encouraging, but I catch them and flatten them above his head, pinning him for a change. He raises his eyebrows, amused.

"Hunter," I whisper against his mouth. "I need to ask you something."

"Yeah?"

"Have you been tested? Recently?"

He pulls back to look at me. "Yeah. When we first moved in together. Just in case." His cheeks flush slightly. "Have you?"

"Yes. Before I moved in."

The admission hangs between us, heavy with implication.

We both planned this, both hoped for this, even when we were pretending it was just business.

"I want you," I say simply. "All of you. No barriers."

"Fuck, Juliet." His eyes search mine. "I've never done that."

"Neither have I. But everything we do feels like the first time," I admit. "I want to feel you, Hux."

He shudders, kissing me hard.

It's different this time and I know it the moment I let him in. All the way in, nothing between us, no latex or pretense or half-measures. There is a terrifying freedom in it, a dizzying sense of reckless possibility, as if I've stepped out past the edge of the familiar cliff and am now in freefall, arms outstretched, trusting that he'll catch me or at least fall with me.

If we have to plummet straight down to our certain death, at least we'll do it together.

I'm on top of him, knees on either side of his hips, and I spit on my hand to lubricate his cock a little extra. He bites his lip and gives me a lustful, hooded expression. "You gonna fuck yourself on my dick?"

"Yes, Hux." I position his cock at my entrance, shuddering with anticipation. "I'm going to burn us both to the ground."

He thrusts up as I impale myself, his cock pushing inside me, raw and perfect, every inch a shock to the system. His piercing hits my g-spot just right, feeling so damn good. I brace myself with hands on his chest, his heart thundering under my palms. I ride him, my pace starting slowly.

My intention isn't to dominate or punish. I want to be seen. I want, for once, to not be afraid of what a man will do with all of me. Hux didn't hold back earlier when I was on my knees for him. The least I can do is give him everything I've got.

His hands roam my thighs, gripping tight, then softening, then gripping again as if he might lose his place. He reaches up and cups my tits with both hands, thumbs teasing my nipples until I arch my back and moan. Maybe he already knows that they're my secret weakness. My cheat code. He works it without mercy or hesitation. Each brush and pinch sends a jolt of pleasure straight to my core, winding me up tighter and tighter as I grind down onto him, chasing the friction that will tip me over.

"You're so fucking beautiful," he croons, low and amazed, like he's still not sure this is real. "Look at how well you're riding my cock. God, your tits, your mouth, your thighs. I *can't*. I'm losing my mind."

Every word, every curse, is like cool water being poured over my sunburned flesh. I crave his words, his praise, his coming apart. Every inch of my body flushes, sweat beading on my skin as I move harder, faster, drunk on the way we fit together. The bed creaks beneath us, wood hitting drywall with a slow, steady rhythm that grows frantic as we do.

My lips tip up as I wonder how hard I'll have to work to get him to demolish this frame, too. How long will it last? Not long, I hope.

He sits up, burying his face in my chest, licking and biting. Then he's sucking my nipples until I moan, until I scream, until I can't remember my name. The sensation is so sharp, so good, that I almost sob with it. I clutch his head to me, tangle my fingers in his sweat-damp hair, and fuck him with everything I've got, wanting to be ruined by it.

Fuck it, I *am* ruined by him.

He's close. His hips jerk, and desperately grinding deeper.

He wants to make me feel it, like he's trying to get under my skin. I want him to lose control. I want him to break.

When I come, it crashes over me like a tidal wave. Violent, relentless, washing away every defense I ever built. I scream his name, not even bothering to muffle it. I dig my nails into his shoulders and ride him through the aftershocks, shaking, grateful, stunned.

But he doesn't stop. He shifts, twists us so I'm flat on my back and he's above me. He pins my wrists to the mattress and pounds into me with a single-minded focus that borders on obsession. There's sweat dripping from his forehead, his jaw clenched as if he's in pain, his entire body vibrating with the need to let go and the fear of what will happen when he does.

"Come for me again," he growls. "Give it to me, Firecracker. I want to watch you fall apart."

He lets go of one wrist and brings his hand down between us. He rubs my clit in hard, tight circles. The world whites out. Stars behind my eyes, toes curling, lungs empty of air. I shatter for him, again. And this time it's not just physical. It feels like something is breaking open inside, like he's touching parts of me that have never seen daylight. It feels like being baptized and born anew.

He loses it. Burying his face in my neck, he clutches my waist. He comes so hard I feel it in every cell, every vein, every nerve ending. His hips snap, pumping, as he fills my pussy with lashes of his hot cum. His cry is low and desperate, my name muffled in my hair. I hold him as he trembles through his orgasm, his hands tightening on my body until I'm sure he'll leave marks.

"Oh, Monroe," he mumbles. Tension seeps from him as he kisses me, fumbling, desperate. "*Fuck*, baby. Fuck."

I smooth a hand over his messy dark blonde hair. I'm not

sure I can speak yet, so it'll have to do. He carefully shifts his weight so that I'm lying partially on his body, our limbs tangled, our breath hard.

God, that was reverential. It was *life*-changing.

Everything that usually swirls in my brain is gone. He makes the static in my brain quieter.

I notice a sketchbook half-hidden in his bedside drawer. Without thinking, I reach for it and flip it open.

The drawing on the current page takes my breath away.

It's me. But not sexual or idealized. It's intimate in a way that goes deeper than physical. Emotional and honest. He's captured something in my expression that I didn't even know was there, some softness I only show when I think no one is looking.

"Huxley," I breathe.

He tries to take the notepad from me, his face flushed with embarrassment. "You weren't supposed to see that."

"Don't." I hold it away from him, still staring at the drawing. "This is beautiful. This is how you see me?"

His mouth flexes as if he's not sure what expression he wants to make. "Sometimes. When you think no one's watching."

"I love it." The words come out more intense than I intended, but I mean them. "No one's ever looked at me like this, let alone drawn it."

He relaxes slightly, but I can tell he's still self-conscious about showing me this side of himself.

"I used to write and sketch a lot," he says quietly. "Before everything got complicated. It's the only time my brain shuts up."

I flip through a few more pages, seeing sketches of his teammates, letters scrawled in his intense, blocky half-cursive, diagrams of X's and O's on a hand-drawn hockey rink outline. Arrows cut across the diagram, tracing a path that feels less like strategy and more like choreography. There's control in it, discipline, and an instinct for movement that goes far beyond brute force.

"You're really talented, Hux."

He tries to downplay it. "It's just a hobby."

"It's more than that." I close the notebook carefully and set it back inside his bedside table. "I get to look at myself how you see me."

"I hope I did a good job of making you look like a smokeshow," he jokes. "I would draw your brain too, but it might be a little weird."

"I like weird things." I lay my head against his shoulder.

We lie there in comfortable silence for a while. I think about how this weekend was supposed to be part of the strategy. A move on the chessboard. A way of selling our relationship to the world.

But it's become something terrifyingly outside the bounds that we tried to set up.

Something real.

Lying there with him, feeling more exposed and more safe than I have in years, I realize I don't know what scares me more. Losing this thing we've built, or letting myself keep it.

Because keeping it means admitting this was never fake. Means acknowledging that somewhere along the way, I stopped playing a role and started falling for the man behind it.

Means risking everything on the possibility that he might choose me when this is all over.

And Juliet Monroe doesn't gamble with her heart.

Except apparently, she does.

Apparently, she already has.

Chapter 34

Hunter

The kitchen sink backs up Tuesday morning while Juliet's getting ready for work. I hear her muttering about it from the bedroom, followed by the sound of her opening and closing cabinet doors like she's going to find a magical solution in there.

"Problem?" I ask, appearing in the doorway.

She's crouched under the sink in her work clothes, hair pulled back, looking frustrated. "The disposal is being stupid. I think something's stuck."

"Move over."

She shifts aside without protest. I slide under the sink cabinet to look. It's not complicated, just needs the disposal reset, and the drain cleared. I take about ten minutes to fix it.

"There," I say. I wash my hands and wipe my hands with a dish towel. "Should be good now."

When I look up, she's staring at me with something soft in her expression.

"Thank you." Her voice has this quality I don't hear often. Genuine gratitude, but also something deeper. I can tell that she's touched that I noticed. I think fixing things without being asked is pleasing to her.

I'll have to make a note of that.

It's not a big moment. Just basic household maintenance. But it hits me hard anyway. That kind of intimacy. Trust. Affection. The way she looks at me like I'm useful for more than just hockey stats and public appearances.

It's quiet, but it's mutual. I can see it on her face that this feels like something to her too.

Like a turning point.

Oh *fuck*. Oh, fucking fuck. I might have serious feelings for my fake fiancée.

I've had a lot of things in my life. Money. Ice time. Rage. Enough anger to fuel a small city and enough adrenaline to keep me going when everything else falls apart.

But I've never had peace. Not like when she's sitting next to me with her feet in my lap, reading some article on her phone while I flip through game footage. Not like when she hums under her breath while making coffee in the morning, unconscious and content.

Not like this.

The realization follows me to practice, where I'm completely useless. I can't focus on drills, miss simple passes, get my ass handed to me in scrimmage because my head is somewhere else entirely.

"You good, Hunt?" Silas asks during a water break. "You look like you've seen a ghost."

"Fine," I lie. "Just tired."

But I'm not tired. I'm terrified.

Having serious feelings for Juliet might change everything. It certainly makes this whole arrangement infinitely more complicated. It forces me to view the expiration date on our contract as a countdown to unhappiness.

Am I happy? Not completely, but happier than I was when I lived alone. Juliet has brightened my days.

I'm still processing this earth-shattering revelation when my phone buzzes. Text after text, missed calls, the notification storm that means something bad has happened. Shit.

The first headline I see makes my blood turn to ice.

"Hockey Mom Breaks Her Silence: Darla Huxley Opens Up About Life with 'The Chainsaw'"

Then another: *"Mother's Heartbreak: Former Agent Details Son's Volatile Behavior"*

And another: *"Exclusive: Inside Hunter Huxley's Troubled Family Dynamic"*

Darla's face is everywhere. Perfectly composed, playing the role of concerned mother to perfection. The articles are careful, walking the line between sympathy-generating and legally actionable.

She claims I've always been volatile. That "The Chainsaw" isn't just a hockey nickname; according to her, it's who I am behind closed doors. Mom depicts herself as a frightened mother, abused and cast aside by the son for whom she sacrificed everything.

Disgusting.

Mom doesn't say anything concrete. Nothing I could sue her for. Just twisted little implications and promises of a "full story" coming soon.

"Christ." I can't breathe. My ears are ringing. All I can think is, *what the fuck. What the actual fuck.*

I gave my mom everything. I worked my ass off for years, built a career from dirt and determination, and handed her the keys to it all. She was my agent, my mouthpiece, my fucking power of attorney. I let her take more than her share, again and again, because she was my mother. I wanted to believe she loved me.

But it was never enough.

I will never be enough for her.

And if my mother says that I'm a monster, how the hell can I expect anyone else to believe me? How can I expect anyone to stay? Especially someone like Juliet. She's all bright fire and sharp intelligence and polished professionalism. This mess is no place for her. Juliet doesn't deserve to be dragged down by my family's dysfunction.

I drive home in a haze, bracing for the fallout. Juliet will pull away, start making exit plans, and remember that this is supposed to be temporary anyway.

But instead of pulling away, Juliet goes to war for me.

I find out about it when I'm almost home. Silas texts me a link to a live stream. "Dude, your girl is handling business."

Juliet is standing in front of a bank of microphones, looking calm and professional and absolutely lethal. She hasn't checked in with me first, hasn't asked permission or run her strategy past anyone. She just dealt with it.

"The Huxley family will step away from media obligations for the time being," she says, her voice steady and authoritative. "Mr. Huxley and his brothers deserve privacy during this difficult time. Their mother is experiencing some troubling personal issues, obviously. And certain news outlets are preying on her weakness to get a cheap story."

A reporter shouts a question about the allegations. Juliet doesn't even blink.

"On a personal note, I've known Hunter Huxley for years. He would never do what his mother is accusing him of. He's known for being The Chainsaw, but that's just a persona. Inside, he has a heart of gold. He's the most decent, principled person I know. And I would say that even if I weren't his fiancée."

My heart tightens in my chest. Decent and principled?

Not words I ever expected from Juliet Monroe. They even *sound* convincing.

Another reporter raises her hand. "Why would Mrs. Huxley lie? What could she hope to gain?"

God, I wish I knew. I wish I had just paid my mom off before she went to a reporter with these crazy lies.

"I think the public should question why someone keeps seeking attention with stories designed to hurt her own children," she says smoothly. "Especially someone with a documented history of exploiting those children for personal gain."

She never names Darla directly. But the implication is razor sharp.

"Mental health struggles are real and serious," Juliet continues. "And sometimes they manifest as a need to control or damage the people closest to them. The Huxley brothers have shown nothing but grace and maturity in removing themselves from a toxic situation."

She spins the narrative so tight it can't unravel. Suddenly, Juliet has turned the spotlight onto Darla's instability, her history, her choices. And somehow, she makes the entire mess look like a mother lashing out, not a son unraveling.

For the second time in twenty minutes, I'm completely floored.

I watch the press conference in total disbelief. I can't believe Juliet did that for me. That she would put herself on the line like that, risk her own reputation to protect mine.

When I get home, I lose it.

I lock myself in the bedroom and sit on the edge of the bed, chest heaving, vision swimming. My fists hurt from clenching them. I want to break something, scream, hide, do something with all this rage and shame and grief that's eating me alive.

None of it would help.

The voices in my head are loud tonight. Darla's voice telling me I'm just like my father. My voice agreeing with her. The reporters' voices, asking if there's truth to the allegations.

All of them echo the same truth. I can't trust anyone. Not even Juliet. This won't last. She'll leave too once she realizes what kind of person she's really dealing with.

There's a soft knock on the door.

"Hunter?" Juliet's voice is gentle but firm. "Let me in."

I stay quiet. Silent. Because what would I even say? How do I explain that my mother is trying to destroy me? How do I tell her that maybe Darla is right, maybe I am too damaged to be worth saving?

I hear a soft clink. A pause. Then the door clicks open.

She picked the lock with a butter knife. Of course she did.

"That's illegal, you know," I say without looking up.

"Sue me."

She walks in like it's nothing. Pretending that I'm not falling apart. She doesn't say a word; she just climbs into bed beside me and curls into my side like she belongs there.

Her hand finds my hair, stroking gently. The touch is so soft, so careful, that it almost breaks me all over again.

"You're not alone," she whispers. "I'm here. It's okay."

"It's not okay," I say, my voice rougher than I intended. "None of this is okay."

"No," she agrees. "It's not. But you're not alone."

I don't deserve her. It's something I know with absolute certainty. Grief, rage, and shame have twisted me, making me too broken and dangerous. I'm too much like my father, no matter how hard I try not to be.

"Why did you do that? The press conference. You didn't have to."

"Yes, I did."

"Juliet."

"What?" She pulls back to look at me. "You think I was going to let her destroy you? Let her spread lies about who you are?"

"What if they're not lies?"

The words slip out before I can stop them. The fear I've been carrying since I was old enough to understand that I inherited more than just my father's eyes.

"They are lies," Juliet says firmly. "I know who you are, Hunter. I've seen you angry, I've seen you lose control. I've also seen you put yourself back together. You're not a monster."

"My mother thinks I am."

"Your mother is sick. And cruel. She's wrong."

She says it with such certainty that for a moment, I almost believe her.

"What if this ruins everything for you? You were defending me when the universe thinks we're engaged. You put your career and your reputation on the line. What if people think you're just as messed up as I am?"

"Maybe I don't care what people think." She touches my jaw so gently, like I'm made of porcelain. "I know you, Hux. The Chainsaw is a made up character. I see you trying to please people, but you don't have to. You can let go."

I suck in a breath. "What if I can't?"

Juliet laces her fingers through mine. "I'll still be here."

I lie there in the dark, her warmth pressed against my side, trying to process everything that's happened. The press conference, the headlines, the way she just walked into my breakdown like it was nothing.

Like she wasn't afraid of me.

Like she wasn't planning to leave.

"I don't know how to do this," I whisper. "I don't know how to let someone care about me without waiting for them to leave."

She lays her head on my chest. "You don't have to know how. You just have to let me."

Her fingers trace patterns on my chest, and I can feel some of the tension draining out of my shoulders.

"I'm wrecked," I tell her. "You know that, right? I'm completely fucked up."

"I know."

"And you're still here."

"I'm still here."

I don't push her away, stop her, or try to convince her she's making a mistake. I'm too tired to keep fighting the one person who always seems to have my back.

"Thank you," I say.

"For what?" Her breath fans against my chest.

"For what you did today. For this."

"You don't have to thank me."

"Yeah, I do."

We lie there in comfortable silence. This is so different from anything I've ever experienced. The way she doesn't need me to be anything other than what I am. She seems to see all my damage and yet she doesn't run.

The way she went to war for me without being asked.

Maybe I'm not too broken for this. Maybe with her I can be something better.

Maybe I already am.

Chapter 35

Juliet

Today is a turnaround trip. We fly into Houston, play a game, fly back. It works best with our schedule. Plus, who wants to be in the middle of a Houston ice storm if they don't have to be?

Calls, scheduling, and trying to wrangle players into media appearances they hate eat my whole day alive. But I love it. I love shaping a story, showing people the best version of this team, of myself. I'm still new here, still proving I'm not just Patrick's ex, and every success is another brick in the future I'm building for myself.

The second I step off the plane in Houston, Hunter is on me like glue. His hand finds my lower back as we walk through the terminal, then my shoulder when we're waiting for our bags. He even grips my hand when he thinks no one's looking.

When an airport employee makes the mistake of asking if I need help to find transportation, Hux appears like magic, growling, putting his arm around me as if he's pulling me out of the way of a speeding train.

"Sorry about him." I blush and roll my eyes, squeezing

Hunter's biceps. "We're completely fine. I'm with an enormous group and a shuttle is going to pick us up."

The guy nods, wide eyed, and disappears. I feel giddy inside at how possessive Hux acts, but I can't let him see that. Schooling my face, I give him a mock stern look.

"You nearly gave that guy a heart attack."

Hunter looks down at me, his hand tightening on my waist. "He's not allowed to hit on you, Monroe."

"Get a hold of yourself. He was just doing his job."

"He was about to ask you out. And he was standing too close to begin with."

"Watch this over the top eye roll to get my reaction to that, Hux." I roll my eyes all the way back, making sure he sees that I think he's being silly.

"You're too nice to random people." He shrugs a shoulder and puts his arm around my neck. "Stick with me. I'll keep them all at bay."

When he flashes a grin afterward, it's pure lizard brain satisfaction. But I know that grin doesn't exist for anyone else.

"Yeah, I can see that, caveman."

He flashes a smile at me, looking entirely too pleased with himself. *Asshole.*

When the shuttle picks up the team, I sink into a seat, sighing as I look out at the Houston skyline. I took countless shuttles here when I flew back and forth from Seattle to Houston. I've never had anybody waiting at the airport for me, though.

Airport pickups were never Patrick's cup of tea. Can't say I blame him; the Houston airport is only about 20 minutes from downtown, but we'll pass nothing but gas stations, grocery stores, and Waffle Houses until we're practically downtown.

"You okay?" Hux nudges me.

Honestly? I've felt better before. I feel weirdly hot; I've felt over-warm since we hit the tarmac at Sea-Tac. I think it's nerves from heading back to Houston and knowing I'm going to have to face Patrick tonight. But I don't tell Hunter any of that.

"Fine." I lean my head against his shoulder. "Tired."

Hux puts his arm around me without comment. I know he's trying to be supportive. The other players seem to handle me with kid gloves, too. They've been treating me like I'm made of glass ever since we got on the plane.

Hunter probably said something to make them act this way. I wish he wouldn't. Or I wish that he didn't have to, I guess.

It would be easier if Hunter were cruel. If he mocked me the way Patrick did when I got overwhelmed or anxious, rolled his eyes and told me to get over it.

But he listens. He notices. He remembers the scent I wear and what brand of coffee I like and how I always check a mirror before I speak to make sure my lipstick hasn't smudged.

And that makes it worse. Because kindness is more seductive than cruelty ever was. It makes me want something more between us, even though it's *insane*. Wanting Hunter is like asking someone to put another hole in my head.

Hunter insists on taking selfies with my phone on the drive. He's never even cared about social media before, but now he's posing for pictures and making sure our Instagram story shows us together in Houston.

Silently telling Patrick to back off, I think.

"Smile like you actually like me," he says. He tugs me onto his lap for another shot and hands his arm around my neck.

"I do like you," I say with a laugh. Suddenly, I realize I mean it more than I should. I really, really like him.

How dare Huxley make me care about him?

He posts them with captions about away games and supporting each other, and I watch the likes and comments roll in. Our fake relationship is so convincing that sometimes I forget it's fake.

"You okay?" he asks quietly as we're unloading at the arena. "For someone whose job it is to talk, you've been really silent."

"Fine. I promise."

He studies my face like he's cataloging every detail. "You sure?"

"I'm sure." I poke him with a finger. "Stop trying to take care of me, you big brute."

Hunter grabs our bags, shaking his head, and guides me toward the building.

I can feel a headache creeping in and feel chills that have nothing to do with the air conditioning. Every sound feels louder than it should.

Of all the days for me to come down with something, I swear.

By the time we get to the arena for pre-game activities, I feel like a truck has hit me. My fever is climbing, my whole body aches, and the fluorescent lights feel like they're drilling into my skull. Hux is in the locker room, presumably getting changed or getting some kind of pep talk from Coach Cross.

I walk into the press room, dreading seeing my ex. The Houston Stars players are just filing in, their press conference before the Havoc's. I lift my chin and make hard eye contact with him as he enters the room, tall, dark-haired, and rotten inside. A sharklike smile breaks out across his face as he heads to the conference table.

He's smirking like a villain, all confidence and calculated charm. I can't believe I ever thought that I was in love with him. He's *revolting*. When a reporter asks about the dynamics of tonight's game, he mentions his ex-fiancée, who's here with the opposing team.

I want to sink into the floor and cease to be, but that's not a choice I get. I have a very public-facing job. Part of it is going to be dealing with my shit choice in ex boyfriends.

"Juliet's doing well for herself," Patrick says. He grins, using the same smile that used to make me feel special. Now it makes my gut churn. "Good for her. Though if she ever wants something real again, she knows she can call me. We all know that what she has with Hunter Huxley is a sham."

God, I loathe him with every fiber of my being. I roll my eyes, but don't respond. I *refuse* to give him the satisfaction of a reaction. But it shakes me more than I want to admit, hearing him dismiss what I have with Hunter as fake. Even though it *is* fake.

Patrick can't know that. He can't see the weakness in me, even if it means trying to hide the symptoms of a brewing illness.

I mop sweat from my brow. My fever climbs higher. I need to tell someone, but none of the women I would normally confide in are around. I can't both Hunter with this either, not when he needs to focus in order to dominate in this game. So I find Coach Ryan in the hallway outside the press room, looking calm and professional as always. Sliding up beside him, I rest on the cool wall.

"I need your help." Hesitating, I decide to give him the short version. "I think Patrick is going to do something hurtful. Someone needs to know in case something weird happens tonight. I… I don't want Hunter to see him giving me shit and lose his mind."

Coach Ryan nods, his expression serious. "Say no more. You need anything, you let me know."

True to his word, when Patrick tries to approach me later near the press area, it's Ryan who intercepts him. He just points right at Patrick and then beckons to him. "You! Come here."

Patrick pales slightly. "I'm just trying to talk to Juliet."

"The fuck you are." He grabs Patrick's arm and yanks him close, then murmurs something in his ear. Patrick's eyes slide to me, but he shakes his head.

Calm and firm, Coach Ryan steers Patrick away without making a scene, physically forcing Patrick to back off.

It's a good thing, too. I keep stealing glances at Hunter throughout warm-ups. He looks like he's vibrating under the surface, always one second away from exploding. His movements are too sharp, too controlled, like he's holding himself back by sheer force of will.

The entire team lines up, grimacing. Something in the Seattle Havoc's water definitely makes them angry. Not a wonderful sign going into a game where I'm hoping Hux doesn't demolish anyone. By the time the whistle blows, I'm shivering, my eyes never leaving #47.

Patrick is gunning for him from the first shift. Chirping him, shoving him after every whistle, trying to bait him into a fight. I watch every second, my heart in my throat, bracing for Hunter to snap the way he always does.

But he doesn't.

He stays calm.

When Patrick shoves him in front of the net, Hunter just shoves back and keeps skating. When Patrick tries to get under his skin with whatever garbage he's saying, Hunter ignores him completely.

No retaliation. No outburst. He plays clean, focused, and deadly.

And when his eyes flick up to the stands, the tiniest smirk appears. It's directed at me and no one else. I feel it piece me like an arrow, notched and aimed straight for my heart.

I feel… *proud* of him. Hunter and I may have started off as the worst enemies, but we've both grown. Become something more. Now my heart races at the sight of Hunter making a logical decision not to go after his antagonist.

I don't know what we are, but we are definitely not enemies.

The other Havoc players take up the slack that their enforcer leaves. Silas goes after Patrick in the second period, giving a nasty bloody nose. Beck gets him with a perfectly legal but bone-rattling hit that makes me wince. Thorne and Grayson start a brutal onslaught, attacking the puck and any Stars player that gets in their way. The Stars are so distracted that they don't have the resources to fight Patrick's battle.

The team leaders don't let up for a second, fighting and not taking an inch of shit, leaving Huxley open to score twice. Connor and Shane even get in on the action, both taking cheap shots at Patrick while everyone else is busy knee-deep in battle. By the third period, Patrick's on the bench nursing a bruised ego and what looks like a sore shoulder.

The trainers haul Patrick off the ice. What a man-baby.

I couldn't care less, though. I turn to watch Hunter like he's the only person on the ice. During a break in play, Hux looks up into the stands and catches my gaze. I make a heart with my hands and he nods, almost imperceptibly, before turning away.

Is it truthful? Maybe not totally. But it'll grind Patrick's gears. Plus, Hux is playing like a hockey god tonight. He deserves to have a girl doting on him and screaming his name in the stands.

When the final buzzer goes off, the Havoc win 3-1. I can't help jumping up and down and yelling for Huxley, although it makes me feel a little dizzy. Maybe not the greatest idea, but I have to let him know I'm excited for his win.

Hunter coasts off the ice at the end of his shift, chest heaving. The bench is buzzing. No fights, no penalties. Just clean, brutal hockey and a scoreboard to prove it.

Cross meets him at the boards, smacking his shoulder. "That's it, Huxley. That's how we win."

Even Thorne nods, sharp approval in his eyes. "Good work."

Hunter's head jerks like he doesn't know what to do with the words. His mouth tightens, but I catch the flicker in his eyes. Pride. Maybe even hope.

It's gone a second later, buried under his scowl. But I saw it. And it makes my chest ache, knowing how starved he is for that kind of praise.

The locker room is electric afterward. I can hear the celebration through the walls as I wait in the family area.

"You get a girlfriend and suddenly you're not threatening to break kneecaps every ten minutes," I hear Shane saying as the guys filter out.

"Still threatening," Jett adds. "Just quieter. Polished threats."

"Fuck off," Hunter mutters, but he doesn't sound angry. "She's my fiancée."

The word hits me harder than it should. Even though it's fake. Even though it's all for show.

I'm Hunter Huxley's fiancée. At least I can pretend it's real.

Hunter stays close to me as we board the plane. I'm trying to hide how awful I feel, but my legs are shaking and my vision keeps going fuzzy around the edges.

"You sure you're okay?" he asks as we walk down the aisle.

"Just tired," I lie.

He keeps a hand on my waist the whole way to our seats, steady and warm and grounding. When we find our seats, I promptly pass out. I have the vaguest recollection of Huxley buckling my seatbelt for me, but everything else is an exhausting haze.

By the time we land in Seattle, I can barely stand. The fever has spiked again, and everything hurts. Hunter helps me off the plane.

He makes a frustrated sound. "Monroe, you can't even walk by yourself."

I mumble something about catching a cab to the hotel, take two steps, and stumble.

Hunter catches me instantly, his voice sharp with concern. "That's it. We're going to the ER."

"No," I manage. "I probably just caught that flu that's been going around the team. I'll be fine."

"You're barely making sense."

"I said I'm fine."

Then I vomit all over the tarmac and go down hard.

When I wake up, I'm back in our apartment, in Hunter's bedroom. I would recognize the scent anywhere. Everything's blurry, like I'm looking through frosted glass. The sheets are cool against my burning skin. The lights are dim. Hunter is beside me, holding a cold compress to my forehead.

"Hey," he whispers when he sees my eyes open. "How are you feeling?"

"Like death."

"The team doctor came by. She says it's just a case of the flu. Nothing serious, but you're burning up."

I try to sit up and immediately regret it. My head feels like it's full of bees, and the room spins violently. Hunter's there immediately, easing me back down.

"Don't get up, Monroe. Just rest."

I drift in and out of sleep for what feels like days. Fever dreams where Patrick and Hunter are fighting and I can't stop them. Nightmares where I'm back in Patrick's apartment and he's telling me again that no man will ever choose me. I shake so hard my teeth chatter despite the blankets Hunter keeps piling on me.

But every time I wake up, he's still there. Bringing me water when I can keep it down. Changing my sheets when I soak them with sweat. Wiping my face with a cool cloth when the fever spikes. Never once looking disgusted or tired even though I'm sure I look disgusting.

He's just… here.

Two days pass in a blur of misery.

Finally, I stir for real. Everything still hurts, but the fever has broken. I can think clearly for the first time since Houston. I look around and spot Hunter scribbling in his notebook. He looks up when I move.

"What time is it?"

"You're awake," he says, relief clear in his voice. "How do you feel?"

"Like I got hit by a truck, but better."

He feeds me a few sips of Gatorade, then some broth, then actual toast when it becomes clear I can keep food down. He changes the sheets one last time and climbs into bed beside me like it's the most natural thing in the world.

He turns on old sitcom reruns and gently strokes my hair while I lie there, wrecked but finally on the mend.

"You didn't have to do all this," I whisper, my voice still weak.

"Yeah, I did."

"Hunter."

"What?" He kisses my forehead, soft and careful. "All I've ever wanted is to be useful to somebody."

The words hit me like a physical blow. This man, who seems so confident, so sure of himself, is just as terrified of not being enough as I am of being too much.

I lie there, stunned by the realization.

This started as a favor. A stunt. Now I'm losing sleep over a man who isn't really mine.

And that's the problem.

"What are you thinking about?" Hunter asks quietly.

"You," I admit before I can stop myself.

"Yeah?"

"You took care of me. For two days. You could have gotten sick too."

"Worth the risk."

"Why?"

He's quiet for a long moment, his fingers still moving through my hair. "Because you matter to me. Because when you went down at the airport, I thought..." He stops, swallows hard. "I thought about losing you, and it scared the shit out of me."

His mouth softens into the smile I know he doesn't give the world. It's unguarded, like it belongs only to me. He's trying so hard to be what I need.

"I thought I was the only one terrified of being too much," I say. "Of being a burden."

"You're not a burden, Juliet."

"What I'm saying is," I prop myself on my elbow. "Maybe you're just as scared of not being enough."

He goes still. "Maybe."

Vulnerability isn't weakness, I realize. It's trust. And I'm not sure I've ever trusted anyone like this before. Not even Patrick, who I was supposed to marry.

"Thank you for taking care of me. For staying."

"Thank you for letting me."

We lie there in comfortable silence, watching terrible sitcoms and not talking about the fact that everything has changed between us. That this isn't fake anymore, hasn't been fake for a while.

That we're both falling for each other and trying to pretend we're not.

"Hunter?"

"Mmm?"

"What happens when this is over? When the five months are up?"

He's quiet for so long I think he won't answer. Then he says, "I don't know. What do you want to happen?"

It's the question I've been avoiding. The one that keeps me awake at night when I should plan my next career move.

"I don't know either," I admit.

Lying here in his arms, feeling safer and more cared for than I have in years, I'm thinking I want to find out.

I'm thinking this man, who fixed my sink and held my hair while I was sick and played the cleanest game of hockey I've ever seen, might be worth the risk of believing in something real.

Even if it scares me.

Especially because it scares me.

"We don't have to figure it out tonight," Hunter says softly.

"No. We don't."

But as I drift back to sleep in his arms, I can't shake the feeling that we're both already in too deep to pretend this is just business anymore.

And maybe that's not such a terrible thing after all.

Chapter 36

Hunter

I'm sweaty, tired, and distracted when I get home from practice. Coach Cross ran us through drills until my legs felt like jelly. Now all I want is a shower and maybe some of whatever Juliet's making for dinner, because it smells *amazing*.

But as I open the door to the condo, I hear her voice carrying from her bedroom. She sounds tense, tight in the way she only gets when she's talking to someone unpleasant.

I slow down, dropping my gear bag quietly by the door. The bedroom door is ajar and I can hear every word.

"I don't understand why you're being like this," Juliet says. There's something strained in her voice that makes my chest tighten.

I should keep walking and give her privacy. But something about her tone stops me in my tracks.

"When are you going to get serious about your life, Juliet?" Her mother's voice comes through clearly from what must be a video call. "You're twenty-six years old. You should have your juris doctorate by now. Instead, you're screwing around with some hockey team."

421

"I am serious about my life, Mom. This is my career."

"This is a distraction. You need to be thinking about your future. Law school, marriage, children. Now, before you're too old to enjoy them properly."

I hear Juliet take a shaky breath. "I am in a relationship, not that you've made any effort to get to know him."

She says it like it hurts. I haven't put a moment of thought into it, but that her parents haven't bothered to really meet me, really get to know me, might be a wound she's been carrying.

Her mom huffs. "The hockey player? Come on."

"I told you I wanted to marry him. What don't you get about that?"

"Juliet, be realistic. This is a phase. Eventually, he'll get bored and leave. You need to be focusing on law school, something to fall back on. You can mess around with him if you want, but you need to be improving yourself."

My hands clench into fists. The casual cruelty in her mother's voice and the way she dismisses what we have like it's nothing makes me want to punch something.

"Why won't you just see that I'm happy?" Juliet's voice cracks. I can hear the tears she's trying to hold back.

"Happy?" Her mother sounds genuinely surprised. "Juliet, happiness is a luxury. You need *security*, darling."

"I'm trying to be happy," Juliet whispers. "For the first time in my life, I'm trying to be happy instead of just successful."

My throat tightens. Because I can hear the truth in her voice. Unfortunately, she's sharing it with her mother, who clearly doesn't deserve it. Juliet glances toward the door and sees me standing there. Her eyes widen, and she waves me away sharply, embarrassment and something like panic flashing across her face.

I move, giving her the privacy she wants. I shouldn't have eavesdropped. A minute later, I hear her end the call, and then she comes out of her room. Her face is tight, eyes wet, and I can see her shutting down in real time.

"How much did you hear?"

"Enough to know your mom was wrong about everything."

She squeezes her fists, her hands are trembling slightly.

"Between her and Patrick, I feel like everyone from my past is coming out of the woodwork to tell me I'm making a mistake." Her voice breaks a little on the last word. "Why are they doing this? What did I do to deserve it?"

She turns like she's about to lock herself in the bathroom.

"Hey," I say, catching her arm gently. "You're not alone. Not unless you want to be."

She doesn't answer right away. She stares at me, throat working, like she's trying to figure out if I mean it. "Yeah?"

"Yeah." I reach for her, walking her back to her room, sitting us both on the bed. I wrap my arms around her and pull her against my chest.

She curls into me and cries. Not the pretty, delicate tears you see in movies, but real, ugly sobbing that shakes her whole body.

I hate it. Feeling powerless is something I truly hate. I want to fight someone, fix everything, make all the people who've hurt her disappear. But I don't know how to do any of that.

So I stay, holding her. I breathe with her until her sobs turn to hiccups and then to shaky sighs, rubbing small circles into her back and wishing I could do something.

"I'm sorry," she whispers against my shirt. "I'm being too much, I know."

"You're perfect," I say immediately. The smile she gives

me through her tears feels like a gift. And the answering curve of my mouth? She's the only one who'll ever see it.

I tip her chin up with a finger and wipe away the vestiges of her tears. "Anyone who says otherwise can take it up with me."

She laughs, soft and surprised.I feel some of the tension leave her shoulders.

"Your mom doesn't know what she's talking about." I look down at her sweet, heart-shaped face. Then I take a breath, knowing what I need to say to her and summoning the courage to say it. It's scary. "You're not a phase for me. I won't get bored with you. You're the best thing that's ever happened to me."

Her eyes are still red-rimmed, but there's something softer in her expression now.

"I don't want to fake anything with you," she says.

My breath catches. "You mean this? Us?"

She nods. "Every moment we're together, I feel more sure that I'm the happiest I've ever been. And that terrifies me because I don't know how to trust it."

"Me too, Firecracker."

The nickname slips out naturally. She smiles for the first time since I got home. We sit there in comfortable silence for a while, her head resting on my shoulder, my arms around her. I can feel her breathing slowly returning to normal.

There's something so perfect about being touched by Juliet Monroe. Usually, I'm worried about a million things. But she lays a hand on my chest and looks at me with those chocolate eyes, and my world quiets. Suddenly, I'm drowning, wanting to dive as deep as I can get into her.

"This is real." I cup her cheek, turning her gaze up to mine. "It might have started off as a convenient lie, but it's so much more than that now."

She inhales sharply and puts her hand over mine.

"I don't think I could ever hate you. Not really. It's nice to hear that you feel the same way, though."

"I've wanted you since the moment I laid eyes on you. And now I have you. You're trapped with me forever. But you don't mind that, do you?"

Her lips tip up in a smile and she shakes her head.

"No, Hux. I don't mind that at all."

My heart pounds. I stare at her for a beat. Absorbing the way it feels to be loved by someone who I'm so entirely obsessed with.

"No more fake shit. I'm not doing fake fiancées anymore. No more fake anything."

"No more," she agrees. "I'm yours, Hux."

"I know, Firecracker."

She looks up at me, her eyes shining, and kisses me. When her lips meet mine, there's not frantic or desperate like we've been lately. We break apart. She's sprawled across my chest, her hair a mess, mouth kiss-swollen and completely bare. No lipstick. No walls. Nothing but *her*.

And fuck, she's beautiful.

I drag my thumb across her lower lip, watching it tremble just a little under my touch.

It was never about the color or about the war paint she wears to face the world. I used to want to be the one who ruined it.

Now? Now I want to be the one who worships it.

"You're staring again," she murmurs.

I press my mouth to the corner of hers. "Can't help it. I'm a lip guy now, remember?"

She laughs. The sound goes straight through me. Because this is real. This moment, this feeling, this woman in my arms who trusts me enough to fall apart and let me put her back together.

Chapter 37

Juliet

The four-city road trip feels like living in a beautiful dream I'm afraid to wake up from.

I stay in Hunter's hotel room every night, which feels indulgent and messy and private in the best way. I spend my days in PR meetings, media coordination, and putting out the occasional fire that comes with managing a team full of athletes with too much money and not enough impulse control.

Beck Tate lands in the hot seat not once but twice for growling at a fan in public. Alex Thorne, his co-captain, is right there with him. He won't stop going on podcasts and opening his giant mouth about anything and everything. It's infuriating what these guys get up to in their downtime.

But at night? I watch every game, seeing Hunter in his element on the ice. I kiss him in public like I'm actually allowed to do it. We fall asleep tangled up together in unfamiliar beds that somehow feel more like home than my apartment ever did. I have the feeling of hanging balanced on a very high precipice, but Hux is here with me.

It feels dangerous and yet the rush is intoxicating. *He* is intoxicating.

He looks at me with those blue-gray eyes, clearly feeling… something. And I'm hooked. I've bought a ticket to this ride, I'm hanging on for dear life, and he knows it.

It makes me ache, the way he softens when no one's watching. Sometimes I think he hates the whole damn world… but then he looks at me and his smile is the exception. He traces patterns on my skin like he's trying to memorize the feeling. He whispers my name, and I'm drunk on it, powerless, beyond infatuated.

I'm not ready for this to end. I'm not sure Hunter is, either. We haven't talked about it in specific, but it seems like we will just ignore the end of our contract and… live together? That part is murky.

There's a stretch in Denver where everything feels close to perfect. I don't use that word lightly, but this? This might actually be it. Waking up next to Hunter, working a job I love, feeling like I belong somewhere for the first time in my adult life.

Could life really stay like this? It's hard to imagine it ending, but also hard to believe it could last. Because it's fragile, I'm trying so hard to hold it. It will break. *It has to.*

My phone buzzes with another text from my mother. A link to some prestigious law fellowship with a note that says, "It's not too late to apply."

I delete it without opening the link, then send back a quick reply

I love my job. I'm not interested.

Her response comes immediately. A condescending thumbs-up emoji.

Someday you'll understand.

I stare at the message for a long moment, then delete the

entire conversation. I'm done explaining myself to people who refuse to see me.

"Everything okay?" Hunter asks, looking up from the game footage he's reviewing on his laptop.

"Just my mother being my mother."

"Want to talk about it?"

"Not really. Feel like distracting me instead?"

He pulls me onto his lap, kissing me until I forget all about condescending text messages and parental disapproval. This? This is the best feeling ever.

The next morning, Ivy shows up at the Denver arena for the morning skate with a red-headed girl who looks like she's running on pure sunlight.

"Everyone, this is Mollie Tate," Ivy announces. Ivy sounds proud, like she's already decided Mollie's going to be a favorite.

Mollie towers over me at five-seven with an extra curvy hourglass build. Her hair is coppery strawberry blonde that falls in a messy wave, catching the light when she turns her head. Freckles dust her cheeks and shoulders, and her blue-green eyes are wide and expressive, practically glowing with nerves and excitement. She's wearing a riot of a floral dress, bold lipstick, and oversized sunglasses shoved on top of her head like she forgot they were there.

"Hi!" she blurts, too loud, too quick. "I'm so excited to be here. This is amazing."

She laughs at herself when the words tumble out, a little embarrassed but not enough to hide her enthusiasm.

"She's Beck's sister, but I found her by accident when I was searching for someone who knows the ins and outs of

TikTok." Ivy beams at her, squeezing her arm. "Mollie's our new social media hire. She'll be working on content for the team channels. I brought her here to dive into the pool headfirst."

Mollie nods so fast I worry her sunglasses are going to slide right off.

"Hi, I'm Juliet." I step forward, offering her a handshake. "Don't worry. It's overwhelming at first, but you'll find your rhythm."

Mollie exhales like she's been holding her breath. "Thank you. I was up half the night writing ideas for TikToks. Then I realized I've never even been in a locker room before. Awkward, no?"

I shake my head, amused. "The only thing they'll notice is if you stand too close to the laundry bins and accidentally swoon at the smell. Avoid those things like the plague and you'll survive just fine."

That gets her giggling, bright and effervescent. I already love her energy.

Beck Tate skates over to us, pulling his helmet off and holding it under his arm. He's also knock-you-out handsome. He's tall with trimmed salt and pepper hair, dark eyes, and cheekbones that could cut. His dark facial hair has flecks of silver in it. "Moll! You made it."

"I did." The radiant smile she gives her big brother makes my heart squeeze. "Are we still on for tonight? You, me, the munchkin, and as many tacos as we can eat?"

Beck nods. "You know it, kiddo."

"Beck!" Mollie looks at the two of us standing here. "No lame nicknames. You *promised*!"

His lips twitch. "Sorry, Mollie Marie Tate. I'll call you by your full name from here on out."

"Go play hockey," Ivy says, dismissing him with a wave. "We're busy over here."

"Sure thing, boss." Beck laughs, putting his helmet on. "See you tonight. Bring those tortillas that Rosie likes."

When he skates away, Mollie sighs. "Rosie is my niece. And she only likes these super fresh tortillas that my neighbor sells from her kitchen because Rosie has great taste."

"You're making me hungry," I chime in.

"Really? Cause you two are welcome to take part in the taco party anytime."

"Tacos are so damn good," Ivy murmurs.

Thorne skates up with a bottle of water, his shoulder pads making his already ridiculously tall frame seem bulky. "Hey."

"We just got rid of Beck. We're trying to work," Ivy chides.

Thorne ignores her and looks at me. "I, uh, might need to talk to you later. I'm not sure yet."

Suspicious. "Why?" I ask.

"I have a situation." He shrugs and glances at Ivy and Mollie. He probably doesn't want to tell me anything in front of them. "I'll monitor it and keep you updated."

"Please do."

Mollie, for her part, seems frozen, staring at Thorne. Her notebook slips from her hands and she nearly drops it. "Hi," she blurts, voice shooting high and thin. "Nice skating out there."

"Moll." Thorne lifts his brows a fraction and gives her a curt nod. "Beck just invited me to taco night."

"Oh!" Mollie's brain is a 50-tab browser, every single page frozen at once. She turns bright pink. "Whatever. Couldn't care less."

As far as statements go, it doesn't seem true. Mollie is quite affected by Thorne, for whatever reason. I have to say I understand, because Thorne is white-hot. Mollie catches our expressions and rushes to give some context.

"Beck and Alex have been besties since sixth grade. We all go way back. And yes, if you were wondering, Thorne has always been an arrogant jerk."

"As much as I love being stuck in this conversation, we have stuff to tackle." Ivy sighs. "Thorne, no offense, but get lost. We're trying to have a meeting here."

Thorne pins me with an intense expression. "See you around?"

"Sure. You know where to find me."

He pushes off the side wall, skating away, chugging from his water bottle.

"Okay." Ivy elbows Mollie gently and Mollie startles. "Why don't you fill us in on your propositions for the team's social media?"

Mollie tucks a strand of brilliant copper hair behind her ear and grins.

"How much do you know about TikTok's algos?" Our blank expressions in response make her grin. "Watch time, engagement, hooks, retention, personalization, freshness, and consistency. That's the order of operations for getting TikTok to eat up your content."

I lean in. "Go on…"

Later that day, we have what feels like our most public date yet. Lunch at a trendy restaurant in downtown Phoenix, holding hands across the table while photographers snap pictures from across the street. I barely notice the cameras. They've become background noise.

"You okay?" Hux rubs the back of my hand.

I realize that I've been staring off into space for a full minute. I smile. "Sorry. I'm just... happy? It's not really something I thought our relationship would bring."

"Our relationship, huh?" He raises his eyebrows.

My face heats. "I just meant... you know..."

"Oh, I know exactly what you mean." He leans in, eyes sparkling. "You're talking about how you're a good girl for me at night."

"Hux!" I duck my head. "I'm not talking about that at all."

He purses his lips and pretends to think. "Are you saying that you don't want to get fucked so hard tonight that we break another bed?"

"Will you keep your voice down?" I squeak. "Honestly, Hunter. You are the absolute worst."

"I know." He smirks, his fingers finding the pulse point at my wrist. "You like it, though. You can't tell me you don't want to slip off to the bathroom for a few minutes and let me ruin that pussy."

My mouth goes dry. "In the bathroom? Here??"

Hux's lips twitch. "There's so much that I want to do with you, Monroe. Do you know how many sex toys I have bookmarked for you? I want to get caught fucking in the supply closet. I want to wake you up with my face in your pussy. In the shower, on the ice, over the phone when I'm away..."

I blink. "You've, um, thought about this a lot."

"Yeah." He laughs, a genuine sound. I haven't gotten a ton of laughs from him but I love hearing them. "You're a fantasy come to life, Juliet. And I don't mean just because you have unbelievable tits. You're smart and funny and you seem to like me even though I'm..."

He trails off, his amusement falling flat. For a second, I see a flash of pain on his face.

"You're what?" I ask, lacing his fingers with mine.

"You already know." When they come, his words are sarcastic. "I'm the Chainsaw."

I consider him for a long moment. Huxley's dirty blond hair falls into his face just so. I brush it back, smoothing my hand along his jaw. He has a healing bruise on his right cheek from a few days ago. His blue-gray eyes study me, his brow creased with concern.

"I don't know who the Chainsaw is," I say at last. "All I know is you, Hux. You're kind and you remember stupid things I care about, like my coffee order. You treat me like I matter." I take a deep breath. "I hope it's not disappointing to say that I hate your alter ego, but I really like you."

He shakes his head slowly, the hair falling back into his eyes.

"You let me take what I need, Monroe," he says, his eyes flashing. "I'm a big brute who needs to be in control. You let me be myself. Not only that, but you seem to enjoy it."

"Yes, Hux, I do. I've loved everything we've done so far."

"Yeah?" He fidgets. It's odd to see such a big guy be uncomfortable. "I love it too, Firecracker."

Moving around the booth, he slides to my side and kisses me. He takes up all the damn space but I don't even care. I tangle my fingers in his overlong hair, sucking in a breath that's pure him. Burnt vanilla, tobacco, and musk. It makes my mouth water.

He pulls back, looking at my mouth, and rubs his thumb over the fullness of my bottom lip. His thumb comes away bright red. "I can't wait to fuck this off you, Monroe. I swear, you've given me a mouth fetish."

"I hate to tell you this, but I'm pretty sure most guys have a mouth fetish."

Hux licks his lips. "Not like I do."

"Oh, yeah?" Heat gathers between my thighs, radiating outward. "You'll have to show me, I guess."

"Deal." He gives me a wickedly dark smile. "Can I take you to bed now?"

My lips twitch. "Almost. Want to pose for a couple of selfies with me? Gotta keep the Gram up to date, you know. It's my job."

"All right, all right." Hunter acts like a Ken doll, letting me move his body around in a variety of poses. I take advantage of his compliance and sneak in a few extras, but he doesn't complain.

On our way back, I post several new Instagram photos. My ring catches the light as my hand rests over his heart. The two of us in bed together, with him shirtless and me wearing his team hoodie. A mirror selfie of us getting ready for dinner, his arms around me from behind.

I post them because I genuinely want to. Because if this were real, if he'd actually proposed, I wouldn't ever shut up about it. I'd be that insufferable person posting couple photos every day and not caring who rolled their eyes.

The thought catches me off guard.

"You're overthinking again," Hunter murmurs against my temple as we walk back into the hotel.

"How can you tell?"

"You get this little line right here." He touches the spot between my eyebrows. "And you go silent."

"I don't go quiet."

"You absolutely go quiet. It's how I know you're plotting something."

I'm about to argue when my phone vibrates. Work emergency. I read about Thorne and some girl he hooked up with last week, who is now threatening to go to the press with what she claims are compromising photos and a story about his aggressive behavior.

I swear to god, hockey players have no self-preservation skills. What would they do without a PR team?

I handle it from the hotel room, sitting cross-legged on the bed with a half-eaten Caesar salad beside me. Twenty minutes and one very pricey nondisclosure agreement later, I solved the problem.

"Nice work," Hunter says when I push my phone away. "Remind me never to get on your bad side."

"You couldn't afford my rates," I joke.

Honestly? I love being in the mix with this PR department. During it all, I fix things and keep the machine running smoothly. Being important. Being *needed*.

It fills some hole deep inside me and leaves me feeling very pleased with myself.

The next day we're in Salt Lake City, after a game where the Havoc absolutely demolished their competition. Hux was an absolute savage, checking and throwing his weight around like he was out for blood. He set the tone for every single shift. And he did it without once getting called out for rough play. The rest of the team fed off it, piling on goals until the scoreboard felt almost unfair.

The press events were mercifully short. A good thing too, since I am running out of steam this far into our trip. The girls are all waiting for the team to finish so that we can catch a ride back to the hotel and crash.

It's been a long week.

Ivy mentions that human resources is final-rounding a

new office gopher for the Havoc. A woman, which makes me extremely happy. The team needs more female energy.

I flip through the profile that Ivy hands me. *Scout Morelli.* The profile picture is cute, one of Scout dressed in tennis gear, smiling at the camera like it's her best friend. Where do I recognize her name from?

Oh, that's right. Team manager Jared Duke emailed it to the team leads. Her résumé came across my inbox with a note about "excellent resilience under pressure." I looked her up, curious.

She is married to Enzo Morelli, a very famous Havoc hockey player who retired and became an agent. He seems like a douchebag, but maybe that's the sort of people pleasing that will help get things done around here. I would certainly like to throw Enzo's wife a bone if I can.

"And that's when I knew I wasn't meant to live in a city forever," Mollie says. "I mean, just think of this hair in the rain!"

Everyone laughs, making me look up from the profile. She points to her smooth red tresses. She's right; I can easily picture her hair getting frizzy in the Seattle humidity.

Mollie looks around the Family Lounge at Ivy, Wren, and Jessa. Jessa and Mollie get along so well that I'm a *teeny* bit jealous. It's hard to resist their sunny attitudes, though. The Coven is in full effect, talking animatedly about some ridiculous plan to buy an off-the-grid compound together and raise goats or rescue dogs or both.

"What if we buy a place in eastern Washington?" Ivy asks. "I'm thinking halfway between Seattle and Spokane. It would be in the desert, but I think if we build something new and dig a well, we can sustain ourselves during the apocalypse."

"That's very important." Jessa nods. "Plenty of privacy.

Scenic views. We could start a cult. Ivy, you'd make a great cult leader."

"Interesting." Ivy taps her chin. "You know, I *have* always wanted to lead a devoted following to a remote locale."

"I'd follow you," Wren chimes in. "If we build a compound, we're going to have to put a moat around it. Ladies, if we're going cult, I say we go full cult."

"All the way, baby!" I agree. Everyone laughs. Just then, Hunter sticks his head into the room, his hair still wet, his dark suit making him look mouthwateringly good. *Yu-um.*

"There you are, Monroe." He beckons to me. "Come on. Two rookies got into a fight in the locker room, so Coach Cross is reaming them out. I'm exhausted, so I'm sneaking us out of here." He purses his lips. "Sorry, girls."

Ivy waves him off. "I'd be ready to get to the hotel too if I had someone like Juliet to cuddle up to."

I stick my tongue out at her. "Don't be jealous. I'll see you guys bright and early tomorrow when we finally fly home."

Ivy chuckles, Jessa gives me a quick hug, and then I head out following my very tall, quite dapper fiancé. Should I call him that? I'm not sure how to refer to him now that we're no longer doing the fake fiancée thing.

"Twenty bucks says Ivy's the one who ends up actually buying property," I say to Hunter as we walk out to a waiting SUV.

"You've built up quite a community here," he comments as he tucks me in the back seat before going around to the other side.

I wait for him to climb in beside me before pressing. "What do you mean?"

"The Coven." His lips twitch. "You all are one TikTok dance away from becoming a girl squad."

"We're not *that* close." I laugh. "We might have been talking about moving to the desert and starting a cult, though."

"See? Men aren't friends that way. I love my brothers and all, but I won't draw up a floor plan for our shared bunker or pick out Kool-Aid flavors."

I grin. "Dark."

He shrugs. "Just saying."

Hunter's right, though. It catches me off guard how clearly he sees it. The way the girls have included me in their plans and their inside jokes, how fiercely loyal we are to each other.

"When did you get so observant?" I ask.

"I think you're always surprised that I notice the most obvious things. You've set the bar incredibly low."

"You're salty today."

His eyes sparkle. "I'm just trying to tell you to expect more. I pay attention to what matters, Firecracker."

The way he says it, like I'm what matters, makes my chest tight. Yeah, Hux is so getting laid when we get back to the hotel.

Chapter 38

Juliet

"**K**eep moving." Hux pushes me through the doorway of the hotel. He closes the door behind him with his foot, unknotting his tie. "Don't even bother sitting down. I need you naked, now."

Hunter isn't the first man to order me to strip, but he's the only one who can say it in that dead-calm, dangerous voice. He's also the only one who makes me want to obey his command instantly, even when it's a terrible idea.

"We haven't changed yet." I arch a brow, moving into the bedroom. "You haven't eaten either."

"Oh, I'm about to eat." A wicked smile settles on his lips.

"You're awful."

"You love it, though."

He stands in the bedroom doorway, tie half-unknotted, jaw tight, shirt already untucked from his slacks. There's a wall of exhaustion in his posture, but his eyes burn with that wolfish, impossible heat.

"Off," he says, chin tilting at the midnight-blue dress I wore tonight. "Now."

I hesitate just to see if I can provoke him. I drag the

zipper down my side slowly, letting the fabric peel away from my skin in increments. His gaze doesn't waver, not even when my bra slides off. I stand there, half-naked, thighs flushed with nerves. He watches as I wiggle out of my panties, a little lacey thing that I wore specifically because I knew that he likes them so much.

Hunter steps forward, closing the distance in two strides. He smells of expensive whiskey and aftershave. Something wild and unruly and uniquely him. He doesn't touch me right away. Instead, he gestures at the bed.

"Sit."

I do, perched at the edge with my knees tight together, trying to decide if I'm more exposed like this or standing up. He bends, retrieves a slim rectangular box from his duffel bag, and sets it in my lap.

"What is this?" I ask, voice small.

"Open it," he says. "You'll need it tonight."

I tear the tissue-wrapped paper, hands shaking a little, and reveal a pink clitoral vibe with a ridiculous white bow on top. The shape is familiar. It's a soft, silicone teardrop, clearly high-end, nothing like the cheap vibrating bullets from college.

"I—" My tongue sticks to the roof of my mouth. "You bought this for me?"

"I was hard as fuck the entire time I was on the site. Just imagining you clenching while you use one of these…"

He sits on the bed beside me, still in his suit pants and dress shirt, and plucks the vibe from the box. He turns it on and drops a kiss on my shoulder. There's a gentle whirring hum, just enough to make my thighs tense.

"Have you ever used one, Juliet?"

I nod. "Yes."

"Good. You want to please me, don't you?" He grabs my

face and stares at me. "I can tell. You want to be a good girl. Do this for me, Firecracker."

He used my nickname, and the sound rolling off his lips is fucking intoxicating. I nod again, my mouth dry.

I want to be whatever he wants. Whatever he needs.

"Lie down," he says. His voice is still even, though my heart is bucking wildly in my chest.

I obey, scooting back onto the mattress, feeling my heart beat in my throat. I expect him to pounce, to put his hands all over me, but he doesn't. He just sits there watching, the vibe in his palm.

"Hands above your head," he says. When I hesitate, he adds, "If you can't follow simple directions, Monroe, I'll tie you up."

I comply, fingers clutching the headboard, every muscle taut with anticipation. Hux leans down and kisses me softly. My nipples pebble in anticipation. The kiss sends a wave of heat curling down my spine, where it pools and settles between my thighs. I clench them.

He hands me the vibe and says softly, "You know how to use it. But you need to keep your hands where I can see them."

I nod, desperate to please, desperate for him to approve of me.

"Good girl," he says. The words make me blush so hard I can feel it all the way down my chest. "Open your legs wide for me, Monroe. I want to see you touching yourself."

I swallow and put the vibrator between my legs, but he stops me.

"Play with your nipples first. Use the vibe, sweetheart."

What a terrible, wonderful idea. My lips part. I hate the idea of anyone seeing me enjoy the toy. But part of me knows that this is for Huxley. It's got to be, right?

My tongue darts out to wet my lips. He watches as I touch the vibe to my nipple. "Aah!"

The sensation is sharp, almost painful, and it makes me jerk away instinctively. But Hux doesn't allow it. He looks at me patiently.

"Keep going."

I circle my left nipple, then my right, each pass sending a jolt straight to my core. My legs tremble, but I keep them pressed together, unwilling to reveal just how wet I already am.

Hunter lets me torture myself for a full minute before he leans forward, grabs my knees, and spreads them open. Wide enough that I feel totally on display. He doesn't even try to hide the way his cock strains against his boxer briefs.

He leans back, testing the weight of his cock with one palm. His piercing winks at me. "Touch your clit, Monroe. But you don't get to come until I say. If you go too far, you'll be punished."

Punished? I imagine Hunter pulling me over his lap and spanking me until I cry out. Okay, now that's an idea I don't hate. But this is supposed to be for him, so I focus on my mission.

I slide the vibe down my torso, across my stomach, teasing the insides of my thighs. Every nerve ending is on fire. I graze it over my clit, just barely, and the sensation is so intense I almost drop the thing.

"Jesus," I gasp, hips bucking up.

"That's it," Hunter says, watching my every move. "Put it right on your clit, Juliet. Let me see you lose control."

I want to impress him. My sole intention is to give him the best show he's ever seen. I close my eyes, turn the vibe up one notch, and work it in slow, deliberate circles. I feel myself getting closer, my breath growing ragged. My body remembers every single time he's made me come with nothing but his hands, his mouth, his words. I want that now more than anything.

But I remember the rules. I pull the vibe away just before I tumble over the cliff, letting myself cool down a fraction. I shudder, needing release, but refusing to break.

Hunter smiles, slow and dangerous. "You really are a good girl, aren't you?"

His words send another shiver of pleasure skittering down my spine.

"Uh huh."

He stands, looming over the bed, and shucks off his dress shirt, revealing all the muscle and old bruises and sharp, familiar ink. He strips off his pants and briefs in a single motion, his cock already hard, already *leaking*.

He takes the vibe from my hand, inspects it, then licks the tip, like he's tasting my arousal. So damn *dirty*. His eyes lock on mine as he does it. "You taste even better than I remember," he murmurs.

Hunter's always so *dirty*. "My God, your mouth is filthy."

The words slip out on a gasp. He grins like I just gave him a medal. "And you love every word."

"*Hux*," I whimper. "Please."

"Please, what?"

I don't even know. "Please… anything. Please, Hux."

He sets the vibe aside and grabs my hips, flipping me over so I'm on my stomach. My ass is in the air, vulnerable. He slides his hands along the backs of my thighs, up to my ass, squeezing hard enough to leave marks.

"Beautiful," he says, voice reverent. "So fucking beautiful. I can see your pussy glistening."

Oh god. I tense up.

He drags two fingers down my pussy, spreading me open, and groans at the sight. "Dripping, already. Such a mess."

He tsks, probing. *Yes. Yes.* I push back into his hand but he merely tsks again. Then I feel a raw slap across my pussy as he murmurs. "Be still, Firecracker."

"God, you're obscene," I groan into the pillow.

He chuckles darkly. "You like me this way."

My eyes bug out of my head. "Hux!"

"Shh. Good girls stay quiet until they're told to speak."

Hunter slides his fingers into my pussy, shallow at first, then deeper, but never enough to satisfy. He moves in and out, gentle and then rough, never quite giving me what I want. I try not to lean into his touch, but I can't help it.

"I really want to come," I murmur, gripping the sheets.

"You will." He pulls out and circles my ass with his thumb. "Relax, baby."

I force myself to breathe, to unclench.

He works his finger into my ass, slow and patient, until I'm gasping. "That's it. Take it. You're so fucking tight, Juliet."

He works both holes, alternating pressure, keeping me just on the edge of pain and pleasure. My clit is throbbing, desperate for contact, but he never touches it.

I reach back, desperate to finish myself, but he grabs my wrist, pinning it to the small of my back. "Stop."

I whimper. "I can't. Please, Hunter, please."

He ignores me. Releasing my wrist, he flips me onto my back, and lies down with his cock in hand. He starts by playing with his piercing, lightly tugging it and gasping. "Mmm."

"Can I–"

"Watch," he says. "Eyes on my cock, baby."

He strokes himself, slow and deliberate.

I can't look away. His cock is thick and perfect, flushed and hard. I want to wrap my lips around it, but he keeps me at arm's length.

"You want it?" he asks, voice low.

"Yes," I breathe. "God, yes."

"Not yet."

He jerks himself off, keeping his eyes on me the whole time. I lick my lips. I feel like I'm going to explode just from the intensity of his stare.

He lets me get close again, lets my hand drift between my legs, but stops me just before I can come.

"Not yet," he repeats, voice rough. "I'll tell you when you can come."

He pulls me down, spoons my body with his, and holds me tight, his thick cock pressed against my ass, his mouth buried in my hair. I can feel his dick twitching where it's pressed against my skin. My lips feel dry.

I'm shaking with need, sweat cooling on my skin, every inch of me unsatisfied.

He kisses my neck, bites down just enough to leave a mark, and murmurs, "Be patient, Monroe."

I make it maybe five minutes before I'm writhing and whimpering. I pretend I'm annoyed, that it's all performative, but it isn't. My whole body aches with need, every cell tuned to the absence of his touch. I grind my ass against him, searching for friction. It gets me nothing except a rough, warning slap to my ass and a muttered, "Not yet. Unless you're ready to say your safe word, I own your greedy little pussy."

There's no give in him, not when he wants something. He buries his face in my hair, breathes in slow and steady, like he's feeding off the pulse of my desperation.

After another three minutes of torture, my personal, unending hell, I twist in his arms so I can see him.

"I need it," I say. "Please, Hunter."

He kisses my neck, soft and possessive. "I know you do, baby."

He holds me tighter, hands splaying wide over my ribs, fingers tracing circles on my skin. But he doesn't go near my tits, and he definitely doesn't touch my pussy.

"Trust me," he says. The seriousness in his voice steals the words from my mouth.

I nod, teeth gritted.

He waits. I can feel his cock throbbing against my ass, but he refuses to move, not even to rut helplessly against me like I would do in his position.

We lie there, bodies cooling. I go a little feral with the denial. My nipples are stiff, aching, desperate for friction. The wetness between my thighs has reached a level of embarrassing I didn't think possible.

Finally, when I'm about to snap, he kisses my cheek, my jaw, the corner of my mouth.

"You're doing so well," he whispers. "I know you can take more."

I shake my head. "I can't. Right here, right now, I'm literally going to combust."

He chuckles, rolls me onto my back, and cages me with his body. I reach for his cock, but he catches my wrist and pins it above my head, the pressure just shy of bruising.

"You know why I'm doing this?" he asks, voice dark.

"Because you're evil?"

He laughs. "Because you're going to come so hard, you'll see god. That's a promise."

I roll my eyes, but the way he says it makes me believe him.

He starts at my mouth, kissing me slow and deep, tongue tangling with mine until I can barely breathe. Then he moves to my throat, biting gently, soothing the sting with his tongue. He makes his way down, worshipping every inch of skin, until he's hovering over my chest.

He takes one nipple into his mouth, sucks it hard. I arch off the bed, desperate for more. He licks one nipple, then moves to the other, biting and sucking until both become swollen, tender, and soaked.

"Oh my god," I gasp, hips rolling up, searching for friction. "I need to come, Hux."

"I know you do." He doesn't oblige. Instead, he kisses his way down my stomach, licking and biting, leaving a trail of heat in his wake. He stops just above my clit, breathes hot against my skin.

He licks his finger and teases my entrance, sliding in slowly, then out, then back in. He adds a second finger, fucking me shallow and slow, never giving me enough.

I'm going to kill him.

He leans up, face just above mine, and watches me as he works his fingers in and out. I struggle to breathe.

"Look at you," he says, awed. "You're desperate."

"I hate you," I whisper. It's a lie and we both know it. I'd let him do anything to me if it meant he'd finally let me come.

He grins, the evil bastard.

He doesn't touch my clit, not even once. He keeps finger-fucking me, slow and relentless, building pressure until I feel like I'll crawl out of my skin.

I sob, not from pain or even frustration, but from the sheer, overwhelming need.

"Hunter, please. Please. I need—"

"What do you need?"

"I need you to fuck me, please, I need to come—"

He watches me, then finally, mercifully, lines up his cock and pushes in, all at once, filling me so completely that I see stars. His piercing bumps my g-spot and my pussy spasms.

"Fuck, Hux. Fuck! Fuck!"

"Good girl," he says, thrusting hard and deep. "That's my good fucking girl."

I don't last. He holds out, fucking me slow and deep, but I can't take it anymore. I come, body clenching around him, vision going white at the edges.

But he doesn't stop. He keeps going, fucking me through it, drawing it out until I'm shaking and crying and begging him to stop.

When I think I can't take anymore, he pulls out, strokes himself twice, and comes on my tits, marking me with thick, hot stripes.

I'm still shaking, body buzzing, when he drags his fingers through the mess and writes his name across my chest.

He pinches my nipples harder than before. "Ah!"

The pain sends aftershocks through my whole body. He waits until I stop shaking, then leans down and kisses my messy thighs, tongue cleaning my skin, licking every drop away.

I'm spent. Completely ruined.

But he's not done.

He grabs the vibe from the nightstand, turns it on, and presses it hard against my clit.

I scream, the sensation too much, too intense, but he doesn't stop. He holds it there, watching my face, waiting for the exact second I tip over into another orgasm. I'll remember the look of hedonistic excitement on his face until the day I fucking die.

The bastard makes me come again and this time it's so

intense I almost black out. He helps me ride it out as my hips buck, my pussy clenching around nothing, every muscle activated.

He finally relents, collapses beside me, pulls me into his chest.

He holds me while I come down, stroking my hair, whispering soft nothings in my ear.

When I finally catch my breath, he kisses my temple.

"Good job, Firecracker," he says, voice thick with pride. "Good girls get to come."

I want to tell him off, but I can barely speak. Am I actually alive? Who knows.

"Was it worth it?" he asks.

I nod, unable to form words. He laughs, the sound low and content. I curl into him, his arms caging me in. I'm languid. Or whatever the word is that's more relaxed than that. Not quite unconscious?

Hux kisses my shoulder like he's been doing it for years instead of two months. He gets me in a way that most people don't. The scary hockey enforcer and the petite bombshell. Who'd have figured?

And that's when it hits me like a punch to the gut.

This won't last.

This trip? It will end. Real life will rush back in. The contract has an expiration date. I can count the days we have left. The number is suddenly, terrifyingly small.

"You okay?" Hunter asks, his voice soft in the dark hotel room.

"Yeah. Just tired."

But I'm not tired. I'm afraid of the end. Beginning to brace for it. Wondering how I'll go back to being just myself after this. After knowing what it feels like to be part of something bigger.

After knowing what it feels like to be loved like this.

Because that's what this is, isn't it? Love. Real, messy, complicated love that doesn't fit neatly into the boxes I've made for my life.

"Juliet." Hunter's voice is gentle but insistent. "Talk to me."

"I'm fine."

"You're not fine. You're spiraling. I can tell because you're doing that thing where you try to solve problems that don't exist yet."

I hate that he knows me well enough to call me on it.

"What if this doesn't work?" I whisper into the darkness. "What if we go back to Seattle and reality kicks in and this all falls apart?"

"What if it doesn't?"

"That's not an answer."

"It's the only answer I have." He pulls me closer, his arms tightening around me. "I can't promise you it'll be easy. I can't promise we won't fuck it up. But I can promise you I'm not going anywhere."

"You say that now."

"I'll say it tomorrow too. And the day after that."

I want to believe him. There is a part of me that desperately wants to trust that this thing between us is strong enough to survive outside the bubble we've created on this road trip.

But I've experienced disappointment before. I've had promises broken and trust shattered. I've learned not to count on things lasting.

"I'm scared," I admit.

"Of what?"

"Of wanting this too much. Of letting myself believe it's real and then losing it."

"What if you let yourself believe it's real and get to keep it?"

The possibility is terrifying and thrilling in equal measure.

"I don't know how to do that," I whisper.

"Neither do I. But maybe we can figure it out together."

I lie there in the dark, listening to his heartbeat under my ear, trying to imagine a future where this doesn't end. Where the contract becomes irrelevant because what we have transcends whatever we originally agreed to.

"Hunter?"

"Yeah?"

"If this were real, if we were really engaged, what would you want our life to look like?"

He's quiet for a long moment and I wonder if the question is too much.

Too hypothetical. Too dangerous.

"I'd want lazy mornings. Finally, he says, "I'd want late nights on the road just like this. Waking up next to you is amazing. I'd want to watch you work because you're fucking magnificent when you're in your element. I'd be excited to come home to you after games and tell you about the stupid things the guys said in the locker room."

"That's it?"

"Other than fucking? That's plenty. That's everything."

The simplicity, the quiet domesticity he's describing, makes my throat tight.

"What about you?" he asks. "What would you want?"

"I'd want to feel like this all the time. All my life, I've wanted to feel like I belonged somewhere. I want… someone who sees all of me and chooses me anyway."

"You already have that."

"Do I?"

"Yeah, Firecracker. You do."

The nickname, the certainty in his voice, the way his arms feel like the safest place in the world. Maybe he's right. Maybe I do.

Maybe I've had it for a while and I'm just too scared to acknowledge it.

I fall asleep to the sound of his breathing and the feel of his fingers in my hair. For the first time in weeks, I don't dream about endings.

I dream about beginnings instead.

Chapter 39

Hunter

I know the Christmas season has started purely because of the influx of Christmas and winter-themed cards I've received in the mail. Thanksgiving is still a few days away, and yet the glut of holiday cards, smiling photos of the Havoc management, my dentist's family, and my agent has filled my inbox.

Juliet is gone, at the arena, working with the new social media team. My lips twitch as I think about her.

Should we do a Christmas card together? The opportunity to take over-the-top, cheesy photos in Christmas sweaters and mail them to people I hate – namely Patrick Delacroix – appeals to me. I guess it all depends on how Juliet is feeling about us at the moment.

We've been together for four months now. The original contract was only for five. Juliet has made quiet comments about our time running out. Does she plan to stay?

That's the question, isn't it? I need to figure out how to convince her I'm serious about trying to make a relationship work.

I'm standing in the foyer, sifting through a stack of mail, when I see it. Another package addressed to Juliet, same careful handwriting as before. Same local postmark. No return address.

Darla Huxley.

What could she be contacting Juliet about this time? I don't even want to know. I take it straight to the patio and burn it without opening it. Watching the flames grow, consuming whatever poison my mother thought she could spread this time. The smoke smells acrid, wrong. I stay outside in the freezing air, watching the flames burn and gutter, until there's nothing left but a pile of ash.

There's a knot in my chest that won't loosen, no matter how much coffee I drink or how long I stare at the ceiling. My thoughts are a mess.

Mom. Juliet. My hockey career. Everything good in my life feels like it's balanced on a knife's edge. It's so fucking precarious.

I need to hit the ice. The cold, the quiet, the rhythm of blades cutting through silence can soothe this ache in my chest.

My feelings for Juliet have grown so broad and so deep. I refuse to lose her. Not now, not ever.

I text my brothers.

Rink. Now. Just us.

The arena is empty except for the Huxley brothers. No coaches, no cameras, no expectations. Just three brothers and an ice rink that has carried us through everything.

"What's up?" Jett asks, scanning my face.

"Here." I drag two resistance sleds onto the ice, tossing the belts to my brothers. "Suicides."

"Shit." Silas sighs. "Are you serious?"

"Yep." I grab the third sled and loop the belt over my

head, strapping myself in. My brothers do the same. "Let's go from the halfway mark."

"Are you sure you wouldn't rather just talk?" Jett whines.

I ignore him, dragging my sled to the center red line. Silas mutters something to Jett as they line up. I glare at both of them.

"Are we gonna do this or not?"

"Yeah, yeah." Silas leans down, eyes forward. "Say when."

"Go."

We push off, hauling the heavy sleds. I stacked them with thick metal plates, so every stride burns. At the blue line, we stop and pivot back to center. The starts and stops are brutal, the sleds yanking against us.

My lungs are on fire by the end.

Silas doesn't even wait for me to call it. He pushes off again, relentless. By the time we finish a full set, my legs are shaking, sweat dripping into my eyes.

Jett drops to his knees, bracing his hands on them. "Bet you wish you'd just talked now."

"We needed the cardio." My chest heaves, heart pounding.

Silas shakes his head. "You dragged us here for a reason. Spit it out."

"Later." I tug at my straps. "One more set."

Jett groans but he sets up again. That's him in a nutshell. He'll complain, he'll crack jokes, but when it matters, he'll do it anyway. Jett has always been that guy. Loud, reckless, the friendliest face in the room, a fuckboy without shame. But he was also the one who kept us alive when Dad died, smiling through it so Silas and I didn't see how much it wrecked him.

Silas is the opposite. Moody, gruff, with eyes that cut through everything. He never says much, but when he does, you listen. Growing up, he'd sit in the locker room, daring anyone to test him. He still does. He's a wall.

We finish another round, and I unstrap, bent over and gasping. Sweat soaks through my shirt. Jett sprawls on his back on the ice, arms wide, dramatic as hell.

"God, I missed this," he says. "Just us."

That hits me harder than I expect. Just us. It has been too long since we were only brothers and not teammates with the weight of the world on us. Too long since we remembered how the rink saved us after Dad died. We'd sneak in before school, skate until our legs gave out, and collapse on the bench in silence. That silence was safety.

"Remember Dad yelling from the stands with that busted thermos of coffee?" I ask.

"Yeah," Jett says instantly. "He'd scream like every scrimmage was the Cup Final."

"Best part of the day," Silas adds quietly.

The words hang between us, heavy.

"After he died… this was all we had," I say.

"Yeah." Jett huffs a humorless laugh. "I hated feeling like I had to be him. Like I had to hold it all together. I was a kid too."

"You held it together," I tell him. "If it weren't for you, we wouldn't have made it."

He shakes his head. "And you, Hunt, you ate up Mom's bullshit until she turned on you. Silas had to live with her for five more years. None of us got out clean."

Silas shrugs. "I stayed at the rink. Pretended she didn't exist."

The truth of it settles on me like a stone. Jett's grin, Silas's silence, my temper. We all built armor to survive. None of it saved us.

"I keep waiting for Juliet to see it," I admit. "To realize I'm not okay. That I'm just a mess in a jersey."

"She already sees it," Silas says flatly. "And she doesn't care. That's the difference."

Jett pushes himself up, smirking. "She looks at you like you hung the moon. She'd fight anybody who tried to hurt you. Including Mom."

The words stick deep.

We sit there for a long time, sweaty and raw, saying things we've never said before. For once, I don't feel like I'm carrying it all by myself.

When we finally leave the ice, I feel lighter. Not fixed. Just less alone.

We clomp off the ice, skates grinding against the rubber mat in the tunnel. None of us bother unstrapping the sleds from where we ditched them by the boards. My shirt sticks to me, sweat cooling fast in the drafty corridor.

The locker room feels almost too quiet without the rest of the team around. Just the three of us again. I drop onto the bench with a groan, chug half a bottle of Gatorade in one go, and tip my head back against the wall.

For a while, the only sounds are us breathing, bottles cracking open, water dripping somewhere in the background.

Jett finally breaks the silence. "Remember that night Dad died?" His voice is low, not playful for once. "We went straight to the rink. We skated until the sun came up."

I swallow, throat tight. "Yeah. It was the only place that made sense."

Silas kicks his feet out, still in his gear, arms folded across his chest. "I was a kid. I didn't even know how to process it. You two kept moving, so I did too."

"You looked pissed the whole time," Jett says.

"I was," Silas admits. "At everything. Mom. God. At the

fact that Dad wasn't coming back. Hockey was the only thing that didn't lie to me."

We sit with that. The ache of it never fully goes away.

"You know what I remember?" I say. "That you both showed up for me. Even when Mom was feeding me bullshit about being her golden boy. Even when she turned it around and tried to break me. You never left."

Jett shrugs, but his eyes are sharp. "We're the Huxleys. We don't leave each other."

Silas nods once. "We survived because we had each other. That's not nothing."

For a second, I can't breathe around the lump in my throat. The three of us are scarred as hell, but we're still here. Still together.

I look at them, really look, and feel it settle in my chest like solid ground. Whatever else happens, I'm not alone in this world.

After a quick shower, I drive home wrung out emotionally but clearer than I've been in weeks. When I walk into the apartment, Juliet's in my bed reading a paperback, wearing one of my old team shirts.

My heart does something funny in my chest at the sight of her.

She looks up when she hears me. I can see the exact moment she registers that something's different.

"Everything okay?" she asks, setting her book aside.

I'm in my jeans and Henley, my hair still wet, but I climb into bed beside her and pull her close.

"It's been a long day." I say against her hair.

She doesn't ask questions, doesn't push for details. She holds me, her fingers tracing patterns on my chest.

"You're different," she murmurs. "Are you okay?"

"Different how?"

"Quieter. But not in a bad way. It seems like you're actually here instead of thinking about seventeen other things."

I push her hair back from her face. "Talking to my brothers helped."

Her lips quirk. "Good. They love you, you know. Even when you're being impossible."

"I know." I press a kiss to her temple. "And I have you. You tolerate me."

"I do more than tolerate you. I would say that I like you."

"Yeah?"

She shifts in my arms and she whispers, "You make me feel too much and it scares me. I hate it. I need you and I don't know what to do with that."

The vulnerability in her voice, the admission that she needs me, breaks something open in my chest.

"You've never trusted me," I sigh, the words coming out harsher than I intended. "Not really. You're always waiting for me to prove you right and run away."

She pushes back immediately. "That's not true!"

"Isn't it? You're always braced for me to let you down."

Juliet sucks in a breath, her brown eyes impossibly dark. "That's not about you; that's about me. Patrick and my parents and everyone else who made promises they didn't keep broke me."

I grab her chin with two fingers. "But I'm not them."

She purses her lips, softening.

"I know that. But knowing it and feeling it are different things."

We stare at each other for a long, loaded moment, the accusation in my voice still vibrating in the air. Juliet's jaw works. I can see the white heat of anger and hurt flicker across her face, but then she surges forward, kissing me with a force that knocks the breath from my lungs.

It isn't gentle. It isn't sweet. There's nothing apologetic or hesitant about the way she crushes her mouth to mine. Our teeth clacking, lips bruising.

Her hands knot in my hair. She tugs just hard enough to snap my head back, like she's daring me to flinch, to fight her off, to be the man she expects to leave. I don't. I dig my hands into her hips and drag her on top of me, answering her with the same open-mouthed desperation.

The rhythm of our bodies turns frantic, clumsy. My hands slide up her thighs, under the hem of my old shirt. She arches into my touch, nails scraping along my jawline. I feel the scratch of them for real, a living stinging line, like she wants to mark me and leave evidence for the morning after.

I want it. I *need* Juliet to mark me as hers.

I flip us so she's on her back, pinning her wrists above her head. She stares up at me, daring me to say what I'm thinking, to call her bluff. I don't know whether I want to fuck her or yell at her. Maybe both. Maybe it's the same thing right now.

I bite her lower lip, not hard enough to hurt, but she makes a soft sound. Half gasp, half challenge. I feel it all the way through my chest.

I husk out, "Where's my good girl gone?"

She grunts. "Don't know. I'm the only one here now."

She wraps her legs around my waist and claws her shirt off her body, leaving it bunched around one wrist. Beyond her beauty, there's more to her. She's alive under me, every nerve ending firing, every muscle taut with need and defiance.

I want to memorize her like this. Raw and furious and real. I want this to be my memory every damn night as I fall asleep. Snaking my head into her hair, I tug her head back, running my lips down her throat and collarbone.

"Don't stop," she whispers. "Don't you fucking stop, Hux."

It's not a plea; it's a fucking command. She's not afraid of me. And she's not going anywhere, at least not tonight.

For a few seconds, there's just the sound of clothing hitting the floor as I strip her panties off and scramble out of my clothes. She sucks in a breath when she's naked before me, exposed, but I'm not after that today. I don't have the patience to tease her.

Lining up my heavy cock, I push into her, sucking my teeth. "Fuuuuuuck, Monroe."

We both go still for a second, breath catching. Then it's frantic again, hands and mouths and hips slamming together.

"Hunter!" She bucks against me wildly. "Fuck, you're so big."

Without missing a beat, I thrust against her, going as deep as I can.

"Too big?"

"Not for a second." She claims my lips again.

She's loud and unashamed, making noises that would make a church-going lady blush. I answer with my own wordless low growls, the sounds I haven't let myself make since I was a teenager.

She scratches lines down my back, marking me again. And I lose control, pounding into her with a force that would terrify me if I could think straight. I want to carve myself into her memory, make it impossible for her to forget me even if she tried.

Monroe meets me with every step, every thrust, holding me in place with her clutched hands and her eyes.

When we come, it's loud, messy, uncoordinated, like everything else about us. Afterward, we're both breathing so hard it sounds like we've run a marathon. Damn. I really need to hit the gym for more HIIT cardio biking.

I roll off her and pull her tight to my chest, not willing to lose that contact, not even for a second. Her skin is damp, her hair tangled, and she's still shaking. I brush a strand of her hair off her forehead and she wraps her arm around me, clinging to me like I'm the only thing strong enough to keep her grounded.

"Hunter." Her lips move against my neck.

"Yeah?"

There's a pause. "I do trust you. It's just scary."

"I know. It's scary for me too."

"What if we mess this up?"

"Then we mess it up together."

She laughs softly. "That's not very reassuring."

"It's the truth, though. We're both fucked up, Juliet. But maybe we're fucked up in ways that fit together."

"Like broken pieces that make something whole?"

"Something like that."

For the first time in weeks, the knot in my chest has loosened. Not gone, but manageable.

"Hunter?"

"Mmm?"

"Did you have a bonfire while I was at work? I saw the ashes on the patio."

"Ah." My shoulders sag. "My mom sent you another package."

Juliet looks up at me, concern filling her eyes. "Are you okay?"

"Am I okay?" I let out a humorless laugh. "I'm not the one being stalked by my future husband's psychotic mother."

Her eyes widen. "Is that what you are? My future husband?"

"There's no rush," I assure her. "But eventually? Yes. For now, I'm more worried about you being harassed by my mother."

"It's not that serious." Her arms slip around my neck. "I know you'd protect me from anything if you had a choice."

Her belief in me is something I don't know if I deserve. But I will hold it close. For the first time, I let myself hope that maybe I am enough for her. Maybe this thing between us is strong enough to survive all the damage we both carry.

"We're going to be okay," she says.

For the first time, I think she might be right.

Chapter 40

Juliet

I wake up to my phone buzzing like an angry wasp. Notification after notification, text messages, missed calls. I rub my eyes blearily. That kind of digital chaos means something *bad* has happened.

I sit up, glancing over to find that Hux is gone. I'm not sure when we started spending the night in the same bed, but the emptiness of what should be his space is eerie. Grabbing my phone, I blink several times.

The first thing I see when I unlock my screen makes my stomach drop to my feet.

It's a video of Hunter from several years ago. He's wearing a purple and gold U of W jersey, so it was probably senior year of college. Hunter and two other players, both dressed in red and white jerseys, are scuffling. The guy goes down with Hunter on top of him, swinging. From this angle, it looks like Hux is a giant and he's beating up on some scrawny kid from high school.

I watch, tense. The third guy yells something inaudible. Hunter leans into the guy on the ground, the thwacks getting louder. I see a fight on the ice that went too far, where he completely lost control. It's brutal, raw, hard to watch. He looks like a completely different person.

Wild. Dangerous. He's the kind of angry that *scares* people.

"Oh shit. Shit, shit, shit." I scroll down.

The comments are outright hostile. People calling him violent, unstable, a ticking time bomb. Some are tagging the team directly. Others are saying this is who he's always been, that the past few months have all been an act.

I feel sick. Not because I believe any of it, but because I know how hard Hunter has worked to curb his impulses. I know how scared he is of being seen this way again. I know exactly what this will do to him.

What should I do? How can I protect him when this is already out there? My heart is in my throat. I have to figure out how to spin this.

My phone rings. It's Coach Cross.

"Hello?" I answer, already wincing.

"Juliet. Have you seen the video?"

"Just now. How… how bad is it going to be for him?"

There's a second's pause. "It could be bad. The video accumulated half a million views in the three hours since its upload. Havoc needs to come up with a response. I'm calling you personally to make sure you know how much Hunter needs this to just go away. He's already skating on thin ice with the league."

"The video is damning, sure. But it's old. Surely the NHL can't penalize him for it."

Coach sighs. "Maybe not. But if we don't make this story vanish, and fast, it's going to be at the top of the pile the next time he gets so much as a time out. A minor infraction will bench him. Major infractions will get him kicked out of the league altogether. The NHL can't mess around with guys who think are genuinely violent."

That makes sense. Last year, a crazed hockey defender in New York essentially terrorized his girlfriend, and the police arrested him. The NHL got shamed when a whole documentary came out about its attempts to downplay some incidents in the guy's past. They don't want to get burned again.

"I understand. I'm on my way in."

"Actually, can you work from home today? I don't want you walking into a media circus if they're camped outside the arena. The press knows that you're Hunter's fiancée."

"Right." I frown. "Yeah, of course. I'll get a statement together."

If I'm going to do this right, I need an awesome cup of coffee. I grab my laptop and head downstairs to The Secret History. The doors are open and the lights are on, but I'm the only customer here so early.

Étienne looks up from polishing a wine glass behind the bar. "Hi. We're not open yet."

I give him a small smile. "What if I just want a cup of coffee while I work? I won't bother you. I just need to be… not at home."

His eyebrows rise, but he just nods and waves to the bar.

"Take your pick. Do you want a latte or an Americano?" He waves at the small espresso machine.

"Oh, latte, please." I slide into a seat. "Oat milk if you've got it."

He gives me a cool smile. "You got it."

I spend the next half hour crafting a statement. Not a defensive denial or an excuse. Something that acknowledges the truth while highlighting Hunter's growth.

"Hunter Huxley has been transparent about his past struggles with anger management. What you see in this old

footage is not who he is today. Over the past season, he has consistently showed his commitment to personal growth and team leadership. We support players who take responsibility for their actions and work to improve themselves. Change takes time. We're proud of the progress Hunter has made."

It's calm, careful, defending him publicly without asking permission first. He doesn't need saving. He *deserves* someone in his corner.

Then I reach out to the friendliest reporters, the ones who've always treated me with some respect. I give them the statement and I seed it with little reminders of Hunter's charity appearances, his time with kids at the charity tournament, his donation to the SPCA.

I can't erase the video, but I can bury it under a mountain of evidence that he's more than one violent clip.

Finally, I log in to the Havoc socials and start reshaping the narrative. I loop Mollie in so that she knows what I'm doing. Then I schedule clips of Hunter smiling with fans, laughing with teammates, dropping autographed jerseys in the stands.

My job is to make sure that when people search his name today, they see more than that brutal fight. They see the man I know.

When I get home that afternoon, the light from the large picture windows is already fading to gray. I find Hunter sitting on the couch in silence, his laptop open in front of him, watching the video repeatedly.

He doesn't speak when I walk in. He doesn't look at me either. I can feel the shame radiating off him like heat.

I don't push. I know Hux too well for that by now. Trying to force conversation or push platitudes will just make him lock up. I just walk over and touch his shoulder gently.

He finally looks at me. The devastation in his eyes makes my chest ache.

"Did you see it?" he asks. His voice is flat.

I nod. "I did."

"Still want me now that you've seen what I'm really like?"

The question hits me like a physical blow. That's what he thinks? That this video from years ago is his true self and everything else has been a lie?

Carefully, I reach down and turn his face to me. "I saw the video. It's not great, I'll be the first to admit it. But I also saw the man who comes home tired and quiet and tries to be better every day. I saw the man who helps his teammates instead of fighting them. I saw someone who tries to talk through problems first before throwing punches."

I run my hand through his hair, soothing him. He's hurting, and it's painful to see.

He murmurs, "*Juliet.*"

"People who grow still carry scars, Hunter. That doesn't make the growth less real."

He stares at me like he can't quite believe what I'm saying.

I sit beside him on the couch, staring up into his face. "I'm proud of you. And I'm not going anywhere."

That's when he breaks. Not with rage or violence, but with exhaustion. Like suddenly he's been holding his breath for hours and now he's finally let it out. He buries his face in my neck. I can feel his whole body shaking.

Huxley is trembling in my hands. I slide an arm around him, needing to hold him close. He breathes against my skin.

"I'm scared that video is all anyone will ever see when they look at me."

I rub his back with one hand. "It's not all I see."

"What do you see?" he asks.

"I see someone who's trying. Someone who makes me want to be better too."

He pulls back to look at me, something vulnerable and desperate in his expression. "You make me want to be the man you see when you look at me."

"You are, Hux. You already are that man."

His expression looks so broken. He stands up, offering me a hand. I take it. He leads me to the bedroom, stripping off my clothes, pulling off his shirt. He takes a minute to drag his shirt over my lips, erasing the bright red lipstick I put on earlier.

Hux takes the rest of his clothes off and drops onto the bed. I straddle him, kissing him, wishing that I could take away the pain he's feeling right now.

When we have sex, it's not rushed or frantic like it's been lately. It's slow. Careful. He touches me like I matter, kisses me like I'm breakable in the best way.

This is what it's supposed to be like, I realize. It's a quiet, reverent intimacy. This is what safety feels like. Trust. Not performance, or proof or transaction. Just love, even if neither of us says the word out loud.

This kind of gentle, intimate sex wrecks my composure in ways that fast and desperate never could.

When it's over, I'm curled against his chest, listening to his heartbeat slowly return to normal. Without warning, I cry.

Not pretty tears. Ugly, gasping sobs that seem to come from somewhere deep inside me I didn't know existed.

He doesn't ask why. He doesn't fix it or make it stop. His hand moves slowly through my hair as he holds me.

"I don't know why I'm crying," I manage through the tears.

"You don't have to know."

"It's stupid."

"It's not stupid."

"Hux," I hiccup. "I'm supposed to h-hate you!"

He brings my knuckles to his mouth and brushes a kiss across them.

"I know, Monroe."

"I don't want to love you. I'm not supposed to. You're a big, mean, awful hockey player and I'm not supposed to want you."

His lips twitch. "I know."

"You don't understand!" I pound a fist into his chest, feeling like a silly child and yet, I can't stop the words pouring out of my mouth. "I've never felt like a normal girl before, because I never understood what love meant. And I hate you, but I realize that I don't hate you at all. And I'm so mad about it. I'm so mad at you, Hunter Huxley."

"I know, sweetheart." He gathers me against his chest and holds me tightly as I whimper.

"You tricked me," I say, lips moving against his chest. "You got me to let my guards down and acted all sweet and now I'm falling for you. Are you happy, Hux?"

He's quiet for a beat. "Honestly? I'm over the moon, Juliet."

I sniffle, feeling pathetic and raw. The feeling of his arms around me and the steady rise and fall of his chest beneath my cheek lull me.

For the first time in my adult life, I let someone see every soft, scared part of me. And he doesn't flinch. He doesn't pull away. He doesn't tell me I'm being too much.

"Better?" he asks when my breathing finally evens out.

"I think so." I wipe my eyes with the back of my hand. "Sorry. I don't usually..."

"Don't apologize."

"But I just completely fell apart on you."

"Good. It's about time."

I look up at him, confused. "Good?"

"You're always so controlled. So careful. It's nice to see you let go."

"Even when it's messy?"

"Especially when it's messy."

I settle back against his chest, feeling wrung out but oddly peaceful. Finally, something inside me that was wound too tight has loosened.

"Hunter?"

"Yeah?"

"Thank you. For today. For not being angry that I put out that statement without asking."

"Are you kidding? You went to war for me. Again."

"It wasn't war. It was just the truth."

"Same thing, sometimes."

He deserves a kiss for that.

Chapter 41

Hunter

At practice that day, I get my ass handed to me. Coach Cross has us bag skating and doing suicide skates. Good for cardio, bad for not feeling like a Mack truck hit you. I'm halfway to being a corpse when I head for the tunnel.

The new team services coordinator, Scout, is waiting in the tunnel. She's got Connor by the elbow, lecturing him about showing up late, while Shane sheepishly hands over a crumpled housing form. She's juggling both without breaking stride, calm as hell while the rookies squirm.

I expect Silas to breeze past her, but he stops mid-step. Watches her. My brother rarely takes notice of the women who work here. Seeing him do it now is unnerving. Scout looks up, catches him staring, and flushes like she's been caught out. He doesn't say a word. She just lingers several seconds too long before moving on.

I don't know what the hell that's about, but I don't like it. Ryan's voice cuts through. "Hunter!"

I cringe. What did I do now?

I brace myself for another lecture about my temper, about

keeping my head down and not giving anyone a reason to doubt the progress I've supposedly made.

But when I sit down, he doesn't come down on me. Instead, he leans back in his chair. "The league is watching you."

My stomach drops. "Coach, I haven't done anything."

"I know." He pauses, studies my face. "Listen. I know that the video that got leaked about you has a lot of extra eyes on you, courtesy of the NHL. But I'm impressed with how you've handled it. Ownership is too. They're very pleased with the fact that you let Juliet make a statement and didn't lash out. Not every player would have the good judgement to let that pass."

I don't know what to say about that. *Impressed* isn't a word that gets associated with me very often.

"You've grown more in two months than most guys do in two seasons," Ryan continues. "Don't stop now."

The words hit me like a puck to the chest. I want to argue, to deflect, to make some joke about how the bar was pretty low to begin with. But something in his expression stops me.

"Thanks, Coach." I manage.

"Don't thank me. Thank whoever's been keeping you grounded."

The back of my neck heats. I know exactly who he means.

After practice, I wolf down a chicken stir fry bowl, then head to an appointment that I'm truly dreading. Juliet brought the idea of doing therapy to my attention last week.

And to prove to my fiancée that I take her seriously, I booked the slot immediately. But now, in the cold light of day, I'm cursing my past self.

The therapy office is nothing like what I expected. No leather couch, no degrees covering the walls. Just two comfortable chairs and a woman named Dr. Sarah Chen, who looks like she could be someone's cool aunt.

"What brings you here today, Hunter?"

I shift in the chair. Even after deciding to come, actually talking about it feels impossible. "My fiancée thinks I should be in therapy."

"What do you think?"

"I think I'm fucked up and tired of being fucked up."

She nods like this is the most reasonable thing she's ever heard. "That's a start. What does 'fucked up' look like for you?"

I talk about anger. How it used to consume everything. How I've been working to control it but some days I still feel like I'm barely holding on. That train of thought progresses to Mom. With some gentle guidance from Dr. Chen, I talk about her and the ways she messed with my head for years.

Once I get started, it's hard to control the flow of words that just pours out of me. Before I know it, I blurt out how scared I am that I'll mess up this good thing I have with Juliet.

"Anger is often a secondary emotion," Dr. Chen says. Her voice is very soothing. "What do you think it's covering up?"

I think about that for a long moment. "Fear, I guess. Fear that I'm not enough. I'm always worried everyone I care about will eventually figure out I'm not worth the trouble."

"And where do you think that fear comes from?"

"My mother." The words come out flat, matter-of-fact. "She spent my entire childhood telling me I was only valuable if I could make her money. If I couldn't perform, I was worthless."

"That must have been incredibly painful."

It's the first time anyone has ever said that to me. Hell,

it's the first time that anyone other than Juliet has acknowledged that what Mom did was wrong, not just unfortunate.

"Yeah." My voice cracks slightly. "It was."

We talk for an hour and forty-five minutes. Dr. Chen tells me a little about trauma responses and cognitive patterns and all the ways childhood wounds show up in adult relationships. She gives me homework. Journaling exercises and breathing techniques, things that sound simple but feel monumental.

"I want to see you twice a week for now," she says as we wrap up. "This kind of work takes time. It takes commitment. But I know that you can feel better. You walked through the door. You did the hard thing."

"Okay." I pause at the door. "Thank you. For not making me feel crazy."

The therapist smiles gently. "Hunter, wanting to heal isn't crazy. It's brave."

I leave her office with her words echoing in my head.

Back at the apartment, I find Juliet curled up on the couch with her laptop, probably working on something for the team. She closes it when she sees me, taking in my expression without commenting on how wrung out I must look.

"How was therapy?" she asks simply.

"Hard. Good? I think."

"Want to talk about it?"

I settle beside her. "Not yet. But I will. Eventually."

She nods, not pushing. She makes space for whatever I need to process.

"Can I ask you something?" I say.

"Always."

"You said Patrick used to make you feel you were too much. Can you uhh… tell me about that?"

Her whole body goes tense. For a moment, I think she's going to deflect. Then she takes a shaky breath.

"Sure. Okay." She sits up a little straighter. "He had this way of making everything my fault. Patrick blamed me for not being supportive enough when he was stressed about work. My career focus made him unhappy."

I listen without interrupting, even though every word makes my hands curl into fists.

"He used to tell me I was lucky he put up with my ambition. Most men wouldn't. He'd say things like, 'You know I love you, but sometimes you're just too much.'" Her voice gets smaller. "He made me feel like wanting things was selfish. He said that my having opinions was exhausting. Like I should be grateful he tolerated my personality instead of asking me to change it."

The shame in her voice makes me want to break something. "And you believed him."

"For a long time, yeah. I thought if I could just be less demanding, less intense, less me, then maybe he'd actually be happy."

"That's not love, Juliet. What he did to you? That's not love."

She looks at me with something fragile in her expression. "I'm still learning the difference."

"You know, someone wise said that love doesn't ask you to change." I reach for her, pulling her against my side. "True love wouldn't ask you to be smaller. It doesn't make you apologize for just being you."

She turns a smile up at me. "Is that what you're learning in therapy?"

"That's what I'm learning from you."

I see a flash of tears in her eyes, but she quickly blinks them away.

"You're secretly charming, Huxley. Under all those muscles and that rough attitude, there is a prince."

My lips twitch. "Only for you, Monroe."

She gives me a kiss, then heads to the bathroom for a shower. I watch her go, her hips swaying slightly. That's my fucking dream girl.

And I finally got her.

Later, while she's in the shower, I sit at the kitchen table and write her a note. Not typed, not rehearsed. Just raw and honest, written in my terrible handwriting on a piece of paper torn from my notebook.

Juliet,

I want to be the man you see when you look at me. I want to be worthy of the way you care for me.

I'm sorry it took me so long to get help. I'm sorry for all the ways I'm still learning how to be better. You deserve someone who has his shit together, but you're stuck with me instead.

Thank you for seeing something in me worth saving. Thank you for not giving up on me when I wanted to give up on myself.

I care about you. More than I know how to say.

H

I leave it on her pillow before I brush my teeth.

We're making dinner together when she brings up my public image again. I'm chopping vegetables while she stirs something on the stove. Both of us move around each other in the simple rhythm we've developed.

"Mollie, the team's social media manager, wants to rebrand you," she says, tasting the sauce and adding more salt. "Move away from The Chainsaw thing."

"Into what?" I can't imagine.

"That's up to you. What do you want to be known for?"

I think about Dr. Chen's words earlier. Choosing who I want to be instead of just reacting to what I've always been.

"I don't know. I've never really thought about it."

"What about The Artist? You're always sketching and writing in that notepad. It's this whole other side of you that people don't see. Oooh, or maybe you could be The Poet."

The suggestion catches me off guard, and I snort. "You think people would buy that?"

"I think people would love it. The tough guy with the secret creative side? That's compelling."

I watch her move around the kitchen, talking animatedly about narrative arcs and public perception. Something settles in my chest.

"I stopped sketching for a while," I say. "A few years ago, some fan found one of my sketchbooks and put pictures online. Made fun of the whole thing. I've always written letters, though."

Juliet stops what she's doing and turns to look at me, her expression fierce.

"Anyone who makes fun of your drawings has no taste. They're beautiful, Hunter. You're an artist. And a fucking poet. I mean it."

The certainty in her voice, the way she's looking at me like she means every word, makes my chest tight.

"You really think so?"

"I know so."

That night, after she's read my note and kissed me, soft and grateful, we lay in bed talking about the future. No more abstract terms. In real, concrete ways.

"I want to keep getting better. I'm tired of being controlled by all the shit that happened to me."

She squeezes my arm. "Good. You deserve to be free of it."

"Will you be patient with me? While I figure it out?"

"Hunter, I'll be patient with you for as long as it takes."

"Even when it gets messy?"

"Especially when it gets messy."

I pull her closer, breathing in the scent of her shampoo, feeling something I haven't felt in years. Hope, maybe. Or just the belief that I could actually become the person she sees when she looks at me.

As she falls asleep in my arms, I think about Dr. Chen's homework assignment. Writing three things I'm grateful for each day.

Tonight, it's easy. Juliet's fierce loyalty. The way she sees my potential instead of just my problems. For the first time in my life, I'm actually trying to heal instead of just surviving.

It's a start.

Chapter 42

Juliet

Jimbo Greene calls asking if I can travel with the team for tonight's quick away game to Las Vegas. It's a turnaround game, where we fly there and head back right after. The management thinks I have a calming effect on Hunter.

Which is fair. He makes all the noise in my head vanish when I touch him. Maybe it's the same thing for him.

Team management wants him to be ready for what's shaping up to be a high-stakes matchup. This game is a big deal and crucial for playoff positioning. Honestly, I needed little convincing to hop on a flight.

Hux seems thrilled with the idea. He spent the nearly three-hour flight with me on his lap, his nose buried in my hair. Apparently, I smell good. I'm not about to protest spending time with him. I'll take all I can get.

I can feel the tension from the team management as we settle into the visiting team's box. Jimbo and Jared are here, watching everything below the box like two predators studying their prey. I do a few interviews while we're up here, filming quick sixty-second sound bites about how the team is excited to face old rivals like the Vegas Suns.

The media coverage of Hunter has shifted remarkably in the last few days. There were exactly two full days of hell after the video emerged, then a goalie from Florida drunkenly smashed his car up and a bystander caught it on film. The sharks circling Hunter flipped over to that story with barely a backward glance.

Reporters are now calling the Havoc *surprising contenders* and praising their *balanced play* and *newly disciplined front line*.

Hunter's name still shows up in every coverage reel, but now it's next to team accomplishments, not tabloid drama. The worst has passed; the world forgot his drama when something juicer appeared. Such is life in a twenty-four hour media cycle.

I'm reading through the latest round of coverage and keeping one eye on the rink when I see her.

Darla Huxley.

She's sitting three rows down, dressed impeccably, and watching the warm-ups with calculated attention. She's not screaming or making a scene this time. Just watching. Waiting.

I can tell the exact moment when Hunter spots her from the way his shoulders go rigid during drills. His movements suddenly get a little too abrupt.

I don't wait to see what she'll do. I excuse myself from the box and make my way down to where she's sitting.

"Mrs. Huxley," I say, sliding into the empty seat beside her. "What are you doing here?"

She turns with that practiced smile and ignores my question. "Juliet! How lovely to see you, hon. I was hoping we'd chat."

"Mrs. Huxley, you're banned from the stadium."

"Oh, really." She rolls her eyes. "There's always someone willing to take a little extra cash to let me in the side door."

Ah. I make a note to tell the head of security about it. If there's someone on the security team who isn't trustworthy, I think he'll want to know.

"You should leave. Hunter has a shot at going to the finals tonight, but he has to be laser-focused. You want your son to win, right?"

She waves off my concerns. "Oh, I'm just here to support my son. Surely there's nothing wrong with a mother watching her boy play."

Oh, so that's the delulu world we're living in? Two can play at that game. I lean forward, smiling, and place a hand on her arm.

"There's everything wrong with a mother who shows up to destabilize her son before an important game."

Her smile falters slightly. "I raised him, you know. Everything he is, I helped create."

"Hunter is good because he chose to be," I say, my voice steel wrapped in silk. "His heart stayed soft even when life tried to make it hard. You don't get to claim credit for that just because you gave birth to him."

"Hon, you don't understand our relationship—"

I cut her off, unwilling to listen to more. "I understand perfectly. You're a woman who exploited her own child. Now you're trying to insert yourself back into his life when it's convenient for you. That's not motherhood. That's manipulation."

Darla's composure cracks just enough for me to see the calculation underneath. "You think you know him better than his own mother?"

"I know he's worked incredibly hard to become the man

he is today. And I know that work has nothing to do with you. He'll succeed in life despite you, Darla."

"You're just a trashy, no good slut," Darla hisses. "He'll tire of you. Then I'll be back in his life and you'll be gone."

I roll my eyes. "Our relationship is none of your business."

She grabs my arm, her fingernails suddenly digging into my skin almost hard enough to break the surface. "Maybe I should just save my son from the heartbreak and make sure you disappear."

"Is that a threat, Darla?" I stand up, smoothing my skirt. Keeping a smirk off my face is hard. "For the record, I'm not fucking scared of you. You're not welcome in Hunter's life. Enjoy the game. But if you try to approach either Hunter or me afterward, security will escort you out. They're right behind us, monitoring your every movement."

She looks up, and the two burly guards I brought to keep tabs on her are standing three rows back, eyes on her. I walk away without looking back, my heart pounding but my step steady.

Instead of heading up to the box, I go down to the tunnel, standing and watching Hux dominate the ice. Every time I deal with his mom, I'm a little more impressed that he turned out as good inside as he is.

The game itself is electric. Hunter plays like a man possessed, but in the best way. Controlled. Focused. Deadly in all the right ways. When the other team tries to bait him into penalties, he just skates away. When they get rough, he gets smart.

They win 3-1. Hunter gets two assists.

The roar of the Dome is different tonight. Not Chainsaw chants demanding blood. Not fans waving foam saws like weapons. This is pride. This is joy.

They're cheering because Hunter outskated the Stars. Because he set up the winning goal. Because he played *smart*.

Reporters crowd the glass, scribbling notes, murmuring about redemption. I can just imagine what they are writing. *Chainsaw grows up. Huxley dominates with discipline.*

On the bench, Thorne claps him on the back. Hunter barely reacts. He lifts his head, scanning the crowd until his eyes lock on mine.

I'm already standing, clapping like my heart might burst. When his gaze catches mine, I make the smallest nod.

And he smiles. Not the angry, sharp smile the fans are used to. A real one. My knees nearly give out from how much it floors me.

"That's my man!" I scream. He flashes me a grin. In the hubbub, I feel like I can get away with claiming him as mine. No one can hear me over the roar of the crowd.

After the game, Hunter finds me in the hallway outside the locker room. He doesn't say anything about Darla, but I can see in his eyes that he knows what happened.

"Thank you."

"What, for standing up to her?" I smile up at him. "You don't have to thank me for that."

"Yeah, I do."

"It's just the cost of doing business." I push up on my tiptoes, kissing him gently. "You're worth it. Trust me."

He slides his hand along my jaw. "What did I do to deserve you?"

"Just lucky, I guess," I tease. I decide not to tell him about the vague threat Darla issued. He'd only be more upset about it if he knew. I'll definitely tell the Havoc's security team about it when we get back to Seattle, though.

Hunter throws an arm around my waist as we exit the

arena. We're walking to the team bus when Alex Thorne appears beside us, his expression grim.

"Huxley, we need to talk. Your mother just cornered me and asked me to give you this."

He hands Hunter an envelope. Even from a distance, I can see Darla's careful handwriting.

Hunter's jaw ticks. He takes the envelope, and without opening it, tears it in half.

"If she approaches you again, call security," Hunter says.

"Already done. I've alerted building management too. She's not welcome at our facilities." Thorne hesitates. "I'm just making sure you're both all right."

I hug Hux's waist. "We're fine. Mrs. Huxley has just realized that we've cut off her oxygen supply, so she's making her death rattle extra dramatic. It should be over soon."

After Thorne leaves, Hunter looks at me with something raw in his expression. "I can't keep doing this. She's never going to stop. Not unless someone makes her stop."

"What are you thinking?"

"I'm thinking it's time to let the lawyers handle it. Criminal charges, restraining order, all of it."

I study his face. I can see the exhaustion there, but also the resolve.

"Are you sure?"

"I'm sure. She threatened you tonight just by being here. She's harassing my teammates. This ends now."

I bite my lip. "I didn't mention this, but she did actually threaten me."

"She what?!" He grips me and looks at me, eyes scanning my face. "What did she say?"

"She said something about saving you the heartache and making me disappear. It was really vague and hand-wavy."

"I'll kill her," he hisses. His entire face is a dark thundercloud. "I'll fucking kill her. I swear to god."

"Baby." I put my hand on his chest, imploring. "Don't freak out. I wasn't even going to mention it to you because her threat made me laugh. I'm only telling you because I think it could be the ammunition you need for a restraining order."

He wraps a hand around the base of my neck and hauls me against his chest. "You're goddamn right I'm going to get a fucking restraining order. I'm going to bury her so deep in legal shit that she'll never get out. She can't just threaten you and think I won't react."

"She wants your reaction. If you call her and tell her off, she's just going to threaten me anytime she wants attention."

A growl sounds deep in his chest. "Fuck her."

I let him console himself by holding me close for a few more seconds. Then someone yells for us to get on the bus. We hurry to climb aboard, but Hunter is in caveman mode. He makes me sit on his lap and won't even let me talk to Jett when his brother tries to tease me for being too needy.

"Fuck off!" Hux grates, pulling me further into his lap and cradling my head close to his chest. "No one talks to us for the rest of the night."

Because I know he's a wounded animal, I stay close, not resisting his possessiveness. He needs to protect me today, and I need him to feel satisfied by that.

A few days later, we're sitting in the team's legal offices. The conference room feels like a tomb as the lawyers lay out everything. Financial documents, bank records, email threads showing the systematic way Darla isolated Hunter from other advisors.

The scope is staggering. Not just the money she stole, but the forged documents, the shell companies, the way she manipulated a teenager who trusted her. There is a lot of proof that she tried to do the same with Jett and Silas, too.

"The evidence is substantial." Marilyn Adams, the team's lead attorney, smiles grimly. "We can file for a restraining order immediately. The criminal charges will take longer to process, but given the dollar amounts involved..."

"She could go to prison." Hunter's voice is flat.

"She could, yes. If that's what you want to pursue."

Hunter stares at the papers in front of him, at the proof of his mother's betrayal laid out in black and white. It's a number north of two million dollars.

"I want to move forward with both the restraining order and the criminal charges. My mom threatened Juliet. She can't just be out there, allowed to roam free, plotting ways to hurt us."

"I think that's a wise decision." Marilyn clasps her hands. "Of course, we don't have discretion over criminal charges. We'll take our evidence to the district attorney, and they will make up their own minds. But I think we have a powerful case." Her eyes twinkle. "And the team has always bankrolled the DA's election ambitions. I'll work that into the conversation if I need to."

"Thank you so much," I say. I look at Hunter, who looks haunted. "Obviously, Hunter is making a really tough decision here, but I'm sure he's thankful to you, too."

"Don't thank me." Her smile is sharp enough to cut. "I live for this stuff."

Hunter grunts, standing. "Let us know if you need anything."

I grab his hand, lacing our fingers together as we exit. We're making steps. Big, decisive steps. And it feels momentous.

In the car afterward, Hunter is quiet for a long time.

"Are you okay?" I ask.

"I will be. This is the right thing to do."

"Even if it means she goes to prison?"

"Especially if it means she goes to prison. Maybe that's what it takes for her to understand that actions have consequences."

He reaches over and takes my hand.

"Thank you for being there today. For handling her at the game. I'm blown away that you haven't run for the hills yet."

"Where else would I be?"

"I don't know. But I'm grateful you are here anyway."

I put my hand on his leg, content, as he pulls out of the parking lot.

That afternoon, Jimbo Greene surprises me by showing up in the PR offices. I glance up and am quite startled by his sudden appearance.

"Oh! Mr. Greene!" I shove myself up as I shut the laptop I was gazing at. "I didn't know you would be here today."

"Please." His eyes twinkle and he waves me down. "Call me Jimbo."

I clear my throat. "Sure, Mr. Greene. I mean… Jimbo. What can I do for you?"

"Outstanding work this season, Juliet," he says. "Hunter's transformation has been remarkable. A lot of that credit goes to you."

My stomach twists at the public praise. I've never been

comfortable in the spotlight, preferring to work behind the scenes.

"Thank you, sir. Hunter's done all the hard work himself."

"Maybe. But everyone needs someone in their corner." He pauses. "Which brings me to why I wanted to talk to you. How would you feel about taking over the entire PR department?"

I blink. "What?"

"Director level. Your own team. Full budget authority. Significant salary increase." He studies my reaction. "You've proven you can handle crisis management and long-term strategy. We'd like to make this official."

The offer hits me like a physical blow. Everything I've worked for, everything I've wanted, handed to me on a silver platter.

"I..." Tears spring to my eyes before I can stop them. "Yes. I'd work my butt off for this team, sir."

Jimbo looks startled when I hug him. He allows it for exactly one second before stepping back.

"Good. We'll discuss details next week."

I spend the rest of practice in a daze. Ignoring my laptop, I head down to watch the guys practice. Hunter plays with such sharp focus and intensity; I stare vacantly as I process what just happened.

I got the promotion. The recognition. The validation that my work matters. I want to shout to the rafters if I didn't think it would interrupt the players on the ice. I'm *buzzing*.

When Hunter emerges from the locker room, I'm waiting for him, like always.

"How was practice?" I ask.

"Good." He studies my expression. "You look like you have news."

"Jimbo offered me the PR director position."

Hunter stops walking and turns to face me fully. His face lights up. "Juliet, that's incredible. Congratulations."

"Thank you."

"You deserve this. You've worked so hard."

He kisses me right there in the hallway, not caring who sees. Not that we've ever hidden our so-called relationship, exactly. But there are no cameras around today. When we break apart, he's looking at me like I hung the moon. "I'm proud of you."

"I'm proud of *us*."

That night, we celebrate with takeout, two episodes of Detective Saga, and cheap wine on the couch. Hunter scribbles in while I read through the preliminary job description Jimbo sent over.

"This is everything you wanted, isn't it?" He doesn't look up from whatever he's working on.

"It is." I cock my head. "Are you worried I'll change? Get too busy for this? Because I won't. I promise."

"No. I'm excited to watch you run things. You're going to be incredible at it." The simple confidence in his voice makes my chest warm.

"What are you drawing?" I ask.

He shows me the sketch. It's me, curled up on the couch with paperwork scattered around me, completely absorbed in reading. He's captured something in my expression I didn't know I had. Determination, maybe. Or just contentment.

"You make me look beautiful." I say.

"I just draw what I see."

My heart hums and I have to kiss him after that. How could I not?

Chapter 43

Juliet

My mother has been a busy little bee, it seems. That much becomes apparent when the second job offer arrives on a Wednesday morning via FedEx. Thick cream paper, embossed letterhead, the presentation that screams prestige and money. Riley, Rawls, and Associates wants me as part of their celebrity PR team. The salary figure makes me blink twice.

"Oh *god*." I sputter.

It's not just more money. It's life-changing money. The kind that comes with a corner office in downtown Los Angeles, a team of junior associates, and my law school tuition fully covered if I want it. *Whoa.*

I set the letter on the kitchen counter and stare at it while my coffee grows cold. What strings has Mom pulled to get this law firm to offer me so much money? I didn't apply, so she clearly told someone to make me an offer. She must've gone deep to get me such an incredible job.

But the law school bit sticks in my craw. It's never enough. I'm never going to satisfy my mom.

Hunter finds me there an hour later, still in my pajamas, the unopened contract sitting on the counter between us.

"What's that?" he asks, kissing the top of my head as he reaches for his own mug.

"A second job offer. A big one."

He goes still. "How big?"

I slide the letter toward him, watch his eyebrows climb as he reads. When he reaches the salary figure, he lets out a low whistle.

"Juliet, this is incredible." He hesitates. "You'd have to be crazy not to take this. When do you start?"

The assumption in his voice, the immediate certainty that I'd take it, makes my chest tight. "I don't know. I still haven't decided yet."

"What's to decide? This is everything you've worked for."

"Is it?" I pull a face. "It's just what my mom wanted. Although this law firm intends to bring me on to head their PR team."

"What's wrong with that?" He sets down his coffee and turns to face me fully. "Talk to me."

I think about how to explain it. How to put into words the shift that's happened inside me over the past few months.

"Three months ago, I would have taken this without hesitation," I explain slowly. "It represents everything I thought I wanted. Status, money, recognition in my field."

"But?"

"But now I think about what that life would actually look like. Twelve-hour days managing crises for athletes I don't care about. Living in a city where I don't know anyone. Starting over somewhere that doesn't feel like home."

Hunter is quiet for a long moment. "You'd be giving up a lot to stay here."

"Would I? I'd have to leave you."

He sucks his teeth, silent on that point. Maybe he doesn't want to influence me.

I stand up and move to the window, looking out at the city that's become ours. The coffee shop where Hunter brings me lattes on busy mornings. I've tried jogging unsuccessfully at the park a few times. The arena where I've built something that matters.

"I used to think success meant climbing as high as possible. Getting the biggest title, the most money, the most impressive business card. That's what my parents taught me matters. But what if that's not my definition of success? What if success means being somewhere you're valued for who you are?"

He looks at me with a hesitant expression. "Are you saying you want to turn it down?"

"I'm saying I want to choose what I actually want instead of what I think I *should* want."

Hunter crosses the kitchen and wraps his arms around me from behind. I lean into him, feeling the solid warmth of his chest against my back.

"What do you actually want?" he asks quietly.

"My plan is to keep developing what we started. I want to run the PR department at the Havoc and make it into something special. I want to wake up in this apartment with you and not have to pretend this is temporary." Turning in his arms, I face him. "I want this to be real, Hux. Permanent. Not a contract with an expiration date, but an actual life we're building together."

The look in his eyes when I say it makes my knees weak. It looks like I've just given him something he was afraid to ask for.

His voice is rough. "Are you sure? Because there's no guarantee. We could break up tomorrow and then you'd have given up this opportunity for nothing."

"Do you want to break up?" I ask.

Hunter shakes his head. "Fuck no."

I rub my hands over his chest in a soothing motion.

"We could break up tomorrow if I take the job. At least if I stay, we'll find out what we're actually capable of together."

He kisses me then, soft and grateful and full of something that feels like relief.

"For what it's worth," he murmurs against my lips. "I think you're making the right choice."

I smile teasingly. "Even if it means I'm stuck with you?"

"Especially if it means you're stuck with me."

That afternoon, I call Riley, Rawls, and Associates and politely decline their offer. The recruiter sounds shocked. She increases the salary by twenty percent, throws in a signing bonus, and asks if there's anything they can do to change my mind.

"It's a generous offer," I tell her. "But I'm exactly where I need to be. Not to mention that I don't enjoy getting jobs through nepotism."

"What do you mean?" she asks.

My cheeks stain. "My mom called in a favor from someone at your firm. Didn't she?"

When she answers, she sounds puzzled. "I saw you on the news, speaking for the Seattle Havoc. I brought your name to the hiring committee. There must be some mistake, Miss Monroe."

My eyes widen. "Oh! I just... assumed. I'm sorry."

"Does this change your mind about joining our team?"

"It doesn't. But I appreciate you reaching out to me. The

job offer is amazing. But…" I suck in a breath. "I'm happy where I am for now. Thanks for even considering me."

"Of course, Miss Monroe. Stay in touch."

After I hang up, I sit in my office at the arena and think about what I've just done. Six months ago, I would have called this professional suicide. Now, it feels like the first truly honest decision I've made about my career.

That evening, Hunter surprises me with takeout from my favorite Thai place and a bottle of champagne.

"What are we celebrating?" I ask.

"You choosing us. You deciding to stay."

"It wasn't really a choice. Not once did I think about what I'd actually be giving up." I kiss him on the lips, my fingers curling in his shirt. "Giving up wasn't part of the equation. I just finally figured out what actually matters to me."

"And what's that?"

"You. Us. Building something real together instead of just collecting achievements I don't actually care about."

"I love you," he says, his voice rough with emotion.

The words floor me. I thought maybe he was falling for me, but to hear it said out loud is a revelation.

I blurt out, "Oh, Hux. I love you, too."

He bites his lower lip, eyeing me.

"No more expiration dates? No more pretending this is temporary?"

"No more pretending anything. This is real. Permanent. Whatever happens, we figure it out together."

That night, we have sex with the desperate tenderness that comes from knowing you're exactly where you're supposed to be. He touches me like I'm precious, like I'm home, like I'm the best decision he's ever made.

And for the first time in my adult life, I let myself be

completely present. Not thinking about what comes next or what I should do differently. Just here, in this moment, with this man who sees me clearly and chooses me anyway.

Just real.

Chapter 44

Hunter

I check the invite again as we step under the glowing arches of Chihuly Garden and Glass. *The Seattle Havoc Foundation cordially invites you to the Annual Winter Benefit Gala to support Youth Arts Programs in Washington.* I just hope we don't have to be here too long. Crowding in a building to rub elbows with other rich people doesn't sound nearly as good as going home and peeling Juliet out of her fancy dress.

Her ass is tempting and I'm sure I don't see any panty lines. Is she commando or does she have one of those lacy little thongs on? I growl as I follow her through the heavy glass door.

The building itself is a work of art, all glass walls and impossible curves, lit from within so every surface gleams. Inside, the sculptures immediately catch my eye; they are massive explosions of color that look as if they originated from the ocean floor or the core of a star. Chandeliers made of twisting blown glass hang overhead, catching the light and scattering it across polished concrete floors. Beyond the main gallery, the Glasshouse rises in a cathedral arc, a wall of glass opening onto the Space Needle framed above us. The whole place hums with money and spectacle, every corner staged to impress.

Juliet turns to check that I'm still with her. I reach out and grab my girl, pulling her to me. She wrinkles her nose, entertained.

"We won't be here forever."

"Good. I'm more interested in having you naked and riding my face than being here."

"I know, Hux." She smiles as she smoothes a hand over my lapel. "But you look very handsome in this tuxedo."

"I look better fully naked with my head between your legs."

Her eyes heat. "I won't argue with that. Now come on, let's socialize for a few minutes. See, be seen. Then you can take me home and fuck me."

God, this woman. I press my half-mast cock against her hip and she gives me a knowing look. Taking my hand, she tugs me into the crowd.

We do the meet-and-greet thing. I let her lead, the way I always do at these events. Pose for a few photos with donors and team executives. Listen as she explains who's who in the crowd.

Juliet's gaze flicks across the room. "That girl over there? The brunette in black by the Havoc execs. Is she the new trainer?"

I follow her line of sight. Scout Nash. And handily, Silas is standing twenty feet away, pretending not to stare holes through her. What the hell?

That's twice I've caught my brother glaring at her. What did she ever do to him?

"Yeah," I murmur. "She just started last week. She's married to Enzo Morelli."

"The agent, right?" She purses her lips. "As I remember, he was an all star on the Havoc roster a few years ago."

"Yeah, that's Enzo. Public cheating mess, splashed everywhere. Honestly, I feel bad for Scout." I shake my head. "He's a bad person and a brilliant agent. Can't imagine he's a decent husband. But he makes me a lot of deals."

She blinks. "He's your agent?"

"Yeah. I hate the guy, but he's really aggressive about getting me the most money for every single deal. Rude, but lucrative."

"Mm. I feel bad for Scout. She looks like she could use a friend."

"You should go rescue her," I suggest.

Juliet's brows lift, but before she can say more, her posture shifts. She goes rigid in a way that makes my protective instincts flare.

I follow her gaze across the room. A polished woman in pearls and a steel-gray dress is moving toward us with predatory grace. On her arm is a tall man with thinning hair who looks like he'd rather be anywhere else.

Her parents.

Juliet goes completely quiet, which is never a good sign. I step closer, my hand finding the small of her back.

Her mother reaches us first, all fake smiles and calculated charm.

"Juliet." She air-kisses her daughter's cheek. "So lovely to see you, darling. And Hunter, right?"

The way she says it makes it sound like a disease.

I extend my hand. "Nice to see you again, Mrs. Monroe."

She ignores my outstretched hand completely, looking me up and down like I'm a stain on an otherwise pristine carpet.

"You can call her Melissa." Her dad steps in and shakes my hand. "Tom Monroe. Good game last week."

"Thanks. The team worked really hard."

Juliet's mother examines the engagement ring on Juliet's finger with clinical detachment.

"What a wild choice of ring." She sighs, as if I'm not standing right here. "At least he plays the doting fiancé well."

Juliet stiffens beside me. I can practically feel her retreating into herself.

I can't help it. The words come out before I can stop them.

"I love your daughter," I say evenly, looking directly at her mother.

Both parents blink in surprise. Her mother's smile goes brittle at the edges.

"How sweet," she says, like I just told her the weather forecast.

When her mother moves, I move with her, sidestepping. "No, I think we should talk. I've watched Juliet tiptoe around and try to pacify you for months now. God knows what a lifetime of being told that you're not good enough has been like. Hellish, probably."

"Hux." Juliet tugs on my arm. She hisses, "This is not the time or the place."

"I'm sorry, Juliet. But we need to hash this out here and now."

Melissa's gaze darts around. She's very aware of the gala attendees swirling around us. "Can we go somewhere more private?"

"No. What I have to say to you won't take long." Juliet has stopped tugging at my hand. Now her gaze is just downcast, which makes my heart twist in my chest.

Her mother huffs. "Well? Go on, then."

"You raised a daughter who is strong. Rigid, but I can see now that she got that from you. She's principled, fast on her feet, and smart as a whip. She's in PR, which I get that you don't love. And she chose me as a partner. I agree with you. I'm not nearly good enough for her."

Her mom, her dad, and Juliet all look at me with surprise. I guess that's not what they expected a 6'6" hockey player with anger issues to say. I press on.

"But I'm devoted to her. I'll do anything for her. Juliet's living her life, maybe not exactly the way you had planned. But she's found something that she's good at. I mean, really *fantastic*. And she's got me for whenever life throws her curveballs. I'll always have her back."

Melissa's eyes soften. She looks at Tom, her lips pursing. He clears his throat.

"I'm glad that you two found each other. You seem well suited," he acknowledges.

"We are," Juliet agrees, finding her voice. She looks up at me. "We're very much in love. We're going to get married and have children and live a blessed life. I want you both to be a part of that. I want you to walk me down the aisle, Dad. Mom, I want you to be a grandmother."

She gets emotional, clinging to my side. And I love that I get to be the one that stands up for her. All of my life, I've been a chainsaw, a battle axe, a grenade. But now I get to be her place of shelter. I've never been so fucking ready to go to battle for anyone.

"She won't get to see either of those things happen unless you give her your blessing. I think you love your daughter in your own way. But you're hurting her. I won't stand around and watch her lie down and take it."

"I never meant to hurt you, darling." Her mom presses her

knuckles against her lips, distressed. "You're my only daughter. My pride and joy. I'm sorry if I made you feel... less."

Her dad chimes in. "We love you, Juliet. I hope we've never made you doubt that."

Juliet runs her hands down her dress, flushed. "I love you both so much."

A waiter comes by, brandishing a silver tray. "Hors d'oeuvres?"

"No." Tom clears his throat again. "I think it would be wise if we planned a time to talk this through when it was just the three of us, Juliet." I scowl at him, making him raise his hands. "Or the four of us, if Hunter needs to be there."

"Perhaps we could all go to dinner this week," Melissa says. "I don't want our private affairs aired out here. But... we are glad to see you thriving, sweetheart. Even if you are in some little PR job and not a name partner at your own law firm. That's... okay."

A growl escapes my chest, but Juliet's hand lands on my lapel, stopping me from making my displeasure known.

"Thanks, Mom. I would love to go to dinner, just the four of us. I'll text you and we'll set something up."

I expect a hug between them, but I'm disappointed. Melissa just steps forward and squeezes Juliet's arm. "Okay, darling. I'll look forward to that."

"It was nice to see both of you." Her dad clears his throat awkwardly. "Well, we should let you two circulate."

Juliet exhales hard, like she's been holding her breath for an hour. Her hand finds mine, squeezing tight, and when she looks up at me, her eyes are glossy. "Thank you," she whispers.

"For what?" My voice comes out rougher than I mean it to.

"For saying what I couldn't. For… seeing me." She presses her lips together, like if she says more she'll unravel right here in front of everyone.

My chest pulls tight. I don't know how to take her gratitude without fumbling it, so I just nod once, thumb brushing over her knuckles. "Always, Firecracker."

She leans in a fraction closer, like she wants to say something else, but before she can, Jett's booming voice cuts through.

"I was looking for you. The new social media girl wants all three Huxley boys together in a photo. I say we take one where we all stand side by side and hold Juliet up like she's a queen reclining on a bed. What do you say, Miss Monroe?"

"I think that sounds great." I look down at Juliet. She nods.

"Let's do it." She seems ready to dismiss the heavy topics we've just been talking about for the time being and have a little fun.

Jett steers us toward the step and repeat they have set up in one corner, where Silas waits, brooding. Juliet stays close, still holding on to my arm. I pull her hand to my mouth and kiss the back. She can hover right by me whenever she wants.

Later, back at the apartment, Juliet walks in and heads straight for the bedroom without saying a word. I give her a minute before following her.

She takes off her shoes. She looks beautiful right now, distracted from her routine. Stripped bare.

My eyes burn into her. I've never loved someone. What if I do it wrong? Am I feeling it right? It's overwhelming, like being swept away by the roaring sea.

Then she turns and smiles at me. Suddenly, like magic, my fear recedes. Her deep brown eyes are soft but steady.

"I turned down that job offer," she says.

"I know."

"Are you disappointed? That I'm not the woman who would take the bigger opportunity?"

"Are you kidding? I'm relieved. Selfishly completely relieved that you're staying."

"Why?"

"Because I can't imagine my life without you in it. What we have right here is worth more than any job title or salary increase."

She rolls toward me, pressing her face against my chest.

"I love you," she says. "Even when my mother makes me feel like I'm seventeen again and nothing I do is good enough."

"You are good enough. You're more than good enough."

We lie there for a while, my fingers brushing through her dark hair, softer than silk. I think about how different tonight could have been. How six months ago, I might have let her parents' dismissal get under my skin. I might have gotten defensive or angry or tried to prove something.

Instead, I just held steady. I let Juliet process what she needed to process. I reminded her of her worth without making it about my ego.

Growth, Dr. Chen would call it.

"Hunter?" Juliet says sleepily.

"Yeah?"

"Thank you for not punching my mother."

"Oh, Firecracker. The night's still young."

She laughs. I feel some of the tension drain from her body.

"I'm proud of you. How you handled tonight was impressive. You were exactly what I needed."

"What did you need?"

"Someone in my corner who wasn't trying to fix

anything. Someone who just saw what was happening and stayed steady."

I press a kiss to the top of her head. "Always."

"Promise?"

"Promise."

Chapter 45

Juliet

Tonight's game against Edmonton has the arena charged with excitement. The crowd is on its feet before the puck even drops, chanting Hunter's name, roaring every time he touches the ice. This is what we've worked for. This moment where he's not just tolerated but celebrated.

I should think about PR angles, media obligations, and which sponsors are watching from the boxes. Instead, all I can think about is Hux. The way he moves on the ice with purpose instead of rage. The way he's transformed from the man who couldn't get through an interview without losing his temper.

They win 2-1. Hunter gets an assist and plays the steadiest hockey of his career. No stupid penalties, no unnecessary hits, just solid, reliable play that helps the team control the game.

In the post-game interviews, when they ask him about his performance, he thinks about my words from months ago.

"I'm just trying to be the guy my team can count on," he says. "Steady. Reliable. Someone who holds the line when things get chaotic."

The reporters eat it up, but he's not saying it for them. He's saying it to me. And I eat it up with a spoon.

After he's showered and changed, I find him in the hallway, like always. He lights up and kisses me. "There you are. I've been waiting for you."

I'm the only one who gets to see him like this. Warm, genuine, happy to see me. I'm a lucky woman.

"No, I've been waiting for you," I say, wrinkling my nose. "Are you okay? That bump to your head you took on the ice might have been harder than it looked."

He smirks. "You might have to nurse me back to health, Dr. Sexy."

"You stay the dumbest stuff to me sometimes." I can't repress a smile. "Good thing I love you."

"It's a splendid thing, Monroe."

I shake my head, smiling. "Let's get out of here, Hux."

Hunter offers me an elbow and I take it, my heart light. I definitely made the right choice when I turned down that other job. It might have been more money, but who would make terrible jokes to me?

We're walking to the parking garage when I see him.

Patrick.

He's leaning against a concrete pillar, uninvited, smirking like the smug piece of trash he's always been. My whole body goes rigid.

"What the hell is he doing here?" I mutter.

Hunter doesn't answer. He just steps in front of me, creating a barrier between Patrick and me.

Patrick strolls up, slow and cocky, like he owns the place. From the corner of my eye, I see a fan recording the interaction with interest. *Great, just what I need.*

"Didn't think I'd see you two still playing house." Patrick looks me up and down with that familiar condescending expression. "Figured this loser would've dumped you by now."

I don't flinch, but I can feel my whole body going tense.

"Walk away," Hunter tells him quietly, his voice deadly calm.

Patrick ignores him completely, focusing on me like Hunter isn't even there.

"Maybe little Juliet really has a thing for damaged goods. She always did like your charity cases. First me when I was struggling, now this washed-up bruiser with anger management issues."

Hunter steps closer. "Say one more thing."

Patrick's smirk widens. He knows exactly what he's doing.

"You think she really loves you? Please. This is just what Juliet does. She finds broken men and tries to fix them because it makes her feel important. Makes her feel needed." His voice drops, making sure I can hear every word. "She's just weaponizing that tight little body and her fake concern to get what she wants. You're just the latest project."

Hunter's fist connects with Patrick's jaw before I can even process what's happening. His punch is so strong that Patrick goes skittering across the concrete like he's not a 6' athlete.

"Fuck you!" Hux seethes. "She doesn't want you, fuck-face. She's forgotten you. Move the fuck on!"

Patrick staggers to his feet, squaring off. I grab Hunter's arm.

"Hux, please. Don't. This is what he wants," I implore.

"Yeah, *Hux*," Patrick says, mimicking my voice. "Be a good boy and fuck off. Juliet probably wants to be with a real man–"

"Fuck you, Patrick!" I yell. "As if I would ever let you

touch me again. You couldn't make me come once in five years. Hunter had me *screaming* his name the first time he went down on me. I get fucked three times a day, every day. Four times if he's on the road."

My face is red from shouting at Patrick. Something flashes, catching my eye. Shit. I forgot that there was a camera. I definitely shouldn't have said anything, but Patrick really knows how to get under my skin.

"Easy, Firecacker." Hunter grabs me and walks me backward. "You were right. He's not worth it."

Patrick steps toward us, his posture threatening. I know that Hunter is about to end his whole career right now if Patrick doesn't back down. He might literally kill him. Thankfully, security finally appears, the guards putting themselves bravely between the two hockey players. You couldn't pay me enough money to break up that fight.

There's blood on Patrick's lip and fury burning in Hunter's eyes. I step in front of Hux, my voice shaking.

"This man is stalking me. Get him out of here," I tell security, pointing to Patrick.

Patrick shouts, "He just proved me right, Juliet. You're both pathetic."

I don't look back as he's dragged away. I refuse to give him the satisfaction.

"Are you okay?" I ask Hunter once we're alone.

He shakes his head. "I'm sorry. I know I fucked up. That's exactly what he wanted me to do."

"Hunter." I tug at his sleeve. "Don't be so hard on yourself."

"I just couldn't let him talk about you like that. I couldn't—"

"I know why you did it."

"Are you mad?"

I think about it for a moment. Three months ago, I would have been furious. Would have seen it as a professional catastrophe, a sign that all our work had been for nothing.

Now I just see a man who loves me enough to lose control when someone tries to destroy me.

"No," I say finally. "I'm not mad."

But something else is building inside me as we drive home. Something bigger and more terrifying than anger. Patrick's words keep echoing in my head, not because I believe them, but because they've triggered something I've been trying not to think about.

Back at the apartment, I pace in front of the windows while Hunter sits on the edge of the bed, watching me with concern.

"Talk to me." He says.

I keep pacing. If I stop moving, everything inside me is going to explode.

"Patrick told me I was too much. Too intense. Too ambitious. That I should be grateful he put up with me. And I believed him because I didn't know what love was supposed to look like. I thought it was supposed to hurt. I thought it was supposed to require a sacrifice of who you are."

Tears are streaming down my face now.

"And then you come along and you make me feel everything. Every messy, complicated, terrifying emotion I've spent my whole life trying to control. You make me want things I never thought I could have. You make me believe I deserve them."

My voice breaks completely.

"I love you. And it terrifies me. It terrifies me how much I need you. How much I want you to stay. How much it would destroy me if you left."

I'm sobbing now. Ugly, gasping sobs that shake my whole body.

"I know you want to run," he says, his voice soothing.

I nod, unable to speak. Hux's voice is emotional.

"I'm staying right here, Monroe." He takes another step. "I'm not going anywhere. Not tonight. Not tomorrow. Not ever, if you'll let me stay."

I swallow, feeling overwhelmed. "What if I can't do this? I'm so badly damaged, Hux. What if things get tough and I run away because I'm too scared?"

"Then we'll figure it out together." He offers me his hand, waiting.

Waiting for me.

"What if I hurt you?"

He continues to hold out his hand. "Then I'll forgive you, baby."

"And what if you hurt me?"

"Then I'll spend the rest of my life making it right."

I stare at him through my tears. This man, who's seen me at my absolute worst and is still here. He's still choosing me.

"I don't know how to do this." My voice is small. Broken. "I don't know how to be loved like this."

"Neither do I. We'll learn together."

I take his hand, scanning his face. "I'm terrified."

"Me too."

Like I'm drowning, I fall into his arms. I let him hold me while I grieve for the girl I was, who never knew she was worthy of this kind of love. I spent so much time protecting myself from the very thing I needed most.

"I love you. I adore you, and it's terrifying, and I don't know what to do with it."

"Just feel it." His hand strokes my hair. "Don't control it

or analyze it or make it into something manageable. Just let yourself feel it."

"I don't know how."

"You're doing it right now."

We stand there for a long time. Me crying, him holding me, both of us finally admitting how scared we are of this thing between us.

When my tears finally subside, he pulls back to look at me.

"Better?"

I nod and wipe my face. "I think so."

Hux kisses me then, and I kiss him back with desperation. I know that this kiss won't chase all my fears away or strengthen me. But his touch silences my demons. It drives away the darkness.

What more can I ask than that?

Chapter 46

Hunter

The suspension comes down twenty-four hours later. Two games for conduct detrimental to the league. The same bullshit they always trot out when they want to make an example of someone.

"Fuck." I am pissed, but I also know Patrick deserved what he got, which tempers my feeling. Plus, he's benched for five games for flying to my city, laying in wait for us, and starting the fight.

I should be furious about being suspended. Six months ago, I would have been. I would've raged about the injustice of it, about how Patrick baited me into it, about how the league always punishes the reaction but never the provocation.

Instead, I just feel tired. And strangely... *relieved*. Patrick deserves to be punched.

"You okay?" Juliet asks from the kitchen. She's making coffee with the focused attention that means she's trying not to hover.

I peer over the back of the couch. "Yeah. I think I am."

She brings me a mug and settles beside me. "Talk to me."

"I don't know. I keep waiting to be angry about it. The suspension, missing two games, Patrick getting exactly what he wanted." I take a sip of coffee. "But I'm not."

"Why do you think that is?"

"Because for the first time in my life, I defended someone I love. I can't regret that. Even knowing the consequences." I look at her. "He said those things about you and I couldn't let it stand. I'd do it again."

"*Hux*." She rolls her eyes. I love the way she huffs out my name.

"I know it was stupid. It plays right into the narrative that I'm still the same guy with anger management issues. But I'm not sorry."

"Well..." She's quiet for a moment, processing. "The league called just now."

I frown. "And?"

Juliet bites her lip. "The clip of Patrick going after me is everywhere. Reporters, players, even fans from rival teams are saying you did what anyone else would've done. The narrative flipped overnight."

I blink, not trusting what I'm hearing.

"They can't keep you out," she says. "If they suspend you, it looks like they're siding with him. The league hates bad optics more than anything."

For a moment, I can't move. I'd braced for weeks of headlines calling me a monster, another punishment for losing control. Instead, people are calling me the man who defended his fiancée.

Juliet slides her hand into mine, steady and sure. "You're going back sooner than they wanted. For once, everyone is looking at the real you."

I blink. "What?"

"Someone recorded the whole thing. Patrick calling me a charity case, saying I weaponize my body, all of it. You are obviously defending me. It's everywhere." She slides me her phone, open to Instagram. "People are calling him a misogynistic piece of shit. His own team fined him and benched him *indefinitely.*"

I scroll through the responses. Thousands of comments supporting me, condemning Patrick, calling my punch justified. *Whoa.*

"They're saying you're a hero for defending me," Juliet continues. "People say any decent man would have protected his fiancée like that."

"Public sentiment is a hell of a thing," I say, echoing her words from months ago. "I guess we can't exactly drop the whole fiancée charade soon, though."

"I suppose not." Her lips tip up and she plays with her engagement ring. "I'm pretty attached to this ring now."

I arch my eyebrows. "Are you saying you never want to take it off?"

Juliet wets her lips with her tongue, studying me, then looking down at her ring again.

"We aren't there, Hux. We both deserve to date each other for a while. Get dressed up, go out on the town, have long conversations late at night about where we want our lives to go. When we agreed to have this fake engagement, we skipped all this incredibly important stuff that you normally start a relationship off with. I don't want to miss one second of that stuff with you." She glances up at me through her lashes. "I mean, if you want that."

I'm genuinely touched that she gives a fuck about me. I'd do anything for this woman. Of course I'll go back to the beginning and take it slow.

"I'm going to tell you the truth, Monroe. If you'd let me, I'd walk you down the aisle tomorrow. I have already decided about you."

She touches my jaw, smiling softly.

"Don't get it twisted. I love you, Hux. I just want us to have the luxury of getting to know each other again for at least a few months before we talk about… you know, getting engaged for real."

"Baby, I love you. I've waited years for you. I'll wait a lifetime if you insist on it. My position is crystal clear. My heart is yours."

Her lips part. "Oh, *Hux*."

There's that nickname again, expelled so gently from her lips. I lean in to kiss her, smiling.

I'm in no rush. When my girl is ready, I'll be waiting.

The next evening, I'm back on the ice for what should have been my second suspended game. The crowd gives me a standing ovation when I skate out for warm-ups. It's not something I expect and I have to blink hard to keep my composure.

Then, I play the best game of my entire career.

After the game, which we win handily, the media wants to talk about everything except hockey. They want to know about my relationship with Juliet, about the personal growth, about whether I'm really changed or just better at controlling myself.

"Both, I guess," I say honestly. "I've changed, but I'm also human. When someone attacks the woman I love, says vile things designed to hurt her, I'm going to react. Maybe not always perfect, but I'm going to react."

I look at Juliet, who is blushing like a schoolgirl. I arch a brow, wondering whether she's wearing one of those lacy little thongs that I love so much under that short navy dress.

"Do you regret hitting him?" a reporter asks.

Oh, yeah. For a second, I forgot that the cameras were here. Juliet has that effect on me, always dragging my mind away from the parts of life I don't like.

"I regret that it came to that. But do I regret defending my fiancée? Never."

The reporter leans forward. "Some people say this proves you haven't really changed at all."

"Some people said I'd never change to begin with." I shrug. "What people think is beyond my control. I can only control my actions going forward. And going forward, I'm going to keep working on myself, keep being the teammate and partner I want to be, and keep protecting the people I love when necessary."

"Even if it costs you?"

I bob my head. "Yeah, man. Especially then."

Juliet smiles at me, her gorgeous chocolate eyes telling me every single thing she feels. God, I'm lucky that I get to take her home, real fiancée or not.

Later, back at the apartment, Juliet is curled up on the couch with her laptop when I find her.

"Working?" I ask, settling beside her.

"Reading coverage of your interview. You did well."

"I told the truth." I shrug my shoulders.

"That's what made it good." She hesitates, then closes her laptop and turns to face me. "Can I ask you something?"

"Always, baby."

She smiles, then schools her expression. "Are you happy? Thrilled?"

The question catches me off guard. "Why do you ask?"

"Because a few months ago, you looked like you were angry at the world all the time. And tonight, even after everything with Patrick and the suspension, you looked like you belonged out there. It seems like you were exactly where you were supposed to be."

I think about it for a moment. "Yeah. I think I am happy. For the first time in a long time."

"Good. You deserve to be happy."

"So do you."

"I am happy. Scared sometimes, but happy."

"What scares you?"

"This. Us. How much I want it to work." She pauses. "What if we mess this up?"

"Then we mess it up together. But we won't."

"How can you be so sure?"

"Because we've already been through the worst parts. We've seen each other at the messiest, most broken, most terrified. And we're still here."

I pull her closer until she's curled against my side.

"We're not perfect, Juliet. We're never going to be perfect. But we're real. We're honest with each other. We fight for each other. That's enough."

"Is it?"

"For me, it is."

She's quiet for a long moment. "I love you."

"I love you too."

I know there is more that she wants to say. I can read it on her face.

"What?" I nudge her gently.

"This is the last time I'm going to ask, but..." She blows out a stream of air. "No more contracts? No more expiration dates? We're done with all that, right?"

Ah. That old chestnut. I cover her hand reassuringly.

"We're done, Monroe. No more pretending this is tempo-rary. This is real. Permanent. Whatever happens, we'll deal with it."

"Promise?"

"Promise."

Two Months Later

The phone vibrates against the kitchen counter. Unknown number. Normally I'd let it go, but something in the pit of my stomach twists and tells me to answer.

"Hello?"

There's a pause, then a voice I haven't heard in months. Raw. Thin. But unmistakable.

"Hunter."

My chest tightens. Mom.

I glance toward the living room where Juliet is curled on the couch with her laptop, her feet tucked under her, hair spilling loose over her shoulder. Curious, she looks up, but I shake my head. She doesn't press. She knows who it must be.

"Mom," I say, the word sticking in my throat like glass.

"I only get ten minutes," she rushes. Her voice is scratchy, like the cheap prison phone is chewing her words in half. "I —I wanted to tell you I'm sorry."

The words hang there, thin and brittle.

"You're sorry," I repeat flatly. "For what, exactly?"

She's quiet for a beat. "For everything. The money, the contracts. For… for how I treated you. I wasn't well."

I rub a hand over my jaw, feeling the grind of my teeth. "You were well enough to sign my name on checks you cashed. Well enough to sell me out for interviews."

"I thought I was protecting us." Her breath shudders. "I thought if I could just keep you afloat, keep you visible—"

"That doesn't even make sense, Mom."

"Well."

Silence crackles on the line. I almost hang up. Then she says it fast, like she's been building to this the whole time.

"Well?" I prompt.

She sounds tearful. "I need your help, Hunter. Please. The appeal hearing is next month. If you testify, if you say I never meant harm. If you just speak for me, they might reduce my sentence. I could be out. I could see you again."

And there it is. The real reason. Not because she misses me. Not because she loves me. Because she wants something.

I lean against the counter and let out a long, rough sigh. "I should've known. You only ever call when you need something."

"No. That's not true—"

"It's exactly true. Every time. As a kid, when you needed me to cover for you with Silas. When you wanted me to keep Jett quiet. When you needed someone to haul your ass home after you disappeared for three days. Every time, you've wanted something. And I gave it, because I was too young and too stupid to know better."

Her breathing goes ragged on the other end. "I'm your mother."

I laugh once. "You stopped being that a long time ago."

"I can change." Her voice breaks. "Just give me a chance. Don't let them leave me here. It's…it's hell, Hunter. I can't sleep. I can't think. The women here… they look at me like I'm nothing. You don't know what it's like."

She's sobbing now, the sound scratchy and desperate. Once, it would have cut me in half. I would have scrambled to soothe her, to fix it, to believe her. But now all I feel is tired.

"I can't get you out," I say flatly. "It's not up to me."

"You could try."

"Not anymore." I look over at Juliet again. She catches my eye, her expression steady, grounding. My chest eases. "I have a wife now. A life you're not part of. And that's not changing."

She goes quiet. Just the sound of breathing, wet and broken, echoing through the receiver.

Finally she whispers, "Do you hate me?"

The question slams into me. I think about all the years she shaped my anger, taught me that love was something you earned by bleeding for it. About the stolen money, the interviews, the humiliation. About the letters I wrote to her and never sent.

"No," I say. "I don't hate you."

"Then why won't you help me?"

"Because hating you would mean I still care enough to fight with you. What I feel now is worse for you. I feel sorry. Sorry that you don't have what I have."

"What's that?" she snaps, defensive even in chains.

"Someone who loves me wanting nothing in return."

I glance again at Juliet, who has set her laptop aside and is watching me carefully, her head tilted, her eyes soft. My throat loosens.

"I feel sorry for you, Mom," I say. "Because you'll never know what it's like to be loved like that."

She makes a strangled sound. "Hunter, wait—"

The line goes dead.

I stare at the phone in my hand.

Juliet crosses the room and slips her hand into mine. She doesn't ask questions or pressure me at all. Just her touch, grounding me in the present. She leans into me, her head resting against my chest. I breathe her in, citrus and warmth and the faint perfume she always wears, and my heartbeat steadies.

I wrap my arm around my wife and let the weight of the call fall away. For the first time in years, I don't feel chained to anyone. I feel free.

Chapter 47

Juliet

Four months later, people fill our apartment from wall to wall, and I've never loved the chaos more.

Hunter's teammates sprawl across every available surface, mixed in with my girls, who showed up with wine and attitude in equal measure. The noise is incredible. Laughter, clinking glasses, overlapping conversations, and Jett's terrible attempt at karaoke in the background.

Scout's on the couch with Wren and Ivy, laughing about something. Across the room, Silas is definitely not watching her, which means he absolutely is. Scout throws back her head, cackling. Silas's expression tightens and his fists clench. If his posture got any more rigid, he'd snap in half.

What is going on there? I make a note to ask Hux about it later. There's definitely a vibe between those two.

I stand in the kitchen, ostensibly checking on the lasagna but really just taking it all in. Watching Hunter's teammates rally around him without hesitation. The Patrick drama is old news now, barely mentioned except as a proof that Hunter's the man who stands up for people he loves.

I watch him with his brothers across the living room.

Silas claps him on the back while saying something that makes Hunter throw his head back and laugh. Jett makes some dry comment that has them both grinning. Hunter doesn't have to be the loudest or the angriest to earn respect. They trust him. Even without his fists.

"You look happy." Ivy says, appearing beside me with an empty wine glass.

"I am happy."

"You deserve it."

She refills her glass and heads back into the fray, but not before squeezing my shoulder.

The evening passes in a blur of food and laughter. I help serve dinner, floating between groups, pouring wine, listening to Grayson's ridiculous story about a broken stick and a mascot that apparently terrorized him for three periods.

For the first time in my professional life, I don't feel like an outsider in a man's world. This is my world too. The strategy, planning, and wins are all mine. I'm not hiding behind being perfect. I'm just being myself.

Hunter catches my eye from across the room where he's deep in conversation with Ryan about defensive positioning. The look he gives me makes my knees feel weak and my stomach flip in the best possible way.

After everyone leaves and we've cleaned up the worst of the mess, we collapse onto the couch together. I'm curled against his side, my feet tucked under me, feeling pleasantly tired and wine-warm.

"That was fun." I say.

"Yeah, it was. I enjoy having everyone here."

"Me too. It felt like..."

"Like what?"

"Like home. Like family."

He's quiet for a moment, his fingers tracing patterns on my arm.

"Juliet?"

"Yeah?"

"I want to marry you."

The words hang in the air between us, simple and profound at the same time.

"Is that a proposal?" I ask, trying to keep my voice light even though my heart is racing.

"It's a statement of intent. The proposal will be better. I promise."

"Will it involve my ring?"

"Unless you want a bigger one. I'll get you the biggest fucking ring you've ever seen."

"I don't need the biggest ring, Hunter. I just need you."

"You've got me. Forever. There's no getting rid of me, Monroe."

I bite my lip, her eyes sparkling. "Forever sounds pretty good."

We sit in comfortable silence for a while, both of us processing the weight of what we've just said to each other.

Hux heaves a sigh. "I want a house."

"What kind of house?" We've talked about moving eventually, but we haven't really made any plans.

"A *real* one. With a yard. And space! And lots and lots of privacy. I want to fuck my wife and have her scream my name with no nosy neighbors poking their heads over the fence."

"Hux!" I say, poking him in the ribs. "Besides, I like this place."

"*Monroe.*" He catches my fingers and turns my hand over to kiss my palm. "I like this place too. But I want something that's just ours. Something no one else has ever lived in."

The idea sends a little thrill through me. "That sounds perfect."

"Yeah?"

"Yeah. I want a house with a yard. What I want are Sunday mornings in bed and late dinner parties. I want to wake up next to you for the rest of my life."

He grins and suddenly stands up, scooping me off the couch in one smooth motion.

"What are you doing?" I yelp, laughing despite myself.

"We should go to Vegas. Tonight. I'll book the tickets right now."

"Hunter!"

"I'll carry you through the chapel myself."

"Easy, tiger," I say, still laughing. "I'd love to marry you. I really would. But let's plan it properly. I want to tell the girls. Let me pick out a dress. I want to do it right."

"Right how?"

I shrug. "I want you. Everything else is just details."

He sets me down on the bed and gathers me in his arms.

"I love you," he announces, his nose in my hair. "I love you so much it's probably illegal in several states."

"I love you too. Even when you're planning to kidnap me and drag me to Vegas in the middle of the night."

"That was a romantic gesture."

I laugh. "That was insanity."

"Same thing."

I kiss him then, deep and full of promise. When we break apart, he's looking at me like I'm something miraculous he can't quite believe is real.

"So we're really doing this?" He asks.

"We're really doing this."

"Thank God for that."

The next morning, I wake up to find Hunter already

sketching at the kitchen table. He's working on something new. Not his usual portraits or game scenes, not any letters, but architectural drawings. Floor plans.

Well, his idea of what architectural drawings should be. He's done them all with a red pen. It's endearing.

"What are you working on?" I ask, wrapping my arms around his shoulders from behind.

"Our house." He grins. "I was thinking about what we want. Open kitchen, gigantic windows, space for a studio, plenty of bedrooms for babies."

"Babies? You're planning pretty far ahead."

He shrugs a shoulder. "You told me you want a big family. I agreed. I don't see any reason we should wait."

"You're impossible." I shake my head at him. "House first, then wedding, *then* we can *talk* about babies."

"I'm hurrying this process along as fast as you'll let me."

"I know, Hux." I study the drawings. He's thought of everything. A home office for me, built-in bookshelves, a patio for morning coffee. "It's perfect."

"Yeah?"

"Yeah. When do we start looking?"

"I already called a realtor. We have appointments this weekend."

I laugh. "You don't waste time."

"I've wasted enough time in my life. I'm done waiting for things to happen."

"I see that." I steal a kiss because his lips are very close and extremely tempting. Though when are they not?

I think about how different things are now than they were a year ago.

How I went from trying to prove I belonged somewhere to actually belonging somewhere.

How I found not just love, but a home. A family. A future I never dared to imagine.

And how sometimes the best things in life come from the most unexpected places.

Sometimes they come from fake engagements and PR emergencies and falling for the one person you're supposed to keep at arm's length.

Love isn't about being perfect for someone. It's about being real with someone. And Hunter and I are as real as it gets.

Chapter 48

Silas

I hate this place.

The Secret History pretends to be classy with its dark wood and amber lighting, but it's still just a bar full of loud people saying nothing important. I'm stuck at the edge of our usual table, nursing a soda water while my teammates laugh at jokes that aren't funny. I should just go upstairs to my condo, but I haven't been here for very long.

Don't want to be accused of being hostile. We're all flying to Vegas tomorrow so my brother can get hitched and tonight, everyone is celebrating. Beer flows, the music is loud, and my little group is getting fucked up.

I don't want to be the voice of reason, telling the other players that they shouldn't drink, shouldn't eat bar food, should just stay home and rest so we can bring it in the next game. So I just keep to myself. My presence is required; my commentary isn't.

Can I get away with working on a Sudoku on my phone? Maybe in a few minutes. Let everyone get a little more drunk first.

Hunter's across from me with his arm around Juliet,

looking more relaxed than I've ever seen him. She whispers something in his ear, and his scowl melts into something disgustingly soft. I don't get it. How the hell did he trick someone like her into marriage?

She's everything the Huxley brothers aren't. Polished. Smart. Lovely. I wouldn't apply any of those words to us three malcontents.

"You look thrilled to be here," Jett says, dropping into the seat next to me.

I grunt.

"Come on, Si. When's the last time you talked to someone who wasn't blood related or wearing skates?"

I purse my lips. "I ordered a black coffee from the barista this morning. That counts."

"You should have a drink. Go into the main bar, meet some girls. Take someone home." Jett smirks. "Hell, take a few home. Enjoy your life. YOLO, or whatever."

I snort. "That's more your speed."

"You're absolutely right." Jett stands up, clapping me on the shoulder. "I'm heading out there right now. Come meet me when you tire of running stats in your head, man."

"Not going to happen." I say it more to his back, because he switched focus the moment he saw the doorway between the private room and the main bar. Say what you will about my brother, but he is laser-focused on whatever his target is. He'll likely find a girl, lock in on her, and have her ready to get out of here in twenty minutes flat.

I've seen it happen many, many times.

The doorway darkens, then bursts into warmth as Jessa Laramie stumbles in from the rainy Seattle night. She is laughing as she shakes water from her hair, golden brown curls tumbling free from a damp cardigan hood. Her cheeks are flushed pink from the cold, freckles bright against fair skin. Her hazel eyes sparkle as she takes in the crowded room.

Scout Nash follows a moment later, steadier in her steps but no less soaked. Her dark honey brown hair clings in loose waves around her face, drops of water sliding down her jaw. She moves with quiet grace as she shrugs out of a rain spotted linen jacket and drapes it over a chair. Her moss green eyes sweep the room, careful and observant.

She doesn't even look at me.

Jessa is the team's logistics coordinator. She helps with short-term housing or how the team gets from point A to point B. And Scout seems to be a personal assistant that the team shares. She grabs coffee, copies schedules, and gets dry cleaning. A gopher, more or less. The two women laugh together as Jessa tosses her jacket onto the nearest table and makes a face at Scout.

"Told you the umbrella would flip inside out," Jessa teases, wringing water from her sleeve.

Scout smiles, quiet and knowing, and nudges Jessa's hip with her own as she unbuttons her coat. Their laughter blends, Jessa's sparkling, Scout's gentler, like wind chimes beneath bells. Then Jessa slips back out through the doorway with a quick promise to find towels, leaving Scout scanning the crowded table. Every chair is full except one. Her eyes land on it, hesitation flickering before she moves closer.

She sits down next to me.

Scout looks over at me, biting her lip. "Sorry. This is the only seat left. You don't mind, do you?"

I don't mind, but I just shake my head stiffly. Her shoulder length hair's curling from the rain and smells vaguely like eucalyptus leaves.

I tell myself not to notice.

"What're you drinking?"

I glance down at my tumbler. "Soda water."

"I see." Her green eyes study me. "Are you not drinking because of hockey? Or for another reason."

It surprises me she knows to ask that question. Then again, she was married to Enzo Morelli. He probably wasn't a hockey player when they were together, but she has been around a lot of hockey players.

I answer, "Hockey. During the summer, I'll have a beer or two."

She smiles. "Sure. Have you tried the nonalcoholic beer they serve here? It's locally made. I've seen Olivier serve it before."

"Yeah. That's usually what I go for. But the main bar is packed, and I'd have to wait in line. That's a definite no for me. I don't like crowds."

"That's funny." Her eyes sparkle. "You play in front of a huge one every game."

"That's… different."

She pushes to her feet. "I'm going to get a drink and grab you the beer you like. If you save my seat, you can tell me how it's different when I get back."

"I don't want–"

But she's gone, already heading through the doorway. My brows rise. I wasn't expecting her to be pushy. It only takes her a minute to return with a can of Sprite for herself and a bottle of beer with a familiar blue label on it. She sets the beer in front of me, then pauses.

"Oh. I didn't ask if you wanted a glass. Let me grab it."

Scout turns and I have to actually stand up to catch her arm. She jumps at my touch and I let go, returning to my seat.

"I don't want a glass. Sit down."

She looks at me uncertainly. "Are you sure? Because it–"

"Sit," I growl.

Eyes widening, Scout slides into her seat. "Jeez Louise."

My mouth almost twitches. Almost. "Thanks for getting me the beer."

"Don't mention it." She takes a sip of her Sprite, pursing her lips.

"So how do you–" I start.

"What's– oh, haha–" she says at the same time.

We both chuckle awkwardly. I look at her more carefully. Scout is pretty, the kind that doesn't need effort. But there's something guarded behind those green eyes. I wonder what she's keeping safe.

She shakes her head. "Sorry, you go."

"What's your story?" The words come out before I can stop them.

"My story?"

I already regret asking. Conversation leads to questions, questions lead to expectations. But she's looking at me now, waiting.

"Everyone's got one."

She twirls her hair around her finger. "I take care of people. Always have. Sometimes they don't want it, but I do it anyway."

"Sounds exhausting."

"It is." She studies my face like I'm a mystery to her. "What about you?"

I shrug. "I play hockey."

"I know. But what else?"

"I'm not sure what you mean." My brow furrows. "What else would there be?"

She narrows her eyes at me and pins me in place.

"I bet you're one of those guys who's like… a secret genius at math. Or maybe a piano prodigy."

I snort. "I am not. Hockey is just my thing."

"Hmm." She props her face in a hand and looks at me. "I'm going to figure you out. There's always more than meets the eye."

I'm about to tell her she doesn't know anything when my agent enters the room. The temperature drops five degrees, and it has nothing to do with the icy Seattle weather outside.

Enzo Morelli strides in like he owns every room he enters. Expensive suit, predatory smile, the presence that sucks all the air out of a space. He's a normal feature at the Secret History. He was a Havoc player for a long time, then he transitioned into being the best, most cutthroat agent on the west coast.

He's my agent. Hunter and Jett too. And he's inked us plenty of colossal deals. But why is he here right now? Tonight is supposed to be close friends only.

I turn to see Scout going pale as she spots Enzo. Actually white. There is obviously some beef there. Not that I wouldn't expect there to be.

"Shit," she whispers, shoving back from the table. "I need the bathroom."

She's gone before I can blink, cutting through the crowd like she's running from something dangerous.

Enzo looks at her as she leaves, then approaches our table with that confidence that comes from never hearing no. He's probably pushing forty, with silver in his dark hair, tan that screams expensive vacations. Way older than Scout, by any count.

"Gentlemen." He doesn't ask before pulling up a chair. "Mind if I join you?"

Hunter nods. "Enzo. What brings you here?"

"Congratulations on the engagement," Enzo tells Hunter, raising his glass. "Surprised you landed someone so far out of your league, little lady."

Hunter's jaw tightens but Juliet squeezes his arm. "Thank you," she says smoothly. Hunter glares at him.

Enzo's attention moves around the table, cataloguing. When he gets to me, something sharp flickers in his eyes.

"Silas. We should talk about your contract."

"Not up for renewal until next season."

"Smart players think ahead." His smile doesn't reach his eyes. "Besides, there are other opportunities. Endorsements. Media. You could double your income with the right choices."

I take a drink of the beer Scout ordered. There's something else here he's not saying.

"Saw you talking to Scout. I just want to warn you there. It wouldn't be smart to get distracted by the wrong attention. A player in your position needs to be careful about associations."

The words hit like cold water. I set down my beer slowly. "Meaning?"

"Nothing specific. General advice. Seattle's a small market. Reputations matter. That's all."

He glances toward where Scout disappeared. When he looks back, his smirk says everything.

"You don't know what you're talking about."

"Don't I?" He leans closer, voice low. "I make it my business to know everything about my clients. Their strengths, weaknesses, potential complications."

Hunter's paying attention now, that dangerous edge creeping into his voice. "Problem here?"

"No problem," Enzo says, standing. "Just friendly advice about the future."

"My future's fine."

"Of course." He smooths his jacket. "Just remember what

we discussed, Silas. Seattle's wonderful, but it's unforgiving to those who don't play by the rules."

He's gone as quickly as he came, but the poison he left behind lingers.

"What the hell was that?" Jett asks. "Did you invite him here?"

"Nope. I wouldn't invite Hunter's agent to his elopement party."

Juliet chimes in. "He seems to show up wherever Scout is. It's happened twice this week. Four times last week."

My brow lowers. "What a fucking stalker."

"I think I should go check on her." Juliet gets up. "Will you order some fries?"

I let the conversation swirl, taking over, without directing it. All I know is that Scout ran the moment Enzo appeared. He felt the need to warn me away from her specifically.

Which means there's a story. A complicated one.

I look towards the back of the bar. She's still going. Part of me wants to find her, make sure she's okay. The smart part knows I should leave it alone.

Scout Nash is pretty. Sweet. And apparently way too much trouble.

I can't afford trouble. Not in my career, not with the walls I've built, not with the peace that comes from keeping everyone at a distance.

But I'm scanning the crowd anyway. Looking for dark hair and green eyes.

Looking for trouble, whether or not I can afford it.

Chapter Forty-Nine

Thank you for reading ***Dear #47, You're the Worst***. I loved every second of writing this book and I'm so thankful to you for being a reader! As a special token of my gratitude, I've written a bonus epilogue. It features your favorite characters – Hunter & Juliet. Scan the QR code to head to the bonus matter!

Here's a list of all the couples in this series!

Dear #47, You're the Worst - Hunter & Juliet - Enemies to lovers, fake fiancé

Dear MVP, You're Ice Cold - Silas & Scout - Enemies to lovers, grumpy x sunshine (different series, shared characters) ***Say Yes to the Nemesis*** - Ryan & Wren - Enemies to lovers, brother's best friend

If you loved this book, please consider leaving a review. It's the best way to let me know that you want me to write more books like this one!

Acknowledgments

This book would not have been possible without with my awesome beta readers Lizzy, Donna, and Patricia. Thank you all for taking the plunge with me as I try out a new subgenre.

About Vivian Wood

Vivian likes to write about troubled, deeply flawed alpha males and the fiery, kick-ass women who bring them to their knees.

Vivian's lasting motto in romance is a quote from a favorite song: "Soulmates never die."

Be sure to join her email list to keep up with all the awesome giveaways, author videos, ARC opportunities, and more!

Vivian's Works

Seattle Havoc

Hockey Romance

Dear #47, You're the Worst

Dear MVP, You're Ice Cold

Wildflower Lane
Small Town Rom Com
The Accidental Honeymoon
The Always Bridesmaid
Say Yes to the Nemesis

Cape Simon
Small Town Romance
The Grumpy Boss Agreement
The Fake Fiancée Proposition

Sinfully Rich
Steamy Billionaire Romance
Sinful Fling
Sinful Enemy
Sinful Boss
Sinful Chance
Sinful Teacher

Billionaires Ever After
Steamy Bad Boy Romance
His Best Friend's Little Sister
Claiming Her Innocence
His Fiancé To Keep
His Lovely Virgin

Hush Hush Club
Forbidden Billionaire Romantic Suspense
Such A Good Girl
Such A Spoiled Brat

Married At Midnight
Forbidden Billionaire Romance

Deal With The Devil
Wed to the Devil
Vow to the Devil

Ruined Castle Trilogy
Forbidden Billionaire Romance
The Single Dad
The Nanny
The Caress

Broken Slipper Trilogy
Forbidden Billionaire Romance
The Patron
The Dancer
The Embrace
Possessive

Fifth Avenue Villains
Fifth Avenue Devil

Royally Rich
Forbidden Royal Romance
Cruel Heir
Sinful Princess
Pretend Princess

King's Capture Duet
Dark Billionaire Romance
King's Capture
Queen's Sacrifice

Addiction Duet
Angsty Dark Romance

Addiction
Obsession

Other books
Wild Hearts

For more information….
vivian-wood.com
info@vivian-wood.com